Speak of the Devil

A Tyranny of Angels
book 2

Speak of the Devil

Isobel Lynn

Paperback ISBN: 979-8-9885306-2-6

Ebook ISBN: 979-8-9885306-3-3

For Mika

Prologue

The moon was at the right position in the sky. The correct number of candles were lit and carefully arranged. A gentle night breeze toyed with each flickering flame. It was the perfect evening to conjure the demon king.

The angel and the woman he possessed crawled across the floor of her art studio and meticulously scraped sea salt into a perfect circle with a painting knife. Possession was not a complicated dance. There were only three real requisites—the possessed must be human, living, and willing. In contrast, conjuration was a tangle of arbitrary requirements depending on the spirit one wanted to call. But the watcher Azazel had been summoning spirits of his own ilk for eons, and by now, it was second nature to him. No matter how much he loathed forcing the presence of incorporeal beings, he had to admit he had a talent for it.

The woman he possessed—the artist—was no stranger to Azazel. In fact, he'd been acting as her muse for years. How he'd worried over her reaction when he finally revealed his true identity, but she hadn't flinched. She hadn't even doubted. And when he'd asked permission to enter and possess her body, she'd just given it.

Now he moved his partner like a puppeteer, nimbly pulling her arms and legs over little walls of salt, careful not to disturb the words and symbols already organized within the circle. He felt her give in to every tug. It was like hypnosis, the way he took her, and she never fought any of it. She truly had nothing left to lose. He, on the other hand, was on the cusp of losing her.

Azazel had always been a better dancer than he was a conqueror. His talents were in beauty and presentation. He loved the spectacles of music, color, twinkling lights and well-placed mirrors. He loved glitter and sequins and all manner of bawdy, extravagant theater. He was an artist and a craftsman. Even the magic circles he fashioned had something about them, some indescribable quality. They were elegant, and Azazel knew it. He stood back in the woman's body and admired his own work through her eyes. Of the few virtues the angel possessed, humility was not one of them.

When Azazel was satisfied with his circle, he knelt outside it, spread the woman's arms, and began to sing. Even in her human tongue, his voice was magnificent. The song he sang was powerful. It included the Ineffable Name—a key that opened the gate to another universe. It harnessed the natural laws of his old world and applied them handily to his new one.

The song drew to a close, and Azazel began the summons in earnest. He spoke in Portuguese, the woman's native language. "I command you, Ashmedai, appear in my circle in fair and comely form, without noise or deformity. Come now, demon—visibly, peacefully, affably—without delay. Speak to me with a clear and perfect voice. Answer to your names: King of Demons, Aeshma Daeva, and Asmodeus." He paused and saw the circle waver and steam. Just to speed the process along, Azazel added one last name to his spell. "Appear before me now, Ash darling."

The wind howled, but the candles burned steadily. The hairs on the woman's arms stood on end as though held by a magnetic force. The incorporeal mingled with the corporeal world as the demon in question drew in the dust he needed to build his body.

Ashmedai never did appreciate the effort that went into conjuration. He was a prickly academic who would not forgive an interruption, no matter how necessary the conjuror deemed it. He appeared within the circle, a book in one hand and gold-rimmed spectacles in the other, his jaw clenched, his mouth pouting.

He'd heeded the command most accurately, however. *Fair and comely* he certainly was, though it was no trouble for him. The demon king stood tall and proud. He'd taken his original form, as he loathed putting effort into anything outside his studies. His black hair was shaved to the scalp. He had deep, russet skin that drank in the candlelight and glowed like a gem. His eyes were spectacular, hooded and brooding. His mouth was a downturned Cupid's bow with the slightest dimple in his lower lip. He looked just like his mother. Azazel had always thought so.

"Speak, Ash."

Ashmedai scowled. "Why am I in Brazil? How dare you? We were finished with each other. We had an understanding."

"Forgive me, darling, but I didn't have the time to spare. I need Raphael's weapon. Something's come up."

Ashmedai positioned his spectacles on the bridge of his nose, which was the only hawkish feature on his otherwise heart-shaped face. He squinted down at the woman whose body Azazel occupied. Then he removed his spectacles. The demon king had an eye for the unseen. He could glimpse the polaroid flash of a person's past and future when he put his mind to it, and he almost always put his mind to it.

Azazel braced himself. "She's dying, Ash."

"I can see that."

"I need the sword."

Ashmedai sighed. "Every mortal dies, Azza." His informality was more to pacify than show affection.

"She's only twenty-three."

"People die young." Ashmedai shrugged, a graceful gesture if Azazel ever saw one. The demon king really was the picture of his mother. "It isn't uncommon, especially these days."

"Please, Ash. You know why this is important to me. You must. If you can't see it, put your spectacles back on and look, for god's sake."

Ashmedai did not. Instead, he glanced around the studio, eyeing multiple easels and stacks of canvas, all in varying stages of completion—the color, the texture, the applied gold leaf reflecting candlelight. "Is this all her work or is some of it yours?"

"It's hers." Azazel was becoming impatient. "I need the healing sword, Ash. I did you a great service once. You owe me this."

Ashmedai shook his head. "The service you performed was payment for my releasing you. Anyway, don't tell me you didn't enjoy binding Raphael. You hated him as much as I did."

"You could never have bound him without me."

"And you could not have overcome him if I hadn't taken his weapon. We defeated him together, you and I. And we did it each for our own reasons. I owe you nothing."

"A favor then, please. I'll be in your debt." Azazel wished he was dealing with a lesser demon. Ashmedai was no one to trifle with. The demon king was as old as they come, born to a watcher, though no one knew which. His mother, Naamah, had been a lover to many of the fallen ones. Her kindness and beauty were legendary among them. Azazel had not forgotten her—he had been one of the first to accept her comfort—but Ashmedai was not his son. No, the demon king's father was undeniably cherubic, and Azazel was not. Every once in a while, he wished he had fathered the boy. Just now, he could have used a familial relationship to his advantage.

Instead, he had to beg. "I'll give you anything, Ash darling. Think it over. You may need me again someday, and I'll be there for you. I swear it. Is that not worth something to you? You don't even have to retrieve the sword. Just tell me where it is. Or better yet, you keep it. Just bring it here and heal the girl. Please. It's such a little favor. Surely you can see the value in such a little favor."

Ashmedai donned his spectacles once more, stepped to the edge of the circle, and held out his hand. Azazel reached inside and let the demon touch the outstretched fingers of the woman he possessed. This way, Ash would get a better sense of her. He would see how precious she was. He had to. After several minutes of stillness, the demon king withdrew his hand. "Is she really the last?"

Azazel nodded. "There are no others. I've searched the world over."

"I'm sorry, Azza." Ashmedai pocketed his spectacles and sighed. "But I can't bring the sword to you. I lost it in a wager years ago. I don't even know where it is anymore."

Azazel nearly laughed, but the somber expression on Ash's face told him this was no joke. His rage was belated but all the more fiery for that. "You lost it?" He rose up and up. His ever-brightening body shook the walls around them with the force of a small earthquake. "Why would you gamble with something like that?"

"What did I need with a healing sword? I'm already dead."

Azazel screamed, furious. The woman slumped to her knees as he returned control of her body to her. She looked up and saw the demon king watching her. "What's happening?" she croaked, exhausted.

Ash glanced up at the raging angel. "If I were to hazard a guess," he said in Portuguese, "I'd say a tantrum." He blinked slowly, polished his nails on his lapel, and winked at the woman to calm her. Then he took a deep breath and hollered up at Azazel. "How this is supposed to improve your situation is beyond me! But if you release me from this confounded circle, I might be able to help you find the sword!" He glanced down at the woman. "Dona Artista, do you want to know how long you have? I can tell you."

She shook her head. "No, but I don't want to wait for him to calm down either. He used my body to capture you." She smiled and held out her hand for Ashmedai. He took it and squeezed as she said, "I will use it to set you free."

The woman broke the circle with one foot, and Ashmedai stepped across the barrier, intentionally scattering more salt as he did. "I can see why he values you, Dona Artista," he said with a smile. "You're full of fire, aren't you?"

Chapter One

Michael's feet were raw and bloody. His lips cracked, and his stomach ached with hunger. But if he died right now, he would die happy. He couldn't stop smiling. In fact, his cheeks were sore from it. He loved everything about the woman beside him. He loved the way she tucked the tips of her fingers between his and the way her voice always sounded a little hoarse, like she'd lost it after a night of singing. Most of all, he loved that she was alive. He'd come so close to losing her.

They'd walked all night and most of the morning down a quiet, Mexican highway. Every once in a while, Michael reached down and tousled Bryony's hair to keep her scalp from burning. She had a fair complexion, and the sun had not been kind. The terrain around them was coastal and rocky with little in the way of shade. She'd gotten some color from her time in the Black Armada, but not enough to protect her from an entire morning of exposure. Michael had carried her on his back some of the night, and now he tried to walk in such a way that she could hide in his shadow. Still he couldn't help but worry.

"What's wrong?" Bryony's voice tugged him from his thoughts. He glanced down at her and smiled. She'd pushed her bangs from her face, and the combination of sweat and salt left them tangled and messy.

"It's nothing."

She groaned. "An evasion if I ever heard one." She was exhausted. He could tell by the way her voice petered out.

"It's just . . . Do you need to rest? We can rest. Or I can carry you again."

She shook her head. "I'm good."

He decided not to call her out on the obvious lie. She wanted to be strong, but she was going to need water and shade soon, and the empty highway seemed to go on forever. "Please, let me carry you."

"Not right now." She stood on her toes to whisper, and he crouched to hear her. "It's embarrassing in front of all these people."

Hallucination. She was worse off than he thought. He tried to remind himself she wasn't in mortal peril. She was a god, if only a little one, and her life was sustained by worship—specifically Michael's worship, as of yesterday. He would not fail to sate her, but that didn't mean she couldn't suffer. As Michael understood it, heatstroke was not a pleasant business.

He tilted her chin up and studied her eyes, which looked even bluer than usual, framed by her reddening cheeks and long, walnut hair. "I'm going to carry you. Don't worry about the people. They can't see us." He bent down and scooped her into his arms. She protested only a little before her head lolled onto his shoulder and she muttered something about needing to feed Shakespeare.

Though her former pet crow had turned out to be the shapeshifting trickster Loki, Michael didn't correct her. "Shakespeare's doing fine. I'm sure someone's feeding him." He rolled his eyes because it was probably true. Loki had stolen Bryony's congregation somehow. Someone was most definitely feeding him.

Michael carried her another mile at least and tucked her head under his chin to keep the sun off her face. When he saw what he thought was an abandoned building off the highway, he started to jog. Bryony needed shade immediately. She needed water too.

The building was a single story, long and orange like a sunset against the backdrop of a blue-green sea. And it wasn't abandoned. It was a hotel in fact, apparently still in operation. The front patio was a colorful mosaic shaded by a lattice of climbing vines, and the doors stood open. Michael ducked into the lobby and was relieved to find their ceilings more than high enough for him. Mexico often delighted him for this reason among others—high ceilings, outdoor spaces, warm people. He straightened up and cleared his throat.

The woman behind the counter glanced up from her magazine. It took her a beat or two to react, but Michael was ready for it. People all over the world were more or less the same. No matter the gender, the language, the culture, their reactions tended to blend into one echoing refrain. "Oh!" The woman's mouth fell open, and she rounded the desk to approach him. She spoke Spanish, but Michael had been traveling up and down the coast long enough to learn it. "You're huge! Welcome, I mean." She blushed. "My god, how tall are you?"

There it was. Michael smiled down at her. She had a pleasant, round face and wore a cotton blouse with a floral skirt. Her hair was braided and wrapped into a bun. Michael gave her his practiced answer. "More than two hundred, less than two fifty. I haven't measured in a while. But please . . ." He nodded his head, indicating Bryony. "I think it's heatstroke. We've been walking all day."

The woman caught a glimpse of his feet and gasped. "Oh, no no no. You poor dears." Then she shouted, "Toño!"

A lanky man entered the lobby, looking more than a little annoyed to have been called so unceremoniously. "What do you want now, woman?" He stopped in his tracks and crossed himself when he saw the giant in the lobby. Michael supposed the man wasn't used to looking up at anyone.

"Toño, get the girl cooled off. Give her water if she'll take it."

Michael let Bryony slide from his arms. She wavered on her feet until the other man caught her and led her away. Michael watched after them as long as he could.

"Don't worry for her, Señor. Antonio will take good care of her." The woman smiled and gave Michael an appraising look. "Now, tell me, do you have a place to stay for the night?"

He shook his head.

"I thought not. You'll stay here, both of you." It was more command than request. The woman held out her hand in greeting, and Michael took it. "My name is Gloria."

"Michael," he said. "And thank you, but I'm afraid we have no money. I'd be happy to work for the room if there's anything you need."

"Oh, there certainly is." Gloria returned to her place behind the counter and turned her logbook to Michael. "I've just the job for you. Sign in, and you'll be our guests for the night. Tomorrow, I'll put you to work."

Michael thanked her. Then he bent at the waist to sign his name but stopped short. Everyone who joined the Black Armada gave up their family name. You were called by the ship you worked on, but *Michael of Dragonfly* was hardly acceptable in this case. Before joining the armada, Michael had no family name. He had no family at all. His hand hovered, waiting for a surname to come to him—any surname—but his tired mind did not supply one. The heat of shame crept under his collar and threatened to color his cheeks. He quickly wrote Bryony's full name after his and passed the book back to Gloria, hoping she wouldn't notice.

She looked down and read the names. "Welcome, Señor Moss. We have a comfortable room ready for you and your wife. Please follow me."

Wife? *Michael and Bryony Moss* did sound rather like a couple. He didn't know the ethical opinions of the hotel owners, how they might feel about his sharing a room with a woman who was not his wife. They might separate Bryony from him, and that was unacceptable. He gulped and let the error stand. "Yes, thank you."

Gloria led him down a spacious hallway to a room bathed in natural light. A sliding glass door stood open on the far wall and let the sea breeze play with linen curtains. Terracotta tiles cooled his bare feet, and the bed, clothed all in white, looked unbelievably inviting. Bryony already lay stretched out on one side of it. Antonio sat beside her and held a wet cloth to her forehead. Every once in a while, he would dip his fingers into a glass of water and massage the inside of her wrists. Michael watched the man's gentleness and quietly decided he would do everything these people asked of him, no matter what it was.

The first clue Bryony got that she wasn't sleeping in the captain's quarters aboard *Dragonfly* was that the ceiling looked wrong. Instead of the dark wood of her alcoved bunk, she opened her eyes to a bright, white ceiling with an electric fan spinning slowly overhead. So the sensation of gentle rocking hadn't been from the ship. It was just her head. She groaned.

The room was comfortable, light and breezy, the bed soft and clean. She'd been laid out on a large bath towel and, to her horror, stripped to her underwear. Beside her, Michael slept on the floor, comfortable as a cat in awkward repose. There was an open bottle of water on the nightstand. She sniffed it and took a gulp. Water never tasted so good. She took a deep breath and tipped her head back, finishing the bottle in seconds. Then she tucked the towel around herself and began to explore.

They seemed to be in a hotel room with a patio door that opened directly onto the beach. There were no ships on the horizon. Bryony's heart broke a little when she remembered how she'd left the Black Armada. The commodore had sent her to the depths—a mercy killing if ever there was one—and Michael had dived in after her. Everyone in the armada most likely thought her dead, but why had they abandoned Michael? Was his inability to let Bryony die really so unforgivable? Or perhaps their dislike of him went deeper than she'd originally thought, and this was just a convenient excuse to be rid of him.

She scowled. Her heart was still protective of him despite his imposing size. He would stand up for anyone but himself. She stood over him and watched him sleep. His clothes were stiff with dried sea salt, though his black hair looked soft and clean with loose curls at the cut ends. Honestly, did he ever need to wash it? She brought a damp rope of her own hair around to her face and examined it. It smelled like unfamiliar shampoo. Her body, too, seemed to have been cleaned of sand and salt. Her bra and underwear had mostly dried, but the damp made it clear they'd not been removed for the bath. At least she was wearing her good underwear.

When Bryony heard a knock at the door, she cracked it despite her state of undress. A thin man held out a laundry bag and two robes. "Good evening," he said. His English was slow and careful, but he managed it quite well. "For your clothes." He handed her the bag and robes. "Leave them outside your door tonight, and we will wash."

"Oh." Bryony tugged the offered gifts through the door without opening it further. "I mean, thank you . . . um . . . sir." The man smiled, and several crescents deepened around his mouth like multiple parentheses, an aside within an aside. Bryony couldn't help but smile back. She let the door open a touch more.

"My name is Antonio," he said.

"I'm Bryony."

"I know. Welcome. I'm glad you're feeling better." He reached into his pocket and pulled out a neatly wrapped package. "For your husband." Bryony took it, failing to completely hide her confusion. Antonio helpfully misinterpreted her expression. "Bandages. For his feet."

"Oh! Of course. Yes, thank you." But *husband?*

"Are you hungry?"

"Yes," she answered without hesitation. She was starving, and she would bet Michael felt even worse. They hadn't eaten for a day and a half.

"We will bring dinner."

Bryony wanted to ask why this man was doing so much for them. Michael must have arranged something. Perhaps he'd even pulled something off. She didn't want to spoil whatever he had planned, so she kept her responses short. "Thank you."

She breathed a sigh of relief after closing the door. What had Michael done? She hesitated to wake him. He looked too peaceful. His cheeks were tinged with pink, his lips rosy as ever. But despite having walked in the sun all day, the rest of his skin was still pale. Was that due to his lineage? His father was the Angel of Death and a seraph, which explained his abnormal height and obsessive nature. Did it affect his complexion as well? There was still so much she had to learn.

"Michael." She knelt on the floor and touched him gently, knowing it was unlikely to wake him. Next, she ran her fingers through his hair. Nothing. Finally, she prodded him until his body rocked from her touch. "Wake up. You have to wake up now."

He groaned, and his eyes fluttered open. As soon as he took her in, his arms shot up and wrapped around her. He tugged her down until she was flat against him. "Thank god," he said with a deep sigh. "You're all right."

She tried in vain to pry herself from his arms. "Of course I am. I can't die, remember?"

He squeezed her tighter. "But if you lose a limb, it won't grow back."

"Was I in danger of losing a limb?"

"In a sense." He released her just enough that she could lift her upper body and look into his charcoal eyes. His irises and pupils were like a single, black void against the whites. If she looked into them long enough, she was certain she would eventually find stars. "You were seeing things that weren't there," he said. "I didn't know if the damage was permanent."

"Oh." She didn't recall much of the morning, which she'd just attributed to physical exhaustion, but it was apparently much worse. All she needed as proof was the look on Michael's face. He pulled her back into his chest and held her tightly. "Michael?"

"Hm?"

"Who, um . . . Who took off my clothes?"

He let her go and sat up. His eyes flicked to the towel, still wrapped around her chest, and back to her face again. His cheeks colored, and he cleared his throat. "I had to cool you in the bath. Your clothes are hanging to dry outside. Antonio was gone by the time I . . . I swear I would have asked first had I been able."

She smiled to reassure him, but the idea that someone, anyone, had been able to strip and bathe her without waking her made her stomach turn. At least it was Michael. At least—

"Bryony." He interrupted her thoughts. "You were always safe, I promise. Please don't feel violated."

"Tall order."

He looked positively helpless, propped against the bed, head and shoulders well above the mattress. "What can I do?"

Bryony forced another grin and tossed the laundry bag at him. "Strip. They're washing our clothes tonight, and I don't want to be the only one in my underwear."

"Right." He nodded and began to unbutton his shirt. "Though you realize if I lose these, I can't easily replace them." He shifted his shoulders and let the fabric drop. Bryony couldn't help but stare. How did he make such a mundane action so delightful to watch? "I suppose they'll want me presentable tomorrow," he said, and he stood to loosen his belt. When he sat on the bed and kicked his pants from his ankles, Bryony realized he was now more naked than she'd ever seen him. Funny, he didn't seem any more vulnerable. His dignity was an impenetrable fortress, apparently. He stuffed his clothes in the laundry bag and set it beside him. "Now we're on equal ground. Do you feel better?"

She did not.

Michael wore well-fitting, navy boxers, which she was certain he'd made himself. Everything he owned was so perfect for him it was easy to mistake him for an average-sized man in a room full of undersized furniture. In fact, many people did not know him for a giant until they found themselves standing beside him. She herself had mistaken him when she'd first met him. He made the world around him look too small, as though the architects of every civilization had simply miscalculated their designs. Maybe that was why the power in his build never failed to surprise her. He hid his strength well—he had few bulging muscles to advertise it—but when he moved, she saw the iron in his arms, his chest, his stomach, his thighs. *Like a python,* she thought. *You don't know its strength until it's wrapped around you.*

"You should get washed up," she said. "I'll bandage your feet when you're done."

He grunted an affirmation and stood. When he passed by her, he paused, and his hand came to rest on her head. "Don't go anywhere," he said, curling his fingers into her hair. "Please."

CHAPTER TWO

M ichael had to find ridiculous, rather creative ways to get the upper third of his body under the showerhead. He'd taken for granted the handheld shower on *Dragonfly*, but how he missed it now. Once he washed the blood and sand away, he could see how raw his feet were. All this was mere inconvenience, though, compared to the problem he faced with the hotel robe. It did not, he noted with a frown, serve its intended purpose in the least. It was short and barely closed around him.

The indignity of it all had Michael blushing before he even left the bathroom. He sat down and considered his predicament. He and Bryony had only just begun their relationship. He wasn't about to stroll out of the bathroom naked as the day he was born and spend the rest of the night that way to boot. That said, his clothes were in desperate need of a wash.

"Hey, Michael." Bryony's voice sounded far too close to the door. "They brought us dinner. Can you believe it? It smells so good. You'd better get out here before I eat it all."

So the staff had already returned for his clothes. No choice, in that case. "We have a . . . a bit of a problem." He leaned his forehead against the door.

She was quiet a moment. He took a deep breath and thought of the best way to explain, but Bryony beat him to it. "The robe doesn't fit you, does it? Hang on." There was a rustling, and then a light knock on the door. "This should work."

Michael cracked the door, and Bryony slipped a bedsheet to him. He took it, grinning. She knew. He didn't even have to tell her. The fact that she'd guessed his need before he voiced it brought him close to tears. He was used to making his own path through the world, unaided and unheard. This only confirmed his conclusion that she would be with him for the rest of his life. He would accept nothing less. She was everything. She was more than the whole world put together.

He shook the thoughts from his head. *Stay grounded.*

The sheet was long on him, but he folded it and wrapped it around his waist. He felt ridiculous, but Bryony didn't seem to care. She wore the robe she'd been given and looked magnificent as usual. "Look at this!" She gestured to the little round table in the corner. "They gave us a whole bottle of tequila. Why are they being so generous?"

Michael wanted to tell her people were just that kind. He loved the delight in her face, but he didn't want to lie. "I've agreed to help them out with some things tomorrow."

"Help with what?" Bryony sat at the table and began piling rice onto her plate.

Michael followed suit. "Something they can't do on their own. Don't worry about it. It's not a big deal."

"What, are you changing lightbulbs or something?" She laughed and opened the tequila.

"Nothing so strenuous, I'm sure." Michael offered his cup, and she poured him several shots. Then she poured roughly the same amount for herself. She seemed to have learned nothing from her last hangover. Well, he supposed they could both use some festivity after the ordeal they'd been through. He drank deeply and ate his fill.

By the time Michael finished his dinner, the sun had dipped below the horizon. He sat alone at the table and stared out at the darkened silhouette of the sea. His life had always been haunted by the sea. There was just no escaping it, was there?

From the bed, Bryony broke into his thoughts. "Are you gonna sleep okay? You can tuck your knees up, can't you? I won't let you sleep on the floor again."

He turned to her and blinked. "Where did you find those?" She sat cross-legged with a spread of playing cards before her.

"In the nightstand," she answered matter-of-factly. Her voice had gone down an octave, due in no small part to her third glass of tequila. "You were busy being pensive, so I decided to entertain myself."

He smiled and moved to join her. "I was just reminiscing."

"About what?" She laid another card down, red on black.

"Staying on the beach like this reminds me of when I was young, before I joined the armada. I used to wander the coast, living in abandoned vacation homes. There was no shortage of them in those days. I would stay in one until the cupboards were bare. Then I'd move on to the next."

Bryony frowned and blew her bangs out of her eyes. "How old were you?"

"Young. I don't know exactly. I tended to measure my life in inches rather than years. I joined the armada at around six feet."

"That sounds so lonely." She drank the last of her tequila and stared down at her game of solitaire. "I think I've lost."

"You haven't." Michael rearranged several of her piles to give her a fighting chance. "It was lonely, living that way. That's probably why I started reading romances. There were a lot of them left behind. They made the days pass more pleasantly." He laid the last stack of cards and sat back. "There. That should buy you a few turns."

She leaned over to examine the cards, and Michael looked away from the place where the robe gaped at her chest. The tequila seemed to be getting to him too. God she was beautiful. He remembered the cool feeling of her lips against his, the way her shoulder blades moved under her skin when she caressed him. He leaned back, closed his eyes, and tried to think of something else—anything—but he could still feel her on the bed beside him. Every time she played a card, he felt her weight shift. It was going to take every ounce of self-control he had not to sweep the cards from the bed and press her into the mattress the way he wanted to.

"No, I think I really have lost," she said.

He opened his eyes and looked down. The cards were a blur. He couldn't bring himself to care about them anymore.

Bryony leaned in to gather the deck, and her robe parted further. Michael tried to swallow his desire, but it was no good. He shouldn't have joined her in bed, not when his own head was spinning from the liquor. He felt like a vampire craving after blood. He closed his eyes again as she laughed. "You didn't help me win after all," she said triumphantly, as though she'd just won a wager they never made. "You just helped me lose more slowly."

"Sometimes that's all you can do—delay your loss." Was that his voice cracking? He was losing his own struggle, and he needed to delay it. But if he stood up and walked away now, he'd be admitting his loss in more ways than one. The bedsheet provided little in the way of modesty, and his own body was working against him now. He squeezed his eyes shut and thought about how he and Bryony would survive from here on out. Surely he could stress himself out enough to get his mind off the fact that the hem of her robe inched up her thigh a little more every time she moved. She neither noticed nor cared—he just had to follow her example.

"Oh, well." Bryony tapped the deck against the nightstand and slipped it back into the drawer. "Solitaire's a stupid game anyway."

And that, for some reason, did it. Michael's entire body surrendered and his brain along with it. So much for delaying his loss. He cupped her cheek, drew her close, and kissed her hungrily.

She rose up on her knees and pivoted into him, straddling his lap like she had on the beach. The movement seemed automatic for her, like a dance step she knew by heart. It enabled him to lift his knees so he could support and kiss her without slouching. Already, she knew how to love him, how to seamlessly rise to meet him.

He touched her collarbone and traced it, taking a path to its center and down between her breasts to the base of her ribcage. Then he slipped his hand into her robe and curled his fingers around her bare torso. When she coaxed his tongue into her mouth, he actually moaned. There was something deeply familiar about the way she tasted. It was electric, nostalgic, the memory of a home he never knew. Her skin was warm but seemed to cool as his own body heated. Soon she would feel like ice melting on a desert stone. She would feel like life, like the quenching of an endless thirst. He slid his hand further under her robe, around to her back, and heard the slightest shush of fabric as one sleeve fell from her shoulder.

Damn. He'd gone too far. He knew it even as his eyes fell on one naked shoulder, one bared breast. He paused and slid the robe back over her shoulder.

Thank god he'd had the strength to stop, though he'd taken things beyond what he knew was prudent. He leaned back and stared at her reddened cheeks, her parted lips. He breathed an apology. Bryony just blinked at him, shook her head, and shrugged out of the robe completely.

Michael held his breath and gripped the sheets beneath him. The power of this current was too much to bear, and he could feel himself begin to lose his footing. He hesitated, and she smiled at him. "Don't worry," she said. "I know your boundaries. I won't cross them." She leaned in and whispered, "Don't tell anyone, but I'm not really that drunk."

When her lips brushed his ear, it finally knocked him off his proverbial feet. He drew his knees up steeper, and she slid into his chest. She pressed her body against his, and he lost himself in the shape of her. Skin against skin for the first time in his life. She was so soft, almost cold now compared to his fevered flesh. He crushed her to himself as her hips, softened by the robe still tied around her waist, rocked into his. Clearly, strict control was no longer an option.

It was agony. Each time he kissed her, he had to bow to meet her, which created space between them. He was uncomfortably hot without her body pressed against his. He found her cooling tongue, and she caressed him with her hands, mercifully giving him the touch he needed. When he couldn't stand the rift any longer, he abandoned her mouth and pulled her body closer. The way she shifted her weight to please him, dug her fingers into his sides, and rolled her body into his made it clear how badly she wanted him.

Waves of pleasure coursed through his veins as he found her rhythm and matched it. He never wanted the feeling to end. Then a sudden, alarming sensation tugged at him. In all the books he'd read, in all the love scenes he'd consumed, he'd never read anything like this. It was a pull, a catch in his chest. His heartbeat grew erratic and kicked up a notch. His breath caught and quickened. It was as though someone else breathed through his lungs. Someone else had taken hold of his heart, and it beat at an unnatural pace.

Through a fog of confusion, he thought he heard Bryony mutter, "Do you smell incense?" And then she went completely still.

She breathed in time with him but didn't move otherwise. Michael took her by the shoulders and held her at arm's length. He gazed down at her upturned face. Tears welled in her wide eyes. Her mouth gaped. He recognized the look, and the shadows now dancing on the walls around him were only confirmation of what he already knew to be true. She couldn't move. He straightened his legs to lift her off his lap, and caught a glimpse of his own limbs, of the writhing fire he'd become.

Bryony must have opened her eyes when she smelled the smoke—sweet this time, for some reason—and the sight of the seraph had paralyzed her, as it always did, as it always would. She could no longer kiss or reassure him. She could no longer be willing, ready, eager. He scrambled away from the bed, backing into a corner as the light faded. How hadn't he noticed it straight away? How had he missed the change in the room? He must have closed his eyes.

"Bryony." He called to her from across the room. "Please, be okay. Please."

When at last she shifted and groaned, he sighed, audibly relieved.

Most people found it nearly impossible to move at the sight of the seraph in Michael. It stunned and held them. Some wept. Some even dropped to their knees. But the seraph was never revealed without Michael first drawing his father's sword. So why now? He was traversing uncharted waters, and it terrified him.

"What happened?" Bryony's voice was wary, nervous.

He stared down at his own hands. "I don't know. I can't . . . I'm so sorry." She slipped back into her robe, clutching it closed at her chest in a way that made Michael cringe. "I'm sorry," he repeated, his voice even weaker this time.

"It wasn't your fault, was it?"

He shook his head. "I don't know how it happened. I've never been with anyone before. I didn't know this was part of it. I almost wonder . . . Am I being punished?"

She scoffed. "For what? You didn't do anything wrong."

"I wanted to." Admitting that was a step he hadn't planned to take, but it was true. If she'd pushed him, even a little, he would have done whatever she asked. He would have given her anything. There was even a moment, in the thick of his frenzy, when he thought he could understand the choices his father had made.

"Don't be ridiculous." Bryony squared her shoulders and patted the bed beside her. "No one gets punished for something they *want* to do."

He tightened the sheet around his waist and approached her, hesitant. "I don't know. Maybe I should sleep on the floor."

"Don't you dare." She darted toward him, grabbed his wrist, and reeled him in. "It's just one of the hazards of dating a seraph. Brought it on myself really." She was trying to make him smile.

He slouched against the headboard and stared at his feet hanging off the foot of the bed. "You're making it worse."

"How?"

"Your kindness." He reached over and caught a strand of her hair between his thumb and forefinger. "I want to be with you."

"You can."

"Not like that." He stared at her mouth and tried not to think about how she tasted. "Not if there's a chance you could be paralyzed."

"Maybe it was just a fluke, a one-time thing."

He shook his head. "Didn't you feel it? The pull?"

"What pull? I smelled incense, and when I looked to see where it was coming from, you were all"—she wiggled her fingers in the air—"wavery. Was that you? That smell? I remember smelling smoke before, but this time it was . . . different."

"It was sweet," he agreed. "I know. That's new too. I don't know what I did wrong. Maybe I just took things too far."

"Psh, no." She dismissed his idea with a wave of her hand. "If anyone took things too far it was me, and I'd do it again." She grinned, but it was a façade, and Michael could see through it. She toyed with his fingers while she thought. "Raeni could move some when she wasn't looking directly at you—I remember that—and Loki. So why can't I?"

"I don't know. I wish I did. My father is the only angel I've heard of who has this problem. It's more pronounced in him than it is in me. Anyone who sees him falls prostrate before him. I knew I'd inherited it. I just didn't know it would be triggered by . . . you." His voice caught. Bryony slid close and kissed him. Her mouth was soft and warm, an indication his own fever had faded. He squeezed her shoulders and kept her from coming too close.

"I love you," he whispered after she turned out the light. Some part of him wanted to follow it up with, *Please, don't leave me*, but he didn't. Anyone in a relationship with him was going to have to deal with more baggage than most, and pressuring her to stay with him would be wrong. Still, if she left . . . He shuddered at the thought.

In the dark, Bryony took his hand and held it tight. "Michael. You know, before the smoke, you made me feel amazing. Honestly."

And there it was—everything he loved about her—surfacing, shining, blinding him to all the ugliness in the world. He wrapped his arms around her and pulled her close. All he wanted to do was protect her forever. All he wanted to do was keep her and serve her. He kissed the top of her head, closed his eyes, and fell asleep with his arms around his god.

Chapter Three

Bryony woke to an empty room. She had a vague memory of Michael's weight lifting off the bed, but she'd been too exhausted to open her eyes. She might even have dreamed his kiss on her forehead, though she hoped not. Her cleaned clothes were laid out neatly. Breakfast had been left on the table and the dinner dishes taken away. She'd never been so waited on in all her life.

She dressed and brushed her teeth. Her hair was an unruly mess, so she wetted and knotted it at the back of her head, carefully combing her bangs down until they behaved the way she thought they should. Her cheeks were red and tight, obviously burned. More than anything, she wanted to pin her black veil in her hair and drop it down over her face, but she didn't have it.

Outside the room, the hall was all warm colors and undusted corners. High ceilings—hung with fabulous, wooden chandeliers—arched overhead. Bryony loved the place at once. The hotel had an air of deterioration about it, which only made it more beautiful to her, more like a place she belonged. But instead of the empty, tomblike atmosphere she would have expected, she heard many guests laughing and talking amongst themselves. She guessed there were at least twenty voices coming from the lobby, but when she finally saw the crowd, she realized she had grossly underestimated.

A line of people snaked out the door, children hanging on the arms of their guardians. And at the head of the snake stood Michael. He had an arm around a woman who grinned at a man with a camera. Bryony's stomach tightened at the sight of the measuring tape pinned to the wall beside him. Her hands balled into fists at her sides, but she couldn't bring herself to interrupt. She stood at the far end of the lobby and bit her tongue.

Michael crouched to shake the hand of a boy who couldn't have been more than seven and only came up to his hips. The boy laughed, questioning him in Spanish, and Michael answered with an easy smile. Bryony softened a bit. Children were different. It was adults behaving like children she couldn't abide.

The line shifted forward again, and Michael looked up to see Bryony staring at him. Oblivious to her discomfort, he grinned and strode toward her. She flinched as he drew the eyes of the crowd to where she stood.

"Did you sleep well?" He bent down to hug her.

She murmured into his ear. "What is this?"

"The hotel's been struggling, so I agreed to help them get people in the door."

"So you're a tourist attraction?"

"It's not like that."

"Isn't it?"

Just then, a woman's voice rose above the rest, and Bryony heard her say, "Su esposa." The crowd let out a collective sound of understanding, followed by numerous shouted questions.

Bryony murmured, "What did she say?"

Michael blanched. "They think you're my wife. I didn't correct them. I didn't know if they'd let us stay together otherwise."

The crowd pressed in, and Bryony took several instinctive steps back. A middle-aged woman with two teenaged children shouted a question to Bryony that made Michael's ears turn red. Bryony glared at her and said, "No hablo español." She knew how to say that at least.

But the tourist would not be discouraged, or perhaps she just couldn't take a hint. Either way, she held out her hands in a gesture whose meaning became immediately clear as soon as the English version of her question left her mouth. "How big?" The woman giggled, and her daughter chided her.

Bryony recoiled. "That's so rude." She turned to Michael, saw the blush in his cheeks, and felt it creeping into her own. "How do you say *that's rude* in Spanish? And don't lie to me."

He muttered, "Eso es grosero."

Bryony turned to the tourist and fumed. "Eso es grosero. Do you understand? How dare you?"

The tourist withdrew, but she hardly looked adequately shamed. Michael said something to the woman behind the counter, who nodded. Then he led Bryony back to their room. After he ducked through the door and closed it behind him, he leaned back against it and heaved a relieved sigh.

Bryony did not feel relieved in the least. "We're leaving," she said. "Now. They can't treat you that way."

Michael closed his eyes and shook his head. "They're just curious."

"That was not *just curious*! That was uncalled for and disrespectful and . . . and vulgar."

"They're not all like that," he said, pushing a hand through his hair. "Most of their questions are innocent." He blushed, and Bryony wanted to scream at every last tourist who embarrassed him. "Anyway, we can't leave yet. We've got nowhere else to go."

"We'll think of something." Bryony began to pace. Nothing would feel more appropriate than angrily packing her things right now, but she didn't have anything to pack or any bag to pack it in, for that matter.

Michael crossed the room and sat at the foot of the bed. "We'd be out on the streets."

"Good," she snapped.

"No. Not good. You didn't see yourself yesterday. I can't go through that again. I can't." He dropped his head into his hands. "If these people want to give us a place to stay and food to eat, and all I have to do is answer some questions and take some pictures to help their business, it's the least I can do. Please think this through before you do something you can't take back. I've been on the streets before. It's cruel, Bryony. I don't want that for you." He lifted his head again. His eyes were pleading. "Let me do this for you. Please, I want to do this for you."

"No." Bryony crossed her arms and stared down at his bandaged feet. "Not for me. If you do it, you do it for yourself and not for me. Do you understand? And the second you want out, you tell me, and I'll drag you from this place myself."

"It's a deal." He held out his hand, and Bryony had to uncross her arms to take it. As soon as she did, he pulled her in and hugged her. "Thank you for defending me. It's . . . not something I take for granted."

"Of course." She couldn't help adding, "But why don't you defend yourself? Why do you let people walk all over you? First the armada and now this. To these people, you're just a photo opportunity. They just want a story to tell. Why make excuses for people who don't really know you and don't want to?"

"Because *you* do." He cupped her face in one hand. "I don't care what anyone else thinks. They can make up all the stories they want. The only one who matters knows the truth."

She fought to keep from softening too much. "How do you always turn it around like that? This wasn't supposed to be about me."

"Sorry." He pulled her in once more and kissed her throat until she felt her anger melt like honey in a cup of tea. "But it will always, always be about you, now and for the rest of my life. I don't want it any other way. You're my world now. Nothing else can touch me." He sat up straight and smiled down at her. "On the bright side, I've finally been measured. I'm two hundred and thirty-nine centimeters."

She blinked up at him. "That doesn't mean anything to me."

"Oh, right." He grinned, misunderstanding. "It's seven feet, ten inches."

"No, I mean why do you think that matters to me? Why do you think I care about what number they put over your head? It doesn't define you."

"I know that." He grinned again, and Bryony tried not to notice the dimple on the left side of his mouth. "It doesn't define me, but it does give me more time."

"What do you mean, *more time?*"

"My growth has slowed. Remember how I told you I used to measure my life in inches? Well, I stopped because it always devastated me. By my old calculations I had ten, maybe fifteen years left to live, but my growth seems to have slowed. If things continue on this trajectory, I could have as much as thirty years left."

Bryony frowned even as she saw the disappointment creep into his face. "What do you mean? You told me nephilim only die by violence or suicide. You'll live as long as you want to."

"It's not that simple, Bryony. When I grow too big—"

"We'll build a bigger home. We'll live in a circus tent if we have to." Her eyes pricked and stung with the tears she held back. "You don't get to just pick a height and quit when you reach it."

He sighed and finished his sentence. "There won't be enough resources to sustain me. It's the way things go for my kind. You know that. I never hid it from you."

"But you were supposed to fight it at least." She backed away from him. "You were supposed to try. Why? Why do you just roll over like this? We'll grow our own food. We'll run a ranch. I'll spend my days stealing everything you need to live. Just don't kill yourself!" She choked on the words.

"Oh." Now he seemed to understand. Bryony wouldn't go down without a fight, and she couldn't bear anything less from him. "I'm sorry, my love." *My love.* "I honestly thought you'd be pleased. I've always expected a shorter-than-average lifespan. I guess I neglected to tell you, didn't I? I just assumed you understood."

"How could I?" She glared at him. "I don't know any nephilim other than you."

"Neither do I." He bit his lips in a nervous gesture she'd just begun to notice he had. "But it doesn't matter now. I have so much more time than I thought. I'm sorry it turned out to be less than you expected."

"That's an understatement," she muttered.

He shook his head and spread his hands. "This is ridiculous. We don't even have to think about this right now. I can't understand why it's worrying you so much."

"Because it's my lifespan too!" The words flew from her mouth before she could stop them. She hadn't even seen them coming. But as soon as she spoke them, she knew they were the only way to make him see reason. "It is, isn't it? I assume you can't worship anyone while you're stretched between worlds. So how long do we get to live, Michael, since it's entirely up to you now?"

All the color drained from his face. Finally, he drew a deep breath and stood. "I should get back. I was only given a ten-minute break."

"What?" So in order to avoid their current argument, he'd circled back to the old one. "You can take as long as you want. You're not the property of this hotel." He was backing toward the door. "Michael!"

"This is the only way I can provide for you right now." He sounded just as frustrated as she did. "Just let me do this. Please? So you don't have to sleep on the streets tonight? I really don't mind. We'll talk about the rest later."

And then he left. Bryony watched the door close and sat mute for several seconds before she found her voice again. "But I *have* a house!"

People were never really a problem for Michael. If they wanted to ignore him, he was fine with that. If they wanted to bombard him with questions, he was fine with that too—within reason, of course. People were people, and they'd never done him any real harm. Bryony, it seemed, had a different experience, and Michael was disappointed in himself for not understanding that sooner. Trust was in short supply for her, and she quickly rose to the bait whenever Michael's dignity was on the line. Part of him was touched. Another part wished she would just let things go. She would have to get used to little intrusions if she intended to make a life with him. He became a public figure wherever he went, whether he liked it or not. It was so much easier to assume people had the best intentions. If he allowed himself too much bitterness, he would break.

He completed the rest of his shift with as good an attitude as he could manage. Children held their hands up to his, marveling at the difference in size. Taller adults tried to reach high enough to touch the wall beside his head. More than a few young women blushed when they introduced themselves, which gave his ego a boost. But all the while, he thought of Bryony sitting alone in their hotel room, quietly seething. By evening, Michael had worked himself into a knot of nerves. He could barely keep his hands from trembling when he held them out for photographs.

He wasn't the right partner for Bryony. If she was smart, she'd team back up with Loki, gather a new congregation to sustain her indefinitely, and walk away from Michael forever. She'd been functionally immortal before she met him. How had he expected her to react upon learning that his lifespan, and consequently hers, would now be even shorter than average? Honestly, he hadn't expected anything, and that was the problem. He hadn't thought about how it would affect her because he'd never really dealt with the knowledge himself. He'd just filed it away under *Inevitable Things* and then done his very best not to think about it.

Now he had no choice but to think about it.

After seven, Gloria thanked Michael and let him go for the night. By the time he reached the door to his room, all the fear he'd barely stifled throughout the day surfaced. His heart pounded, and his palms began to sweat.

If she was smart, she would walk away.

If she was smart, she'd be gone.

Despite his own obsessive thoughts, he was still shocked when he opened the door to their hotel room and found it empty. His breath caught. She was gone.

The nightmare scenario Michael had imagined over and over again had come true. She'd left him. She'd really left him. He searched the room like a thief, turning over what was there, even looking under the bed in one desperate, ridiculous moment. "No, no, no, no, no." His own frantic voice echoed in his ears. The room thoroughly upended, he started down the halls, opening every unlocked door.

Nothing.

Nothing.

Nothing.

He went outside and checked the parking lot. No sign of her. "Damn it!" He checked the beach—a long jog in one direction before he sprinted in the other. He did the same on the highway, jogging south in his bandaged feet before the nagging thought that she might be headed north turned him around. None of it made sense. He was irrational. He couldn't pick a course. She could be anywhere. This was a waste of time.

He stopped running, though his heart wouldn't quiet. Why hadn't he just talked to her like she wanted? Why had he walked away? He couldn't berate himself enough for his own stubbornness. He turned back toward the hotel. Bryony was somewhere beyond his reach. Come morning, she would need a place to shelter, water to drink, food to eat, and she didn't even speak the language. He had failed to protect her.

CHAPTER FOUR

Bryony began her afternoon in high spirits. By evening, she was exhausted but still feeling optimistic about her plan. She wove between tables with a broom and dustpan, sweeping the floor of the hotel's terrace restaurant. It felt good to work again, to have a hand in her own future.

The chef had taken her on with very little prodding. Michael's presence gave the restaurant more business than one person could reasonably manage. All Bryony had to do was mention that she had experience in a kitchen, and the chef had her chopping vegetables immediately. His English was halting but understandable, and Bryony found the work conducive to learning a little Spanish herself.

Her plan was to make enough money for train tickets home. Then she would take Michael to her house—assuming it hadn't been burned to the ground by angry congregants—and invite him to live there. That way his public life would be his own choice, not a means to shelter. She needed him to have a choice. She needed to know he wasn't exploiting himself for her sake. She guessed about two weeks of work would do it. Two weeks and they would be on their way home.

It was the last hour of her first shift. A few stragglers still sat at the bar. Bryony had cringed when the odd customer pointed her out to others at their table. But most of her work was in the kitchen, so she didn't have to deal with unwanted attention often. Anyway, it would all be worth it, she told herself, and by the end of the evening, she actually believed it.

Everything was going swimmingly, in fact, until Michael himself strode out onto the terrace. He was drained of color, slick with sweat. His mouth held a striking grimace, and his hands were tight fists at his sides. He made a beeline for her, never minding the people at the bar who turned on their stools to watch the drama unfold. He crossed the floor, plowing through unoccupied chairs like a cannonball. Something was most definitely wrong.

Bryony shrank back when he reached her, expecting to finally see his full temper. Instead he dropped to one knee and scooped her into his arms. He squeezed her so tight she dropped the broom and dustpan. All the while, she heard him muttering, "I thought you were gone. I thought you were gone. I thought you were gone."

Out of the corner of her eye, Bryony saw her new boss watch with his arms crossed and one eyebrow arched. She gave him an apologetic smile. He shook his head. "Go," he said, waving his hand at her. "Come back tomorrow."

Bryony wriggled out of Michael's embrace and took him by the hand. "Come on." She led him off the terrace and onto the beach. She walked with him until they were halfway to their private patio. He could have his outburst here—away from customers—but he didn't. He just stood there, swaying, exhausted. His chest heaved with the air he greedily took in.

"What happened?" she asked. "Why are you all sweaty?"

He had a few false starts before he answered. "I . . . I thought you were gone."

"Gone where?"

He pushed his hair off his forehead, and it stayed that way, clinging with sweat. "Gone."

"You thought I left you?" She could hardly believe it. He didn't nod, but he didn't need to. The pained look on his face confirmed it. "Oh my god, no! I just wanted to get a job so we could buy some tickets home. I have a house, Michael. We don't have to live in a hotel or on the streets. I just wanted to do something to help."

"I thought you were gone," he repeated. The refrain was starting to get to her. She'd seen him like this once before—the day she "broke" him, as Raeni had put it. It was becoming increasingly clear that the end of this relationship would be the end of him.

"Why would I leave you?" Bryony lowered her voice. "You're everything to me."

He choked on his next words. "Because I shorten your life. Because being with me is too public for you. Because I . . . I can't control the part of me that paralyzes you. How can you be okay with all that?"

"Well, I'm not." She shrugged. He was right that she'd been uneasy with the direction her life seemed to be taking, but she saw it as a problem to be solved not run from. "But none of that's your fault, Michael. And I did sign on for this, you know. I knew you'd be different."

"You couldn't have known it would be like this."

"No, I couldn't. I don't know what's going to happen tomorrow either, and neither do you. But we'll deal with it together. That's the whole point of—" She couldn't finish. He'd lifted her into his arms and then dropped to his knees so her feet could touch the ground. As soon as he loosened his hold on her, she finished her sentence. "A relationship."

For a brief moment, he cupped her face between his palms. Then he dropped onto his hands and bowed his head. His entire body went rigid. And then she felt it—that rush, that warmth and fullness. The high. *Worship.* "Michael." She tapped him on the head. "Stop. I don't need it yet. Please."

"I know," he said through gritted teeth. He gripped the sand like he could pull the whole beach up with him. "Just . . . give me a second." He was fighting his nature, but not successfully. Bryony couldn't stand to watch him. If he lost this struggle, he might lose his mind along with it. Love and worship could never comingle. It's what had driven his father mad. So, amid another wave of ecstasy, she cleared her throat and began to sing.

Bryony's singing voice was not something she was proud of. In fact, she was damned ashamed of it, and she hoped Michael would be too. She'd never been able to carry a tune. Her little brother used to beg her to sing just so he could hear her parents beg her to stop. Now she sang with all her heart. The only song she could think of in her haste was *O Holy Night*, which she was certain she'd butcher adequately. She began timidly and raised her voice as her confidence grew. Michael's worship wavered but only a little, and she dared to think her singing might not be that bad after all. Then she came to the line, *Fall on your knees!* And she sang it at full volume.

Michael shot up and covered her mouth with one hand. "Stop, for the love of god." He laughed when she narrowed her eyes at him. He pulled his hand away, and she spat out the sand that had gotten in her mouth.

Hardly worth the humiliation, she thought, but then again, it had worked. Michael looked at her with adoring eyes, but that was all. Adoration, she could handle. "You didn't have to go that far," she said.

"Oh, yes I did. Believe me." He grabbed her shoulders and kissed her. He was becoming more aggressive with his affection, and Bryony rather liked it. He splayed one hand against her back and bowed his body as she arched her own, locked in his ever-deepening kiss. He wrapped his long fingers around her thigh and coaxed her leg up, brushing one thumb across her knee as he did. His skin began to warm. *Good.* Bryony didn't taste a hint of worship in him any longer. It had been replaced with what might indelicately be described as abject lust.

As flavors went, Bryony was hardly a stranger to lust. She'd been a fumbling teenager in the backseat with the best of them. She'd never been so careless as to do anything that might result in pregnancy—contraception being scarce in their modern age and angels being the terrifying, puritanical overlords they were—but she'd been a lonely girl, and certain boys her age became far friendlier when you gave them what they wanted. She'd taken some pride in pleasing them. It was a gift, she supposed, and sometimes you had to give gifts to make friends. But the boys were never so friendly to her afterwards, and she frequently found herself just as alone as she was at the start.

Michael distracted her from her memories, first by slipping his tongue into her mouth, which she audibly appreciated, and then by pulling away and staring over her shoulder, which she liked significantly less. "Don't turn around," he said, and she immediately wanted to. "Close your eyes." She did, and he lifted her into his arms and carried her down the beach. "Don't open them yet."

She hoped whatever he had planned included a soft spot to recline and some privacy. She was feeling extremely amorous, which could be the result of chasing a shot of worship with a long, sensuous kiss. Or she could stop overanalyzing everything and just accept the rather mundane fact that she was attracted to her own boyfriend.

When Michael set her down again, the sand was wet under her feet and the ocean an even louder roar in her ears. He turned her around and said, "Okay. You can open your eyes now." And Bryony stood stunned before an ocean of crashing, frothing bioluminescence. Michael draped his arms over her shoulders and pulled her back against his thighs. "Look down," he said. The sand under her feet glowed. She took a step and laughed. It was as though the entire beach was wired to respond to her touch.

"Is it dangerous?" she asked.

"No. Maybe try not to drink it."

She bent down and drew a circle in the sand. It luminesced and faded. She wrote her initials next, followed by, *I love you, Michael* . . . "What's your last name?" she asked him, realizing how ridiculous it was that she didn't already know it.

He hesitated. "I don't . . . really have one."

She looked up at him, puzzled.

"I never gave myself a surname, and my mother never gave me hers. I honestly don't even know what it was."

Bryony frowned. His first name had already faded, so she rewrote it in the sand and followed it with *Moss*. "There. You can have mine." His eyes lit up. He looked about to cry. "Don't make me sing again," she warned.

"No. No, I won't. It's just"—he smiled down at her—"a first."

"It's no big deal."

"Of course not." But she could see by the way he had to stifle his grin that it was a big deal to him. For a brief moment, he seemed to deliberate and finally come to a decision. "Life is short." He crouched, wrapped his arms around her, and walked her into the surf.

"What are you doing?" She laughed.

"Going for a swim." The waves rose and pushed against her. When they receded again, she felt the power behind their pull, and every muscle in her body tensed. "Don't be afraid," Michael said into her ear. "I won't let go of you. Just watch the sea. The angels say it's dead, but they're wrong. You can still see Rahab in the movement of the tides. Despite his own death, there's a world of life and light in his grave. It's so beautiful, isn't it?"

He dropped to his knees and set her on her feet but continued to anchor her, his hands curled around her ribcage, as the ocean rose and fell from her chest to her hips. All around her, the sea glowed with a ghostly light. Every breaker burst into sparkling life. She spread her arms and watched the luminescence flow between her fingers like smoke. But if she was honest, just now, it wasn't the sea she found beautiful.

She murmured, "Michael, I've been thinking about what happened last night." He tensed but she went on. "About the seraph. We've been intimate before, on *Dragonfly*, but last night you were drunk. That was new, wasn't it? Maybe that explains it. Maybe the seraph shows itself more easily when you're drunk."

"So I just have to stay sober?"

"Maybe." She shrugged and turned to face him. "Maybe we should test it." She dragged her hand down his shirtfront, let it slip under the water, and felt for herself how much he wanted her. His grip on her tightened. She hesitated, blushed, and offered what she could. "I can take you home if you want."

He bowed over her, one hand at the small of her back, drawing her close. "Right now?"

"Only if you want."

He breathed shakily into her ear. "But we don't have tickets yet."

She laughed because he'd misunderstood. The romances he read were old ones. He didn't know the modern euphemisms, and she loved that about him. In some ways, he was every bit as naïve as she was. She decided not to correct him, not to tell him she meant to relieve his tension with her hands and take him *all the way home*, as the boys from her youth liked to say. Instead, she caressed him beneath the waves and asked, "Do you want me to stop?"

He shook his head. "But I should warn you. If you go on . . ." His breath hitched as she increased the pressure of her touch.

"If I go on?"

"If you go on, I'll be forced to repay you."

She laughed again, this time because *she* had misunderstood. She'd thought perhaps he meant to warn her about climax, assuming she was unfamiliar with the concept. But no, he meant to flirt, and she had every intention of playing along. "And how do you intend to do that?"

He detached his mouth from her throat to murmur, "I could show you."

"Could you?"

He nodded. "I could, but you're wearing entirely too many clothes." With that he stood, lifted her into his arms, and took long strides toward the beach like a creature emerging from the deep.

"Where are you taking me?" she asked.

He practically growled his answer. "Home." So he was a fast learner. "It's not home if you're not there with me."

CHAPTER FIVE

The particular darkness of a moonless night made the spectacle of bioluminescence even more stunning. But as they approached the silhouette of the hotel's guest rooms, Bryony thought she and Michael could have used a bit more light. Rows of identical sliding glass doors and private patios greeted them. Bryony murmured, "Which one is ours?"

"I . . . can't tell."

"We'll have to go all the way around and walk in through the front."

Michael shook his head. "We're not presentable."

"Just a little wet. We're on our honeymoon, aren't we? People do all kinds of crazy things on their honeymoons."

"I didn't mention a honeymoon to them."

"But they think we're married. You can just slip it into conversation that we're meant to be on our honeymoon. Then they have to forgive us for spontaneity. It's a rule."

He let out a low, husky laugh as they turned to walk along the beach. "Is it?"

"Absolutely, it is." She kicked up the sand and continually glanced at the glowing surf. "Newly married couples aren't acting like themselves. That's why they say *the honeymoon is over* when you start acting like yourselves again."

He chuckled. "I don't think that's what that means." He may have gotten her joke, but by the sudden warming of his hand, she could tell it was more than a joke to him. She was certain, if she could see him now, he would be blushing furiously. Was the idea of marriage actually turning him on?

She decided to test her hypothesis, a little proud she even remembered the word *hypothesis*, let alone what it meant. "So we have to act like a married couple from now on, don't we? How do you say *my husband* in Spanish?"

"Mi esposo," he answered, his skin growing warmer.

"I can remember that." She grinned. "And how do you say *I love you?*"

Warmer. "Te amo."

They passed the end of the hotel where the landscape rose into a magnificent cliffside. She made a play of practicing her Spanish. "Te amo, mi esposo."

He stopped walking. He was positively radiating heat. "You're doing this on purpose."

She just smiled.

Michael returned her smile with a look that bored a hole all the way through her. "I can't wait another minute, let alone ten." He lifted her and laid her down in the sand before joining her. She shrieked in delighted surprise. "You've no one to blame but yourself." He nuzzled into her, and Bryony was thrilled. She'd been afraid the beach had become a sacred place to him, like a church. But he seemed more than willing to turn it into a bedroom. He planted one knee between her legs and slipped a hand under the hem of her shirt.

"Te amo . . ." she whispered into his ear. "Mi esposo."

He kissed her mouth and settled himself against her thigh. His hand found the buttons on her jeans and made quick work of them. But when his fingers slid lower, she caught his wrist and stopped him. He immediately drew back. "What's wrong?"

She bit her lip and agonized over how to put her worries into words when she herself didn't know exactly what they were. "It's just . . . I've never been on the receiving end of . . . this sort of thing." Her heart pounded and her body was sweating under his. The heat rolling off him felt like sitting too close to the fireplace on a cold winter's day—the slightest discomfort mingled with enough pleasure that she knew she would never move away.

"Do you want me to stop?" He repeated her own question back to her.

She shook her head. "I just wanted you to know before you started. I've heard . . ." God this was hard, talking so openly, but she supposed she would have to get used to it. "I've heard some things can be painful at first."

"Oh, that." He grinned. His being simultaneously less experienced and more knowledgeable than she was made for an interesting dynamic. "This shouldn't hurt at all." He paused, and a look of concern crossed his face. "You'd tell me if it did, wouldn't you?"

"Should I?"

His eyes went wide. "Yes! You should."

"Okay." She let go of his hand. "Show me."

"With pleasure." He settled back against her, bringing his forehead to hers, letting his breath warm her before he kissed her again. He slid his hand back under her waistband. "And I'll go slowly." He kissed along her jaw and made his way down to her neck. His tongue barely grazed her skin as his hand inched lower. "So slowly."

He rose to her mouth again and kissed her, tasted her, consumed her. His fingers tenderly massaged her until she couldn't even think anymore. She was lost in the world he created. He made his own desire evident in the way he pressed himself, hard and heavy, into her thigh. He wanted her so badly she doubted he could help himself anymore. If she was honest, neither could she. Her back arched involuntarily. Sand clung to her sea-soaked clothes, and she felt the grit of it against her bared skin. It reminded her of the day he'd saved her life. She vaguely realized how vulnerable she was now, half naked on the beach. But Michael's body, vaulted over her, felt like shelter.

Her breath came quick and ragged. Each sweet trespass of his tongue and the beckoning motion of his fingers followed the beat of the same silent drum. Soon, the undulation of his entire body against hers became an overwhelming pulse. She could almost hear it. Every inch of her skin came to bright, electric life as her heart beat in time with the rhythm he made.

And then she smelled incense.

Immediately, Michael withdrew his right hand and covered her eyes with his left. "Don't look." His voice was pinched and panting. "It's happening again." He trembled, this time with fear rather than desire. When the smoke cleared, he lifted off her, and she felt the chill night air on her overheated skin. He groaned in frustration, and she thought he could not have more perfectly expressed how she herself was feeling.

So it hadn't been a fluke after all, and it hadn't been the alcohol. Now the seraph surfaced without the sword. Every time Bryony saw it, she would be stunned, paralyzed, and it seemed to make an appearance whenever she and Michael reached a certain level of intimacy. *Damn.*

He sat beside her, his knees tucked to his chest, his head in his hands. She tried to suppress her own fears and comfort him. "It's okay," she said. "You caught it in time."

He turned his face to her in the dark. "It's not okay. We can't keep doing this. If anyone saw that . . . If they find out what I am . . ."

"They won't."

"Bryony, they'll kill me."

Bryony lay awake most of the night agonizing over why she hadn't worried for Michael's safety when she definitely should have. Angels were feared and hated all over the world, and she didn't think people would make much of a distinction between an angel and a half angel. In fact, she had little doubt most would relish the thought of a mortal angel—one who could suffer, one who could die. She'd been so used to thinking of Michael as the massive, serpentine beast who wielded the death sword. She'd forgotten he was also human, a pacifist, and far too trusting.

She went to work early that afternoon, chopping, prepping, and setting up tables. She was glad for the rush when it came. The more she had to do, the less time she had to chat with her boss, who couldn't stop going on about the mysterious light he'd seen last night. "You think it was an angel?" he'd asked. "I hope not." Others had seen the light, too, but no one seemed to have any idea of its origin.

After three weeks, Bryony began to smile more at the customers. She started to wait tables, her Spanish improving by the day. The tourists became less loathsome to her now that she saw them through Michael's eyes. She even managed to take the same question that had so enraged her the first time she'd heard it without blushing or throttling the person who asked. "Eso es privado," she'd answered with a good-natured smile. *That's private.*

Apparently, Gloria was telling every tourist the story of how a giant had turned up on her doorstep with nothing, and how her hotel had saved him and his wife. Michael refused to take donations, so people brought their money to Bryony instead, and she was happy to pocket whatever they were willing to give. Her experience as a healing god made taking gifts from strangers an easy routine. Sometimes it was the only way to survive. That the gawkers thought to give Michael anything at all warmed her heart. And it gave her something pleasant to dwell on when she lay next to him at night with her legs tucked between his knees, completely, agonizingly chaste.

The day Bryony and Michael left, the hotel gave them a beautiful send-off. There were trays of little cakes and plenty of beer on the house. They were gifted travel kits and toiletries. Gloria even gave Bryony a pink sundress, which Michael could have told her was not his wife's style. But Bryony had been so excited to finally go home, she wore it gladly, and it looked beautiful on her.

The first leg of the trip was pleasant enough. Even as a child, Michael had been fond of train stations. They were a safe place to shelter in a pinch. If anyone asked, he would explain that his mother was on her way—he'd just been too excited and arrived too early. Sometimes, a kind person would offer to bring him a sandwich while he waited, and he always accepted gratefully, as he was always, always hungry. Even now, the station looked like a cathedral to him, but without the rows of pews and candles, and sadly, without the pipe organ.

Bryony returned from collecting their tickets and sat on the bench beside him. "We have a few minutes. Do you want to get lunch?"

They ate at the platform, Bryony's expression becoming more mischievous with every bite she took. Eventually, Michael couldn't stand it anymore. "Okay, you have to tell me what you keep grinning about before I lose my mind over it."

"Don't joke about losing your mind." She pointed the corner of her sandwich at him and then bit it off. "I'm just excited to show you the present I got you."

He couldn't help but smile back. "My love, what have you done?"

She held up a finger while she chewed and swallowed. "If I tell you, it won't be a surprise. Oh, fine." She didn't even wait for him to protest. She wanted to spill her secret so badly. "I upgraded our tickets and got us a sleeper cabin."

Michael tried not to choke on his last bite. She really didn't know. He was going to have to break it to her. "Bryony, I'm not sure you realize how small those cabins are."

She cocked her head and continued to look like a kid who'd just blatantly cheated at cards and was certain she'd get away with it. "Ooh, but I *just* upgraded because they had one left. I doubt they'll let us change back now." She pulled two lollypops from her pocket. "Strawberry or pineapple?"

Michael pushed a hand through his hair. This was not going to be a pleasant trip at all. "None, thank you."

Bryony unwrapped the pineapple and shoved the strawberry back into her pocket. "Well, if you don't like the cabin, you can just sleep in the observation car." She popped the candy into her mouth, and the sound of it knocking against her teeth sent shivers of the very best kind down Michael's spine. How could he ever say no to her? He would find a way to fit into a sleeper cabin if it killed him. He would fold himself into thirds and stay that way for the full two-day trip.

As soon as he stepped aboard the train, Michael was anxious to sit down. He had to bend over almost double to make his way to the cabin. This was going to be hell. At least it was hell in good company. But when Bryony opened the door to their cabin, he had to eat his own words. The space was so much more than he'd imagined. There was a long bench on one side that would unfold into a double bed in the evenings, and beyond it, floor space for days. "What is this?"

She grinned around the stem of her lollypop. "Special access cabin." She quoted what he was certain had been written on the brochure. "For people with mobility challenges and special needs." She shrugged. "I told them I was traveling with you, and they told me this cabin hadn't been booked yet, so I upgraded. Check out the bathroom. It actually has a shower in it."

Now her excitement was infectious. Now he understood what it was about. He sat on the bench and let his legs stretch out across the cabin. Instant relief. People didn't tend to realize how much of one's height was in the legs. Bryony, for example, came up to his stomach when standing, but if they both sat, her head rose to his shoulders. He almost always preferred to sit when he could, especially if the ceiling was shorter than he was. This was nothing short of a miracle. He took Bryony by the hand and tugged her down beside him. "You"—he reached into the pocket of her pink dress and snagged the strawberry lollypop—"are a gift."

She could not stop smiling. "Luckily, we have no luggage to take up space."

"A gift," he repeated, his voice low and honeyed. He leaned in, kissed behind her ear, and murmured, "And I want to unwrap you right now."

She laughed, and her throat moving under his lips was exquisite. "Don't get ahead of yourself," she said. "We have to get home first."

God she had no idea how much she tortured him. "I can kiss you at least." He pulled the candy from her mouth and kissed her. She tasted like saccharine pineapple, and he was certain he would never taste the flavor again without remembering this moment. The frustration of the last three weeks coalesced, and heat rose to his cheeks. She must have felt it, too, because she quickly pushed him away.

"Not here," she whispered.

He groaned. "Then you're going to have to be much crueler from now on because kindness is . . . Honestly, it's a bit of a turn on for me." Her eyebrows shot up. He didn't usually speak so candidly, but he was quickly becoming comfortable with her. And to hell if it wasn't the absolute, albeit embarrassing, truth.

"Really?" she said, incredulous.

"Fair warning."

"Oh, you aren't kidding, are you?" She took her lollypop back and stared at the ceiling in thought. "So matrimony and kindness."

He grimaced. "And hard candy."

She burst out laughing and drew her legs onto the bench to kick him playfully. "Wow." She turned the lollypop in her mouth, letting it drag against the back of her teeth. "So now that I know what your buttons are . . ."

"You'll be careful not to push them?"

She curled her toes into his side. "Not at all what I was going to say."

Michael grinned and stared out the window as the train lurched to life.

"We'll be home in two days." She stretched and her legs were suddenly in his lap, her skirt pushed up past her knees. "I can't tell you how glad I am that our stupid, public honeymoon is almost over."

The word *honeymoon* found him and ate away at his resolve a little.

She went on teasing. "I do hope, once we get there, we can finally live like a normal husband and wife. I mean do you think we should even have a ceremony, or do we just consider ourselves married already?"

He brought his knees up and tried to breathe. "So you intend to use all the information you've gained—which I freely gave you in a show of good faith—against me."

She spun the candy in her mouth one more time. "You told me to be cruel."

He knew the broad smile he wore now gave him away completely. She was merciless, and he loved it. But what he loved about her teasing wasn't the way it drove his need so much as the way it drove her confidence—the way she sat a little straighter, touched him a little more freely. She felt powerful, and he wouldn't have taken it from her for the world. No, he wanted to watch her shyness fall away. Now that they were away from the crowds, she was like another person entirely. He loved both versions of her. But this version he saw so seldom, he would give anything to capture it in a mason jar and watch it glow all night before releasing it back into the wild.

Chapter Six

Every day, Bryony had to remind herself that Michael actually liked the company of people. If she'd been alone, she would've been happy to hide away in her private cabin for the entire trip. But Michael wanted to sit in the observation car with its windows that stretched from the floor and arched overhead. He was happy to chat with total strangers and answer the same questions again and again. *How tall are you? How do you fit in a car? How much do you eat?*

At night, Bryony tugged the mattress and pillows off the top bunk and latched it back in place so Michael had room to sit. There was no chance he would be able to fully recline anywhere in the room. At least he looked more comfortable than he'd be in a row of seats. She turned out the light and positioned the mattress on the floor. Michael had piled pillows behind his back and sat propped in the bunk staring out the window.

He glanced down at Bryony. "What on earth are you doing?"

"Setting up my bed."

"No, you aren't. Get up here." He gestured for her to sit beside him. The lower bunk was a double after all. "We've been sharing a bed for weeks. I think we can handle it."

She scrunched up her face. "I don't think we'll both fit."

He reached over and pulled her onto his lap. "Just for a moment then."

She reclined into him like he was an easy chair, and he kissed the top of her head. They both listened to the clacking of the train on the tracks and watched the land roll by in the night. The moon was new and the stars bright on the horizon. "Do you miss navigating?" she said absently. In her mind's eye, she could see him measuring the stars with his sextant and chronometer, charting their course at his work table.

"A little," he answered. "But not as much as I would have missed you." He wrapped his arms around her and squeezed. "No, I made the right choice."

"You never doubt it?"

"Never." His voice was soft, but she felt it vibrate against her back like thunder. "Do you imagine I'm following you home while pining away for a lonely life at sea?"

Bryony didn't answer because the answer was *yes*. It shamed her—her own lack of confidence, her doubt that she could ever make up for what she'd taken from him.

He sighed and held her tighter. "Think of my devotion as a non-human trait if that helps you to believe in it. Devotion is where I'm most comfortable. Because of what I am, I need to adore you. I need to follow and protect you." He brought his mouth closer to her ear. "I need to hold you in the dark and dream about what it will be like to cross your threshold. These aren't things I had before you came into my life, and I ached for them. Couldn't you tell? I don't think I was subtle about it."

"No, you weren't." She recalled his romance novels, corner-worn and spine-cracked like they were for study rather than pleasure, like he was preparing for the most important exam of his life. "You just seemed so content."

"But I never wanted contentment. I wanted to burn up and know. I was an unlit candle. I swear, I wouldn't be happier unused and unloved. So set me on fire, Bryony Moss. It's what I was made for."

Late in the night, Bryony woke to a rush of worship. Michael had fallen asleep behind her, his arms still wrapped around her. He must have been dreaming—worshiping in his dreams. That was how natural the act was to him, and Bryony chose not to stop it this time. She told herself it was because she didn't want to wake him, but if she was honest, she'd also grown hungry in the last few days. She hated that she needed this from him, but she did.

When they disembarked the following day, Bryony told him what had happened in the night, and he apologized, not for the worship but for letting her go hungry. "Well," she mused as they waited for their taxi. "Now that we've got a good handle on my schedule, we can start to wean me off."

He blinked at her. "No."

"Just half a day at a time. What am I at now, three weeks? We'll go three weeks and half a day, and see how that works out."

"Absolutely not." He was adamant.

Bryony pouted. "But what if I want to be weaned off? What if I want to prove that gods can be saved?"

"Bryony, it isn't your job to prove anything. You were tricked into becoming a god. If anyone should risk their life to fix this, it's Loki."

She scoffed. "I highly doubt he'll risk anything for anything. Really, I don't mind. I'm almost certain it can be done."

"And I am certain you won't become a test subject because I won't allow it."

That was the end of the conversation. Michael would hear no more of it while they waited, and Bryony wasn't comfortable bringing it up in the taxi.

Martha's van was still parked at the beach where Bryony had left it the day she joined the Black Armada. At first, she had a hard time believing no one had bothered to steal it. But as she struggled to open an unlocked door and grabbed the key from a glove compartment that refused to latch closed again, it began to make sense. The van may as well have been made of rust. Had she not known otherwise, she would've assumed it didn't run, but the damned thing had always been as reliable as its owner. Bryony turned the key in the ignition, and the beast immediately roared to life.

Michael was equally impressed. He sat with his knees angled sharply despite having the passenger seat as far back as it would go.

"Apologies in advance for this little jaunt of the trip." She spoke playfully, but she meant every word. They had to drive over a mountain pass to the east. If she pushed it, she figured they could make it before night. But so many hours in a seat built for someone almost half his size was bound to be uncomfortable.

The closer they drew to Martha's Café, the more Bryony's stomach churned. Within miles of home, she turned off the road and jumped out, expecting to be sick. She paced, crouched, and hugged her knees with a frustrated groan.

Michael followed her out. "Do you need me to drive?"

She snapped back up. "Can you?"

"It's been a while, but I'm sure I can manage." He shrugged. "It's hardly rocket science."

"Martha's van is more art than science."

Michael squeezed her shoulder and led her back to the van. "It'll be okay, you'll see. People aren't as unforgiving as you think they are." How did he read her so easily? He folded himself into the driver's seat and drove the rest of the way.

It was hypnotic, watching the country hills roll past like a green-and-gold sea. Bryony hadn't seen these hills since she'd left with Shakespeare, following his harebrained scheme to find and kill the deadliest godhunter in the world. Well, now that same godhunter was following her home. She'd found him all right. She'd just neglected to kill him. She'd fallen in love with him instead. Like an idiot. She supposed she was lucky the godhunter had been every bit as tenderhearted and foolish as she was. He had, after all, somehow managed to fall in love with a god and an outright con.

Bryony was so lost in her anxiety, she didn't even notice they'd pulled up to Martha's Café until Michael said, "Is this it?"

She jerked her head out of her hands and saw the little cabin that used to be like a second home to her. It looked smaller than she remembered. "I can't do this," she muttered.

Michael stared at the café with a dreamy expression. "It's cute."

"I really can't do this." Bryony opened the door and jumped out. She decided to leave the van and walk home. Martha would figure it out. No problem. But it was too late. The woman must have heard the familiar roar of her faithful engine because she came jogging out of her café, wiping her hands on her apron with a look of utter shock on her face.

Bryony froze like terrified prey. Part of her demanded she run and run now. Another part was nagging her to keep calm. The third and loudest part told her with absolute confidence that it would be prudent to prepare for the worst possible outcome. *No, really. Martha hates you. Look at her expression. She knows you played her for a fool. Would you forgive something like that? Could you?*

But Bryony had forgiven such a thing and worse, hadn't she? With Loki.

The pessimistic side of her was quickly proven wrong when Martha closed the distance between them, pulled Bryony into her long arms, and hugged her so tightly she could scarcely breathe. "Oh, sweetheart, you came back. Thank god you came back. You have no idea how worried I was."

"I'm sorry." Bryony sniffed, on the verge of tears.

"Oh, no you don't." Martha pulled back and dabbed at her own eyes with a cloth napkin. "You don't owe me any kind of apology."

Bryony's voice was thin and small. "But I lied to you. For years."

"You listen to me. You saved my husband's life. You gave me so much more time with him. I will never, ever not owe you for that. It's *what* you did that matters. Do you understand? I don't care the story you told in the process." The slam of the driver-side door and Martha's astonished gasp told Bryony that Michael had finally emerged. "Oh! Who's this?"

Bryony didn't get the chance to introduce him. Another voice—an exceptionally familiar one—shouted from the door of the café. "That's him! That's the godhunter!" It was Shakespeare, or Loki, or whatever name he went by these days. He looked like an ordinary man. His hair was tied back and his ginger beard cut short. Bryony couldn't help but notice he was also wearing an apron. "Get him away from her!" he shouted. "He tried to murder her. He's half angel!" Bryony could have slapped him for revealing Michael's secret so carelessly.

Martha stepped back and Michael froze. Only Bryony found tongue enough to respond. This was Shakespeare after all, her pet crow turned trickster, who'd lived with her for the last ten years, through many trials, mutual teasing, and much stealing of food. "He did not try to murder me, you ass. I'd be dead if not for him."

But Loki only had eyes for Michael. "Not so tough without your sword drawn, are you? Huh? Still a coward? Still too scared to fight me man to man?"

Michael just sighed. He didn't seem at all intimidated by Loki's blustering. He turned to Martha and held out his hand. "Pleased to finally meet you, madam. I'm Michael. I've heard so much about you."

"Likewise." Martha took his hand, all cordiality and calm. "My goodness, how tall are you?"

Michael didn't miss a beat. "Seven feet, ten inches. I've just been measured, as it happens." He was grinning like a kid announcing straight A's to a parent. "I'm quite pleased to finally know it because it means my growth has slowed."

"That's so good to hear, Michael. But you must tell me, are you really the godhunter?"

Loki broke through their wall of civility. "Of course he is, Marty. Would I lie to you?"

Yes, Bryony thought.

Michael continued to ignore the shapeshifter. "I'm afraid that's true, madam."

"Oh, call me Martha. We're not formal here. Looks like our little god has won you over, has she?"

Michael smiled. "One hundred percent."

Loki pointed an accusing finger. "That snake seduced her!"

"Oh, shut up, bird." Bryony spun on him. "If anything, it was the other way around. And if anyone here's a seducer and a liar, it's you. You have no right to talk."

Martha continued her conversation with Michael as though Bryony and Loki didn't even exist. "We should have known she'd go about things her own way. She never was one to follow tradition."

"She is very, uh . . . diplomatic." Michael blushed.

Martha laughed. "Michael dear, do come inside. You must be famished after all that driving. Oh, where did you come from anyway?" She led him into her café as he told her about their travels. Bryony and Loki both stared after them, open-mouthed and pink with unsatisfied rage.

It hit Bryony all at once that Martha had not only forgiven her, but missed her and was happy to see her. Before she quite understood why, she'd burst into relieved tears, and Loki was beside himself watching her howl. "Oh, for Christ's sake." He pulled her into his arms and held her like an old friend. "You ridiculous girl. Of course she was going to forgive you."

Loki was warm and solid, and his voice sounded like home. "I missed you so much, Shakespeare," she said without thinking, and it was the unmitigated truth. Yes, his lies had unseated her identity and everything she thought she knew about her life. Still somehow, this trickster, this monster had slipped into the empty place her family had left in her heart.

"I missed you too," he said. "You know, I really did. And you can call me Bill."

She pulled back. "Bill?"

He grinned, his eyes still full of mischief. "Get it?"

Bill Shakespeare. She rolled her eyes and hugged him again. "Okay, Bill. Does Martha know the truth about you?"

"I should hope so, since you just outed me as a bird." He stepped back and looked down at her soberly. "But it's Martha and only Martha who knows. To everyone else, I'm your friend Bill. I came here to tell them the truth about you and offer them the trinket that allowed you to heal them."

"And they believed you?"

"Of course they did. A few left town in a flurry of indignation, but the rest are still here, as is the sword. They come to me when they need it now. It's only a matter of time until someone steals it and starts charging fees, but never mind. How are you?" He narrowed his eyes. "And why the hell are you here with the godhunter?"

She glared back at him, glad to finally be free of her sentimentality enough to do so. "He's not a godhunter anymore. Anyway, why do you hate him so much?"

Loki started back toward the café, and Bryony followed. "I don't get along with snakes," was all the answer he gave.

"He spared your life."

"Only because of your siren ways and you know it."

They entered and found Michael sitting in a chair at the end of their regular booth, the curtains pulled aside to make room for him.

"Oh, now he's going to invade our turf, is he?" Loki snarled.

"Yes, *Bill.* And he's going to live in my house, too, so I hope you have somewhere else to hang your hat."

"Done and done, Ms. Moss. I now live behind the café, thank you very much. I have my favorite person and my favorite meals within arm's reach at all times." He watched Martha come from the kitchen as he slid into the booth, giving Michael a highly indelicate side-eye.

Bryony sat across from him and picked up a menu. It hadn't changed at all, and something about that was a comfort to her. Martha was the same. Loki's attitude reminded her that he was indeed still Shakespeare. She couldn't help feeling that she hadn't lost much of what mattered to her really. And she'd gained Michael. Just now, Martha stood beside him and tapped her pad with a pen. "Order another," she said. "I imagine you need it. It's all on the house. It's always on the house for our mistress, and it always will be." Michael blushed and thanked her.

After she left, Loki leaned in and stage whispered to Bryony. "I just adore her, don't you? I've never met a more generous, levelheaded human in my life. She simply cannot be defeated. Did you know she ran this café without help while her husband was sick? She worked morning, noon, and night to maintain this beautiful business while she cared for him, and I'm just . . . Well, you know me. Anyone who can produce this kind of quality service in such trying circumstances is not to be underestimated." He leaned back, apparently pleased with his enthusiastic accolades.

Michael did not play along. He asked his question at a normal volume. "Are you in love with her?"

"Don't be disgusting." Loki scoffed. "Must everything be a romance to you? I admire the woman, that's all. And if you knew my wife, you'd never think to suggest such a thing. My wife is unequaled in loyalty, beauty, and courage. *Unequaled*, I swear it."

"I remember reading about your wife when I was young." Michael leaned in and spoke with a sincerity that threw Loki completely off his game. "She sounds like an amazing person. Remind me, what's her name again?"

Loki softened immediately. Bryony had never seen him speak with such tenderness, not even of his favorite meals. "Sigyn," he answered. His eyes glossed over with what Bryony could only assume was eons of history. "And she is. Amazing."

"Where is she now, if you don't mind my asking?"

"Oh, here and there. Who can say?" Loki smiled at his memories and appeared to tuck them away again, as though he'd just removed a photograph from a pocket, kissed it, and quickly put it back. "When you're immortal, all the years seem to melt together. She's having a fine time, wherever she is, and we'll meet up again next century and tell each other everything. I'm sure to have forgotten you by then."

"She's a Jötunn too?"

Loki rolled his eyes. "Interesting assumption coming from you. No, she's a god. And don't go saying I have something in common with you. I'm certain that's what that sentimental look on your face means. I'll never have anything in common with a snake."

Michael sipped the water Martha had brought for him. On the surface, he appeared to take Loki's hatred in stride. But Bryony sensed some of that old loneliness creeping up on him, and she was not at all pleased. "Don't you have a snake for a son?" she said to her old crow. "I'm certain I heard that somewhere. A giant serpent, right? Circles the earth and all that."

Loki slid from the booth and stood, staring down at Bryony with eyes like fire. "Don't."

"Well?"

"Well, I liked you better when you thought I was a bird, that's all." The shapeshifter ground his teeth at her. She could see his jaw work under that magnificent beard, and she didn't care. "Fine. Yes, one son happens to be a serpent—from a previous relationship, mind you—but I make no claim on the bastard. He's a miscreant." Then he delivered a final blow, clapping Michael on the shoulder to punctuate every word. "He just. Never. Stops. Eating. Speaking of which, I should go help Martha in the kitchen. Her work load just doubled, didn't it?" And he stalked off.

Bryony shook her head. "Sorry about him. He was always kind of a mean little bird."

Michael nearly choked on his water. "*Little* is definitely not a word I would use to describe him."

"Is he a giant? I thought I remembered hearing that too."

"It's more complicated than that," Michael said, shrugging off the irony. "I hesitate to call anyone who can change his size at will a *giant*, but the essence of who he is isn't small. He's . . ." He stared up at the ceiling as though the right word was hiding among the fabrics draped there. "Elemental." He glanced back down and smiled. "Let's just say you're lucky to be on his good side. I doubt anyone else could bait him like that and get away with it."

"Ha!" Bryony couldn't help thinking of Loki as the little, black crow who begged for treats and tucked his head under his wing when he was tired. "He's not so scary. He's just ill-tempered."

Michael sighed and reached over to take her hand. "I'm glad he's your friend, but no matter what shape he takes, he's not of this world. Try to remember that. Don't take his alliance for granted. It's never been a sure bet. He can easily become a force of destruction on one bitter impulse, and he has. Loyalty is not his strong suit."

Bryony thought a moment. "I don't know. He seems entirely loyal to Martha. Even when he was a crow, he sang her praises endlessly."

"I think she reminds him of his wife. If the stories are true . . ." Michael paused a moment and frowned at an idea Bryony could not begin to interpret. "Sigyn followed him to hell."

Chapter Seven

Though the walk home would have been short enough, Martha insisted they keep her van. "It's dark out, and I hardly need the old beast," she said. "I only held on to it for sentimental reasons. I want you to have it. Take it, I insist."

Michael wondered what could make one person feel so much generosity toward another, but when Bryony stood at her own threshold and said, "Welcome home!" to him with that bright smile of hers, he understood completely. He wanted to give the world to her. An old van would not have given him a moment's hesitation.

Her home was a Victorian farmhouse with a heavy front door, a weathered veranda, and peeling blue paint. Michael ducked inside as Bryony proudly went around illuminating every lamp. At the foot of the main staircase, a wooden orb crowned the newel post. Over the years, her family must have polished it smooth with every touch. He noticed a path up the stairs where years of climbing had disproportionately worn away the finish. Every surface spoke of the house's history—the wainscoting, the textured green wallpaper, the fireplace. Oh, the fireplace was magnificent with its dark wood and decorative tiles. He ran his hands over the mantle, letting his fingers trace the scrolls and vines carved into it.

Bryony returned, having given light and life to the entire first floor. "Do you like it?"

"It's wonderful. How long has this been in your family?"

"Oh, years and years." She waved a dismissive hand. "I honestly don't know. My father's family tended to put down roots. My mother's never did. Staying here was her big sacrifice for him, I guess. She really did love him." She laughed. "I'm just glad it has high ceilings. The old houses usually do, you know."

"I know." He grinned at her. "It couldn't be more perfect. Show me the rest."

She bounced on the balls of her feet and showed him the kitchen and formal dining room. There was an upright piano in the parlor with yellowing keys and cobwebs draped like doilies over the top. "Do you play?" he asked.

"No, my father played. Music was never my strong suit. Come to think of it, I don't really have a strong suit, do I?"

She really was extraordinarily hard on herself. Michael wanted to deal a blow to the incessant little voice that seemed to constantly whisper to her that she was *not good enough*. He lifted her by the waist, ignoring her playful shouts of protest, and placed her on the staircase where she was almost equal to his height. Then he stood on the other side of the banister.

"Listen, Bryony. I've been a godhunter more than half the years I've been alive. I don't show mercy. I don't hesitate. No god has ever survived me." His expression grew severe at the memories. "That is, until you. You changed everything. I'm rethinking my entire life, and I wouldn't bet against Raeni and the Black Armada rethinking the way they do things too. If you'd been a master pianist, it would have changed nothing for us." He nuzzled her. He couldn't help it. It was so good to have her stand at his level, to just lean in and hold her. "I never needed a pianist anyway." He brushed his lips against the soft skin under her jaw. "What I needed was a home."

"I'm glad you like the house."

"I wasn't talking about the house."

She smiled and wrapped her arms around his neck. "It's all yours." Then she urged him around the banister and up the stairs. "Come and see the rest."

There was a small library at the top of the stairs with two comfortable chairs and a little table between them. All around the library were closed doors, and Bryony opened them one at a time. Michael glanced into each room as she revealed it. The process reminded him of a winter from his youth when he'd found a beach house with an Advent calendar still affixed to the refrigerator. He'd popped open each little door dutifully on the appropriate day and not given in to the temptation to open them all at once. The chocolate was old and had a bad texture, but he'd eaten it anyway. It was more about the ritual than anything, and Bryony revealing her home in little bursts of enthusiasm felt just the same.

"This is the master bedroom. And here's where my brother and I slept when we were little. This is the bathroom. There's a handheld shower, so I think it'll work for you. Maybe we can raise the curtain up a bit. Oh, and this was my mother's workroom."

So many years of wandering from empty house to empty house made Michael doubt the very concept of *home*. He could never wholly believe in good things that lasted. Even now, part of him questioned his own fortune as he ducked into the workroom and saw stacks of fabrics, a long cheval mirror, scissors, measuring tape, and a sewing machine.

He wanted to cry. He didn't, but he wanted to. *A sewing machine!* He drifted toward it. Was his mouth hanging open? Did he really care? His hands seemed to touch it of their own accord. "Does it still work?"

"Of course it does," Bryony said, beaming up at him. "And it's yours. The whole room is yours now."

Michael had used a sewing machine exactly once in his life. He never imagined he would one day own one. "This is amazing." He turned to face her. "This is . . ." He couldn't find the words, so he just repeated, "Amazing. I love you." Sometimes it was the only thing he could think to say to her. His chest expanded with nothing else. Just, *I love you.*

She laughed. "Do you want to see the attic? It's where my mother kept all her extra fabric. I bet you could find enough to make a change of clothes or two."

He stumbled after her, not wanting to take his eyes off the sewing machine. He touched the casing overhead as he ducked back through the door, imagining the hours he would spend in that room, not quite ready to leave it.

At the end of the hall, he waited as Bryony climbed the staircase to the attic. He needed to gather his thoughts and breathe. His heart was treading too close to worship. It built in him like a pressure. He leaned against a round window frame and pressed his forehead to the stained glass. Through a haze of purple, he could see a little grove of trees trembling in the wind. He focused on the branches, on the sensation of glass cooling his skin, on the woodgrain of the windowsill plucking at his fingertips like the drum of a music box. Somewhere downstairs, a clock was ticking.

Then he heard a gasp followed by, "What the hell?" And he immediately made his way up the stairs after her.

The half-sized, dusty room was stifling, but Michael walked on his knees to Bryony, who stood aghast in the middle of the attic. She had pulled the cord to illuminate a bare lightbulb overhead and now stared down at a litter of papers arranged into small piles like dried leaves in autumn. Most of the papers were yellowed with age, apparently taken from the envelopes that lay alongside them. It wasn't chaos. It was organized. Someone had done this.

"What the hell?" she repeated, blinking at the scene.

"You didn't do this?" Michael already knew the answer, but he still felt obliged to ask.

"Of course not! These are my family's letters. I would never disrespect them like this." She bent down and picked up one handwritten note that lay at her feet. "This one was from my father to my mother. He wrote her love letters when she traveled for performances. I haven't looked at them since he died. Who did this?"

Michael frowned. "Maybe someone broke in?" But no ordinary burglar would take the time to sit and read a person's letters, would they?

"All the doors were locked when we got here," Bryony said. "Every window was closed. The key was hidden where I've always kept it. I don't understand how they got in, unless . . ." Her face scrunched up in thought and suddenly smoothed again in bitter understanding. "Loki." She fumed. "He knew where the key was, and even if he didn't, he could have turned himself into a colony of ants and marched under the door. It was him. I know it. How dare he! He knows how important these are to me."

Michael tried to ignore his aching knees. "But why would he bother?"

She threw her hands up. Her good mood seemed to have taken a turn for the worse. "How can I ever know why he does what he does? He's practically a stranger to me." Michael put an arm around her shoulders, and she turned into him to accept the embrace. "I have to clean this up."

"Later," he said. Her body felt so small all of a sudden. How could he have even thought to worship her moments ago? Worship was a kind of dependence, and she needed him to be there for her, not the other way around. "We'll clean it up together. In the meantime, let's get some rest. If you're even half as tired as I am . . ."

She straightened in his arms. "Oh, of course!" She pulled away and hurried down the stairs. It took Michael a bit more time to crawl after her. As he descended, he heard a loud thud and a scraping sound. When he finally got to the bottom of the staircase, he saw Bryony trying to push a twin bed out of the smaller bedroom. She had turned it on its side, and the feet were caught on the doorframe. He could see it shift this way and that as she tested its position from the other side.

"Let me help with that." He took hold of the bedframe and quickly maneuvered it through the door. Together they moved the whole assembly to the master bedroom. Michael asked where she wanted it, assuming she meant for them to sleep separately. The look on her face told him he'd made a grievous error.

She shifted her end toward a large four-poster bed. "Here," she said. She turned the twin bed sideways and slid it up against the foot of the other. Michael didn't know whether to laugh or cry. She disappeared and returned carrying a rope with which she proceeded to secure the two beds. His hands tensed and relaxed in turn.

Before she had quite finished, he pleaded, "Please stop. Oh, please come here." And he greedily took her into his arms, pulling her down onto the bed with him. The stretch he allowed himself when he finally lay down was heaven after days in taxis, trains, and vans. "How will I ever make it up to you?"

Bryony lay on her side next to him, her head propped on one elbow. "Must you always make such a big deal of little favors?"

He wrapped his arms around her and pulled her in until she was comfortably tucked against his chest. "They aren't little favors," he murmured. "They're enormous, important favors. You'll save the world with them one day."

Bryony woke the next morning, still in the clothes she'd worn the night before. Michael slept beside her with one arm shoved under his pillow, his hair as black as soot against the white pillowcase. Neither of them had found the energy to ready themselves for bed last night.

She dressed quietly, choosing a familiar Regency gown from her mother's old costumes. It felt so good, slipping that black dress over her head. She zipped up the side and pulled a pair of lace gloves from a dresser drawer. She'd just given up trying to wrangle her hair into a braid when something struck the window. Bryony jumped at the sound. Then it struck again. And again. It was a familiar *tap, tap, tap*—more forceful than a twig in the wind, lighter perhaps than a pebble thrown from the ground.

Bryony pushed back the curtain to find a little, black crow standing on the windowsill. *Loki.* She pressed her finger to her lips in an effort to quiet him, and the bird cocked his head. Then he drew back to peck again. "Dammit, bird," she hissed and opened the window before he could wake Michael.

The crow hopped in and waddled across the floor to the bedroom door. Bryony opened that for him too. As soon as he was in the hall, he shifted into a full-sized, completely naked man. "Hello, Bryony," he said, clearly proud of the shocked expression she wore.

She groaned. "Can't you ever turn human with clothes on?"

He looked down at himself and clapped his hands to his cheeks. "Oh, dear! How mortifying. Please accept my deepest apologies and condolences for your maidenly innocence."

"Oh, for god's sake." Bryony fished around her linen closet for a towel, which she tossed to him. "Go and get your pants. I'm certain you left them in the yard."

"That I did. Martha didn't want to wake you, so I told her I'd check to see if you were sleeping."

"And you did this by banging on my window? You're lucky Michael's a heavy sleeper." She followed the shapeshifter downstairs. The ease with which he moved through her house unnerved her, but she reminded herself it had been his home too. Shakespeare would feel comfortable enough to push his way in and stomp around like he owned the place. Seeing him as a man was something Bryony was going to have to get used to.

Loki made his way to the kitchen and opened the back door for Martha, who walked in overloaded with grocery bags. "Grab the rest, will you? It's on the porch." His state of undress didn't seem to throw Martha at all. She was an engine that ran without the slightest hiccup, and Loki obeyed her like a well-behaved retriever. It was frankly astounding.

Martha set her bags on the counter and paused to give Bryony a quick hug. "I thought you might need something in your pantry," she said. "How's your . . . friend?"

"It's okay to call him my boyfriend." Warmth bloomed in Bryony's cheeks when she thought of Michael still asleep in her bed. "It's more than okay, actually."

"No kidding?" Martha laughed and began to stock the pantry with baking goods and dry cereal. "If you don't mind my asking, how far along in the relationship are you? Will we be hearing wedding bells any time soon?"

"Not if I have anything to say about it." Loki stood in the doorway, now fully clothed and carrying three more grocery bags. "They hardly know each other. They met less than two months ago."

"I'm fairly confident I know him better than I know you," Bryony argued. "And I lived with you for ten years."

Loki had bitten off the corner of a block of cheese before putting it in the fridge and now spoke with his mouth full. "That's only because I was lying to you the whole time."

It took Bryony a moment to get past the bluntness of what he'd just admitted. How was one supposed to argue with the truth? "Right. Speaking of that, you're no longer welcome to enter my house uninvited. Do you understand? I can't believe you came back here after everything and just . . . helped yourself to the place while I was gone."

"And what makes you think I set one foot inside this house?" He pulled an egg out of the fridge, cracked it on the counter, and promptly swallowed the innards. "These are still good."

Bryony nearly gagged. Somehow, the things he did as a bird were disgusting to her now that he was a man. "I found the letters. Did you think I wouldn't?"

He blinked. "What letters?"

She was about to argue with him and insist he knew exactly what she was talking about, but his perplexed expression gave her pause.

"The . . . The letters in the attic. My family's papers. Everything's been gone through, scattered."

"I see." Loki sniffed another package and made a face at it. "And you think I wouldn't have the foresight to put things back after I rifled through them?"

"I . . ." Bryony thought a moment. It did seem entirely unlike him.

Martha leaned back against the kitchen counter. "Do you mean to say you had a break-in while you were away? Did they steal anything?"

"No," Bryony answered. "They didn't really break in either. All the doors were still locked, and the key was where I always keep it. Shakespeare was the only one who could get into my house without breaking in. That's why I thought—"

"Believe me," Loki interjected. "I have absolutely zero interest in your family's paperwork. I have zero interest in paperwork in general. I've gotten everything I ever needed to know about you just by asking. In bird form, obviously. You're inordinately keen to talk to animals." He smiled in a way Bryony supposed was meant to be charming, but it produced the opposite effect in her. "Do you prefer the crow? I can change back if you like. It's not a bad shape to be in. Food tastes remarkably better, for one."

"Don't you dare," Bryony snarled at him. "Especially if it means you'll turn up completely naked in my hallway again."

Loki rolled his eyes. "As if you never stripped in front of me."

"I thought you were a bird at the time! And speaking of that—"

"It's not like I got any pleasure—"

"I'm sorry, what? Oh, you'd better think of a compliment now."

"Your breasts are flawless. There. Will that do? Now your turn."

"Children!" Martha shouted to quiet them, and just for a moment, Bryony saw a sliver of Raeni in her. "We have another participant in the conversation. You may want to keep him in mind before taking this any further."

Michael had ducked in so quietly only Martha had noticed him. Now he stood in the kitchen, half frozen between rubbing his eyes and yawning. His cheeks were turning a shade Bryony recognized as embarrassment mixed with anger. She let her dispute die in favor of throwing her arms around him and burying her face in his wrinkled shirt.

"You're up," she said gently. "I'm sorry if we woke you."

"It's all right." His eyes scanned the kitchen, the guests, the food. "Did you go shopping already?"

"Martha did." Bryony pulled away, but Michael kept hold of her hand.

"I didn't help at all," Loki said, his sarcasm evident. "And my thorough knowledge of what you typically keep in your pantry was of no use whatsoever."

Apparently, Bryony wasn't tired of arguing with him. "Knowledge ill-gotten, you ass," she snapped before she could stop herself. "And half of what I kept on hand was for you anyway."

"I know." Loki popped an unwashed grape into his mouth. "It still is. I'm so magnanimous, though, that I'm even willing to share with a snake."

Michael had disengaged from the conversation and was examining Bryony's lace gloves as though he'd never seen anything like them. He bowed over her and murmured, "You look stunning in this. Was it one of your mother's?"

She would never understand his ability to tune out the universe and focus only on the things that made him happy. That quality made him more beautiful than his high cheekbones, broad mouth, and dark eyes ever could. "It was," Bryony finally answered.

"It's good quality." He crouched beside her to examine the seams of her dress. "Did she make this herself?"

"Yes. For a production of *Mansfield Park*." Bryony would have loved to introduce Michael to her mother. She imagined the two of them discussing craftsmanship and technique.

"Did she play Fanny Price?"

He knew the story? But of course he did. Bryony laughed at her failure to predict him when he made it so incredibly easy. "She was Mary Crawford."

"I wish I could have seen her performance."

"Me too." She took his hand and kissed it. "She would have loved you."

CHAPTER EIGHT

"Stop freaking out," Loki mumbled later that afternoon. "You only make yourself more conspicuous." He'd insisted on accompanying Bryony to the shops. Martha had to open her café, and Michael had stayed behind to sew. Bryony had found enough spare fabric in the attic to get him started. Now she intended to buy more. She had a list, which she repeatedly forgot she was holding, crumpled in one fist. In truth, she could scarcely feel that hand anymore.

She was grateful it was Loki who'd joined her. He attracted less attention than Michael, albeit not by much. He walked beside her, tall and confident, in black jeans and a blue T-shirt that brought out the color of his eyes and contrasted the rosiness in his cheeks. Bryony thought his entire outfit was at least two sizes too small, but that seemed to be the style he preferred. Anyway, if you've got it, flaunt it, she supposed.

Loki definitely had *it*, whatever it was. He drew the attention of anyone whose tastes tended toward men, and some—Bryony was all but certain—whose tastes generally did not. The shape of every one of his muscles was apparent through the thin fabric of his shirt. Intentionally. Shamelessly. Adorably. She was reminded of the way Shakespeare used to strut, chest puffed out, head held high. Bryony was perhaps less impressed with his physique than everyone else, being privy to the fact that he could as easily change his shape as his outfit. His well-chiseled chest and biceps, therefore, were not so much the result of hard work and persistence as they were the result of whatever artistry went into choosing a body.

"Is Mr. Steward still here?" she asked.

"Nah, he didn't take the news so well. But his daughter took over for him, and she's infinitely more charming. So not a loss, in my opinion." Shakespeare always did have a way of making bad news into good—Bryony once called him *the King of Sour Grapes*—which was going to be a skill she appreciated now that she was about to learn just how many people actively hated her.

"I still can't believe you told them the truth."

"Neither can I. Could've come up with a sensational story given the time, but as you know, there wasn't any. It was entirely out of character for me."

"I know." Bryony smiled and held open the door to the fabric shop. "I won't forget it." She still hadn't told him that what he'd done had nearly killed her, and she didn't plan to. Shaming a person for doing the right thing didn't seem prudent, especially when that person was not known for his impeccable moral principles.

"Bill!" Julia Steward rounded the counter and gave Loki an enthusiastic hug. Bryony had never met her but remembered her father well. She was a younger woman, perhaps twenty, with mousy hair and big, chestnut eyes. "I'm so glad you came in today." She beamed. Bryony wanted to tell her that "Bill" was already married, but she supposed he enjoyed the attention regardless. Sheepishly, she dropped the crumpled, sweaty wad of paper onto the counter.

"Good lord, Bryony, you were supposed to hold it not murder it." Loki picked up the paper and smoothed it out for her. "Let's see . . ." He began to read the list aloud, and Julia went around her shop gathering fabrics, measuring, cutting, folding.

In the meantime, Bryony ran her fingers along the edges of stacked bolts and wondered at the many variations in color. She chose two fabrics that were not on Michael's list. One was the color of the sea in Mexico. The other was a black satin she thought might make a wonderful jacket lining. It sang against the tips of her fingers and sent shivers all through her. She hoped Michael liked them. If not, Julia told her she'd be happy to take them back.

"I want to formally thank you for saving my mother, and apologize on behalf of my father." Julia folded the fabric and wrapped it in tissue paper. "I know you did what you did to keep the sword safe. And I think, as you reacquaint yourself with some of your former congregants, you'll find there are many who feel the same."

Bryony left the shop carrying a stack of fabrics that hid the lower half of her face and offered a modicum of relief, while the man who used to be her pet insisted on dragging her from shop to shop to inform the rest of the community she'd returned. As though she had any importance now. She wasn't their god anymore. She couldn't heal a soul. She couldn't imagine any of them really knew her, let alone loved her. But again and again, she was proven wrong. Mr. Miyamoto, who owned the local bookshop, even offered her a job.

"I don't have any sales experience," she said, hoisting her bundle a little higher to hide her smile.

The slight Japanese man, who wore bell-bottoms and a brown leather jacket, had always reminded Bryony of a 1960s rock star. "Well, you've served the public before," he said. "I know for a fact you have a good work ethic. And you read, which is more than I could say for most."

"Oh, that reminds me." Bryony set her bundle on his counter. "Do you have any new romances in?"

Mr. Miyamoto stood. "Venturing into a new genre?"

"Oh, no. Well, maybe. It's actually for my boyfriend. He likes them, and he recently lost his entire collection."

As Loki browsed, he glanced over his shoulder and mumbled, "Insufferable man." He sounded like somebody's grandmother. Bryony made a mental note to tease him about it later.

Mr. Miyamoto rounded the corner and started toward a bookcase close to the door. "Here they are. Do you know his favorite subgenre by chance?"

"Subgenre?" Bryony bit her nail.

"What do the covers look like?"

She described them, blushing as she did. If he noticed, he didn't let on, and Bryony was grateful for it. Michael, it turned out, was partial to historical romances, and Mr. Miyamoto—or Ryuhei as he insisted Bryony call him now—had just the book. "It's chock-full of highwaymen," he said with a grin. "Well, there's at least one."

Bryony bought the book and tucked it between the fabrics in her bundle. "Thank you, Mr.— Ryuhei. Thank you for everything."

He held the door for her and invited her to apply if she wanted work. She left feeling a little ashamed that she'd never learned his given name or that of his brother, whose leg she'd saved from almost certain amputation after a nasty run-in with a hay baler. Other than Martha, she'd never taken the time to really get to know many of her congregants. They were a group to her, a whole. They had one want—to be healed. They had one gift—gratitude. Once upon a time, they made her feel warm and full and happy with their worship. Now they were just people, and she would have to discover them anew, one at a time.

Loki strode along beside her without offering to carry a thing. "And now you have a job lined up. See, what did I tell you? You just have to put yourself out there."

"Okay, okay. How many times do you expect me to say you were right? You ought to be tired of hearing it by now."

He tilted his chin up. "I'll never tire of it."

Bryony's arms ached by the time they started up the drive to her home. She was anxious to be relieved of the load she carried, but before she even stepped onto her veranda, Loki stopped her. His grip on her shoulder was iron. "Is your boyfriend in the habit of leaving the front door open?"

She shook her head, and Loki pushed past her, jogging up the stairs and into the house. She wanted to stop him. The intruder was back, and she couldn't help remembering Shakespeare bisected on the deck of *Dragonfly*, his feathers settling around him like thick, black snow. *He's a shapeshifter,* she reminded herself. *He's not a man or a bird. He's elemental.* But Michael was human. She dropped her bundle, flew up the porch stairs, and ran into Loki's back on her way into the parlor.

The Jötunn whirled on her. "Get out!"

She stood her ground.

He growled, "Now is not the time for your stubbornness, Bryony."

She called to Michael, her heart thundering in her ears. Just as Loki began to physically eject her from her own house, she heard the music of the staircase. There was that step that creaked, and through the banister she saw Michael's familiar, bare feet.

"Michael!" She broke free and ran to him. He caught her at the bottom of the stairs.

"What happened? What's wrong?" Michael examined her.

Loki's voice was cold and bitter. "Were you trying to give her a heart attack?"

"I don't know what you mean," Michael said.

Bryony spoke into his stomach where she'd buried her face. "The door . . ."

"You left the door open." Loki finished her thought. "After all that's happened, you didn't think that might send a message that the house had been breached again? She's not without enemies and neither are you."

Michael began to stroke Bryony's hair. "I didn't touch the door. Maybe the wind—"

"Listen, snake, you forget this was my home for a good ten years. That door is too heavy to be moved by the kind of winds they get around here. It's impossible."

Michael sighed like a man dealing with a petulant child. "I suppose I might have forgotten to close it." It wasn't true. Bryony heard the tinge of placation in his voice. A gentle squeeze on her shoulder told her to let it go for now.

"Careless," Loki muttered. "Well, we got your fabrics, not that you deserve any of them."

"I dropped them," Bryony admitted. She'd been terrified. She'd imagined Michael's body. She'd imagined his blood. She'd thought about all he'd survived, just so he could come to her house and die in some ridiculous burglary. She'd overreacted again. "Outside."

Michael smiled down at her and went to retrieve the abandoned fabrics. For a moment, she was left alone with Loki, with Bill, who looked at her with his piercing, blue eyes. He knew as well as she did something wasn't right. Someone had been in her house, twice now. And this time, they'd been in her house while Michael was there. She couldn't blame Loki anymore. He'd been with her all afternoon. There was no clever glint in his eyes. The quirk of a smile he always wore was gone, and an expression of pure concern had taken its place.

Michael ducked back inside, carrying the bundle of fabric under one arm. In his other hand was a pristine, trade paperback. He could have lit the room with his smile. "You got me a present!"

Loki crossed his arms and puffed out his chest. "Don't you go thinking that's from both of us. I had nothing to do with it. I'm personally of the opinion that those books have been a bad influence on you. Made you far too sentimental if you ask me."

"I didn't." Michael strode past the smaller man and beamed down at Bryony. His eyes were little fires of intense desire. "And if it bothers you so much, you'll want to walk away now, because I'm about to get very, *very* sentimental."

CHAPTER NINE

Loki narrowed his eyes like he was about to say something anyone other than him would regret. Then he thought better of it and shrugged. "Eh, Marty needs help with the dinner rush anyway. You know where I am if you need me." He paused at the door and turned back. "To be clear, that was meant for Bryony, snake. You can roll over and die for all I care." And he left.

Bryony stared after him for several seconds before she asked, "Why does he hate you so much? It can't be because you're a . . . a . . ."

"Snake?" Michael finished for her. "It's fine. I happen to think snakes are lovely creatures. I wouldn't be ashamed to count myself among them. Unfortunately, I can't. But I'm close enough for him, it seems."

"Does he hate his own son that much?"

"I don't think so." Michael held the fabrics in one hand and clutched his new book like a priceless treasure in the other. "Come with me. I want to show you something." He started up the staircase.

Bryony followed, but she couldn't let the question go. "Why then? You've never done anything to him. You even spared his life when it came down to it. He should be grateful."

Michael paused and turned back. He towered over her, the elevation gained by the stairs adding to his already generous height. *He will be this tall one day*, Bryony reminded herself. *Imagine it. Deal with it. Be ready.*

"Gratitude can be difficult after a lifetime of abuse," he said. "Your friend has been through hell and come out the other side. Have you not heard what was done to him?"

"If I did, I must have forgotten."

"It wasn't pretty." Michael frowned, and his brow creased. He seemed to be weighing whether or not to tell her. It was different now that it wasn't a myth. The truth was always harder to tell. He scratched his head and decided. "They bound him—the same gods who'd taken him in—with the entrails of one of his murdered sons. They lashed him to a stone beneath a serpent whose venom caused unbearable suffering for any creature it touched. The pain would have killed a mortal man. They say the venom dripped constantly. I don't think the serpent was of this world."

Bryony recoiled as she suddenly realized why Shakespeare had once been so insistent that she fix a leaking faucet in her house. *Now!* he'd shouted. *I can't bear the sound of it anymore.* She'd thought him overdramatic at the time, but she'd misjudged him. She'd misjudged him immensely. "I didn't know," she whispered as shame crept into her cheeks. Why hadn't she fixed that faucet sooner?

"He did have an oasis in his wife." Michael smiled down at her. "Sigyn stayed by his side and caught the venom in a dish, but she had to empty it from time to time. When she did, his suffering was so great, it supposedly shook the earth. I used to think it was just an origin story for earthquakes—you know, like the story of Asmodeus—but now that I've spoken to him, I'm inclined to believe much of it is true."

There was that name again. *Asmodeus.* Michael had mentioned him once before on *Dragonfly*. Bryony remembered that Asmodeus was one of the nephilim but not much else. "Can you tell me the story of Asmodeus?"

"Later," he said. "I want to show you this first." He was excited, giddy even. He led her to his sewing room, bowing low as he entered before her. For a moment, all she saw was his back. Then she saw an unfinished shirt hanging on the handle of her mother's old wardrobe. It was plum colored, and she thought it would look quite fetching on him. "I still have to add the collar and cuffs," he said when he saw where her attention was. "But that isn't what I wanted to show you. Look. I found it with the scrap fabrics, but it was only torn, so I repaired it."

He unfolded a black dress and lifted it by the shoulders so she could better make it out. It was a beaded flapper dress her mother had worn in a stage production of *The Great Gatsby*. Bryony had dyed it black and worn it all of three times before she tore it on a nail. She'd wept over that damn dress. She wept over all the dresses she damaged. Every costume was a little piece of her mother, and she felt the loss of each one keenly. But Michael had stitched this one back together.

Bryony desperately tried to blink back her tears as he lowered the dress and pursed his lips in concern. "I can put it back the way it was if you don't like it," he said. "I made sure I could undo whatever I did."

And Bryony lost all her resolve not to cry. She sobbed. "Don't you dare. Don't you dare put it back."

For some reason, Michael always gave the impression that he was naturally empathic, intuitive in his humanity, but he wasn't. Right now, for example, he held the love of his life in his arms and wondered why she'd suddenly burst into tears. It seemed a potent cocktail of grief and joy. But in his own life, he'd experienced grief as a constant pull, not a jolt of feeling. It was an undercurrent that stole his ability to know joy without also anticipating its loss. What was it like to suddenly realize that someone you loved was gone, to feel it come on like a thunderstorm? What was it like to have it strike you down all at once?

Michael led her to their bed and lay down beside her. She was exhausted, red eyed and rosy cheeked. He combed his fingers through her hair. "Please, be happy," he said. "I don't want to see you cry."

She laughed through her tears. "This is what happy looks like, mister. You'll just have to get used to it."

"No, I've seen you happy, when you saw bioluminescence and watched the stars. I wanted to give something like that to you."

"You did." She scooted closer to him. "Don't you understand? You're giving my mother back to me."

"I am?"

"Yes." She grinned. "Husband."

Electricity crackled in his chest at that word on her lips. "I love you so much. I'd do anything to make you happy." He drew close, kissed her cheek, and brushed his fingers along the line of her neck. "But I should warn you. Right now, I crave you more than hell craves heaven, and you're only making it worse."

"Or better," she offered.

His breath caught as she tucked one knee between his thighs. "Better," he conceded. "Definitely better." He kissed her throat and tasted the salt of the day's activities still lingering on her skin like sea spray. "Tell me when to stop," he begged. "When you smell smoke."

"What if I just close my eyes?"

"The light will penetrate easily." He slid one hand under her dress and let his thumb linger against her inner thigh. "Just . . . Please. I can't bear the thought of paralyzing you again." Her skin began to rapidly cool, which he knew was just the warming of his own. She was a night breeze, a mountain stream, snow and snow and snow. "I need . . ."

He couldn't finish. She'd arched her back and was trying to wriggle free of her dress. He stared stupidly before he realized she could use his help. Once he unzipped it, the gown slipped off her shoulders. He slid the smooth fabric down past her hips and pulled it gently from her legs. His fingers were trembling by the time he got around to unbuttoning his own shirt.

When he was in an equal state of undress, Michael crawled over her and pressed her into the mattress with a fraction of his weight. There was no point in hiding how much he wanted her now, no point in shyness. He moaned and kissed her hungrily.

"I love you." The phrase tumbled from his lips with each exhale. He couldn't help it. The seraph had taken his tongue, and he spoke without thinking. "I love you." It was too much. He knew it was too much, but he was of two minds and two bodies. The seraph demanded permanence—her love, her bones, her promise. The man demanded passion—her breath, her flesh, and every sound he drew from her lips. He was close, so close to losing control. For once, both halves of him were in total agreement.

"Stay," he whispered and slipped a hand between her legs. "Stay." He spoke in time with her gasping breath. Somewhere, between every kiss, one word had claimed him. There were no other thoughts in his head. There was only the dance of flesh against flesh, the pressure of her hand and mouth drawing his own voice out of him. "Stay." He didn't exist anymore, not outside this moment, not outside that word. His resolve was beaten back by the pulse and momentum. The rhythm, the catch, the pull . . .

"Michael." She broke through his haze of desire. "Stop."

He obeyed without a breath of hesitation, and as he did, he smelled it—incense, sweet smoke. His heart, seconds ago muffled by the frenzy of need, pounded in his own ears. He gripped the sheets and pushed himself off the mattress, away from her. "Thank you," he said shakily, and he meant it. She groaned. He knew she was as frustrated as he was, but she'd stopped him anyway. "Thank you." He fell on her, wrapped his arms around her, and buried his face in the pillow under her head.

"You're heavy." She pushed at him.

"Sorry." He rolled onto his back.

Bryony propped herself on one elbow and laid her other arm across his chest.

He glanced at her and noticed the way her perfect shoulder shifted under her skin, the way her bare hip was accentuated by her position. He quickly looked away. "How are we supposed to do this for the rest of our lives?"

She shrugged, unperturbed. "Learn to love blindfolds?"

He almost laughed—almost—but it was time to be honest. He stared up at the crown molding. "It would be an interesting experiment, but the risk . . . The only memory I have of my mother is of being taken by a stranger from her lifeless arms. She'd been paralyzed somehow, permanently. Later, I learned, she died. I never really thought about why before. Now I wonder, was it her proximity to my father that finally killed her? Is there even a chance I could do the same to you?"

Bryony sighed and absently stroked his arm with the tips of her fingers. "That idea requires some pretty big assumptions. There are just too many variables. Do you even know what her circumstances were? Or his? I feel fine. I promise I'll tell you the second I don't." Her fingers stopped tickling his arm, and she squeezed his wrist in earnest. "I'm not usually an optimistic person, but I feel good about this—about us. That has to count for something."

He fought back his own dread and pulled her against his chest. "I hope you're right."

CHAPTER TEN

Michael spent the rest of the evening lost in a mental tug-of-war. What he believed was right and what his instincts told him to do were irreconcilable. A relationship with him put Bryony's life in orbit with troubles most people couldn't begin to comprehend. But every time he so much as thought about letting her go, adrenaline seized and disconcerted him.

From day one, he'd known this would not end well. He'd seen it plotted like a course on a nautical chart, stretched out before him in an unalterable path. He shouldn't have kissed her. God help him, he should have stopped her from holding his hand. He should have been distant, cruel even. He should have been so much stronger than he was. But now it was too late to go back. There was no way to return the love he'd stolen, probably from someone who could have given her a real marriage.

He tucked his knees to his chest and listened to Bryony shower one wall away. He'd been on the right track in the armada—fighting the angels the only way he could—so why did every choice he make seem to bring him that much closer to becoming his father? *You can't run from who you are,* a voice in his head seemed to whisper.

When he heard the shower stop, he decided to do something useful. "Do you want dinner?" he called to Bryony.

"Sure!"

"I'll make us some." He descended the stairs, his hand trailing along the banister. He fumbled in the dark to find the light switches. Upon reaching the kitchen, he stopped dead. The back door yawned into the night. Someone had been in the house. Again. He scowled and mumbled, "Tricksters," when he remembered Loki had been there that afternoon.

Once the door was closed and locked, he set about making dinner, but the years aboard *Dragonfly* had not taught him much in the way of cooking. Eggs. He could make eggs. So dinner became a haphazard scramble. Still it was food. He'd skipped lunch to keep sewing, and his stomach ached with hunger. He could barely keep himself from eating the ingredients raw. Shame stood in for willpower, and he was grateful for it when Bryony finally appeared in the kitchen and he hadn't yet bitten into an onion like it was an apple straight off the tree.

She wore a pair of jogging shorts with a hoodie, and was still toweling her hair dry. "That smells good. Is it breakfast for dinner? I love breakfast for dinner."

"Lucky, because it seems to be all I remember how to cook." He spooned some of the scramble onto a plate for her. "Sorry."

She seized a fork and sat down at the table. "Never apologize for making me food." She took a bite and made a sound that told him she more than approved. "You're spoiling me today."

Michael's chest swelled with pride. No matter how poorly thought out this relationship was, he could still be good to her. He swallowed the words *I love you*, knowing he'd already spoken them too many times that day. He poured her a glass of the pomegranate juice he'd found in the fridge and sat down with his own plate.

"This is too much." She washed another bite down with juice. "And you didn't have to build a fire in the living room. I doubt I'll stay awake much longer. If you like, I can build one in the bedroom, but it won't be as cozy. Where did you learn to do that? Not on *Dragonfly*, surely."

Despite his hunger, Michael froze with a forkful of food halfway to his mouth. "I didn't build a fire." And there hadn't been one in the hearth fifteen minutes ago.

"Of course you did." Bryony laughed. Then she stopped. "Didn't you?"

Michael stood, nearly toppling his chair in the process. "Someone's in your house. Right now. The back door was open when I came down. I assumed Loki had done it."

Her eyes widened. "It's not him. You should have seen his reaction this afternoon. It wasn't an act."

"Wait here." Michael tried to push past her, but she wouldn't allow it.

"Absolutely not," she said.

"Please."

"I won't let you go alone, and if that's not enough to convince you, consider that the goal might be to separate us."

He sighed. "Fine. Come on." He took her by the hand and quietly led her to the living room. The last thing he wanted to do was alarm whatever might be out there. It was never a good idea to frighten a creature that did not intend you harm, and so far, whoever was doing these things hadn't attempted to harm anyone.

The living room was empty, but the front door stood open again. "This is beyond weird," Bryony muttered.

Michael squeezed her hand. "Are you certain your house was never haunted?"

"Unfortunately." She chuckled. "Ghosts would have been welcome. The place was always too quiet after . . ."

After her family died—that's what she was going to say, only she couldn't. In this house, they'd died. Michael didn't press her, though he wondered how she spent so many years in a place with so many unpleasant memories. *I will give her better ones,* he thought. One more thing he could do for her. He just had to focus on those things. He stared into the fire, which was admittedly cozy. "Bryony, should we go somewhere else for the night?"

He felt her tense at the suggestion. "Not a chance." She squared her shoulders. "This is *my* house. They won't drive me from my own house." Then she took a deep breath and shouted to the invisible intruder. "Get out of my house, whoever you are! You aren't welcome here! I don't care if you build the most beautiful fire in the history of hearths! You don't come in uninvited! It's rude!"

There was a whoosh of air around them. A great wind kicked up and doused the fire. Then, with a shocking jolt, the front door slammed closed. A distinctive emptiness filled the house. It was as though some living, breathing shadow had just sucked the life from the room and fled.

Michael gaped. "Did . . . Did that just work?"

Bryony shuddered and broke into terrified laughter. "I think it did. Oh my god. Was that really a ghost? But I don't believe in ghosts."

"As someone who's dating a future demon, you really ought to reassess."

She let go of his hand and bent down to hold her knees. She was shaking. "Are you trying to suggest that was a demon?"

That hadn't been what he'd meant to say at all, but now that he thought about it, there was no reason to rule it out. "Why would a demon break into your house, read your letters, and build a fire in your hearth?"

She shrugged. "To shake us up?"

"Well, congratulate it because I'm well and truly shaken." Michael's stomach growled its protest at the cooling of his dinner. Now was hardly the time, but his stomach didn't seem to care.

"I'm starving," Bryony said, likely for his sake rather than her own. "Whatever that was, it's gone now. Let's eat and try to get some sleep."

Later, Michael lay on his stomach in bed—toes touching the top of the headboard, a pillow clutched under his chin—and watched Bryony build a fire in the bedroom hearth. The smell of sulfur hit his nostrils when she struck a match and set the kindling alight. Then she doused the lamps, grabbed her own pillow, and joined him at the foot of the bed. Her cheeks were still flushed from the heat of the fire.

I love you. Michael swallowed the words again and buried his face in his pillow. Everything she did for him set his mind to worship. She fed him, housed him, even fought off evil spirits, apparently. He couldn't temper his awe, and a little voice in the back of his mind kept whispering, *You don't deserve her, you don't deserve her, you will never, ever deserve her.* He pressed his face harder into his pillow and muffled a groan.

"Michael?" Bryony's voice broke into his thoughts. The floral scent of her shampoo mingled with the hint of woodsmoke as she moved closer. "Is it bothering you that much? I'd planned to wait until morning to call Martha, but I can do it now. Maybe it really was Loki. Who am I to say it wasn't? I didn't even know who he was for ten years."

He could hear the smile in her voice, but he couldn't return it. "You're so fearless," he said into his pillow. "I don't understand it."

She laughed. "Oh, I've never been afraid of ghosts, even when I did think they were real. They're just dead people really."

"And demons?" He looked up.

Her eyes danced in the light of the fire, and her dark hair glistened, still clinging and damp from her shower. "A demon is just another kind of ghost, right? You taught me that."

"Then I taught you wrong. Demons aren't always acting under their own will, which makes them unpredictable. Never trust a demon, Bryony. If you've attracted the attention of one . . ." He paused and shook his head. "God, what am I saying? You already have, haven't you? I won't live forever, and you've certainly got my attention." He rolled onto his back and watched the dance of shadows on the ceiling. How could he continue this mockery of a relationship without at least giving her the option to get out?

"Why did you choose me, Bryony? You could have been with anyone. You still could. You could have a real relationship with someone normal, someone who could give you real intimacy." He choked on his words. This went against his every instinct. "You could have a family again. You could have children. I won't stop worshiping you if you choose to be with another man. I swear I won't let you starve, so you don't have to worry about that. You deserve so much better than—"

Suddenly, her hands were at his mouth. She swung her leg over his chest, straddled his ribcage, and muffled his protests. "Shut up." She stared down at him with so much anger that, if he hadn't already been backed into a mattress, he would have recoiled. "Shut up, shut up, you massive idiot. What do you think you're doing? Trying to talk me into leaving you? What if you succeeded, huh? What if I just said, 'Well, you certainly have a point there, Michael,' and walked away? What would you do then?" She scowled harder. "After all we've been through. Yeah sure, let's call it quits. I'm tired of you already."

Her sarcasm was apparent, but Michael couldn't stop fear from flooding his veins. The illusion of her absence—her weight lifted, her scent conspicuously gone—washed him away in a storm of dread. His fingers tightened around her thighs as he struggled to see her through tears that blurred his vision and cooled in his ears.

Bryony kept her hands over his mouth as she leaned in and examined his face. "You really are imagining it, aren't you?" She seemed surprised. Michael nodded. "Well, stop." He obeyed, but the tears kept coming. "I said, stop it."

He closed his eyes and tried to focus on her presence, her legs around his ribcage, her weight on his chest, her hands over his mouth. She wasn't gone, but he couldn't stop shaking. This was the closest he'd come to letting her go, and his body, it seemed, wasn't finished punishing him for it.

"Not another word," Bryony said, and Michael nodded in agreement. He'd said too much already. She removed her hands from his mouth. "I won't leave you, even if we have to come to a screeching halt whenever I smell smoke for the rest of my life. Understand? And you've already given me another family. Don't you dare take it away just because you think I need intercourse and a baby."

He stared up at her. Her hair was unraveling from the knot at the base of her neck. Her eyes reflected the heat of the fire, and her hands gripped his shoulders.

"I'm not with you because I need you," she said, and her expression softened a little. "I'm with you because I love you. I'm with you because you're a beautiful person who reads the stars and the sea and ridiculous romances." He brought a hand to her cheek and she cradled it there before she went on. "I'm with you because you sew and make scrambled eggs for dinner, and because you thought of a way to give a piece of my mother back to me. I love the way you move through the world. You always seem so confident. I guess I forgot that you get scared too. Maybe you tell me you love me so much because that's how much you need to hear it."

Michael opened his mouth to deny it.

"Quiet," she said, pressing a hand to his lips again. "It's my turn to talk. Your turn to listen."

He blinked up at her.

"I love you." She removed her hand from his mouth slowly, as though she were a kidnapper afraid he might scream. "So stay." She bent down and kissed him. He slipped one hand around the back of her neck. "Stay," she breathed again. Then she bent to his ear and whispered, "And marry me, Michael."

His body jolted and he sat up, taking her with him. Those words. Had he really heard them? She didn't have his impulses. She wouldn't propose just because she couldn't help herself, but would she do it just to comfort him? "Bryony . . ." he began, but he didn't know how to finish. His insecurities were pushing their way to the surface again. "You don't have to—"

"I'm asking you to marry me. Right now. I'm asking you to be my husband for the rest of our lives. Yes or no?"

"I don't—"

"*Yes* and *no* are the only words you're allowed to speak." She straddled his lap and cocked her head at him. "Well? Do you need more convincing or something?"

He watched her wait on his answer with that ferocious look in her eyes. It was the same look she'd given him the day she pointed a gun at his chest and demanded to be heard. He'd been so proud of her then. "You're terrifying," he said.

She slapped him.

It was a soft strike—there was no sting in it—but it was meant to communicate something words could not. Her cheeks were flushed with frustration, and it made her downright adorable. "Your hands are so small," he mused.

This time, he caught her wrist before she struck him. "They're proportionally appropriate. Now answer."

He brought her palm to his lips and kissed it tenderly. "You already know what my answer is."

"Just say it."

"Yes." He dipped her until she lay back on the mattress and he was on his hands and knees over her. "My answer is yes." He kissed her. His fingers curled around her neck, caressed the base of her skull, tilted her deeper into his kiss. He opened his mouth and let her draw him in until he was completely lost in the taste of her. Finally, he whispered, "Yes," and stilled himself before she had to tell him to stop.

She held his head to her chest and cleared her throat in a failed effort to hide the huskiness in her voice. "That's settled then."

"Yes."

"Good. So we can go to sleep now?"

"Yes." It was the only word he seemed able to say.

Hours later, Michael leaned against the headboard of Bryony's bed—his bed now—and listened to her fitful slumber. She always seemed to sleep somewhere between dream states, unable to fully let go of consciousness. He wondered why and thought about her past. But he couldn't think for long.

The soft, barely perceptible sound of the parlor piano drifted into the bedroom. Michael sat bolt upright. Every muscle in his body tensed. Someone was playing the instrument—someone who had taken the trouble to apply the damper. Courteous or not, the intruder had crossed too many lines, and Michael was not about to let them get away with it. If it was Loki, he intended to catch the trickster red-handed. If it wasn't . . . Well, Michael would have to deal with that problem when it came up.

Carefully, he lifted himself from the bed, but Bryony stirred anyway. "Mmm . . ." she mumbled. "What is it?"

"It's nothing, my love. Go back to sleep." He tried to sound nonchalant, but his voice was pinched. Luckily, Bryony was only half awake and slipped easily back into unconsciousness.

Michael dressed and crept downstairs, already sure-footed, knowing precisely when to duck and which stair to skip because it creaked under his weight. He was quiet as a cat as he made his way to the parlor. Unless they expected him, no one could have known he was coming.

But they did.

The piano was silent, its bench conspicuously empty. Michael took two steps into the parlor before he felt something massive wrap around him and pin him back. A hand pressed hard over his mouth and echoed the gentle silencing Bryony had given him earlier that evening. Only this was far from gentle, and these hands were far from small. Too late, Michael realized that whoever had him now was much bigger than he was.

He kicked but got nowhere. He bit down on the flesh over his mouth, but his assailant didn't flinch. It had been years since he'd felt this helpless. God he was so stupid to have thought he could just investigate quickly without telling Bryony where he'd gone, so stupid to have underestimated an intruder he hadn't identified. A cry rose and died in his throat as he heard a masculine voice hiss into his ear. "Make one sound, and your woman comes with us."

In that moment, Michael knew he was lost. The blow to his head and the following darkness were only confirmation.

Chapter Eleven

When Bryony woke the next morning, she was alone. She blinked at Michael's vacant pillow and sat up in a panic. Where was he? Had she made a mistake in proposing to him? He'd been trying to talk her out of the relationship. What if he really meant it? She kicked off the comforter and leapt up, ready to search the entire town for him if she had to. Then she heard the shower and collapsed back into bed, relieved. One day, she would have to learn to stop overreacting. He was here. He'd just risen before her and decided not to wake her.

After giving herself an appropriately stern talking-to, she decided to put on the dress Michael had repaired the day before. It still fit. She spun around and grinned at her own reflection when she saw a touch of her mother in herself. It had been so long since she'd even tried this dress on. It probably should've been washed after accumulating dust for so many years, but some impatient, childish part of her decided not to care. That same irresponsible childishness told her it didn't matter that the weather was too cool for a short dress, and she put on black tights rather than worry about it.

She was already flipping pancakes by the time Michael appeared in the kitchen. "What do you want to drink?" she asked. "Coffee? Juice?"

He hesitated. "I'll have whatever you're having."

Bryony added more grounds and water to the percolator and set it on the stove to heat. "Sorry I don't have a French press. Maybe I'll pick one up when I'm in town today."

"You're going into town?"

"Of course." She smiled over her shoulder at him. "I want to thank Martha properly for buying all these groceries for us."

"Right." He lingered in the doorway. "You should definitely do that."

Bryony checked the pancakes and decided they needed another minute or two. Then she grabbed two mugs and added cream to one and sugar to the other. Michael looked like he was waiting for an invitation to sit down. She wasn't used to this kind of hesitancy in him, and it worried her. She decided to test the waters and hopefully quell her fears with a casual jab. "You aren't getting cold feet, are you? I could always take the marriage proposal back if you don't want it. I still have the receipt."

That seemed to do the trick. "Oh, I want it." He strode into the kitchen and draped his arms over her shoulders. "Of course I want it, darling." He kissed the top of her head.

Darling? He hadn't used that endearment before, but perhaps he felt differently now that they were engaged. He might have read it in a book and thought it went nicely with engagement.

He took a seat at the table and smiled. "I was just thinking, I hope you don't plan to visit our Martha empty-handed. If you like, I'll whip something up after breakfast."

"Sure. And thank you." Bryony set the table with butter, syrup, honey, and jam. She set Michael's plate before him, spread honey over her own pancakes, and dug in.

Michael took a sip of coffee and made a face.

"Sorry again about the coffee. I really will buy a French press today."

His smile was warm and cheery. "Do you know, I think I might switch to tea after all."

She knifed through her pancakes and stuffed an oversized bite into her mouth to hide her shock. Michael loved coffee. But perhaps his fondness had more to do with his midnight-to-four watch than anything, or perhaps the coffee she made for him really did taste that terrible.

They finished their breakfast in relative silence. Michael seemed unsure about things he usually took comfort in and confident about things he usually shied from. He typically dealt with his food in a careful, meticulous manner, but now he was rushed, carving through his breakfast like he had an appointment in ten minutes and wouldn't be allowed to eat for the rest of the day. And he gulped the coffee he normally would have sipped, as though it were foul tasting medicine he had to choke down.

After breakfast, he went about the kitchen looking for flour, sugar, and baking soda. He grabbed the butter from the table and found bowls and spoons. "It'll have to be a quick bread," he said, holding a bag of herbs in his teeth. "There's not time enough to prove dough, otherwise I'd make croissants." He grinned, and Bryony forced herself to smile back.

She watched him with interest. He measured nothing, pouring the ingredients directly into the bowl like it was second nature to him. He hummed while he worked, and Bryony chewed at her thumbnail. "I thought you couldn't cook anything other than eggs," she said, recalling their dinner from the night before.

"Oh, of course I'm useless if I'm not baking," he assured her. He added the wet ingredients to the dry and wiped his hands on a dish towel. He did not look remotely useless. In fact, he looked like he could find his way around the most intimidating, professional kitchen and whip up something extremely French in the time it took Bryony to comb her hair. She watched him fold salt and herbs into the dough in utter astonishment.

"So what other hidden talents do you have that I don't know about?"

"Hmm . . ." He pressed a finger to his chin and left a smudge of flour. "I suppose you'll just have to wait and find out." There was a mischievous glint to his eye as he grabbed a rolling pin and cheese grater. "I'll send you to Martha with the most mouth-watering biscuits this side of heaven. But when you get back, promise we'll make plans for the wedding. I'm simply beside myself with anticipation, darling, you must know I am."

Bryony felt like Little Red Riding Hood walking to Martha's in a black, hooded cloak with an enormous basket of biscuits hanging off her arm. Admittedly, they did smell delicious, and she had to resist the temptation to devour one on the way. They were still steaming when she walked around the back of the café and found the door to the kitchen.

Martha's kitchen was far from adequate, but the woman performed miracles with what little she had. Her business had begun as a true café, serving coffee and tea in the morning and closing down in the late afternoon. As the community gradually realized her biscotti were as unrivaled as her caffeinated beverages, her business grew. Now she ran a full-blown restaurant from a kitchen that was smaller than Bryony's own. As cramped a space as she had to work with, Martha still welcomed Bryony. "How are you getting along?" she asked.

"Good." Bryony handed her the basket, though it looked like Martha had precious little counter space on which to set it. "Michael wanted you to have these. We both want to thank you for stocking our cupboards. It took a lot of pressure off us."

Martha wiped her hands on her apron, took the basket, and breathed in its aroma. "They smell divine! Did he make these himself?"

Bryony nodded. "Although it was a bit strange. Last night he told me he couldn't cook, and then this morning he whipped these up like he'd never done anything easier in his life."

"Baking is quite different," Martha admitted. "I myself had to learn the art of the skillet when I expanded my menu. At least you know he has the talent for it." She smiled and handed the basket to Loki, who'd just walked in with a tray full of dirty dishes.

"What's this?" He eyed the biscuits suspiciously.

"A gift," Martha said.

But Loki had already stuffed his mouth with one of them. "Is there cheese in these?" The question was barely intelligible through the bite he'd taken.

"And garlic," Martha added. "And is that thyme I smell?"

Bryony shrugged. "He was way too fast for me to keep track of ingredients."

When Loki looked confused, Martha clarified. "It seems Michael baked for us this morning."

Loki immediately spat out what he still had in his mouth. Then he grabbed a napkin and began vigorously wiping the residue off his tongue. "Seriously? When were you going to tell me these were made by the snake? After I died of cyanide poisoning?"

"Don't be so dramatic, Bill." Martha took a biscuit from the pile and bit into it herself. "Goodness, these taste even better than they smell. How can you resist them? I'd risk the poison myself." She chuckled, washed her hands, and went back to the stove. "I hope *the snake* is settling in well." She gave Loki an impressive over-the-glasses look.

"I think so." Bryony wrung her hands, and the gesture did not escape Martha's keen eye.

"What is it, sweetheart? You can tell us."

"Well . . ." Bryony shifted on her feet, hesitating. "I mean he seems kind of . . . different today. I don't know."

The other two occupants of the tiny kitchen reacted at once, and in very different ways.

Martha calmly asked, "How so?"

And every well-fabricated muscle in Loki's body tensed. "I knew it." He scowled. "I knew he'd lay hands on you one day."

Bryony ignored Loki and answered Martha. "He's just more . . . Hmm. How to describe it." She fidgeted with her dress. "He seems happier? Well, not happier exactly. Just . . . louder about it, I guess. And he didn't like his coffee this morning."

"That's nothing." Loki visibly relaxed and grabbed another biscuit. Apparently, he was no longer worried about cyanide. "You make terrible coffee, Bryony. I've always said so."

Bryony rolled her eyes and bit back a grin. It was good to have her old friend again, no matter how infuriating he could be. "It's not just that. He ate so fast. He never eats like that. And the baking. I swear I heard him humming while he worked. He called me *darling* twice."

"You're worried about an endearment?" Martha seemed confused. "And the fact that he had a healthy appetite and hummed while he worked?"

Bryony sighed. How was she going to explain why these things felt so wrong when, to hear them described, they seemed completely reasonable? "It doesn't matter," she said finally. Perhaps she really was overreacting. It wasn't like she hadn't overreacted before—a million times before.

If Martha thought Bryony had fallen off her rocker, she didn't let on. "Excuse my asking, but did anything happen last night that would make him a bit giddy this morning?" She smiled a knowing smile. "Don't answer that if it's too personal. Just . . . keep it in mind. He is a man, after all, and he's quite taken with you, clearly."

Loki groaned and let out a sarcastic echo. "Clearly."

Bryony could feel the color creep into her cheeks. She knew exactly what Martha suggested, and she wanted to deny it outright, if only to minimize her own embarrassment. But now that she thought about it . . . "Well, I suppose we did get engaged last night."

Martha dropped her spatula and her jaw. "You did not!" She rushed in, scooped Bryony into her arms, and swung her around. Bryony was not particularly short, but Martha was quite tall and lifted Bryony easily. "You little weasel, how long were you going to wait to tell us? Congratulations!" She set Bryony down and smoothed her dress for her. "Sorry, I just get so excited about these things. For Pete's sake, Bryony, that explains everything. Of course he's acting the fool this morning. He's beside himself with joy. Oh, get over here and give me another hug. Have you got a date in mind yet? You will invite me, won't you?"

But Loki did not seem at all pleased. During Martha's excitement, Bryony saw him put down the biscuit he was eating. "No, Bryony's right. Something's off. He may be sentimental, but I've seen that bastard eat like he can't stand the sound of his own teeth. I honestly can't imagine him inhaling a plate of food without overthinking it."

Martha released Bryony from her most recent, crushing embrace. "Remind me, Bill. What was the first thing you did after I told you I'd forgiven you for all your lies?"

Loki frowned.

"You ate an entire plate of pasta, didn't you?" Martha grinned like she'd won.

"Yes, but that's me." He ran his fingers through his beard in an almost timid gesture. "And I am *not* him. That . . . thing coddles his food like he's afraid it'll run away if he frightens it."

"Please don't call him a thing," Bryony muttered. "I know you don't like him, but he's still a person."

"Not only do I not like him, but I don't trust him as far as I could throw him when I was a crow." Loki's expression grew far more severe than Bryony felt it had any right to be. "He's a godhunter and a hybrid of the seraphim, the worst breed of angel in the known universe. He's a snake, Bryony. One day, he'll unhinge his jaw and swallow you whole. And if you think that's hyperbole, take some time to read the legends. Please, before you swear the rest of your life to this creature, do a little research. The nephilim eat—that's literally all they do. Plant, animal, and *human.* They would have eaten the entire world if the angels hadn't wiped them out."

Every word out of his mouth set Bryony's teeth a little harder. She wanted to punch him, but she reminded herself that his attitude was a symptom of unimaginable suffering, so she tried to be gentle with him. "That's not fair. There are stories about you, too, you know."

Loki spread his arms in surrender. "Yes, and most of them are true. You shouldn't have trusted me either. I honestly don't know why you ever did, but at least I'm trying to deserve it. I saved your life, didn't I? He was going to kill you, and I saved your life. If you have to trust one of us, it shouldn't even be a contest."

Bryony's fists began to ache before she realized she'd clenched them. She didn't want to reveal the devastating truth, but Loki was leaving her very little choice. She spoke in a low, quiet voice. "You didn't save my life."

"You're so stubborn, Bryony. Of course I did." His cheeks were flushed. "Have you forgotten the way that monster drew his weapon on you? He would have killed you if you'd stayed a god. And now you're going to marry him? Do you even know the kind of children you'll have? Second generation nephilim are no better than the first."

She spoke a little louder this time. "You have it all wrong, and it's my own fault. I never wanted to tell you the truth."

Now Loki looked a little less sure of himself. "What truth?"

Bryony shook her head, but Martha put a hand on her shoulder. "Tell him the truth, Bryony. Teach him how it's done." Loki shot a hard look at Martha, but she didn't begin to back down. "He needs to learn."

"It'll hurt him," Bryony muttered. "And not just him." After all, the absence of Martha's worship had been every bit as deadly as the absence of everyone else's.

"That's part of the process." Martha squeezed her shoulder. "We can handle it. Tell us so we can all move forward."

Bryony swallowed hard. She had to find the strength to do this, for Michael's sake if nothing else. But Michael had warned her about Loki, about how volatile the trickster could be, and she'd be lying if she said she wasn't afraid. She took a deep breath. "You can drift in and out of godhood because you were born immortal. I can't. Human gods just die. When I lost my congregation, I began to die."

Loki croaked out, "What?"

"The only reason I survived was because I gained one worshiper." She choked on the memory of Michael weeping, stumbling, praying a frantic prayer on an abandoned, rocky shore. "And he was enough."

"No." Loki ground his teeth.

"The godhunter is the only reason I'm alive today. He's my last worshiper, and if you hurt him . . . If you kill him, I'll die too."

"No!" Loki's hand flew to the tray he'd brought in. He seized a mug and threw it to the floor. It shattered. His face turned bright red, and he grabbed a bowl. It quickly joined the mug in a pile of porcelain shards. Bryony could feel the energy rolling off him. Michael had been right. This Jötunn was no one to trifle with. He wasn't a joke or a well-meaning fool. He was far from harmless, and she got the distinct impression he was only destroying the dishes to keep himself from destroying the entire café in his temper.

With every crash of her tableware, Martha jolted. "Bill, please. I can't afford to replace them all."

Loki shattered one more plate for good measure and stood panting over the pile. "I won't ally with a snake," he snarled. "I won't give him an ounce of respect. Do you hear me? I don't care what he did! He can't hide his nature from me. Marry him then, Bryony. Marry him because he saved your life after I killed you. But mark my words, there will come a day when you regret it."

"He told me why you hate snakes." Bryony stared down at the broken shards. "He told me what they did to you."

Loki growled, "Stop it, Bryony."

She didn't. "But Michael didn't kill your son. He didn't bind you, and he wasn't the serpent that tortured you. I know it's easier to blame someone else when it's your own people who hurt you—"

"Stop!"

"Your own family."

Before she could say another word, Bryony's mouth was filled with a choking wind. The entire café shook with the anger of the beast she'd provoked. He was energy, electricity, and she felt the evidence of it when her hair stood on end and her skin began to tingle. In a fit of rage, Loki had shattered his own mask, and both Bryony and Martha cowered before the thing he became. They closed their eyes to the heat and the angry, orange light that penetrated their eyelids. To Bryony, the Jötunn's true presence felt too much like an angel's. She tried to force herself to look up, to see the new—or rather very old—shape of her friend. What did he really look like? Was he a wheel, a beast, a serpent himself? But Loki was gone before she could muster the courage to open her eyes.

When the café settled, Bryony saw its owner crouching beside her, protecting her head from debris with her forearms. Martha steadied herself, stood, and helped Bryony to her feet. "Well . . ." She finally broke the silence. "Do you think there's any chance I can convince my customers that was just an earthquake?"

Chapter Twelve

When Michael finally opened his eyes, he wondered whether the blow to his head had affected his eyesight. No shadow, no silhouette, not a single sliver of light penetrated the darkness. He had to take stock of his surroundings with his other senses. The wall behind him felt uneven, rocky, and cold—the ground too. There was a smell like wet stone, damp earth, and stale air. He heard a trickle of water echo from somewhere to his right and felt more dripping down his back. Overriding every other sensation was the headache to end all headaches.

Michael shifted and felt a weight at his waist. A quick examination told him it was a metal ring that had been chained to the wall behind him. It was too small to push past his hips. It must have been clasped around him somehow, and he quickly found the joint that confirmed his suspicion. Had someone made this giant shackle especially for him? Or perhaps it had originally been made to fit an animal. He shuddered at the thought of some poor beast chained up the way he was.

At least he could be relatively certain Bryony had been left behind. *Make one sound, and your woman comes with us,* would not have been a threat if his abductor already planned to take her. That thought was his one comfort. Bryony was still safe and sound asleep. Michael was determined to get back to her before she even knew he'd gone. But when he reached for the death sword he always carried in his coat pocket, he realized he'd left the coat casually draped over a chair in his new bedroom. He was completely defenseless.

"Shit," he whispered.

A long sigh filled the chamber in response, and a hint of flame opened like a tiny eye before him. It was as though someone had struck a match, but he'd heard no sound and smelled no sulfur. The light grew, golden and warm, and he could begin to make out a face behind it. Dark, hooded eyes blinked at him from the other side of the flame. Then he noticed more features—the delicate point of a chin, the gentle curve of a hawkish nose.

"Awake, are you?" His abductor's voice was masculine, dignified, and calm. There was no bluster, no theater behind it.

"Who are you?" Michael asked. The anger in his own voice surprised him. "What do you want?"

The light grew brighter, revealing a lithe body dressed in white shirtsleeves, a herringbone vest, and shoes that appeared to have been recently polished. The man sat with his legs crossed just inches from Michael. "You don't want to know where you are?" he said. "That's the first question I would have asked, were I in your place."

"Well, you aren't," Michael grumbled.

His abductor laughed. "I'll tell you anyway. These caves were carved out by lava thousands of years ago. It's a vast, underground labyrinth. Can you believe no one even knows it exists? We won't want for privacy here. You should be pleased to be held in such an intellectually stimulating environment. Think about how long this marvel has gone unexplored, unappreciated. And now you can appreciate it."

"So give me a tour."

Again, his abductor laughed. There was something uncanny about him. Something . . . almost familiar. "You're cute, you know that? Has anyone ever told you before?"

"No." Michael made a face. "Not since I was a child."

The man across from him seemed in no hurry. His nonchalance was maddening. He smiled a charming smile and removed a pair of spectacles from the right front pocket of his vest. They were folded flat, gold rimmed, and the reflected light seemed to dance in their round lenses. "I tried to see you while you were unconscious, but you were quite well obscured. I found it odd. I have my suspicions as to why, which would explain your height and your lack of surprise upon finding a man who outmatches you."

Michael groaned. "Please, just get this over with."

"Oh, to be young and impatient again." His abductor sighed wistfully. "You fascinate me, I admit. I'd like to keep you for a while if you don't mind. Well, even if you do." He chuckled to himself. "Humor me for a moment. Before I take a closer look, tell me if I've guessed correctly. You're an angel's son, aren't you?"

Michael pinched his lips between his teeth and refused to answer.

"Stubborn." The man smiled. "I'm willing to bet you take after your father that way, whoever he is, considering he openly defied an agreement that's been in place since the great flood."

Michael knew that last comment was meant to bait him into revealing his father. He bit his tongue and glared.

"Well . . ." With an uncommon grace of movement, the stranger balanced his spectacles on the bridge of his nose and reached out a hand. "I'll need some help . . . *Michael*, is it? Your nature obscures you a bit. Take my hand, and we'll get this over with just as you requested."

Michael stared at the hand offered to him. The long, elegant fingers were scarred with evidence of hard labor. Strange. His first impression of this man was that he was a scholar, not a laborer.

"Come," the man urged with a gentle shake of his hand. "When I get what I want, I'll send you straight home to your woman. I promise."

Though safe, Bryony was bound to be frightened when she woke alone. She would wonder where Michael was. Perhaps she would even think he'd left her, frightened away by her proposal. He wanted to tell her it wasn't true. He wanted to tell her he loved her a thousand more times. He shouldn't have suppressed the urge. What if he never got another chance? Before he could lose his composure, Michael reached out and took his abductor's hand.

Behind his spectacles, the man squinted as though he were staring into a blinding light. His body began to tremble with the effort. He growled, "You're a nephil, no doubt, but why so young? And why can't I see you clearly?" He released Michael's hand and pulled the spectacles from his face as though their frames had burned him. He tucked them into his pocket and stood. The little, gold light followed him up like a well-trained firefly. He towered over Michael and actually seemed to be growing as he spoke.

"Whose son are you?" The calm in the man's voice began to waver. "Which angel dared to sire you?" His body widened. Michael saw two batlike wings sprout from his back, uncurling like forest ferns. "I see death in your past and your future. I see death in you now. You breathe it. If I cut you, you would bleed it. I can't see anything else!"

Michael shook his head as the creature—and it was definitely a creature now—rose up before him. Its back bowed against the ceiling before it stopped growing, though Michael suspected it could have become much, much bigger. Sharing its one head were three faces that vaguely resembled a man and two other animals respectively. Its tail whipped across the floor like an angry serpent. Its feet gripped the stone beneath it with the kind of massive talons Michael had only ever seen in illustrations of dinosaurs.

When the beast tired of waiting for Michael's answer, it shook the cave with a howl that made his stomach drop. "Samael!" It seemed to be calling for the Angel of Death himself, furious enough to actually take him on. Then the creature's voice dropped to a low growl. "Samael, you'll come to regret this sin, even if I have to find and punish you myself."

As much as Michael wanted to hate his abductor, he hated his father more. At last, his longstanding grudge was validated. And even though his life was probably forfeit at this point, something about that validation made him brave. "Please!" he called up to the monster towering over him. "Let me help! I want my father to pay for what he did!" He was ready to fight alongside the thing that had chained him to a cavern wall. It seemed they had a common enemy between them. Finally, someone else saw Michael's existence for what it was—a crime, a sin, abuse—and Michael would risk almost anything to bring his depraved father to justice. Almost . . .

His fury died at the thought of Bryony, but it had already done its work. Those elegant hands and that herringbone vest reemerged. And the demon—Michael had no further doubt he'd identified his abductor correctly—showed his teeth in an expression that was half grin, half snarl. "Bow before me then, son of Samael. Bow and swear fealty to your king."

Asmodeus.

Michael was as good as dead.

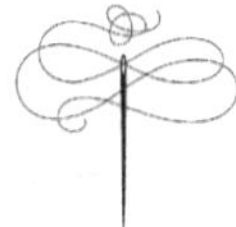

The front door stood open again, and Bryony hesitated to enter. This time, Loki was not with her. This time she was alone, but so was Michael. She needed to prove to herself he was safe, so she screwed up her courage and crossed the threshold.

Inside was too quiet. She had exactly ten seconds to assess the silence before it was broken. Michael came stumbling down the stairs, holding one hand tightly in the other. She saw a flash of blood. "Help," he said, trembling. "I think it's deep."

Bryony's reaction was immediate and instinctive. She rushed upstairs and pulled out all the first aid supplies she had in the house. Then she took Michael into the kitchen and tried to pry his fingers open. "I need to look at it," she said. "It should be washed and disinfected." He begrudgingly complied. His hand was sliced across the palm as though he were about to perform an at-home ritual that required a blood sacrifice. "How did this happen?"

"Oh, it was silly." Michael laughed and winced. "I was cutting fabric. I didn't pay attention to where the blade was and cut right through my hand. So stupid of me, right?"

"I think we've all done something like that at one time or another." But Bryony wasn't so sure. After cleaning the injury, she took a closer look at it. The cut wasn't as deep as it looked at first glance, but it was bleeding heavily. She tsked and opened the gauze package. "You must not be used to my mother's tools. Did you at least get to finish your shirt?"

"I did." He smiled down at her, and Bryony noted the pride in his expression. "I'd hoped to show it to you when you got home. It's cut marvelously well and fits like a dream."

"I should think so since you made it." She disinfected the cut and pressed fresh gauze to it. "Apply pressure to that for me, will you?"

He did as instructed with a quizzical expression. "Is all this really necessary? You are a healing god, after all."

"*Was* a healing god," she corrected. "Now I'm . . . Well, what am I the god of now? Just you, I suppose. But the cut's pretty clean and not too deep. I think it'll be fine in a few days."

Now he looked even more confused, but he quickly shook the expression off and replaced it with an absurdly charming grin. "Of course, that's what I meant—you *were* their healing god, and now you're mine." He bent down low and pressed his cheek to hers. The gesture was unusual for him but sweet all the same. He kissed her as he pulled away, and she was left with a feeling of lingering warmth on her cheek. She removed the gauze and spread ointment over his cut while he stood staring down at her, chewing his lower lip. He looked far more concerned than the situation warranted. "You . . . You will tell me when you need your rite, won't you? Preferably well beforehand. You won't let it get too late."

Was he still worried about that? "I promise not to be careless, Michael, but I still want to wean off worship."

He stiffened. "We won't be weaning you off, darling. That's not how this works."

"I don't think it should be entirely your call." She finished taping the bandage and kissed his palm. "The finishing touch. It'll have to do since I don't have the healing sword anymore."

All at once, Michael's warm expression faded into something decidedly less friendly. She couldn't tell which of her comments had upset him. He quickly composed himself and applied that saccharine smile he seemed to have perfected overnight. "Well, I like to think anything lost can be found again, don't you? Come. I'll show you what I've been working on."

Bryony followed him out of the kitchen and upstairs to the sewing room. He ducked to enter but still managed to bump his head on the doorframe. "Oh, for the love of . . ." he muttered and rubbed his head with his uninjured hand. "That hurt."

"Sounded like it did." She was sympathetic but dubious. Michael was accustomed to ducking through doorframes considerably lower than the ones in her house. But she didn't want to question any difficulties he had that were due to his height. There was no way she could understand what he went through on a day-to-day basis.

"I seem determined to damage myself today." When Michael recovered from the collision, he picked up the plum-colored shirt from the sewing table. He'd given it long, black cuffs and an understated collar. The buttons he'd added were far more decorative than she expected. They looked like they were made of silver lace. "I still intend to embroider the collar to add flair and elegance. What do you think?"

"I didn't know you could embroider." She touched the fabric, more than a little impressed by the finished product. "You usually dress so practically."

"Nothing wrong with practicality in moderation." He folded the shirt and placed it back on the sewing table. "I thought complementing your wardrobe would be an interesting challenge. Couples who complement each other are rare these days but delightful, don't you agree? And I wanted to practice making something appropriate for the wedding. I assume you intend to wear black."

She drew back. "I . . . hadn't thought about it."

The giant's usually resonant voice rose in pitch and picked up pace as he spoke. Martha had been right. He was giddy about the wedding. "We'll have a beautiful ceremony. I'll make you the most gorgeous wedding gown the world has ever seen, but you must promise something in return."

Bryony cocked her head. "What?"

"Promise you'll wear a splash of blue somewhere among all that black. It'll bring out your eyes." He bent down to examine her face and nodded. "Yes, cobalt, I think. You have such striking eyes, darling."

Bryony blushed. She couldn't shake the feeling she was being flattered by a stranger. Michael's cadence, his tone, his language had changed. The way he carried himself had changed. Before, she'd thought he moved like a cobra, coiled and ready. Now he was easier, limber, more catlike. Yesterday, he was steady and even-tempered. Today, his moods shifted in and out of shadow in a way she'd never seen before. Could a marriage proposal really change a man so much? Was the answer different when the person in question was half angel?

Throughout the afternoon, Michael continued to make plans for the wedding. Bryony had never seen him so excited. He talked about décor, colors, flowers. That night, she sat at her vanity in shorts and a T-shirt, untangling her hair after a shower. He built a fire in the bedroom hearth and mused about its garden aesthetic. "What a gorgeous inset. Such an intricate design. You know, what I find so splendid about the Victorians is their appreciation for excess. Everything had to be beautiful in those days. We could do something like that for the wedding. Tell me, do you have a corset?"

"My mother's fits me all right."

Michael pressed a thumb to his lips in thought. "Most ideal to have one made for your measurements, but that won't be a problem. I could have one ready in no time. We'll have a midwinter wedding. Imagine the snow! Do you object, darling?"

"No." She made a face into the mirror. The idea of a wedding had never appealed to her—the attention she knew she'd receive, the small talk she'd be expected to make—but if it made Michael happy, who was she to object? "Can I wear a veil?"

Michael closed the space between them, draped his hands over her shoulders, and pulled her back against his thighs. "I wouldn't have it any other way." He bent down and took in the smell of her hair. "Is that orange blossom?"

"It is." She twisted her freshly washed hair into a knot at the back of her head.

"It smells divine." He caught her wrists before she could finish securing the bun. "If you don't mind . . ." Bryony allowed him to lower her hands and unwind the knot in her hair. "Do you ever wear braids to bed?" She started to shake her head but stopped when he stilled her. "Would you allow me to braid it?" He combed his fingers through her hair. "I'll do Dutch braids. In the morning, you'll have waves."

"Okay." Her heart pounded like it knew something she didn't.

Michael started at her left temple and began to weave. Watching his long fingers work in the mirror was mesmerizing. He braided her hair as though he'd done it a million times before, as though he were playing an instrument he'd practiced since childhood. He braided her hair the same way he'd baked those biscuits, she realized. As he worked, he gathered more and more strands into the braid, and it began to form a wide arc over her ear. When he was finished, he secured it and tugged at the loops to loosen them.

She reached into the top drawer of her vanity and retrieved another tie so he could do the other side. It was perfectly symmetrical by the time he was done. "Where did you learn to do this?" She turned to face him.

He pulled her to her feet and bent to kiss her. "There's a lot about me you've yet to discover."

"I guess so." He'd changed so suddenly, but she supposed she should have expected it. Michael—whose entire body warmed by degrees any time she playfully called him her husband—had been fundamentally affected by her proposal, by her promise to stay. She recalled a conversation they'd had on the beach in which she'd suggested newlyweds don't usually act like themselves. *That's why they say the honeymoon is over when you start acting like yourselves again.* She'd only been half serious at the time, but now she had to wonder whether she'd been onto something. Perhaps he felt he could be himself now that he had some security in the relationship. She tried to smile as she called back to that conversation. "I guess the honeymoon is over, isn't it?"

Michael's eyes widened. He looked to have massively misinterpreted her quip. Then he let his lids drop, and his voice grew low and sultry. "No, darling, it's only just begun." He lifted her in his arms, laid her down on the bed, and kissed her ferociously. For the first time, Bryony felt more urgency in his kiss than his touch. *Who are you?* she wanted to ask, but she didn't want to hurt him. She could get to know him all over again if that's what it took. He was still kind, still gentle. He was still Michael.

Wasn't he?

His hands were practiced and deliberate. He lingered over her bones as always, and when his fingers drifted down to her wrists, a brief moan escaped his lips. He kissed along her jaw and chin before locking onto her mouth again. Something of him was still there—it had to be. She just had to dig deep and find him. He slipped a hand under her shirt and drew his thumb under the curve of her breast. She shivered, and his skin warmed at her reaction, but it wasn't the fever she was used to. Gently, he bit her earlobe and murmured, "You're mine. No one else can have you."

What? She pushed herself up beneath him, and he followed, allowing her to sit. Michael had gone into this relationship afraid. Maybe he wasn't anymore, but she'd never thought him the possessive type. Even now, it felt performative, like he didn't really mean it, like he thought it was what he was supposed to say. Why did he suddenly think this was what she wanted? "You don't have to do this," she said.

His hands dropped away from her. "Do you not like it?"

"No, it's . . . It's not that. It feels wonderful." That wasn't a lie. She hated to put a stop to such a warm, inviting touch. And his kiss had been exciting—like a first kiss—but . . . She cleared her throat. How could she say this without hurting his feelings? *I don't feel like I know you anymore, and I'm not okay with being this intimate until I do.* No, that would break him, and she didn't want to see how the new him broke. The old him had been bad enough.

Instead, she said, "I've been thinking, maybe we should take things a little slower. I know you're uncomfortable getting this close, and I don't want to pressure you. Maybe we should wait until you feel better about it. Honestly, I don't mind. I'd much rather wait than feel like I seduced you before you wanted me to."

Michael sighed and stared down at his hands. He looked almost relieved, but there was nothing unbelievable about that. Too many times they'd pushed their boundaries only to find the seraph waiting for them. "All right, darling," he said.

He removed his shirt and pants, folded them neatly, and placed them on the chair where his coat still hung. He turned out the light, and the warm dance of fire reflected off his skin as he climbed into bed beside her. He snuggled up to her, kissed her head, and breathed in the scent of her shampoo. "I love orange blossoms," he murmured. Then, as an afterthought, he added, "And you."

"I love you too, Michael." But she didn't think he needed to hear it, not like he used to.

She closed her eyes and tried to focus on the rhythm of his breath, the soft touch of his skin against hers. In the dark, she began to doze. And somewhere between dreams, Bryony could have sworn she heard

Michael whisper, "Don't be afraid, little god. You'll get through this in one piece."

Chapter Thirteen

Michael did not bow, and he did not swear fealty. He stared at his captor and opened his mouth to speak, but the demon preempted him. "Don't," he snapped, "call me Asmodeus."

"What should I call you then?"

His captor showed his teeth in a mock smile. "That depends on whose lie you're looking to advance. You can call me the Aeshma Daeva if you're trying to wax nostalgic, but honestly, I don't feel it's accurate. Do I look like an agent of rage to you?"

Michael shook his head, not quite sure what the demon was talking about but absolutely sure what the desired answer to his question was.

"You could call me Ashmedai if you wanted to suggest I had an unquenchable lust for women—that I ravished Solomon's wives even in their . . . 'time of separation.'" Here he made air quotes with his long, delicate fingers. "But if you call me Asmodeus, you'll be suggesting that I killed seven *innocent* men simply because they married a girl I wanted for myself. You'd be lying not only about me, but about Sarah, and that I will not abide."

Michael tried not to let his surprise show. He'd learned both stories as a child and believed them without question. Of course, the king of demons would not be above lying to him, but what would be the motive in this case? He had Michael at his disposal. Anything he wanted, he was going to get through force, not by convincing his captive he wasn't so bad after all. "What should I call you if I don't want to lie about you?"

The demon's true smile was sweet, small, almost doll-like in a way. "You'd call me *Ash* if you were a friend. But in your case, considering your need to supplicate for mercy, I'd suggest *Your Majesty.*"

"You're not my king yet. I'm still alive." Michael regretted his own hubris almost as soon as the words left his mouth.

"Inevitability breeds resentment, I suppose."

In the dim light, Michael noticed that his captor sat cross-legged and hovered an inch above the ground as though he were too good to touch it. The same stones the demon avoided jutted into Michael's lower back in a way that was initially uncomfortable and eventually quite painful. Michael glared at him. "Can we come to the point, please? What is it you want from me?"

The demon frowned. "Such impatience. I should have expected as much from Samael's issue. And to think I was going to challenge you to a game of chess." The way he said *chess* made it sound more like a musical note than a word. He leaned back against nothing and crossed his arms. "I had hoped to discover whether Samael's complete inability to strategize would be passed down to all his children universally. Your brothers and sisters were walking checkmates."

Brothers and sisters? A wave of curiosity doused Michael's anger. The demon king was an ancient creature, and Michael suddenly wanted to ask what else his captor knew about him that he himself did not. He realized he had never in his life spoken to another nephil, and he had so many questions. But how could he begin to ask them of someone who'd abducted him and chained him to the wall of an underground labyrinth? He shook off his own curiosity and mumbled, "Please, don't compare me to my father."

The demon—Ash—watched Michael with interest. His haughty expression had softened into something like sympathy. "Be grateful you know who your father is. There are benefits to understanding your lineage. Some of us are not so lucky."

Michael shifted and heard his chain drag over the stones. "Do you not know who your father is?"

Ash shrugged. "My father was a cherub and a watcher, which narrows it down a touch. My mother, on the other hand, was a prostitute, which does not."

"I'm sorry." Michael frowned, fearing he'd angered his captor.

"Don't be. I'm proud of my mother. She was a good mother and made an honest living. She didn't want to marry, so she didn't. Most women were forced to marry in those days. And what do forced marriages lead to? Do you know?" He sounded like a teacher addressing a particularly dense student.

Michael thought a moment and cringed at the answer he didn't want to voice.

"It's all right," Ash said, barely hiding the disgust in his voice. "Say the word. It doesn't disappear just because you refuse to acknowledge it."

This conversation was wearing Michael down. He didn't understand it. He wanted to go home. He wanted to know that Bryony was safe. He answered, "They lead to rape."

"Good boy. And now you can begin to solve the riddle of why I killed seven 'innocent' men on their wedding nights." A shadow passed over the demon's face, and Michael began to see why an entire civilization had assigned him the attribute of rage. "But enough about me. Let's talk about you and where you keep that magnificent sword you stole."

Sword? So that's what the demon king wanted from him—his father's sword. Michael could only begin to imagine why anyone would want the Angel of Death's indomitable weapon. It took him several long breaths to fortify his answer with every ounce of courage he had left. "No."

"Excuse me?" The demon actually laughed at him.

"I said no." The sword was too powerful to blithely hand over to anyone, let alone the demon king. The consequences could be devastating. Michael trusted very few people to understand just how permanent true death could be, to know exactly what it meant to use that weapon on another living soul.

The demon king stood and towered over him. "I want you to think more carefully about your answer, son of Samael. Until now, I've been courteous. We made our introductions like civilized creatures, and I've given you a reasonable request. You can tell me where the sword is, and after I have it, you can go home to your woman, take a hot shower, and forget about all this. Or you can refuse me and quickly discover why the Zoroastrians called me *the bloody mace.*"

Michael could almost hear his own heartbeat, thunderous in the dark. He wanted to surrender. He wanted to give everything just to see Bryony again, but the only reason the death sword was even up for grabs was because he'd stolen it from his father. He closed his eyes and answered firmly. "I can't give you the sword. I won't."

A monstrous wind howled through the caverns and rattled the chain that bound him. He heard a roar like torrential rain. Sand and pebbles struck and stung his skin. Then there was total darkness and silence, and Michael lost track of the world again.

The whir of the sewing machine was as familiar to Bryony as rain on the roof, and in that cloudy space between sleep and consciousness, she almost believed her mother was alive again. She saw a needle dancing over fabric behind her closed eyelids. She heard her father hum as he stacked freshly laundered sheets in the linen closet. But the fading dream couldn't conjure her little brother's feet slapping against the floorboards as he ran downstairs to get breakfast. Her mind wouldn't allow it. *He's gone. He's gone. He's gone.*

She kicked off the sheets and sat up. Early morning light filtered through the curtains. The sight of her old twin bed strapped sidelong to the foot of the one she slept in brought her back to the present. Sometimes grief crept up on her and took her back in time to when it was fresh. She was glad to open her eyes and find she'd passed through that nightmare and come out safe, albeit changed, on the other side.

Her new family, it seemed, had already started on his sewing. She patted her head and felt the braids he'd woven the night before. They held together rather well, which must have meant she slept better than usual. Odd, considering how uneasy she'd been about the change she saw in her fiancé. The word *fiancé* tripped lightly through her thoughts and made her smile to herself. Change or no change, she loved him, and she was determined to show him how much.

She dressed in Eliza's street clothes from *My Fair Lady*, which included a patched jacket that looked much classier dyed black, in Bryony's opinion. Then she unraveled her braids and shook out her hair. It fell over her shoulders in playful waves. Michael had been right. She practiced her smile, marched to the sewing room, and tapped him on the shoulder.

He sat hunched over the sewing machine, carefully guiding fabric under the needle. At her touch, he perked up. "Look at you!" he cried when he saw her. "You look stunning in waves."

Bryony forced a smile. "Thank you."

"Look what I've been working on." He held up a nearly finished, white shirt with black and gray accents. "What do you think? I decided monochrome would complement your style. Speaking of, where on earth did you get that jacket? Oh, don't tell me. I already know. Of course I do."

"Were you up sewing all night?" Bryony looked doubtfully at the shirt.

"Not all night, but you know, I can't go around with only one set of clothes. It's just not dignified. I plan to make black slacks, devastatingly plain, but one must have something that goes with everything when one's wardrobe is small. I considered a cravat, but I'm fairly certain you'll tell me it's too much."

Bryony shook her head. "You should wear whatever makes you happy."

His eyes widened, and a spark of mischief ignited in them. "Oh, never tell me that, darling, or you'll live to regret it. Promise to keep me on a short fashion leash, will you? Preferably one studded with diamonds." He laughed.

Her smile began to slip, but she caught it and tugged it taut again. "I promise."

He took her hand in his considerably larger one and ducked through the door with her. "Now, let's have breakfast and discuss your wedding gown. I thought perhaps a nautical theme for the wedding and a cephalopod-inspired gown. Nothing overt, mind you. But what do you think of an asymmetrical, cobalt band around the bodice with tentacles of color descending into a full, black skirt?"

Bryony didn't answer, and he didn't press her. He just went on talking about open backs and upswept hair. When they reached the parlor, she was startled at the sight of the yawning front door. But she said nothing, and Michael didn't close it. The kitchen door was also open, but nothing else was out of place. In fact, the entire kitchen appeared to have been scrubbed top to bottom. It practically sparkled.

"Did you clean last night?" she asked.

"Oh, it was nothing." He grinned and pulled out a chair for her.

She glanced down at his bandaged hand. "You shouldn't do any cleaning with that cut."

"I know how to use gloves, darling." He began rifling through the fridge and fished out eggs, onion, mushrooms and a block of cheese. "I was pleased to find our Martha thought to bring you a variety of cheeses. I wouldn't have survived if I'd been forced to use cheddar. Oh, forgive me, would you like an omelet? I hadn't even thought to ask."

"Sounds delicious. But really, you don't have to—"

"Not another word. I'm making you breakfast, and you've no say in the matter."

"Where did you find all this energy?" she mused, more to herself than to him.

Still he answered. "I'm just so happy to finally be sharing your home."

After breakfast, which was admittedly delicious, Bryony went to town with a new list of fabrics Michael wanted. On her way, she stopped by Martha's and ordered a coffee. She needed some time out of the house. Her mind was reeling.

Martha brought coffee and sat down beside her with an almost imperceptible head shake. "You're miserable, and you should be happier than you've ever been."

"I'm just exhausted." Bryony lifted her cup to her lips, but Martha's hand covered it before she could drink.

"Don't lie to me now. No coffee until you tell the truth."

The familiar booth, with its wine-red curtains and copper-penny tabletop, was an oasis to Bryony. If she couldn't tell Martha, who could she tell? She definitely didn't want to forfeit her coffee. "Promise you won't tell Bill?"

Martha drew her fingers across her lips like a zipper.

Bryony sighed and looked away. "I feel like I don't know my own fiancé, and it can't just be the engagement. I've never seen this big of a change in anyone. Granted, I've never known an angel. Maybe that's just how they are, but if it is . . ." She choked but composed herself. "If it is, I wish I'd never proposed to him. I miss him. Is that even possible? I feel like I fell in love with a completely different person, and he's been stolen from me." She hesitated before she voiced her next thought. It implied distrust, but she had to know. "You'd tell me if Bill had been absent more than usual, wouldn't you?"

Martha nodded. "I swear it. Our mutual friend has been with me all day, every day. So unless he can be in two places at once, this isn't his doing."

"I almost wish it was." Bryony stared down into her coffee, realizing she hadn't added sugar. She drank it anyway. "As it is . . . I don't know. It would hurt Michael to know how uncomfortable he makes me now. I can't tell him, but I can't keep it from him forever. At some point, he's going to wonder why I don't really . . . want him anymore."

"Oh, no." Martha knit her brow. "That's not good. Are you sure it isn't just stress? An engagement is a big change, and you're sharing your home with someone new."

"I suppose it could be stress, but I really don't think so. I mean did you have this experience when you first got engaged?"

"No." Martha frowned. "I was nervous, but nothing like this. Of course, I wasn't engaged to an angel, which would give any reasonable person extra jitters, considering." She stood and handed Bryony the sugar. "Sit back and enjoy your coffee. Your secret's safe with me, especially when it comes to Bill. I'm not a hundred percent certain he wouldn't kill your fiancé given the right excuse."

Chapter Fourteen

M ichael had to block his eyes from the sun when he opened them. But as his vision adjusted, he saw that what he'd mistaken for daylight was just a few lit torches affixed to the walls of the cavern. After so many hours in darkness, any light can be mistaken for brilliance, any illusion mistaken for truth. Across the floor, another person had been chained to another wall. He couldn't tell at first whether the figure was alive or dead. It lay curled in a fetal ball with its back to him. It was a small figure. A woman, he thought. Then the figure stirred, and Michael's world spiraled out of control. It was Bryony.

A minute ago, he knew exactly where he stood. He knew denying the demon king Samael's sword was the right thing to do. Now he wasn't so sure. It seemed Ashmedai intended to use Bryony as a bargaining chip. Considering his lineage, Michael didn't stand a chance against that method of persuasion, and Ashmedai had to know it.

Bryony woke and groaned. She pushed herself to a seated position and spotted Michael. "Oh, thank god!" she cried. "I thought I'd never see you again."

Michael stretched his chain, but he couldn't reach her. "Did he hurt you?"

She shook her head. "Who did this, and what do they want?"

"The demon king. He wants the sword."

Bryony's hand flew to her mouth. "What? Don't give it to him!"

"I don't intend to. I can't imagine what he wants it for, but there's no chance it's for anything good." He watched her struggle with her chain and winced sympathetically.

"I mean it, Michael. You have to promise you won't give it to him. Even if he tortures me—and he probably will—you can't give in."

"Please don't say that." Michael hung his head. There was no way he could stand to hear her cries without breaking. It was impossible. His nature simply wouldn't allow it—his nature, which was every bit as unwavering as Ashmedai's . . . Suddenly, Michael understood something fundamental about his captor. It was like finally placing an integral piece in an impossible puzzle. "I . . . don't think he'll torture you. No, he wouldn't do that."

"What makes you so sure?" Bryony folded her arms in a pout that Michael found simultaneously endearing and confusing. Why on earth should she *want* to be tortured?

"Because . . ." He hesitated, rifling through his memories for every story he'd ever heard or read about the demon king. "Because Ashmedai isn't capable of harming a woman. It's not in his nature, and the angelic side of him makes his nature all but immutable."

Bryony frowned. "And you're certain of this? Why? Because he told you so? He could be lying you know."

The echoing drip, drip, drip of water pounded in Michael's ears. His head still ached, and he had to work through a fog of pain to remember the stories he'd learned in his youth. The demon king was a creature of habit. That was why Solomon's men had been able to enslave him in the first place. Every night, Ashmedai came down his mountain to drink from the same well. Solomon's men knew his routine and replaced the water with wine. The demon drank it anyway—he couldn't help himself—and it was only in his drunken slumber that the men were able to manacle him. "They knew," Michael muttered to himself.

Bryony arched one brow and crossed her arms. "What did *they* know? And who are we talking about exactly?"

"Solomon's men. They knew Ashmedai couldn't break his habits, even though it would have been in his best interest. And it isn't his habit to harm women. In fact . . ." He grinned as another piece of the puzzle fell into place. "He seems to go to great lengths to protect them." He thought back to the story of Sarah. "It took an archangel to drive him away from Sarah, but he wasn't killing her husbands out of spite. He was . . . He was acting as her guardian angel."

Bryony bowed her head. "Guardian angels hardly shrink from harming women."

"I know." Michael rolled his lips into his mouth in thought. "I think he meant to be a true guardian, though. Like with the wives of Solomon. According to the stories, after Ashmedai escaped from King Solomon and began impersonating him, his lust for the women of the palace could not be sated. But he just told me that story was a lie, and I think I believe him."

"Why?" Bryony narrowed her eyes.

"Partly because Solomon never sired any giant sons. There would've been stories about it. I think . . . I think Ashmedai never slept with any of Solomon's wives. I think he was trying to protect them too."

Bryony laughed. "From what?"

"From Solomon."

The silence that followed was palpable. Michael watched Bryony, but he couldn't begin to read her. She was sullen, angry. And was that a glimmer of pride he saw twitching at the corner of her mouth? She kept her head down and muttered, "All the same, don't tell him where the sword is. Maybe he'll let me go. When he does, I can hide it somewhere safe."

Michael nodded. "That sounds like a good plan."

They sat in pensive silence until the torches burned out and the cavern was nothing but inky blackness again. And Michael felt a sting in his eyes as he realized how desperately he wanted to see the stars.

Bryony came home to open doors and fires roaring in every hearth. It didn't even surprise her anymore. She'd spent much of the day in town, flitting from shop to shop and buying very little—anything to avoid going home. She'd chatted with everyone who said hello to her, which was clear evidence of just how uncomfortable her own home made her these days. And then she'd run out of places to go.

Michael greeted her with a friendly embrace and a cool kiss on the cheek. She recalled the first time she'd begged to kiss his cheek and the heat that passed between them when she finally did. It couldn't be gone so soon, could it? She fidgeted with the sleeves of her jacket and muttered, "Good evening."

"You're out of sorts." He crouched before her. "What happened? Did someone say something nasty to you? Tell me who it was, and I'll tear the tongue from their mouth."

Her gaze shot up to his, and she couldn't stop her face from contorting into a confused mask. She opened her mouth to speak but snapped it shut again. The Michael she knew was an unmovable mountain. On the surface, insults seemed to roll off him. He was protective but never aggressive, never violent. She whispered, "I don't think I know you anymore."

A blush crept into his cheeks but quickly faded. "You're upset." He stood and took her hand. "I know how to cheer you, but first, dinner."

They ate pasta with ready-made sauce, which Michael insisted on cooking himself. "Even I can boil pasta," he said, but Bryony caught him adding herbs when he thought she wasn't looking. His appetite was voracious, and he made no attempt to hide it. She watched him with mounting concern.

After dinner, Michael prepared a pot of loose-leaf tea and added just a touch of honey to Bryony's cup. Then he took her by the hand and led her upstairs, balancing both teacups like he was a backward child who had run away from the circus to join a home. He sat Bryony at her vanity and set her cup beside her. "Don't move from that spot. I have a surprise for you."

God she hated surprises.

He returned with what looked like a large tackle box. For a moment, she expected him to show her a new sewing kit he'd put together, but she should have known better. This Michael was not the same person she knew from *Dragonfly*. He wasn't even the same person she knew from Mexico. So she really shouldn't have been shocked or confused when he opened the box to reveal a vast array of makeup and skincare products.

"Where did you get all this?" She ran her fingers over the rows of glass tubes, spinning them until they rattled like an odd, percussive instrument.

He didn't look at her when he answered. "Just something I found lying around."

There was a chance he wasn't lying, albeit a slim one. Bryony's mother had kept quite a few boxes of makeup around the house, and it was entirely possible she'd had one stashed away that Bryony had failed to notice. But these products didn't look as old as that. Still she held her tongue. If this was not Michael, then the last thing she wanted to do was let on that she suspected anything. Whoever . . . Whatever this was had to be dangerous, a tiger dressed as a house cat. She knew better than to put it on guard. Then there was the other possibility—one Bryony was loath to consider—that she might have gotten herself engaged to a person she never really knew at all.

"I thought we could try a look for the wedding." He was grinning at her, picking little bottles out of his kit. "I noticed you don't tend to wear makeup. I hope you aren't averse to it. I've so many ideas, and your bone structure is a thing of beauty. May I?"

How could she say no when he asked like that?

He had her turn away from the mirror and crouched before her. "Close your eyes, and tilt your chin up."

She complied. She needed time to think, but as soon as he began, she was completely lost to the process. He slipped a scarf behind her neck and knotted it at the top of her head to hold her hair back. His gentleness sent shivers down her spine. He was sure, steady, and confident as he brushed the colors onto her face. He didn't seem like Michael, but he didn't seem entirely unlike him either. There was something achingly familiar about the way he lingered over her bones. Bryony opened and closed her eyes as he instructed, opened and closed her mouth as he instructed, and moved only when he turned her head with his own hands. She sensed no malice in his touch. It was as tender as it was alien.

Finally, he backed away, pressed a thumb to his lips, and looked approvingly at his work. "It's not perfect, but this was a dry run. It'll be absolutely gorgeous with the gown." With that, he removed the scarf and turned her to face the mirror. And she found herself gazing upon an undeniable work of art.

Her complexion was too fair, but he hadn't bothered to correct it. Instead, he'd worked with it. Everything about the look he'd created was subtle, except her eyes. They were the centerpiece. They were shaded like the sunsets she'd seen on the Mexican coast. Orange and pink and faded blue. He'd drawn a lace pattern from the corners of her eyes that fanned out toward her hairline. It was so intricate she couldn't have retraced the pattern if her life depended on it. And in a finishing flourish, so gentle she hadn't even felt it, Michael had applied gold leaf to the skin around her eyes. It wasn't much, just a glint here and there. It made her skin look as though it had been painted on years ago and was now chipping away to show the gold underneath.

She was speechless.

Michael's smile faded. "Do you not like it?" But before she could answer, he shook off his doubt. "Of course you do—it's positively stunning—but how could I have failed with such a perfect canvas to work with?" As unsettling as the face grinning behind her in the mirror was, she had to believe Michael was in there somewhere. Some things had stayed the same. He was as creative as ever, as gentle as ever. "You're beautiful," he said. "Go ahead and wash it off. I can recreate it at a moment's notice." He stood and handed her a cleanser and towel. "I'll look forward to sleeping in a grove of orange blossoms tonight."

Bryony twisted the towel in her hands. Her honesty was long overdue. If they were going to get anywhere in their relationship, they'd have to start with the truth. "Michael, I . . ." Her voice was quiet, apologetic. "I know I've been cold to you lately. The thing is, you've been so different since we got engaged. I didn't know what to think or how to feel about it."

Did he flinch just then? She was almost certain he did. "Have I really been so changed?" he asked.

Bryony nodded. "I understand if the engagement affected you more than I expected it to. I mean it is kind of a big deal, but . . . engagements don't usually cause such a big change. I just need to remember you're different, right? Your nature is different. I still have so much to learn about you."

He recovered from his dismay, and a warm, flirtatious smile crossed his face. "I look forward to teaching you."

Bryony walked away from him feeling good that she'd finally come clean but less than confident it was the wisest course of action. At the door, she turned back and said, "I love you."

"I know you do, darling."

After her shower, Bryony slipped into running shorts and a tank top and joined Michael in bed. A warm fire crackled and glowed in the hearth. A cool breeze from the open window toyed with the flames and energized the shadows on the walls. She turned to her fiancé and tried to find him buried somewhere behind his own eyes. Then she leaned over and kissed him. He slipped his hand around the back of her neck, under her hair. She tugged him closer and opened her mouth to him. His tongue lingered at the boundary of her lips, almost tentative. For a moment, she could have sworn she felt his skin begin to warm under her hands, but then he pulled away.

"It's okay," she assured him. "I don't feel shy anymore."

He frowned, pulled her into a tight embrace, and kissed the top of her head. "Whatever am I to do with you, sweet god? You give yourself away entirely too easily."

Bryony touched her forehead to his chest and chewed her lip, grateful he couldn't see the expression on her face. She wanted to trust him. She'd decided to trust him and hadn't made that decision lightly, but . . . She shivered in his arms. He noticed.

"Are you all right?" He let her go. "Is it too cool for you? I thought we might enjoy some fresh air tonight, but perhaps I was being presumptuous."

Bryony shook her head. "No, it's not that. Sorry. I'm just not feeling one hundred percent tonight." She lied, but whether she didn't want to hurt him or didn't want to alert him, she couldn't have said.

Regardless, he believed her. "You're not feeling weak or feverish, are you?" He checked her forehead with the back of his hand. "You promised to tell me when you needed a rite. You promised not to let it get too late." He wasn't just worried for her—he was terrified, and it didn't make sense. They were alone together in her home. He could perform a rite at a moment's notice. He had no reason to panic.

Still she couldn't stand to see the fear in his eyes, so she smiled to reassure him. "It's not that. I promise I'd tell you if it was. Come on, Michael, you know I can go at least three weeks."

He leaned back against the headboard and failed to hide his relief. "Well, yes. Of course I knew that, but anomalies, you know." Then he quickly shifted moods. His voice raised in pitch, false cheer covering an obvious tremor. "Speaking of odd occurrences, I found your book in my workroom, hiding in a stack of fabrics. Do you have any idea how it got there? Perhaps it was the ghost." He chuckled and handed her a paperback.

Bryony took it slowly, gazing down at the cover, willing herself not to scramble to her feet at the sight of it. It was the romance she'd bought for Michael on her first day back in town. He would never have assumed it was hers. Her heart hammered in her ears.

It isn't him.

It isn't him.

Merely suspecting she'd been living with an impostor was one thing. She could easily cast doubt on her own suspicions and tell herself she was overreacting again. Now the impostor left no room for doubt, and interwoven with her fear was a familiar, old rage. How dare she doubt herself? Why did she always question her own intuition? Now she'd wasted time, and Michael was gone—taken, likely against his will. She might have wept at the thought, but a mountain of terror overwhelmed her.

She carefully placed the book on the nightstand and calmly got out of bed. "Thanks. I've been wanting to finish this one." She turned and smiled at the impostor. "Bathroom first." Then she walked out of the bedroom and straight down the stairs to the phone in the kitchen.

Chapter Fifteen

The little, gold firefly hovered lazily before Michael's eyes. As it brightened, the cavern came slowly into focus, and he saw Ashmedai levitating an inch over the jutting stones, staring at him. "I thought you might like a meal and a walk," the demon said, smiling.

What he meant by *a walk* was a guided tour of the tunnels, including an opportunity for Michael to relieve himself at the end of a long, chain leash. Like a dog. Michael had been on several of these walks already, and as necessary as they were, he did not enjoy them. "This is humiliating," he muttered.

Ash didn't let his smile slip. "I would have gotten us a hotel room, but I thought it best if we didn't have to worry about the volume of our conversations. Also, this is far more intimidating, don't you agree? Up you get. I'll feed you after."

When the demon rose to unhook the end of Michael's chain, the torches sputtered to life, seemingly on their own, and the entire cavern came into view. To Michael's utter horror, Bryony was no longer there. "Where is she?" he demanded, though he was in no position to do so.

"Perfectly safe," Ash answered. "Although a little worse for wear." He chuckled wickedly.

"You wouldn't hurt her," Michael said, more to convince himself than anything. "I'm certain you wouldn't. She's done nothing to you."

Ash wrapped the end of Michael's chain around his own wrist. "Well, if you're certain. Now walk or I'll drag you. Your choice."

Michael obeyed, and they walked a while in silence. As it happened, Ashmedai was fastidious and insisted on the pit toilet being a good half mile from the cavern where he kept and fed his captives. He wasn't cruel, as captors went, but he wasn't kind either. He was practical to a fault. "Why did you move her?" Michael finally found tongue enough to ask. "What are you doing with her?"

"I'm letting her bathe. There's an underground river near where you were kept. Surely you heard it. She's there."

"That's a lie." Michael stopped walking and felt the irresistible tug of the much stronger demon on the other end of his leash. He couldn't begin to fight the Aeshma Daeva. Only an angel would even consider it—only Raphael ever dared to try.

"Believe me or don't." Ash shrugged in the dim light. "It makes no difference to me."

Michael groaned. How long could this go on? Surely the demon king would tire of his game soon. And then what? Was Michael about to join his brothers and sisters in that hellish afterlife reserved for the children of angels? Over a sword. "Why do you want the sword anyway?" he asked.

"That's not remotely your business, little brother, nor is it mine. I'm just an errand boy fulfilling a contract." He muttered, "Azazel never could manage anything on his own."

"Azazel? The watcher?"

Ash groaned. "Unfortunately."

"Wasn't he bound after the flood?"

"Yes, well I let him out." The demon king rolled his eyes. "To my eternal detriment it seems."

Michael stopped walking again and felt another tug on his leash, more insistent this time. He'd only ever met one watcher—Daniel, the cherub informant of the Black Armada—and Daniel never spoke a word to him, nor to anyone really. He always arrived in the dark of night with a note, which he would surrender only to the commodore. Michael would have loved to ask Daniel questions about the watchers and their children, but Daniel wanted very little to do with him. And Michael, being used to people wanting very little to do with him, never argued the point.

It occurred to Michael that he was wasting a rare opportunity in this abduction. For the first time in his life, he had the chance to talk to another nephil, and not just any nephil—the eldest child of the watchers, the demon king, who had beaten a path for all those who came after him. Perhaps it was a gamble to speak candidly to one's current captor and future king, but Michael took a deep breath and rolled the dice. "How long do I have left to live?"

"You'll find out soon enough, little brother, if you continue to resist my demands."

"No, I mean how long do nephilim live on average? How big do we get before we have to die?"

Ash stopped walking. The false smile that usually graced his delicate features disappeared, and the darkness it left behind was as fathomless as an ocean trench. "The answer to that depends on whether the angels are in the mood for corporeal punishment. None of my contemporaries lived as long as they could have."

No, that couldn't be right. "I thought the nephilim grew too big for the earth to sustain. That was why they killed each other, wasn't it? Because they ate too much, and there wasn't enough to go around."

"Yes, of course that story is almost entirely true." Ash began to walk again, his new pace slower, each step more deliberate and somehow full of fury. "But a true story is made up of the facts you know as well as those that have been hidden from you. No angels will admit they caused drought and encouraged pestilence. No angels tell of how they created a famine so great, even the humans were starving to death. They'll never talk of the discord they sowed, the lies they told to punish the watchers. We were mad with hunger and fear and rage. We didn't know who to blame, so we blamed each other. And then came the flood, the first massacre."

Ash yanked Michael's leash so hard the iron ring around his waist cut into his skin. "You'll live as long as you have friends you can trust, little brother—friends stronger than those who hate you—and that's such a rare thing, I'll wager you don't make it to fifteen feet regardless. Then you'll be just like the rest of us, stretched between worlds until some tyrant or other comes to employ you."

"Then why take poison? Why drown yourselves?" Michael felt a little bolder. The demon king was answering his questions, and so far, the punishment for asking them was not enough to discourage him. "I don't understand why you wouldn't want to go on living as long as you could."

"We were homeless and hated, shamed and killed for sport. We rarely saw our children grow to adulthood. We had no future. Do you know what hopelessness does to one's will to go on living?"

Michael bowed his head. "Almost."

"You'll get there." Ash ground his teeth. "I can't believe an angel dared to sire a child after the second massacre. Samael has much to answer for, but you are perhaps the worst sin he's committed since he turned his back on God."

Bryony held the telephone receiver in one shaking hand and waited. Each ring seemed to last a lifetime. She'd called the only number she had memorized, and considering it was now after midnight, she had little hope anyone would pick up. But someone did.

Loki sounded more than a little annoyed. "Do you have any idea what time it is? Who is this? Martha's asleep and I refuse to wake her unless it's absolutely necessary."

Bryony gulped. "No, don't wake her. It's you I need."

A breath of silence. "Bryony?"

"Please," she whispered. "It's not him. It's an impostor. I should have listened to my own instincts. I should never have doubted myself . . ."

More silence.

"Bill? Bill?"

She turned back to see the false Michael standing behind her, his hand on the cradle, one finger having disconnected the call. He looked completely alien. He wasn't even trying anymore. He was a department-store mannequin—dead eyes, expressionless face—and his body was a tower, blocking her path forward. Luckily for Bryony, her friendly houseghost had left the back door open again. She ran for it.

Outside, she realized her flight was futile. The impostor had only let her run because she didn't stand a chance. He stood before her in an instant, his massive hand gripping her wrist with a strength she couldn't begin to match.

She thought about biting him but doubted it would have an effect. She kicked and twisted, but the more she struggled, the tighter his grip became. Frustration turned to helplessness, and helplessness to fury as she realized she had no recourse. She'd already lost. Somehow, this creature had taken Michael, and now it would take her too. "What have you done with him? Where is he? Give him back!"

The impostor ignored her, his expressionless eyes staring pointedly into the forest. A night wind rustled the leaves on the trees around her. The stars were crisp and bright. It was a beautiful night, and Bryony began to realize it might just be her last. If Michael was killed, then she would die with him. Maybe that had been the impostor's plan all along. Maybe he was another godhunter, one who had to eliminate a god's worshipers to kill it. Maybe Michael was already dying.

Bryony raged at the idea that this monster would steal such a kind and gentle life—a life well deserved and well appreciated—just to get to her. She felt her cheeks redden as she fought her premature grief. "What are you? Why have you done this to us? Explain yourself! You owe me that at least before you kill me!"

The blank eyes turned down to her, and the false Michael spoke at last. "I don't intend to kill you, darling. But if you don't keep quiet, you may die nonetheless. I'm not working alone."

"Neither is she." Loki's familiar voice was hope incarnate.

The impostor loosened its grip on her arm. "And who, may I ask, are you?"

"No." Loki grinned in his infuriatingly confident way. "She asked you first." Bryony almost worried for him. Overconfidence had been his downfall in the past.

The impostor didn't answer. Instead, it grew and grew, and its hand slipped away from Bryony as its height matched first the orchard, then the house, and finally, the evergreens around them. Its skin seemed to melt away, and beneath it, Bryony saw flames. The creature's flesh was like ice and snow, melting at the head and heart, and freezing again at the hands and feet. It was ever dripping, ever moving, like some kind of supernatural glacier with a volcano at its core. Bryony's courage disintegrated as the realization hit. It was an angel. *An angel.* She screamed until her voice gave out and her knees buckled. Her entire body surrendered to fear.

"Run!" Loki jolted her from her stupor. She ran. The forest engulfed her as the light behind her doubled in brilliance. She heard a crack, like the breaking of a giant tree, and another, and another. And she turned back to see.

The angel wrestled with something neither human nor animal. Bryony backed away and hid behind the thick trunk of an old cedar. *Elemental* was exactly how she would have described the Jötunn now. He burned like the filament of a massive lightbulb, but the shape of him was identical to the lightning scars she'd seen in a book on rare injuries. He branched out like the plum trees in Bryony's orchard, dividing and dividing, smaller and smaller, until she couldn't distinguish individual branches anymore, no matter how brightly they shone. The margins of him reminded her of the Milky Way, billions of smaller luminaries creating the illusion of an unbroken band of light.

So this was Loki, her inhuman ally. And her enemy was shaped like a man with four limbs and a head, bipedal even. For a moment, she wondered at how her idea of what made a monster had changed. Then she saw the angel hit and hit hard. The Milky Way flickered and crashed into the forest. Bryony screamed again, but this time, she screamed out a name.

The angel turned, and its mouth opened wide. "Loki?" it said. Its voice sounded like standing at the base of a colossal waterfall. "Is that who I'm fighting? Damn it, little god. You didn't tell me you had a Jötunn on your side."

Bryony ignored the angel. She screamed for her friend again and saw him rise from the pile of timber he'd just created. While the angel was distracted, Loki hit, and the glacial beast melted far more than Bryony thought it should. It stumbled back, and Loki hit again. But the angel easily reformed, ice closing over its wounds like a miracle.

At this rate, Loki was bound to lose, or at the very least, the battle would go on forever. Bryony felt useless as she stood watching a fight between two titans who could crush her and not even notice. An image of the angel's mouth opening wider and wider until it finally devoured the Milky Way nauseated her. She'd grown so accustomed to the idea of living with a half angel, she'd forgotten what monsters they were. Good thing this one was here to remind her. Good thing the bastard had come along to show her what evil really looked like. She let her thoughts fill with hatred for the creature that abused her friend, and she used that hatred to fortify her courage. She ran back into her home.

It was foolish, given the circumstances. Then again, she knew something the angel didn't. It would not have pretended to sleep so close otherwise. No angel could have closed its eyes and breathed so easily within feet of the death sword.

She ran up the stairs in the dark. The whole house quaked as the battle outside raged on. Bryony fumbled in her bedroom by the light of a dying fire. She found Michael's coat draped on the chair. His dividers were still in the breast pocket, and she wrapped her fingers around them for the first time. They hummed like a tuning fork in her hand, almost as though the death sword recognized her. She felt the emptiness behind the weapon—the vacuum, the space a life once occupied. She felt the power too. And as she carried it downstairs, out the back door, and toward the battle in the forest, it became more and more familiar to her. Death was an old friend. She knew exactly how it worked, exactly how to wield it. And in one fluid, instinctive motion, Bryony drew the sword.

She claimed it as her own. It grew and lengthened until it was taller than she was. In her hands, the death sword became an impractical, oversized scythe. *Classic,* she thought, but what else had she expected? She'd grown up on stories of the Grim Reaper. She'd been fond of them. The idea of a cloaked skeleton with a scythe comforted her. The animated bones of a long dead person were far less terrifying than the all-consuming grin of a strange angel.

All angels were monsters. She gripped her own rage like a second weapon and marched toward the battling giants. Her hands trembled, but the scythe didn't. It knew its own power. A bead of poison collected at the tip of its blade like the sword itself salivated, hungry for a soul to consume. Good. This time, Bryony would feed it an angel.

Chapter Sixteen

Another crash echoed deep in the forest, and light shot up through the trees. Loki had successfully led the angel away, but he wasn't faring well. The fractal firelight shrank and faded under the arched body of a glacial monster.

Bryony broke into a run. The scythe in her hand should have been too heavy and awkward to carry, but it wasn't. It felt like an extension of her own arm. It was simple to maneuver, its weight a familiar burden to bear. Though she couldn't have said how, she got the distinct impression the death sword knew what she wanted and conducted itself accordingly. Right now, she had only one desire, and that desire beat like a drum in her chest.

Save him. Save him. Save him.

She found the two battling titans in a circle of felled trees, wrestling like brothers, though they looked nothing alike. The angel hovered over the shrinking, fading Jötunn. Every few seconds, Loki would push back and knock the angel off balance. But inevitably, he was pinned again, and he grew weaker and weaker before Bryony's eyes.

Finally, the angel opened its wide, horrific mouth, and Bryony screamed, "Stop!" She darted in and swung the scythe. Both figures froze. "Stop now!" She came close—too close—to the angel. Fear might have overcome her when the creature turned its attention her way, but her rage was more powerful. "Do you know what this is?" Bryony shouted. "Do you?"

The angel shrank back, and one word hissed from its mouth like steam. "Samael."

"Yes, it was his sword. Now it's mine, and it's hungry." She stood her ground as Loki's body shrank, took human form, and solidified beneath the angel. He was battered and humbled, and Bryony hated to see him that way. He scrambled out from under the beast and backed away until he stood behind Bryony. Once again, the angels threatened her family, but this time she had the means to fight back. "Tell me where he is!" she demanded. "The man you were impersonating. What have you done with him?"

The angel shrank by half. "He's with my partner." Its voice was still inhuman, but its words were clear as crystal.

"Alive?"

The angel nodded.

And Bryony's bottled-up tears finally fell. "Thank god!" she cried. "Thank god, thank god." She was so relieved she almost lost her grip on her weapon, but she caught herself and quickly regained it. "And who is your partner? Another angel?"

The creature shook its head, and again, relief flooded her. But then the angel's terrible mouth broke into a smile, and it was so disturbing, Bryony almost dropped the scythe again. From behind her, Loki steadied her arm.

"Who is your partner?" Bryony demanded.

The angel answered, "It's only Ash, darling."

She scowled. The monster was being intentionally vague. And *darling*? How dare it use an endearment as though they had some sort of relationship? But then she remembered she'd spent the last couple days with this creature, eating with it, sleeping beside it, letting it comb her hair. She shifted the tip of the scythe closer to the beast and relished the sight of it recoiling and shrinking away. "Who is Ash? Answer!"

Slowly, the glacial beast faded, and Bryony was left pointing her weapon at a figure indistinguishable from any other man on his hands and knees—well, almost indistinguishable. It seemed the angel couldn't help an extra flourish or two. He had shoulder-length, turquoise hair cut to a perfect bob and warm, copper-toned skin. His clothes were rich and flowing, timeless somehow, with fitted pants and a long, ornate jacket. He wore all the shades of blue one might find in an ice cave, including one that matched his hair. And, Bryony noticed with a flinch, he had the most intricate, purple design painted around his absolutely stunning, amber eyes. Her fear began to melt, which had to have been his aim all along. He was just . . . too much.

He smiled a charming smile and answered in a perfectly human voice. "Ash is just Ash if you wish to please him, and you *should* wish to please him if you want to get anywhere with him. But he's also known as the Aeshma Daeva or Ashmedai. If you want to enrage him, call him Asmodeus." He chuckled despite his alarming situation.

The name was familiar. Loki bent to her ear and whispered, "The demon king." Bryony tightened her grip on her weapon.

The angel flinched but managed to keep his voice calm. "Don't fret now. I've given Ash strict instructions to release his captive unharmed as soon as we have what we want."

Bryony spoke through gritted teeth. "And what exactly is it you want from us?"

"Only the sword." The angel glanced up but quickly looked away again when he saw the bead of poison clinging before his eyes.

"This thing?" Bryony nodded to the death scythe.

"No, no. Of course not *that* thing. Keep that disaster miles away from me please. I want nothing to do with Samael's cursed weapon." Bryony might not have believed him had she not seen the disgust in his eyes for herself.

"Then you must mean . . ." Right. Raphael's sword. She'd always known someone would come for it one day. She'd just thought it would be . . . "Are you Raphael?"

Abruptly, the angel burst out laughing. He had a musical laugh, but as beautiful as it was, Bryony hated the sound of it. He was laughing at her? "Raphael!" He sputtered. "Spare me, please! Do I look like a seraph to you?"

Bryony steeled herself against her own humiliation. He was teasing her. He was teasing her as though she did not have the nasty end of a death scythe pointed at his head. Yet he was an angel, wasn't he? He should be terrified beyond motion. He should be shaking and cowering. Death was not something he could even contemplate. Unless he was accustomed to it. Unless he'd already lived among mortals and seen too many of them die.

"You're a watcher!" She pointed at him with her other hand now, having lowered her weapon to the ground. For some reason, the idea made him far less terrifying. The watchers had just as much reason to hate and fear other angels as she did. Perhaps this creature was not as dangerous as she'd first assumed.

When he saw Bryony relax, the angel did too, and he shakily rose to his feet. Bryony adjusted the death scythe accordingly. The angel brushed the dirt from his otherwise immaculate clothing and bowed. "Azazel, at your service."

The name meant nothing to Bryony. It seemed Loki had more information than she did because he quickly wrapped his arms around her waist and began pulling her back. "Run, Bryony," he hissed into her ear. "I'll handle him. Don't be a fool."

She shook her head. "You'll be eaten for sure. We work as a team or not at all. Understand? That's the deal, Shakespeare. That's always been the deal." She used the name she'd given him when he pretended to be a crow—when he was her pet, her only family. It was calculated, but she wasn't sorry.

Loki's arms softened around her. "You'll get yourself killed." His voice was warm and affectionate. "You don't owe me anything. You do know that, don't you?" It seemed, for the first time, the outcast Jötunn was beginning to understand that, to Bryony, their friendship wasn't about obligation. She would have fought for him even if he hadn't come to save her. She would always fight for him because he was Shakespeare and for no other reason. "Listen," he said. "Azazel is a captain, not an underling. He's the single most destructive angel in history, the grandfather of weaponry and war. Don't underestimate him."

Azazel frowned, and his frown was at least as charming as his smile. "That's a terribly one-sided résumé. I also invented jewelry, if you don't mind. And mirrors, and makeup, and all the best dances." He counted his achievements off on his fingers.

"Doesn't make up for the war," Loki grumbled.

"I'm sorry, darling, but didn't you used to hang around with Vikings? Have you any claim to pacifism?"

Loki's grip tightened.

"That's enough." Bryony shook free of his embrace and propped her weapon upright. "None of that matters now." She stared at Azazel, squared her shoulders, and made the fiercest expression she could muster. She felt so artificial she might have laughed at herself, but she channeled her mother instead. *Don't break character,* she heard her mother say. *You can laugh after the curtain falls.* "Azazel, what do you want with Raphael's weapon?"

All playfulness fled from the angel's expression. "You must give it to me. Please. She's dying."

"Who?" Bryony and Loki both asked at once.

"My last descendant. She'll not survive without the sword, and she has no offspring." He seemed to hesitate, but eventually he came to a decision and dropped to his knees. "Please, little god. I beg you. I'll return your last worshiper in exchange for my last descendant's life."

The angel was a watcher, Bryony reminded herself. He'd come to earth to oppose mankind and had fallen for one of them instead. She could more than relate. The bead of poison that clung to her scythe turned to smoke and floated away. "For god's sake," she groaned. "Why did you go to all this trouble? All you had to do was ask, and I would have given it to you."

Had she tried, Bryony could not have imagined an angel's jaw dropping for any reason other than to devour, but now she didn't have to. The watcher Azazel knelt before her, his once-monstrous mouth hanging wide open in unadulterated shock.

Michael drifted in and out of sleep, half propped against the jutting rock wall, his chain trailing away from him like shed snakeskin. The torches were lit, and he woke to the sight of Bryony watching him from across the cavern. He was almost certain he was dreaming again. All his recent dreams had been of her. He dreamed of *Dragonfly*, of holding her hand for the first time and silently wanting her more than anything. He dreamed of her kiss, her touch, her laugh. He dreamed of Mexico and the moment he was certain he'd lost her. He dreamed of watching her fall in love with someone else while he was trapped behind a veil of shadows.

"Are you all right?" she asked.

He scrubbed the dust from his eyes with his dirty shirtsleeve and looked again. She was no dream. "I am now. Did he hurt you?"

She appeared to consider the question, and Michael wondered why. Then she shrugged and said, "No. Just as you predicted."

"Good." He breathed deep and let his head fall back against the stones. Had he ever felt this helpless before? He couldn't recall a time. Michael was used to dealing with people smaller than himself, weaker. It was easy enough to practice pacifism when no one ever wanted to fight you. Even the gods he hunted froze in their tracks at the sight of the seraph. Some even fell to their knees before him. One had actually begged for death. He shook the memory from his head. "Did he ask about the sword?"

"Yes, but I told him nothing." She smiled proudly. Her hair was still wet, so Ash hadn't been lying about letting her bathe after all. "I've been working on him, bit by bit. I think he might let me go soon. You were right about him, you know."

Michael sighed and slouched, both relieved and exhausted. He wanted to pull Bryony close and tuck her head under his chin. He missed her touch, missed touching her. There was a good chance he would never be allowed to touch her again, and that thought ate away at him. He should have kissed her more, touched her more, told her he loved her a thousand times more. He was not likely to survive this—that much was clear. He couldn't give a death sword to the demon king or anyone else, for that matter. Whoever had it would gain the power to wipe out every soul in every world they entered. Immortality would be rendered moot.

Bryony broke into his thoughts. "Have you considered where I should hide the sword when I'm freed?"

"No." He hesitated. "More importantly, have you considered how to build a new congregation, in case I don't make it . . ." He trailed off because the expression on Bryony's face was one of pure bafflement.

She quickly recovered. "Well, I suppose I'll just do it the same way I did before."

"You'll have to relocate. Your old congregation knows the truth now. They couldn't force worship even if they wanted to."

Again, Bryony looked confused. "So . . . you don't think you're going to survive this? And if you don't, I'll need to build a new congregation."

"Yes. Sentience takes years to achieve after death. I won't be able to worship anyone, let alone you." He narrowed his eyes. What was the matter with her? Had Ashmedai hit her on the head too? "Listen carefully, Bryony. Here's what I want you to do as soon as he lets you go." She nodded eagerly and leaned in to listen. "Don't go home. Don't even drop by. Go immediately to Martha's and tell Loki everything. He's on your side for now, and if anyone can help you build a new congregation, he can."

Bryony's eyes widened almost imperceptibly. But Michael had studied her face every day since he met her, and he noticed. She mouthed the word *Loki* before sinking back against the wall with a worried look.

Michael tried to console her. "After I die, I'll find my way out of the darkness and back to you. I swear. Even if I can't manifest a body, I'll haunt your house until you tell me to leave. I'll be your ghost until some conjurer finds a use for me. I'll make myself known. Just look for me." He nearly choked on his words.

Bryony didn't look at all comforted. "You won't die, Michael," she said, and she seemed unreasonably certain of it. "Let's just take this one step at a time before we start planning your funeral. Jesus." She pinched the bridge of her nose and muttered, "This is getting more complicated than it needs to be. Maybe . . . Maybe we should consider just giving him what he wants."

"No."

"But why?" She sat up on her knees and spread her palms.

"It's too much power to give away."

"Really?" She seemed irritated now. "It's just an angel's sword. Isn't your life worth more than that?"

"It isn't *my* life I'm thinking of. Believe me, I wouldn't make this decision lightly. I'm sorry. I'm sorry you got involved with someone like me. I should never have allowed it. I knew this would end badly. I just . . . I didn't want to lose you." His voice caught. "But it was wrong. You could be happy without—"

"Quiet." Bryony didn't shout or snap at him. She was calm and in command. She was magnificent, and Michael felt the uncanny urge to obey her without question. "We're not speaking of this any more tonight. The demon made it clear he wasn't ready to release me, so we have some time. Settle down. I can't stand to see you like this." She yawned and stretched suggestively. "God, I'm just so tired. Aren't you?" Her chains rattled as she shifted into a more comfortable position.

At first, her dispassion in the face of things alarmed Michael. Then she began to sing, and her voice hit him like a drug. It echoed through the chamber, turning each drop of water and the rush of the underground river into part of her song. His eyes grew heavy, and his muscles relaxed. He felt like he was floating, sinking deeper into the quiet ocean while a storm raged on above.

But one thought pulled him back to the surface. One idea struck and woke him. Bryony's voice was angelic, beautiful. Her song was haunting . . . and in perfect pitch. He slumped and heaved a long, defeated sigh. "I'm an idiot."

Bryony stopped her song and frowned. "Why do you say that?"

"Because you're not her. She was never really here. I should have guessed it from the start. Isn't that what you're famous for—taking someone else's identity in order to get what you want?"

The hovering gold light returned, the chains around Bryony dissolved, and suddenly, she was gone. The shape of the studious demon sat in her place. Michael expected him to laugh, to enjoy the humiliation he'd caused, but he didn't. Ashmedai just looked disappointed. "Damn. I thought I'd made a perfect imitation."

"It nearly was," Michael admitted. "Except she can't sing."

"A careless mistake." Ash hovered just above the rocks now that he'd revealed himself. His suit was spotless, his shoes polished, his golden spectacles tucked neatly in his vest pocket. "I was so close."

"Don't beat yourself up." Michael relaxed a little. If Bryony wasn't here, it meant she was probably still home, though she must be worried to death by now. He hoped she wasn't alone. "Please tell me she's safe."

Ashmedai rose, crossed the cavern, and laid a hand on Michael's head in an almost affectionate gesture. "She's safe enough, little brother. She doesn't even know you're gone."

"How?"

"Azazel has taken your place. No doubt, he's keeping your woman well fed and comfortable. Although I do worry for him now that I know he'll be dealing with Loki on the side. How on earth did you make an ally out of that time bomb?"

"It wasn't my doing." Michael couldn't help feeling a little proud. "It was hers."

Ash pinched the bridge of his nose. "Good god, this plan was bad from the start, and it's only gotten worse. Azza may love the theater, but he's better behind the scenes. Acting is hardly his forte. Try telling him that, though. And with Loki in the mix . . ." He sighed. "Well, he should be all right as long as he doesn't let his mask slip."

Chapter Seventeen

Had Bryony somehow gotten hold of the Angel of Time's sword—if such a thing even existed—and traveled back one year to tell herself she would soon join the trickster Loki and an equally infamous angel in her living room, she would not have believed herself. But here she was, sitting on her couch beside the Jötunn himself with a watcher in the adjacent chair. The angel's eyes darted repeatedly to the scythe, and he shivered despite the fire.

"Are you cold?" It was hardly the first question Bryony intended to ask, but she couldn't help it. He looked pathetic, and a pathetic angel created so much dissonance in her head, she simply had to eliminate it.

Azazel shook his head.

"Then why are you shaking?"

He gripped the armrests. "I might feel better if you opened the door, darling. Even a crack."

"So it was you." The events of the last few days were beginning to fall into place. "You opened all the doors and windows." And he'd probably built the fires to compensate. "Why?" The question encompassed more than just open doors and windows, but she didn't have the words to voice it just yet. She was still flabbergasted.

The angel answered, "I fear I'm not at my best in enclosed spaces. Being bound in darkness for thousands of years is more than enough to give a body a touch of claustrophobia."

Loki cleared his throat. "Not for all of us."

Bryony shot him a severe look. "An unreasonable hatred of snakes does not make you superior."

The color that crept into the shapeshifter's cheeks gave his shame away. His voice, on the other hand, was all sarcasm and pride. "Look at you all of a sudden, siding with angels. I'm sure your mother would be proud." He stood and strode over to open the front door.

Loki's comment was meant to sting as much as Bryony's had, but it didn't. Somehow, she did think her mother would be proud. All her memories of the woman were the color of courage. And courage, no matter how misguided it was, always made her mother proud. She closed her eyes a moment, took a deep breath, and prepared to negotiate with a watcher. "Take me to Michael."

Azazel knit his brow in sympathy. "I truly wish I could, but I don't know where he is. Ash is due to meet with me tonight, though. If I have Raphael's sword in hand, he'll return your Michael unharmed."

Perfect. This was almost too easy. "Then it's yours. I only ask that you bring it back."

"As freely as you give it, darling, I won't feel the need to keep it for myself. There's only one person I intend to use it on."

"Your descendant?"

The angel nodded as Loki returned to his place beside Bryony. The Jötunn did not look at all pleased. There was a flash of distrust in his eyes—anger, too, though Bryony could hardly blame him after the beating he'd just taken. He sneered. "Your descendant was never supposed to exist in the first place, so why not let nature take its course? Less angelic blood in the world is hardly a loss. Why do you care so much about your line anyway? You're immortal. You can always try again later."

Azazel's eyes widened at Loki's last comment. "You've misunderstood. It isn't *my* bloodline I'm looking to save." A shadow of grief passed over his expression. As quickly as it came, it was gone again, but Bryony had not missed it. Grief could never be subtle to her. It screamed, even if only for a moment. For half a breath or less, it screamed.

She suddenly understood. "It's her bloodline."

"What?" Loki snapped.

Bryony answered without looking away from the angel. "The mother of his children. The dying woman is also the last of *her* descendants."

"Bingo," Azazel muttered with an empty smile.

Loki scoffed.

"No, it makes sense," Bryony said. "Angels bond too powerfully—that's what Michael told me. Their love borders on worship. It's obsessive, unhealthy. Sorry." She apologized to Azazel as a matter of course.

Azazel waved a dismissive hand. "Go on, darling. You're onto it."

"He can't bear the thought that the last sliver of her will disappear forever." She hated to speak such a personal truth about someone other than herself. "He'll do anything to protect it. He can't help it. That's just his nature."

Loki leaned back and crossed his arms. "If what she says is true, then you're at a distinct disadvantage, my angelic friend. Unfortunately for you, as soft as my companion may be, it's me you have to deal with. See, she has no idea where the sword is. It's no longer hers to freely give. I took it from her, and I hid it well. So if you want to get your hands on it, you'll offer me something in return. And that snake you've kidnapped won't be enough, in case you're wondering. Tear him to shreds for all I care."

Bryony suddenly found it difficult to breathe. How could she have been so foolish? After all he'd done, she still thought of Loki as a friend, but he was no one's friend, not really. That was *his* nature. "Why?" she asked him.

"Because you have no idea how to barter, Bryony. You offer asking every time. You never even consider how much more you could get"—he grinned and shrugged—"for less."

How could he do this? Bryony was furious. She'd never been this angry at her old crow, not even when she learned he'd been lying to her for ten years. Every limb on the Jötunn tensed when her fingers curled around the staff of her scythe.

"Hear me out, Bryony." He scooted away from her reflexively. "I'm trying to help you. I'm trying to give you what you've always wanted."

She glared. "What more could I want? I wouldn't give Michael up for anything. He's more than enough." Her knuckles whitened, and Loki stood. A fiery, orange light flickered behind his eyes for a split second. It was the briefest glimpse of his monstrous form breaking through. He was afraid.

Good, she thought. *He should be.*

But Loki wasn't about to give up. "Think back," he said, ever so subtly backing away. "Remember who you were before you joined the armada. Remember what was stolen from you. Surely that snake hasn't completely erased the girl I met in the graveyard, the girl I grew to—"

"Don't you dare try to tell me you ever cared for me, you liar. You've never done one unselfish thing, have you? And I thought you came to help me." She laughed a poisonous laugh. "I should have known it was just another lie."

Loki narrowed his eyes, and she saw another flash behind them, anger this time. For a moment, she realized how stupid she was being. Just because she had the death sword did not mean she could take on a creature like him. *He's elemental.* She'd seen it for herself. But then the Jötunn clenched his fists, and Bryony stared in disbelief as the unrepentant trickster—the traitor who'd lost the love of every god who took him in—actually fought to control his temper.

He breathed deep and closed his eyes. "There is something you want. You've just forgotten it. I'm trying to give it to you." His voice betrayed his sincerity, but he quickly curbed it. "I don't want to owe you anymore, and just paying a ransom for you won't be good enough. It wasn't only your fiancé who was stolen from you. Remember? It was your mother, your father, and your brother."

Bryony spoke through her teeth. "Like you could bring them back."

"You're right, I can't. But would you throw away the opportunity to confront one of the angels responsible for their deaths?"

"They're *all* responsible." Bitter tears welled in her eyes, but she quickly blinked them back. "My family died of influenza, and you know it."

"But why? Why did they have to die of such a preventable disease?"

"Because the angels made it a sin to study medicine." Was he teasing her? He knew all this. He knew it better than anyone else in her life. Why would he question her like this? Why would he torment her?

"The angels?" He laughed, and she realized his persona had finally gotten the better of his fear. He was clever always, the picture of hubris. "Do you mean the guardian angels—those weak, servile creatures who got stuck with the dirty work? Do you really think they'd be able to enforce such a decree if an *archangel* were there to defy it?"

Bryony opened her mouth to question him, but the faintest rustle of fabric reminded her of the watcher behind her. She turned to see him stand, tense and ready.

Encouraged, Loki went on. "Raphael is the Angel of Healing. Unlike the rest of them, his nature demands he fight for mortals. He would have sustained medicine himself if he had to, and a thousand guardians could not have stopped him. Unfortunately, he was bound. So I'll ask you one more time, Bryony. Is your fiancé really enough? Or would you like to try for something more? Because the angel who bound Raphael is standing right behind you, and he's more than willing to bargain."

The river water was icy cold. Every time Michael went under, he flashed back to freediving for the Black Armada. He willed his body to still, his heart to slow, and he let himself sink. He knew his own lungs well. If he could just descend until he didn't have enough oxygen to get back up, he could easily set his own drowning in motion. By the time instinct took over his body, it would be too late. He would be dead, Bryony would be safe at home, and the death sword would be out of Azazel's reach.

On the other hand, if he let himself drown, he would become a demon, and a demon could be summoned. Trapped at the center of a conjuring circle, Michael would have little choice but to give up the sword. By all accounts, conjuration was the end of free will. No, it made more sense to stay alive as long as he could. He kicked his feet and resurfaced.

The demon king waited for him on the banks of the dark, underground river. "Feel better?" he asked.

Michael hoisted himself from the water onto the rocks, feeling even colder after he emerged. "I would have preferred a hotel."

"Well, this isn't your honeymoon. At least I allowed you to bathe." Ashmedai's downturned mouth quirked into a smile as he stared shamelessly at his captive's shivering, naked body.

But Michael had become too accustomed to humiliation to let it bother him. "I doubt you're allowing it for my sake."

The demon sat in his characteristic way—without quite touching the ground—and rolled his eyes. "Yes, I was positively dying to see your manly physique. However could you tell?"

"I was referring to the inevitable smell."

"Obviously." Ashmedai winked.

It was the strangest thing in the world. Though Michael would have told anyone he'd been abducted by a fiend, this sarcastic little spat felt almost friendly. Apparently, he'd become somewhat comfortable with his demonic abductor. He picked up his shirt and began to scrub it against a stone.

Ash leaned in to watch him as though the concept of laundering one's own clothes was completely alien to him. "Answer a question for me, if you will. Why haven't you surrendered the sword? You're a nephil. By all accounts, you're madly in love with the woman I pretended to threaten. I was certain you'd crack long before she did—your nature being what it is—but you haven't. Instead, you gambled with her life based on little more than my rather ambiguous reputation."

Michael lifted his shirt out of the water, examined it, and decided it could do with more scrubbing. "I'd be gambling with even more lives by giving you the sword. There's no telling what Azazel plans to do with it, and I can hardly expect you to be honest about it."

"Who needs honesty?" Ash crossed his legs and stretched his arms. "There's a limited amount of evil he could do with it regardless. Do you imagine he intends to corner the market and overcharge for his services?"

"Overcharge for what?" Michael stopped washing his shirt and gave all his attention to the conversation. "You mean like a godhunter for hire?"

"Godhunter? Wait . . ." The demon king's expression shifted smoothly from confusion to amused enlightenment. "We're not talking about the same weapon, are we? All this time. Christ, what a fiasco! My dear little brother, Azazel seeks the archangel Raphael's weapon, which we understood was most recently in the hands of an obscure healing god in the Pacific Northwest. You were an unexpected complication, but I decided to make the best of you. Now I see I've wasted my opportunity most egregiously."

Michael knelt speechless at the edge of the river, his wet shirt dangling like a dead fish from his hand. They wanted the healing sword? He'd accepted the eventual loss of his own life, made peace with the fact that he might never see Bryony again, and all for nothing. They only wanted the healing sword. Ash was absolutely right that Michael would have told him everything immediately had he understood. "Your plan really was terrible," Michael said at last.

"I take no responsibility for it." Ash shrugged.

"Had you been clear from the beginning, I could have told you I have no idea where Raphael's sword wound up, and neither does Bryony. We don't even know what it looks like anymore. Azazel won't get much by deceiving her, but if he'd just told her what he wanted, I'm certain she would have done everything in her power to help him find it."

The demon king dropped his shaved head into the palm of his hand and groaned. "Oh, Azza's not one for being direct—not if he can stage an elaborate performance starring himself."

"Says the demon who just spent days pretending to be my fiancée."

"Don't be ungrateful. I was trying to get the information from you gently. I don't have to be gentle. It's perfectly within my nature to abuse men, as you well know, and I'd have no qualms whatsoever about teaching a lesson to an insolent future-demon like yourself." Despite the airs Ash put on, just making the threat seemed to exhaust him. He massaged his brow. "So if it wasn't Raphael's sword you were protecting, whose was it?"

Michael didn't answer.

Ash stared at the ceiling in thought. "There are a number of bound angels whose weapons you might have claimed. Was it a watcher?"

Still Michael kept his mouth shut.

"But you mentioned godhunting. No watcher's weapon could kill a god without first stripping it of its immortality."

Abruptly, Ash stood. He snatched the end of Michael's chain from the ground and, hand over hand, began to reel his hostage in. Michael was forced to crawl to keep from being dragged. All the while, the demon king grew in size, and Michael fought the unpleasant but pervasive urge to grovel.

"Here's the thing," Ash began, absentmindedly twisting the chain around one giant finger. "As little as I like Azza and as much as I would prefer to be rid of him, he doesn't deserve to die. He's an imbecile, but he means well. So if your woman has a weapon that can kill an immortal at her disposal, I'm going to need you to fess up."

It was over. Michael didn't stand a chance. Even if he didn't answer, Ashmedai would simply go and find out for himself. Michael spoke quietly at first. "The sword is Samael's." Then a little louder. "It's my father's sword." Own his lineage and maybe it would do him some good. The name had to count for something.

Ash wrenched the end of the chain, and Michael looked up to see a furious half cherub staring down at him. "Bullshit," he said with all three of his mouths. "Samael is not bound, and you wouldn't last half a second in a fight with that monster."

The iron around Michael's waist dug in, and he cried out involuntarily. "It's the truth! I stole it when I was a child. I don't know why he hasn't come for it since. He just hasn't."

"And I suppose you left it at home when I took you." The demon king was suddenly human again, curling his fingers under Michael's chin, examining his face for lies. "So you're telling me that my feckless employer is currently tangling with a woman who has the Angel of Death's sword within arm's reach and *Loki* at her beck and call."

When he put it that way, Michael wondered why he'd ever worried for her at all.

Chapter Eighteen

Azazel's abject terror did not escape Bryony's notice. She now had no doubt regarding his guilt. This was the angel who'd bound Raphael—the angel who'd killed the source of all medicine—but right now, he didn't look like an angel. He looked like a man. He was so colorful, so bright, so musical in his movements and everything he did. It didn't seem right that such a person should be afraid.

"Darling . . ." Azazel began, but his voice petered out when Bryony pointed the tip of the scythe at him.

She should have killed him. She should have plunged the blade into his heart before she could have second thoughts. She should have aimed it at his immortal soul, wherever that was. But all she could manage to do was ask, "Did you?"

Azazel took a step backward. "If you understood what he'd done to me . . ." He paused and fought back a smile. "I'd say Raphael was no angel, but the idiom hardly applies in this case."

Was this what Michael felt whenever he confronted a god he intended to kill—this weight? Azazel was lucky on several counts. He'd lived with Bryony for days and never harmed her. She'd gotten to know him. Even in his angelic body, he looked halfway human. And he was not an ophan. "What are you anyway?" She let her curiosity get the better of her.

The angel cocked his head.

She clarified. "You're not one of the cherubim or seraphim. You're not an ophan. What are you?"

"Oh." He relaxed a touch, but one shift of the scythe sent him back to his stiff, soldier's stance. "One of the ishim, I'm afraid. Only a lesser angel, you see? No great threat to you or anyone else."

From behind Bryony, Loki laughed derisively. "Azazel, the grandfather of war, not a threat? That's hilarious. So how did you manage to subdue and bind an archangel if you're mostly harmless?" Bryony could almost hear the question he stopped short of asking—*And how were you able to beat me?*

"I had help, darling." Azazel seemed unable to suppress his personality, even when he feared for his life. "And I'm not entirely without talent."

"What did Raphael do to deserve it?" Bryony asked. She, of all people, understood that reputations were not always accurate.

Azazel stood before the fire and shrugged. "I only repaid him in kind, you know. Of all the watchers, I alone received Raphael's special treatment. The archangel had strict instructions on how to deal with me, and he obeyed to the letter. If only you knew what it was to be bound. I cannot begin to describe it."

Loki interjected. "Did you forget who you're talking to?"

"Not in the least, Jötunn. I hoped you might be able to empathize. We've so much in common, you and I. Our children died at each other's hands. Our bodies were bound in torturous prisons. We were both unfairly punished for our mistakes."

"*I* was unfairly punished," Loki growled, but he stayed behind Bryony. "I was partly responsible for the death of one god. How many wars would not have existed without you? You want to talk about the Vikings? Every weapon they used evolved from one of yours. Every drop of blood they spilled is on your hands. Then you had the audacity to bind the Angel of Healing. How many people do you think died prematurely because of that? I can name three for you right now if you want to know. So can she. You gave mortals weapons, and then you stole medicine from them. You've been stacking the deck against them from the moment you arrived in their world. And you don't think you deserve to suffer for that?"

Azazel bowed his head, and Bryony couldn't help admiring the way his turquoise hair reflected the firelight. "I was trying to even the playing field," the angel said. "I didn't mean to stack the deck as you say. We each taught mortals something for their own protection. Every other captain had a useful lesson to impart. What did I have? Eyeliner? My weapon is the essence of beauty. What were they supposed to do with that? So I gave them metalsmithing."

"You gave them blueprints for blades and bullets."

"Yes." Azazel spoke to Loki but kept his eyes trained on Bryony. "The nephilim were hunting and eating them. Humans would have gone extinct if we'd done nothing."

Loki wasn't finished. "They'd have been far better off if you really had done nothing. You created the nephilim in the first place."

"That's an error I will own." Azazel glanced down at the dwindling fire. "May I?" Bryony nodded her consent. He didn't bother with the poker now that his cover was blown. He reached into the fire with his bare hands and rearranged the logs. Then he added a couple more, and the hearth sprang back to life. "We were wrong to couple with women," he said. "But we'd never met them in the flesh before. We weren't familiar with love's pull. Even those of us who married out of obligation to our chief captain fell completely in love with our children. How could we not? Have you seen infant nephilim? They're irresistibly cute." He smiled at some distant memory. "Little petals."

The angel sat, and Bryony felt her grip on the scythe loosen. How Michael had managed to kill all those gods was beyond her, it seemed, and curiosity was getting the better of her. "Were there no female angels?" she asked.

"Not a single one." Azazel folded his hands in his lap. "And I'll tell you a secret, but you must swear never to reveal it." It was an obvious pretense, but Bryony couldn't help playing along. She nodded and leaned in. Azazel smiled. He was beginning to feel more confident about his own survival, and he was right to. "Darling, there are no male angels either."

"No!" Bryony gasped in exaggerated fascination. She felt as though she were back in *Dragonfly*'s galley, gossiping with Rose as they prepped meals together. "So why do you always appear as men?"

"It's habit mostly. In the beginning, it only made sense. If you're visiting a hostile country, disguise yourself as someone with power. These days, I must say, the masculine wardrobe is sadly utilitarian, but it's easiest for me to manifest this body for extended periods. Well, I do try to make the best of it."

Bryony nodded in agreement. "You do make a beautiful man."

The angel's face lit up. "I do! Thank you so much for saying so."

Loki threw his hands up in disgust. "Well, I see you two are becoming fast friends. I'm clearly no longer needed here, so I'll be off. It's late. You know how to reach me." He bent down and pretended to kiss Bryony's cheek. In the process, he whispered, "Do *not* take your hands off that weapon. Beware, Bryony." He straightened and brushed nonexistent wrinkles from his shirt. At the door, he turned back. "Let me know when you've come to a decision, angel. I'll make my position clear. Unbind Raphael, or you get nothing, and if you harm her, you lose the chance to bargain altogether."

Then he was gone, or at least he seemed to be. Bryony couldn't help wondering if he'd become one of the moths that flew in through the open door and fluttered around the electric lights. She liked to think he had. It made her feel less alone.

The room went quiet after Loki left. Somehow, his presence had made it easier to talk. Bryony wanted to close her eyes and pretend it was Rose sitting across from her, telling her all the armada's secrets. Subterfuge was so much easier than sincerity. But it wasn't Rose. It wasn't even human. And worse than that—worse still—it was an angel.

Yet Azazel wasn't just any angel, was he? He was a watcher. He was fallen. Bryony cleared her throat. "So . . . your big crime, according to the archangels, was teaching? I'm beginning to see a pattern with them."

The angel managed a smile. "As much as I would love to let you go on thinking so, it isn't entirely true. Our first crime was insubordination. Our second and most grievous was reproduction. Teaching was hardly the only sin we committed."

"Okay." She chewed her lower lip. Angels were such baffling creatures. Could someone really sin if they intended no harm? Sometimes, awful things just happened. Surely the archangels knew that. "No, I still don't get it. How is reproduction a sin? You couldn't have known whether your children would be good or evil. I mean maybe you could have raised them a bit better."

That was the end of Azazel's discomfort. He laughed, and his laugh was full and mirthful and lovely. "Bless you, child. That is the epitome of understatement." When he'd caught his breath, he explained. "Angels are born immortal. We were never supposed to reproduce. Birth and death, as you know them, don't exist in our world. Individuality itself is rare. We naturally operate as . . . How can I put this? Well, have you ever been bitten by fire ants?"

Bryony thought about it and shook her head.

"They're magnificent little beasts, you know, the way they synchronize. If you come upon a nest, you'll find them crawling up your leg, gentle as kittens. They get into position without even a pinch. Then the multitude strikes as one. They act with one will, one mind. We were like that. Some of us still are."

Azazel reached over and adjusted the fire. It was unnerving the way he used his bare hands, but Bryony reminded herself he was partly made of fire. She waited patiently until he resumed his story.

"When our universe collided with yours, it was catastrophic. A number of worlds were involved, it seems—the Jötnar wouldn't be here otherwise, though they do tend to keep to themselves. I only know how it affected the angels. The rules of our worlds, yours and mine, blended. Immortality found its way to mortals through worship, and angels began to think independently. Some of us resisted the change, especially the ophanim and seraphim. Others leaned in. The cherubim found it easy to manifest flesh. The ishim had a talent for chatting up mankind."

"Like you're doing now," Bryony added.

"Sure, if you like. It was never in question that angels intended to rule this world, but there was disagreement on how to go about it. Most of the seraphim and ophanim insisted we manipulate mankind from our own realm—all disembodied voices and allegorical dreams, you know. But those of us who became watchers were convinced . . ." The angel wrung his hands, and his eyes darted once to the scythe. "Forgive me, darling, it was a long time ago. But we felt a . . . more direct approach was called for."

"Go on." Bryony wasn't about to stop him with righteous indignation. He was giving her everything.

"We watchers originally came to prove our method. We manifested flesh perfectly and bound ourselves to it, certain we would succeed. But we hadn't accounted for the strength of hunger, thirst, exhaustion. And fear. Some of us were permanently traumatized from just the proximity to mortality. When we failed to thrive, we begged men for help, but they knew us for the impostors we were. They'd already begun to call us watchers when they noticed we didn't sleep through the night.

"Men refused to help us, but in secret, women taught us to survive. In turn, we fell in love. We loved independently, which was as unprecedented as the love itself. Some of us fell right away. The rest took our time." Azazel's eyes glazed over with some haunting memory, and he smiled to himself. "I didn't love her in the beginning, you know. I thought she was plain." A burning log crackled and split, but the angel didn't seem to hear it. He was daydreaming. It was such a human thing to do that Bryony felt uneasy watching it.

After a few minutes, she interrupted his reverie. "Azazel?"

He looked up, jolted from his memories. "Call me Azza, darling—all my friends do. *El* is an honorific I no longer deserve."

Bryony frowned at the word *friends*, but Azazel just smiled and went on. "The moment we coupled with women, we uncoupled from each other. We became individuals. We had children with no idea how to bring them up—to be honest, most of us hardly tried—so our sweet petals grew up lost and angry. Not all of them were monsters, but enough of them were. And they were mortal. I think that was the sin that stuck. We had created mortal angels.

"As punishment, we were made to watch them turn against each other. They fought, and they died. It was torture, watching them die. And the way our wives grieved the loss of their children—we had to watch that too. The epithet *watcher* came to mean something far crueler than it originally had. Then the archangels came for us. I didn't see color again until the day Ash freed me and asked me to help him bind the archangel Raphael. As I later learned, Raphael had also been sent to punish Ash for his misdeeds, and Ash holds an even longer grudge than I do."

After an uncomfortable silence, the grandfather clock chimed, and Bryony jumped at the sound. Azazel stood and said, "Speak of the devil and he shall appear. Let me talk to Ash alone. I'll ask him to bring your fiancé home as an act of good faith. It seems I'm no longer dealing with you when it comes to the sword."

"I'm sorry for that," Bryony said, and she meant it. The angel wasn't the avatar of evil she'd expected him to be. He was just impulsive, and there had been unintended consequences to choices he'd made long ago. Few people could say they'd never made a mistake or accidentally hurt someone they never intended to hurt. Life was messy and unpredictable. It always knocked the wind out of you if you lived long enough. If only someone had warned the watchers.

The angel reached out and squeezed the tips of her fingers before heading to the kitchen and out the back door. Bryony stared at her hand in disbelief. An angel—a real angel, not a nephil—had been touching her for days. She blanched. A monster had kissed her, braided her hair, done her makeup, and oh god! What was this, some kind of warped slumber party?

She tiptoed into the kitchen and stood adjacent to the open door to listen.

"Ash darling!" Azazel tried to play nonchalant, but he was as bad at that as he'd been at playing Michael.

A second voice grunted. "What on earth are you doing in that body? A bit careless, don't you think?"

"I'm afraid the jig is up, as they say. We need to return our hostage and regroup. They don't know where the sword is, and the person who does has made other demands."

"You mean Loki? Please tell me you're aware of his involvement in this."

"Of course I am, darling. What kind of fool do you take me for?"

"I take you for the large, garish variety, personally. Have you been threatened yet?" The second voice sounded decidedly less benign, and Bryony did not like it.

"Threatened? I don't know what you mean." Azazel laughed. How strange it was that she could already tell his false laugh from his true one. They were not remotely the same.

The demon king seemed equally unimpressed. "Azza, drop the act and bring her out here."

"Who?"

This was painful to listen to, and it was only going to get worse. Bryony took a deep breath, squeezed the staff of her scythe, and stepped into the doorway. The person she saw waiting for her with crossed arms and a tapping foot was the last person she would have guessed to be Asmodeus. She had pictured a hulking, massive creature with wild hair and long claws. Instead, he looked . . . well manicured. He had a svelte figure, a shaved head, and delicate features. He wore a black suit with shoes she could only guess would have cost a fortune if he'd bought them. Maybe they weren't even real. He was far from terrifying, so why did she shrink back when he looked directly at her?

He sneered. "I see you found your fiancé's sword and made good use of it, you resourceful little thing." In seconds, he was before her and dragging her onto the lawn by the front of her dress. She didn't even have time to swing the scythe before he released her again and wiped his hands on his jacket as though she were filthy.

"Temper, Ash," Azazel sang.

"Let me do my job, Azza. You conjured me for a reason, remember?"

Bryony was stunned, but not so stunned she couldn't be sorry that Loki was no longer here. However powerful the watcher Azazel was, the demon king did not seem the least bit intimidated by him. Nor did he seem intimidated by the death sword, which wasn't at all what Bryony had expected. It was like pulling her trump card only to find it had been a deuce all along. She trembled.

"That's right, I'm not afraid of you or your stolen sword." Could he read her mind? "I died thousands of years ago, and I've seen millions of deaths since then. I've even caused a fair number of them. I'm quicker than you are, and if you try to aim that thing at me, I'll decapitate you before you can even swing."

Azazel tsked. He seemed more amused than anything. "Such harsh words."

The demon king was not hearing it. He continued to speak to Bryony. "Had I known you were more dangerous than the nephil, I would have handled you myself instead of leaving you to Azza."

Bryony's jaw dropped. "More dangerous?"

"You've made a powerful ally, and you have an even more powerful weapon at your disposal. Now stop wasting my time, and tell me what's going on. Wait. You know what? I'll just see for myself." He reached into his pocket and withdrew a pair of gold spectacles. Lightning fast, his hand was on her wrist. She heard the slap of skin against skin before she even noticed he'd reached for her. His grip was firm as he balanced the spectacles on the end of his nose and looked down at her. Then he released her. "I see," he concluded.

Bryony could not keep up.

Azazel patted her shoulder from the greatest possible distance. He was clearly still nervous about the scythe. "Don't fret, darling. Ash has a particular talent for seeing the past and the future all at once. The spectacles help him to focus. He says it all jumbles together otherwise, and he can't make much out."

Ash shot daggers at the angel. "Azza! Stop speaking to her like she's on your side."

"But she is on our side. She offered to give me the healing sword at once. It's her Jötunn who's hiding it from us. You must have seen that much when you were wearing your clever little accessory. It only just happened."

The demon king bristled at that. "What I saw was that this woman is a con and has been for years."

Bryony took offense. "I quit doing that!"

"Only just. I still don't trust you."

She wanted to shout, *That's not fair!* But it wouldn't have been true. A gust of wind blew her hair into her eyes, and she pushed it back with a huff. "I'm not lying. I don't know where it is. I almost died when it was taken. Surely that stood out to you. Here. Look again if you have to." She offered the demon her hand, but he only slapped it away.

"Death is too bright to make out, so I saw nothing of the kind."

"You at least saw Michael save my life. You must have."

Ash winked. "I also saw what followed, if you catch my meaning." She blushed, and he burst out laughing. "*Now* who's the liar and who is the fool? You've got to put up a better guard, woman. You're too transparent." He stroked his chin in thought and finally made a decision. "All right, I believe you. So tell me what your ex-ally wants in exchange for the sword, and we'll try to get it for him."

"You won't like it, Ash," Azazel warned. "But you mustn't take it out on her."

The demon glared, and Bryony could not have said whether she shivered from the chill or his disapproving gaze. She steeled her courage and dove in. "Loki wants Raphael. He wants you to bring the archangel back."

Ash closed his sharp eyes for a breath and a half. He didn't scream or shout. He didn't destroy anything. He spoke one word in a voice that was terrifyingly quiet. "No."

Azazel pushed in. "Consider it, Ash."

"That disgusting proponent of forced marriage is at the bottom of the sea where he belongs. He's the property of Rahab now, and Rahab is too dead to return him. We couldn't get him back if we wanted to, and I most certainly don't. You'll have to find something else to trade. The answer is no." The unyielding way he pronounced the word *no* was louder than any furious bluster could have been. The demon king had spoken, and there was simply no way around it.

"But, Ash," the angel said, "you know there's a way. And Raphael is the only one who could begin to right the wrongs done to mortals."

Bryony took the opportunity to beg. "Yes, please let's try. What harm could it do?"

Azazel sucked air through his teeth as though she'd just said the worst thing she could possibly say, and Ash let out a cruel laugh. "What harm? You humans really don't know much of anything anymore, do you?"

"Don't be so hard on her, Ash."

"*Don't be so hard on her,*" Ash mocked. "Who's worse, a demon who tells you the truth straight away, or an angel who offers false hope and then lets you down when it matters? What do you say, Ms. Moss?"

Bryony didn't answer. She found herself leaning on the scythe rather than holding it up. She was so tired. Talking with Azazel had given her such energy, such hope, but talking with Ash was draining her.

The demon went on. "Well, now you'll hear the truth from me, and you can decide what to do with it after you've processed it. I'll give you three days." He was resolute. That wasn't a good sign. "The only way to unbind Raphael is to temporarily raise Rahab from the dead. And the only way to do that is to conjure an angel who either has dominion over death or can defeat it. There are only two. Can you guess who they are?"

She gulped. She could guess one of them easily enough, but she didn't want to say his name aloud.

"Listen." Ash stepped closer and stooped until he was face to face with Bryony. "I'll only say it once. Samael must not be summoned, especially now that you have his weapon. Death will almost certainly follow in his wake, and he's impossible to control. He does not honor his contracts. The only other option is to conjure the archangel Michael, who is . . . How do the kids say it nowadays? Mad as a hatter."

The archangel Michael—her fiancé's namesake—was mad? She couldn't imagine it. What did a mad angel look like? How did one distinguish them from the supposedly sane angels who went around consuming whole cities?

"You do not want to meet the archangel Michael," Ash concluded. "I swear to you. You don't want him to even know you exist." He straightened his stance and hovered like a ghost about an inch off the lawn. "I'll leave the rest of the explanation to you, Azza. Hopefully, you don't regret involving this soft little heart you've found, because *you* are going to have to break it."

And then he was gone.

Chapter Nineteen

The first time Bryony swung the death scythe, she aimed it at the ground. It seemed a harmless way to take out her rage until Azazel cleared his throat from several feet away. "Those plants will never grow back, you know," he said.

She stared down at the patch of death she'd created in her own yard and tried not to care. There was apparently no harmless way to wield Samael's weapon. She was beginning to see why someone like Azazel might want nothing to do with it. But the sword was hers now, so she dragged it by the handle back into her house. Azazel followed, which she thought was extraordinarily brave considering the weapon she carried. The head of the scythe thundered across her kitchen floor.

"Don't worry, darling," the angel said, false cheer coloring his perfect voice. "We'll find another way to get him back."

"Will we?"

The question was bitter and sarcastic, but Azazel responded anyway. "There's always another way."

Bryony recalled saying something similar to Shakespeare back when he'd insisted she had to kill the godhunter or die by his hand. She felt decidedly less optimistic now. "If I could give that demon what he wanted, I would. Doesn't he know that?"

"He does." Azazel followed her through her living room to the base of the stairs. "Ash just thinks you're capable of more. He thinks if he pushes you hard enough, you'll figure it out. His expectations have always been unreasonably high."

She whirled on him at the newel post. "Well, tell him I'd sacrifice the whole world on an altar to save Michael if I could, but I can't. I don't have what he wants." She started up the stairs, the head of the scythe thumping after her as she went. "God I'm so selfish," she muttered. "I don't care about anyone else anymore. If I had my way, you'd have the sword and I'd have Michael, but the rest of the world would stay the way it is. How is Loki the hero of this story all of a sudden? Why is he the only one fighting for real change?"

The angel waited at the bottom of the staircase. "Because you and I have each filled our hearts with only one person. We don't have room for anyone else."

Bryony bowed her head at the top of the stairs. "What's happened to me? When did I start thinking like a goddamned angel? Sorry," she added hastily.

"No apology needed. As far as I'm concerned, I stopped being an angel the day they made me a watcher." He hesitated, seemed to come to a decision, and followed her up the stairs.

She didn't stop him. He'd been in her bedroom the last several nights pretending to be Michael. At least, this time, she knew who he was. She dragged the scythe to her room, propped it near her nightstand, and dropped onto her mattress like a giant paperweight. "What if I *am* too soft?"

"I'm still here because you're soft." Azazel sat beside her. "I know to hear Ash talk you'd think I was a third-rate angel. I'm not, darling. My name is hardly unknown, and if you continue to be just as soft as you started, I dare say you'll soon find out why. Brittle crumbles. Bitter repels. If you want to catch a wasp, you've got to build a web, little orb-weaver. And the strength of every web is in its silk."

Bryony stared down at her own small hands. She didn't want to ask, but she knew her years of blissful ignorance regarding the angels were coming to a swift and irreversible end. "Is it true what he said? Has the archangel Michael gone mad?"

Azazel dropped his head into his hands. Bryony was all but certain he would refuse to answer, but she'd never been good at reading people. It turned out she was equally bad at reading angels. "The archangel Michael is . . . complicated. They called him our general, but his role was far more nuanced than that. He had a thought and so did we. He had an impulse and so did we. Ever since our world collided with yours, he's been . . . off somehow. It was small changes at first. We would have two conflicting ideas, followed by a strong conviction that both were true. We knew without question that Michael was the word of god, the only connection we had to the divine. At the same time, we began to doubt the existence of that god, and doubt is . . . Well, it's like poison to angels."

Bryony lay back and stared at the ceiling. She was so tired—so, so tired. "But if your leader lost his mind, why did you let him continue to lead? Why didn't you fight him?"

"Some of us did. We broke off into factions. Samael was the first to break away—though I suspect it was more a matter of spite than principle—and his host followed. Then Shemjaza made the decision to leave, and he took two hundred with him, including myself. Raphael remained neutral through it all, though it's still a mystery how he managed it. To those of us who uncoupled from Michael, it was obvious he'd become muddled and confused. He is, for lack of a better word, quite mad. But to those who still cling to him, *we* are the traitors—we're the ones who are confused. Sometimes, I wonder whether they aren't right. Then I meet someone like you."

Here, Azazel took her hand. He was still comfortable touching her, apparently. He drew his thumb gently over her knuckles, following their contours like it was second nature. He touched her almost exactly the way Michael did, and she suddenly flushed at the thought of how he must have learned it.

She sat up. "Did you . . . Did you watch us together? When Michael and I were intimate, did you watch us?"

The angel looked taken aback. "My god, darling. I'm not a voyeur if that's what you're implying." He withdrew his hand. "Is that what you think we did, Ash and I? I swear we left you alone when you were together."

There was sincerity in those amber eyes, but Bryony wasn't sure she could trust it. "Then how do you know the way he touches me?"

"You mean like this?" He reached up and traced the line of her jaw. He trailed his hands down to her shoulders, painting her bones with tenderness before moving on to her wrist. If she had closed her eyes, she would swear it was Michael.

She snatched her hand away. "Yes, like that."

"Forgive me. It wasn't intentional. It was merely our common heritage."

"What do you mean by that?"

Azazel grimaced, and the look was almost comical on his otherwise perfect face. "I hate to steal the uniqueness from your relationship."

"Please, just tell me." God she was tired.

"You know angels are repulsed by change, death, and decay. Likewise, we're attracted to things that last. Of your entire, positively stunning body, what will remain most unchanged are your bones."

"So . . . you're both attracted to things that last?"

"Yes, little orb-weaver." He was trying to cheer her with the unusual endearment, and for some reason, it was actually working. "We're often commitment fiends as well. No doubt, he spoke of marriage far too early in your courtship?"

She blushed. That too? She didn't want to confirm it. Michael's predilections seemed such a private thing to reveal to a stranger, no matter who that stranger was. But then a thought occurred to her so suddenly, she couldn't help but blurt it out. "Hard candy! Oh, for crying out loud. Now it makes sense."

Azazel grinned. "My goodness, but for a man who doesn't want to be seduced, he seems to have shared quite a few of his weaknesses with you."

She took offense. "He trusts me."

"As well he should." The angel stood. "You look exhausted, darling. You should shower and get to bed. I'll see you in the morning." He turned to go.

"Wait." She wasn't sure why she'd stopped him, but the idea of being alone in her house drew her chest in tight. "You can stay if you like."

"Here?"

"Yes." She wrapped her arms around herself and clutched her own elbows. "I just thought . . . If you needed . . ." Oh, who did she think she was fooling? "I'm terrified, and I don't want to be alone."

His eyes widened. "Do I count as company, or would you rather I retrieved your Jötunn?"

She tried to smile at him. "You count."

"Darling, that is perhaps the sweetest compliment I've ever received. I'll forever endeavor to deserve it. If you don't mind a few open windows, I'll stay."

"I don't mind." She paused and decided to try out his less formal name. "Thank you, Azza. And I swear I'll do whatever it takes to save your . . . Can I just call her your granddaughter? I don't know how many *greats* to add to it."

His eyes lit up, and he laughed. "Why are you so delightful?"

"I'll take that as a *yes*." She blushed. She'd never been able to take compliments without blushing. It didn't seem to matter whether the giver was human or not. "I'll do whatever it takes to save your granddaughter, even if I have to fight Loki for the sword myself."

A deafening roar shattered the silence in the labyrinth, and the stone behind Michael split. He closed his eyes and covered his head with his arms to protect himself from falling rocks.

"Stop cowering," said a familiar, disturbingly close voice.

Michael glanced up and jolted at the sight of the demon standing over him. "What was that?" he asked.

"My temper." Ash showed his teeth. "I'm not happy with the way this contract is progressing." For the first time, Michael noticed, his captor wasn't hovering an inch off the floor. He wasn't wearing shoes either, and despite his otherwise human body, he still had inhuman feet. They matched the color of his skin, but they were scaled and had talons like an enormous bird. Three long toes pointed forward, and one sharp talon turned back. Suddenly, the demon's wings materialized and punched the roof of the cavern, sending more rubble down on Michael's head. "Don't stare. It's rude." Ash's eyes flashed once, and then he was calm again. "And do yourself a favor, little brother. When you're a demon, avoid contracts with watchers at all costs."

Michael looked warily at the ceiling above him.

"It'll hold," Ash assured him. "What good would it do me to kill you now that you're my hostage?"

"Wasn't I always?"

"You were Azazel's hostage. Now you're mine."

"I don't follow." Indeed, it was nearly impossible to keep up with the quickly evolving situation.

"Azazel contracted me to help in the retrieval of Raphael's weapon. Now they're demanding the archangel himself, and I've not agreed to that. My employer has changed the terms. The contract is void." He growled under his breath, which Michael was grateful for. He didn't think his ears could take another full-fledged roar. "Oh, they can try to bring the bastard back, that oaf of a watcher and your impulsive woman, who has, by the way, taken full ownership of the sword you stole and unmasked your double. I dare them to try it. If they so much as breathe in the direction of Raphael's resting place, you're going to be missing some parts."

Michael had two distinct reactions to this news. First, he had to stifle a smile. Bryony had taken the death sword and successfully defended herself with it. She was resourceful and alive. Michael had never been so proud, nor could he be gladder to have left his weapon behind. Then the full implication behind Ash's tantrum hit. "Wait. You know what happened to Raphael?"

"Of course I do. Who do you think stole his sword in the first place? It was no small feat, I assure you, which is why I still don't understand how a child walked away unscathed with Samael's weapon." He squinted at Michael as though he were looking at a portrait through extremely foggy glass. "It makes no sense."

But it was all starting to make perfect sense to Michael. "You bound Raphael."

"Ha!" Ashmedai scoffed. "I commissioned the job, obviously. Do you think there's any demon alive who could bind an archangel alone? No, I needed help. The only conjuror I knew who could not only bind his superior, but had the right motivation to do it was the watcher Azazel. He barely resisted when I told him what I wanted. He was more than eager to do the job in exchange for his freedom. I can't understand his willingness to even consider bringing the bastard back now." He punched the floor and the cavern shook. "No, I should have expected it. Azza's gone soft for your woman, which is bad news for you. And that's why I'm telling you, avoid contracts with watchers, especially if there's a woman involved. They're weak for women, the watchers. They always have been."

Was it possible? Had Bryony somehow won Azazel to her side? But who was Michael kidding? Of course she had. He'd seen the process before with half the armada and Loki. Even Michael himself had fallen for her. Then he had a thought that made his stomach turn. "Azazel won't touch her, will he? He won't . . . He won't touch her." He could feel the color rush to his cheeks, the fury building in his chest.

Ash just laughed at him. "Oh, I don't know. They seemed pretty cozy to me, and Azza was dressed to impress."

Michael's body lurched forward automatically, but the ring around his waist held him fast. He didn't know why he reacted this way. He had nothing to fear. Bryony hated angels. Didn't she?

"Ah, there's that nephil jealousy I remember so well." The demon king laughed again, heartily this time. "I was wondering when it would finally rear its head."

But Michael's mind had already wandered. He pictured every intimate moment he'd shared with Bryony, but in his place, his merciless imagination substituted a man who was just the right size—a man who could kiss and caress her and never once paralyze her. He imagined the life she would have, how she might grieve for him but ultimately be grateful she had ended up with a superior partner, an angel who would never age or die. His breath grew shallow as he held his face in his hands and wept.

He was so lost in his own cruel fantasy he hadn't noticed that Ashmedai had stopped laughing. "Stop crying, little brother," the demon king demanded, nudging him with one foot. "That's an order from your king."

Michael sobbed.

Ash glowered and muttered, "Insolence. You really are just like your father." Then he sighed and crouched down. "Listen. The watcher Azazel does not want your woman. She's not his type. There's only one woman who's currently Azza's type. In fact, this entire endeavor is to prevent the death of her last descendant, some artist in Brazil who's overly fond of gold leaf, in my opinion. The last drop of his wife's blood exists in a body that's dying, as mortal bodies tend to do, and Azazel will turn the world upside down to stop it. I guarantee you, now that his cover is blown, he's not going to waste any more time seducing your little . . . What is she to you anyway?"

Michael didn't hesitate to answer. "She's everything."

"Ah." Ash wrinkled his nose. "So you've truly coupled with her. I was hoping you were just getting your kicks while you had the flesh to do it. Well, I'm sorry for you. Love is often a terminal disease for us. It would have been better to avoid it."

"I tried," Michael groaned.

"I'm sure you did." Ashmedai reached out and ruffled Michael's hair. It was so demeaning Michael had to remind himself who he was talking to. This demon was thousands of years old. Ash treated Michael like a lost kid because, to Ash, he was one. The demon king reached over and pinched Michael's chin to examine his face. "I still can't see you well, so I'll have to ask. Have you consummated your union yet?"

It was such a straightforward question that Michael had to pause a moment to be sure he'd heard it right. "Excuse me?"

"How would you rather I put it? Have you made love to her? Have you copulated? Have you fucked her?"

"Stop!" So it was to be more humiliation. Except that twinkle of cruelty was no longer in Ash's eyes. He was in earnest. The entire ordeal made Michael extremely uncomfortable.

Ash took it all in stride. "If you haven't, then you should relax. Azza will only have done what it took to mimic you. If your relationship with your woman has not progressed to sex, he won't have gone that far either. That should quell a fair percentage of your worry, correct? She's not been deflowered."

Deflowered. Michael couldn't help rolling his eyes. "That isn't my worry. If he'd even tried, she would have known him for a fraud." He didn't want to think about how that could have been the very way she'd unmasked the watcher.

"You don't say. How?" As soon as Ash responded, Michael realized he'd made a grave mistake. Once again, he'd piqued the interest of the demon king, who now sat and made himself comfortable.

Michael opened his mouth to protest but closed it again. He recognized another opportunity and hated the idea of wasting it, humiliation be damned. If he was ever going to learn about his own nature, Michael would have to swallow his pride and tell his predecessor everything. "When I draw my father's sword, the seraph in me shows itself."

"Resonance." Ash nodded like an eager field researcher. "Go on."

Michael looked down at his lap and forced himself to continue. "When she and I come close, it . . . It happens then too." He looked up again and saw the demon king staring at him, wide eyed and open mouthed.

"Already? That's incredible!"

"You say that like it's supposed to happen."

"Only in the very best of circumstances." Ash grinned and patted Michael on the knee. "Congratulations, little brother. You've found a partner with whom you resonate. Although it usually takes years of courtship. Did something happen to accelerate your bond? A shared trauma perhaps? A near death experience?"

That was a little too on the nose. "How did you know?"

Ash waved a dismissive hand. "I've seen it dozens of times. You're not as unique as you think you are. You've just formed a more powerful bond. Now, when you two are in synch, your body will resonate with hers, so those faint wisps of seraph you hide will grow louder and louder until they can't be ignored. It doesn't only happen with sex, although I believe that's the most common catalyst. I've seen it with dance, prayer, and song. Of course, song is unlikely to work for you if she's incapable of harmonizing." He laughed.

As the demon spoke, something in Michael began to relax. This had happened to other nephilim. It wasn't just his own deformity. "Is there any way to stop it?"

Ash instantly stopped laughing. "Why on god's green earth would you want to do that? You've achieved perfect resonance. You'll feel her pleasure, her pain. It'll be amplified in your own body—her tension, her climax, her release. You won't even have to ask her whether what you're doing is good. Do you know how many men would kill for that kind of feedback? Do you know how many angels struggled to achieve resonance with their own lovers and failed? Have you any idea how lucky you are?"

Every word Ash flung at him hit Michael like a shard of glass, and he leaned further and further away from them. "Lucky? Why would I want to make love to a partner who couldn't consent? I thought you were against that sort of thing."

Now Ash looked truly baffled. "What are you talking about?"

"She can't move once the light hits her eyes."

"Oh? *Oh!*" Ashmedai stood and began to pace. There was something captivating about the way his taloned feet clutched the stone as he walked. "Of course." He tapped a finger to his own temple. "You inherited Samael's curse. I didn't think it could be passed down. This is fascinating. Terrible for you, though. Truly, I am sorry." He didn't sound at all sorry. "But tell me, little brother, does this also happen when you resonate with your father's weapon?"

Michael nodded. It didn't seem advantageous to hide the truth at this point.

"Your victims collapse when they see you?" Ash asked.

"They find it extremely difficult to move."

"And do some of them weep involuntarily?"

Michael grimaced. "A few."

"A weaker form of it then." Ashmedai stopped pacing and crouched to examine Michael again. "If only I could see it."

"Why would you want to?"

"For educational purposes, of course. Samael's curse is a mystery to all of us. We don't even know that it's a true curse. It's certainly not a blessing. Humans, angels, and demons alike—they all fall before the Angel of Death. They retch or weep or shudder in horror. Some think it's what finally drove him over the edge. I believe the archangel Michael has been the only one to completely resist it. He didn't get away unscathed, though."

Michael wanted to ask what happened to the archangel, but he was afraid of the answer. If the only angel in the world who could defeat his father had been weakened . . . No, he didn't want to know. "Thank you for answering my questions, Ashmedai."

The demon king stood and patted him on the head. "No problem, little brother. And now that I'm privy to your most intimate secrets, I think you can start calling me Ash."

Chapter Twenty

I t hadn't been an easy decision, leaving the death sword behind, and Bryony had not made it lightly. She'd tried to transform the thing into a less conspicuous shape with no luck. It wanted to be a reaper's scythe, and there was simply no arguing with it. She couldn't guard the weapon twenty-four seven. She needed to sleep, and taking a giant scythe with her into the shower would hardly be prudent. What if she slipped?

She decided it would be equally imprudent to take the scythe to Martha's Café. It was rarely advisable to bring a weapon to a peace talk, and she intended to speak to Loki as a friend. At the very least, dragging a giant scythe through town would make a spectacle of her, and she was already garnering much more attention than she wanted with her angelic companion. No, it made more sense to shove the scythe under her bed and hope to god no one else broke into her house looking for angel swords.

Azazel walked beside her and exuded charm. His turquoise hair looked vibrant in the morning light, and his amber eyes positively glowed. His smile was unnaturally perfect, and his outfit unsuitably loud. If she was honest, though, she would admit he looked gorgeous, like a tropical oasis in her gray little world.

When they arrived at Martha's, Bryony entered through the front and sat at her private booth. Azazel joined her and took in his surroundings. "How charming," he said.

Before long, Martha found them and stood ready to take their order. "And who have we brought along today?" she asked. "A new friend?"

"Yes." Bryony decided his abbreviated name would be less conspicuous. "This is Azza. I met him yesterday and wanted to show him your place."

"A pleasure, Azza." Martha extended her hand, and to Bryony's utter shock and just a touch of horror, Azazel kissed it.

"The pleasure is entirely mine, I assure you." He grinned, and Bryony loudly cleared her throat hoping he'd get the message and turn down the charm. He didn't. "This is a palace, I must say. How on earth did you get it up and running in such a sparse little town?"

The usually unflappable Martha blushed for perhaps the first time Bryony had ever seen. "The uh . . . The town wasn't always this sparse, but thank you."

"The truth takes no effort at all, darling."

"Martha." Bryony interrupted before Azazel could charm Martha right out of her own café. "I wondered if I could have a private word with Bill."

Martha tapped her pen on her notepad. "Well, he's on kitchen duty right now, but I suppose he's due for a break. Go on then. I'll take over for him. In the meantime, would your friend like any coffee or tea?"

"Oh, he's definitely a tea drinker."

Azazel answered, "Tea would be lovely, thank you. But to be honest, I'd be more than thrilled if you showed me your kitchen. I could help you out while you're short-staffed."

Martha hesitated, and Bryony felt the need to explain. "He made those biscuits you liked."

"Oh!" Martha was taken aback. "But I thought that was Michael."

"I was mistaken." The answer was hasty, but Bryony must have looked a sight because Martha didn't question her further. "It turns out Michael truly cannot cook." She tried to laugh and failed miserably. "Will you two give me a minute to get Bill out of the kitchen before you go back? He's not entirely comfortable around my friend."

"Goodness, is there no one that man can get along with?" Martha pocketed her pad and pen and gestured for Bryony to head on back.

"Sometimes I wonder the same thing," Bryony muttered. Last night's battle flashed through her mind just as she reached the kitchen. Loki had almost lost the fight, and what would Azazel have done to him then? She didn't want to imagine it. "Bill?"

Loki turned, and she saw him in full kitchen regalia. He wore a white apron and held a spatula in one hand. His beard was neatly trimmed and his long hair tied back. He looked positively domestic. It was almost impossible to see him as the fractal firelight he had been the night before.

His greeting wasn't warm. "What are you doing here?"

"We need to talk."

"Do we, though? I think I made myself quite clear."

She gulped. This was not going to be easy. "Yes, you did. I just . . . I need to know why. Please. Martha said you could take a break."

"Oh, and I suppose you two get to dictate what I do with my breaks now, do you?"

Bryony couldn't help her own exasperation. "You're immortal, Bill. What's ten minutes?"

"Fine." He removed his apron, balled it up, and tossed it onto the folding chair that always propped the back door open.

The morning was crisp and pleasant. Bryony had always been fond of the fall, although it meant harder times were ahead. When she was a child, her parents had kept the worries of winter well disguised, and her days had passed in blissful ignorance. She recalled piles of colorful leaves rounded up and then scattered by the wind and her own little feet, frozen blades of grass that crunched when she walked on them, and a warm fire when she found her way back home. It would have been glorious to walk alone and reminisce, but she had come here for a reason, and it wasn't a pleasant one.

"Please, don't do this," she said after several minutes of walking in silence. "Please, Loki." No one was around, so she used his oldest name—the oldest one she knew—in an attempt to placate him. It didn't seem to work. She tried another tack. "Are we really going to just let someone die when we could so easily save her? Are we that heartless?"

Loki picked up his pace. "First, we have no way of knowing this mystery woman even exists. It could all be a scam. You and I should both be aware of that possibility, considering. We've fleeced so many people together, Bryony. To this day, I have no logical explanation for why you're not more skeptical."

That stung. "I just don't understand why you're doing this to me. I thought we were family."

At that, Loki stopped walking. His weakness, it seemed, was the same as hers—family. He'd lost his own long before Bryony was born, and perhaps he craved a new one as badly as she did. He turned to face her. "I'm not doing this to hurt you."

She looked up into his alarmingly blue eyes. "Then why?"

He spread his arms and shook his head at her. "Because my god, Bryony, you can't begin to strategize. You don't even see it, do you? You're winning! Why are you so eager to give up now? You're on a roll, girl. So let me be the bad guy for a while, and we'll keep playing the long game together."

She wrinkled her nose. "The long game? Is that what you think this is?"

"That's what I know this is."

"You're wrong. I'm not winning anything. I've lost Michael."

He shook her by the shoulders. "You've *gained* Azazel! Do you have any idea who he even is? Didn't you learn anything about angelic history while you were doing all that reading in the Black Armada?"

"No." She shook him off. "I was too busy reading medical texts. I didn't have time to learn about angels. I don't care about their history. I hope the world forgets it one day, and we can all go back to our normal, monster-free lives."

"Oh, for crying out . . ." He grabbed his own head and curled his fingers into his skull. "You! Are going to make me say something I regret later. I can't stand people who don't know their own potential. You've won *Azazel.* He may not be much in hand-to-hand combat—"

"He beat you," she muttered.

Now the Jötunn's face was burning red, which gave Bryony some small satisfaction. "I was trying to save your house, you ungrateful brat. I could have ended him right there if I hadn't needed to be careful."

She rolled her eyes. "Sure." It was good to fight with Shakespeare again, like old times. She'd always enjoyed ribbing him and watching him bluster and boil. She imagined his feathers all fluffed and his beady eyes blinking back at her.

"You're infuriating," he said.

"Ditto."

"Bryony Moss, you will listen to me right now, or I swear to Odin I'll stop speaking to you for the foreseeable future." He was so perfect when he was angry. Bryony couldn't help but smile at him, and he immediately softened at the sight of it. "You insufferable woman. Listen to me. Azazel may not have much in the way of brute strength, but he's an unmatched magician and the most powerful conjuror to ever walk the earth. I was mad to tangle with him, and had I known who he was from the start, I probably wouldn't have. Now, for some mysterious reason, the son of a bitch likes you."

She couldn't help but take offense. "It's not a mystery, Bill. I just promised I'd try to save his granddaughter."

"Good, and you keep on promising him." He took her by the shoulders again and looked directly into her eyes. His earnestness was not lost on her. "Keep him in your corner, Bryony. Let *me* be his villain. Most likely, your fiancé is alive and Azazel's descendant has time. Believe me, we would not be negotiating with him if she didn't." He sighed and dropped his hands. "You're winning," he said one last time. "Let me carry you over the finish line, just this once."

They walked in silence a few minutes more until Loki appeared to have a revelation. "Hang on. Please, tell me you didn't leave an angel at home with the death sword."

"No," Bryony answered.

"Then where is he?"

She shrugged. "He's back at the café."

Loki's shoulders tensed, and he shouted, "What?" Then he turned an explicit shade of rage-pink and ran back to the café at a speed Bryony was certain no world champion could match.

She walked back to the café alone. When she arrived, she saw the tall, blond man holding Martha in his arms. He looked like a protective father who'd just found his lost child wandering aimlessly in a shopping center. Bryony imagined him saying, *Don't you ever do that to me again! You hear me?* to Martha. Instead, he snarled, "Get him out of here," to Bryony as soon as he saw her.

As Bryony passed by, Martha said, "Sorry. I don't know what's come over him all of a sudden."

"Oh, Bryony knows." Loki's eyes flickered orange in the morning light. Bryony suddenly remembered what he was and who she'd managed to piss off, and she hurried into the café.

Azazel was in the kitchen humming to himself over a mixing bowl. He seemed perfectly content and docile. Someone would have to speak to Loki about his overprotectiveness when it came to Martha, but Bryony decided the best person to do that would probably be Martha herself.

"Let's go, Azza," she said, and she led the angel out the front. All eyes were on him as they left the café. All eyes had probably been on him from the start. He was quite a whirlwind character to have blown into a small town like this, with his stunning colors and his ridiculous charisma. Even the clothes he manifested were works of art.

He somehow managed to look both modern and eighteenth century at the same time.

They walked together down the lane Bryony knew so well. The branches overhead were bare and brown, and wet leaves covered the ground. "So," Azazel began, "how did it go?"

Bryony just bowed her head.

"That bad?" He heaved a deep sigh. "I suppose I shouldn't have expected better. That Jötunn reminds me of Ash. They're equally hardheaded, and neither one is likely to give in any time soon. It's a shame we're caught in their crossfire."

"Yes." But it was Bryony's crossfire, too, wasn't it? To hear Loki talk, she'd been in on it from the start, setting up a risky con with an enormous payoff. "Loki said she has time, your granddaughter. Is that true?"

"A few months at least. A year at most."

Bryony cleared her throat. "Is she . . . in a lot of pain?"

"None." Azazel stared at the web of branches above them and smiled a devastated smile. "Hopefully, she won't feel it until the very end."

"Then how do you know she's sick?"

"Ah, well." He pushed his perfect brows together and frowned. "I'm a touch ashamed to admit it. But possession is not all speaking in tongues and frothing at the mouth, you know. Long ago, artists were said to have daemons or muses to inspire them. I was hers."

A knot began to form in Bryony's gut. "You possessed her?"

"Occasionally." He smiled wistfully. "We made art together. She's a rare talent, but of course, she is *my* granddaughter. One day, while occupying her body, I felt part of her that hadn't been there before. It was her, but it wasn't. The following month, it had grown. Such a ridiculous disease, cancer."

Bryony chewed her lip in thought. How could she make him understand? She didn't want to behave like a con artist anymore. She needed to try something different. She needed to try the truth. "Loki says Raphael would never have let medicine die."

The angel just stared at her.

"Loki says . . ." She picked up her pace and dug her fingernails into the heels of her hands. "He wants you to bring Raphael back, and he isn't going to budge on it. He . . . He says we're playing the long game this time."

"The long game?"

"It means we have to be patient. We have to make sacrifices for a bigger payoff in the end."

"Payoff?" He narrowed his eyes. "*We?*"

This conversation was getting more and more precarious. Bryony bowed her head. Her past was hardly a secret now. "The thing is, Ashmedai was telling the truth about me. I am a con . . . *was*. I became a god by lying to the people of this town. I let them believe I had healing powers, when really I'd just found an abandoned angel's sword. Well, it turns out Loki had stolen it, but at the time, I thought it had been abandoned. I think, to him, the long game is just how we operate."

"Loki didn't steal the sword." Azazel looked annoyed, and Bryony could only hope he was directing his annoyance at the Jötunn instead of her. "He won it. Ash has never been able to resist a wager, and it seems Loki took advantage of that. At the time, the healing sword was little more than a trifle to Ash. He hasn't cared for a mortal since Sarah. Probably, he's decided caring for mortals just brings too much trouble." The angel shot Bryony a sharp look. "I'm beginning to see where he's coming from."

Bryony gulped. She'd really made a mess of things this time, hadn't she? She'd given away Loki's strategy and possibly lost her only other ally in the process. "Please don't be angry," she muttered.

"Angry?" The angel pursed his lips at the word. "I'm furious, darling. I'm positively incandescent, but I'll keep my temper until I hear the full story." His expression was too serene. It revealed nothing of how he was feeling, and Bryony got the impression that was because he'd stopped trying. An angel must take pains to imitate human expression. When they lost their composure, they might simply stop applying the effort. She suddenly regretted leaving her scythe behind. "I would like an answer to one burning question if you don't mind," he said.

Bryony nodded and tried to subtly put some space between them as she walked.

"I would like you to explain to me why Loki is playing a *long game* to free an archangel who, frankly, deserved what he got. What in the world does a Jötunn want with Raphael?"

Here was Bryony's opportunity to abandon the truth and lie her way out of this. She could come up with a story about how Loki had his own vendetta against Raphael and wanted to settle it his way. Something like that. But she didn't. She seemed to have lost the talent for deceit somewhere along the way. Anyway, she got the impression this angel would easily see through a lie. "He's doing it for me," she admitted.

"At your request?"

She shook her head. "No, I didn't ask for this. It's his plan, but he's doing it for me, for who I was ten years ago—someone he seems to have lost."

"And who were you ten years ago?"

Her house was in view, but Bryony didn't want to go in. She stopped and stared at the place. There were too many memories locked behind those doors, and she suddenly felt too weak to face them. She answered Azazel's question. "I was angry." She couldn't look at him anymore. If she did, she knew she wouldn't be able to continue. Sharing this part of her life with an angel seemed so fundamentally wrong.

"I had a family once—a father, a mother, a little brother. We lived in this house together until they got sick. It came on so fast. It was some kind of flu. They say before the massacre there were vaccines and treatments, but not anymore—not for my family. My brother . . ." She choked but pushed through it. "My brother was so young. He was so young, and he took so long to die. I tried everything to break his fever. I wiped his brow with a wet cloth because I'd read that in a novel somewhere. I fed him ice. I gave him my father's whisky . . ." She sobbed and hated herself for it. Then she rubbed her face on her sleeves and willed herself to go on. "I gave him whisky to dull his pain because of some stupid show I'd seen. It only made him sicker. It became my whole life, watching him die. It became who I was. And when he was gone, I wasn't anyone anymore . . . until I found this hatred, and I hung on to it, and I used it to survive. That's who I was when Loki found me."

She glanced up to see the angel staring down at her. Suddenly, she didn't care whether he was angry with her. She didn't care about anything. "It didn't have to happen that way. One little shot could have prevented it if the angels hadn't gotten rid of vaccines. So I'm sorry for what Loki's putting you through, but I don't think he's wrong."

Azazel took too long to respond, and when he did, it could not have been further from what Bryony expected. She'd readied herself for an explosion of rage. Instead, he said, "Please, darling, may I embrace you?"

"I—" She'd already begun to defend herself but stopped short when she found she didn't need to. She nodded, and her once bitter enemy wrapped his arms around her and pulled her into his gold-embroidered jacket.

He held her a long time, and she found his embrace every bit as warm and inviting as his personality. When he spoke, his voice was low and soothing. "I know what it is to lose a child. I know what it is." His breath shuddered at some ancient memory of grief, and Bryony was sorry to have reminded him of it.

Azazel swayed a little and cleared his throat. "Do you know, when Raphael bound me, he didn't speak a word? That's what I recall most about that day—Raphael's silence. If you knew him, you'd understand. He loved to talk, especially to mortals. He was an incurable gossip. You could have an entire conversation with him without saying a word. So unlike a seraph." He chuckled. "Sometimes I wondered, when I was sane enough to think, whether he'd been quiet because he hated what he had to do. Sometimes I wondered whether he would have done it had he been able to completely free himself from Michael's pull. I suppose I should find a way to ask him."

Bryony pulled back and scrutinized his expression. Was he saying what she thought he was saying?

He smiled down at her. "But you'll have to be willing to help, darling. I'll never manage to conjure an archangel on my own."

Chapter Twenty-One

"I wish you wouldn't watch me eat."

The demon king had given Michael a plate of food, made himself comfortable across the cavern, and then proceeded to stare. Every once in a while, he drew a notebook from his pocket and scribbled something in it. He was done pretending to be Bryony, done pretending to leave Michael alone in the dark. All his tactics had failed him, so now, it seemed, he resorted to being endlessly present. "Why?" he asked. "Ashamed of your appetite?"

"No, I—" Michael stopped himself. It would have been an obvious lie to deny it. He groaned and stuffed another pickle into his mouth.

"That's what I thought." Ash unbuttoned the collar of his shirt and rolled up his sleeves. "You really should try to get over it. You are what you are. Don't make yourself miserable over something you can't control."

It was good advice, but Michael knew he was unlikely to take it. "How bad does it get?"

"That depends on how long you live." Ash unlaced his shoes and removed them. His taloned feet uncurled in the most grotesque way. They should not have fit into those shoes. "I doubt you'll live long enough to have a lasting effect on the food supply. Soon enough, your only concern will be who your next master is and whether he'll make you do something unthinkable. You'll wish you were alive again and agonizing over whether to eat that third sandwich."

Michael groaned and swallowed a mouthful of bread. "That's not very comforting."

"It wasn't meant to be." The demon king yawned and stretched as though he actually had a body. Apparently, old habits died hard. "All I'm trying to say is life is short. Eat whatever you want. Ditch the shame. Enjoy your appetites while you still have them." He winked. "*All* your appetites."

Michael raised an eyebrow and frowned. "That's fairly inappropriate, considering."

"Considering what?" Ash jumped to his feet. "I am your king! I order you to enjoy your lunch! There. Is that better?"

"Not really."

The demon king sighed. "Take my advice, little brother. Try to appreciate your life while you still can. It doesn't get better from here. You've a home, a fiancée, and a steady supply of food. Each year of existence will only get darker for you. I don't mean to depress you, but it's true. I wish someone had told me as much when I was young."

Michael looked up from his meal. His captor was unfathomable and frustrating. "Why would you take it all away then?" He dropped his plate. "If I only have a few years left to enjoy the good things in my life, why would you steal them out from under me like this? What kind of person are you? Am I going to survive this or not?"

Ash's eyes widened. "The cheek! Lecturing *me*? Do you have a death wish, son of Samael?" He chuckled at his own joke and knelt in front of Michael, crushing the plate under his knee without the least indication he'd felt it. "I'll tell you why I'm doing this, but only because I like you. You remind me of myself, maybe a little less intelligent, but still . . . Whether you survive this ordeal is entirely up to your woman. She and my *ex*-employer mean to unbind Raphael, but in order to do that, they'll have to conjure an archangel to raise Rahab. Not just any archangel, you understand. They'll have to conjure the archangel Michael."

Michael blinked. "Why is that a problem?"

"Are you winding me up, little brother?"

"That would be a mistake on my part," Michael admitted.

Ash leaned back on his heels and nodded. "Absolutely, it would. So you're telling me you see no problem with your precious fiancée summoning the *archangel Michael,* under the tutelage of—and I have no idea how to stress this enough for you—the accused source of all earthly evil, the watcher Azazel?"

"I thought the source of all evil was Samael."

"Samael?" Ashmedai made a face. "Samael is the punishment not the sin. Now listen closely while I educate you. An angel cannot conjure another angel. It's impossible. Only earthly hands can draw the circle, and only an earthly tongue can recite the summons. Azazel is uniquely skilled at conjuration—I'll admit that—but he can't do it without a host. Are you getting this? Azazel will need a willing host, a body to possess. So where do you think he'll find such a body?"

"Bryony." Michael sat up straight.

"Good boy. Now you're getting it. But that's not the worst part."

Michael couldn't imagine anything worse. He'd already begun pulling at his chain in a desperate attempt to break it.

Ash just shook his head. "The archangel Michael hasn't been in his right mind for as long as I've existed. Who do you think perpetrated the most recent massacre, the one that eliminated every scientist and educator from the face of the earth? Let's narrow it down, shall we? Who do we know wasn't involved? Samael and his host weren't involved. The watchers weren't involved. So if it wasn't the rebellious and the fallen, who was it?" He tapped a finger to his temple. "The loyalists. And who do the loyalists obey?"

"Enough!" Michael rose to his knees. His entire world was collapsing around him. Suddenly, his own name repulsed him. He hadn't just chosen it to anger his father, though that had been his primary motivation.

He'd looked up to Michael, even occasionally wished the archangel had been a father to him instead. "Let me go!" he roared. "Release me now! I'll stop her myself!"

Satisfied, Ash sat back and crossed his arms. "Good. You're exactly as angry as you should be, but I think it's better if we do it my way. She'll be more pliable if she fears for your life rather than fearing your wrath. I have her pegged as the rebellious type, and I know I'm not wrong." He grinned and patted the pocket that held his spectacles. "I've seen it for myself."

As soon as Bryony entered her home, she opened all the doors and windows while Azza built fires in every hearth. Already, they'd developed a routine. Perhaps that was the reason Azza wanted to try possession right away. "We only have three days, and I need to see where we stand," he said. "We may already be well coordinated."

But Bryony wasn't so sure. What if she was making a horrible mistake? What if Azazel was a far better con artist than she could ever hope to be? Oh god, she was going to let him inside her. She began to hyperventilate at the thought.

"Goodness! Sit sit sit." Azza guided her to the couch. "You'll pass out before we even get started."

"I'm not . . ." She panted. "I'm not sure I can do this."

"Of course you can. All you have to do is let me in." His voice grew soft and rhythmic. "Relax. Allow. Trust." She tried to focus and failed. "You're too tense, darling. Do you need some tea?"

"I think vodka would be a better choice in this case." She laughed.

Azza sat beside her. "No alcohol. Not yet. It's our first time. We need to be clearheaded." The way he spoke about it sent the blood to her cheeks. He winked at her. "If it helps, remember I'm not a man." His body began to change. He didn't grow the way he had before, but his flesh dissolved into ice and fire. He became that glacial creature that melted at the center and froze at the hands and feet. His heart was as warm and alive as the fire in the hearth.

Bryony began to tremble.

"I'm not a man," he repeated. "And I'm not a woman. I'm not a demon. I'm not Azazel." His frozen hand drifted to her cheek. "My darling, I am you." He leaned in, and she felt the sharpness of his hand passing through her own flesh. She jolted, but he continued his slow, rhythmic speech. "I'm nothing without you, nothing but the echo of a song you remember from a long time ago. Where did you hear it last? Can you recall? Try to remember where you heard that song before." His voice became a whisper, and then it was nothing but a thought. *That song playing over and over in your head.*

The sensation began as a tingle, like blood rushing back into a limb, except the limb was her entire body. Then her extremities became ice cold, and she shivered. At last, fire erupted in her chest. She grew feverish, hotter and hotter. She fought it. She screamed. A figure crashed into the hearth and shattered like glass. Bryony jumped up after it. "Oh, no! What did I do?" She tried to gather the pieces together, but they slipped through her fingers. He was too close to the fire. He was melting. She panicked. "Azza!"

In seconds, he was a puddle on the floor with a hovering, flaming heart. The puddle froze and began to build, and before his body was quite finished Bryony heard the angel's familiar voice wheeze, "Rejection is never easy."

"But I didn't mean to reject you."

"Don't fret, darling." In seconds, he'd reformed his angelic body. More slowly, he found his color and looked like a man again. "I was overly optimistic," he said, his voice quiet and weak. "But I needed to know. I haven't possessed anyone other than my granddaughter in a long, long time. I seem to have lost my touch. All that means is we need to practice."

Bryony squared her shoulders. "You want to go again?"

"Oh, no no no. At least, not until after I teach you to dance." He took her hand in one of his and slipped the other around her back. "First a waltz."

Bryony was not a good dancer. More than once, she stepped on his feet, got distracted by her own apology, and lost the rhythm entirely. On top of everything, the angel was singing, and she could not for the life of her tamp down her goosebumps. Angels, she had always understood, were musical creatures. Their songs could drive the hardest heart to weep, or they could drive a man mad if they wanted to. Azazel was no exception. He provided the music, but it was far too beautiful. Bryony lost herself to it.

"Try not to think too much." Azza interrupted his own song. "Just move with me. There are no other requirements. You can't possibly do this wrong. Just let go and allow me to lead. Open your eyes, darling." He lifted her chin until she stared up into his amber eyes. They glowed with the fire. They were mesmerizing. "Watch me." Eventually, he was all she could see. Her own home was so out of focus she couldn't have even told him which room they were in. "Good," he said.

Again, the angel began to sing, and this time she felt it in her bones. It warmed her, his song. It led her. She could have closed her eyes and still known exactly what he was going to do next. He let her go, and she knew where and when to step without his touch. "How are you doing this?" she whispered.

I'm not, he answered with a thought. His inhuman voice echoed in her head. *We are.*

"This is so weird," she murmured, and Azazel burst out laughing.

He clapped his hands, and she snapped out of her daze. "Let's break for dinner."

Dinner? On cue, Bryony's grandfather clock chimed to let her know it was already six. "How did it get so late?" She would have guessed they were breaking for lunch, had anyone asked.

"You were focused on me and not the time."

But that didn't seem right. Somehow, dancing with an angel had stolen hours from her. She was starving. She hadn't felt that either, her own hunger. It was quickly becoming apparent why even willing possession was undesirable. Even if you'd given permission, you could still lose track of your own body. A spirit could keep you for years, and you might not know you'd lost more than a few days.

Azza made her dinner, which she repeatedly told him he did not need to do. "Don't be ridiculous, darling. I've wanted to show off for days. You have no idea how disappointed I was when you told me your fiancé couldn't cook."

Dinner was exquisite. Azazel preferred everything to be buttery and rich. Bryony silently thanked Martha for supplying her with good wine, which had narrowly prevented a disaster when Azza couldn't find any and Bryony didn't know whether she even had it.

After the meal, the angel retrieved a pad of paper and a pencil and replaced her plate with it. "Are you comfortable?" he asked.

"Yes."

"We'll practice drawing the circle next." He stepped behind her and placed both hands on her shoulders. Soon she felt the chill of ice where his skin used to be. "Every conjuration requires a lure and a net. The circle is the net. Are you ready?" She wasn't, but Bryony nodded anyway. Azazel leaned into her until his voice was at her ear. "Give me permission, darling. I won't hurt you. Try to remember that song from before. You know the one. Dance with me."

And she felt those pins and needles, the sting of ice, and the heat of fire at her breast. She closed her eyes and tried to breathe through it. She thought of dancing, how she'd known what to do before she needed to do it, how she'd anticipated her partner's every move. She listened for his voice and heard it rise up inside her like a song she couldn't forget. *Beautiful*, the voice said. *You're a natural talent.*

Bryony got the impression that wasn't the entire truth, but she let it go as her arm moved to pick up the pencil. Whether he'd moved her or she'd moved herself didn't seem to matter. They moved together.

But when she looked down and saw herself begin to draw without an inkling of what she was drawing, an alarm went off inside her.

And there was a crash and a pile of shattered ice behind her.

This time, Bryony knew not to panic. Azazel would reform in a minute or two, and he did, perhaps a little more slowly this time. Was she wearing him out? She hoped not.

"What happened this time?" she asked when he stood before her again.

He wavered on the spot. She reached out to catch him, but he never quite fell. "We need to practice digital dexterity." He smiled a weak smile. "Tell me, do you play the piano?"

"You're exhausted," she said.

"Yes."

"Then you should rest."

"We have to do a month's worth of work in three days. I'm not sure I have time to rest. You picked up broad movements quickly enough, but you're bound to have a weakness. Everyone does."

Bryony insisted. No one worked well when they were exhausted. She made him tea and let him sit by the fire. She had no idea whether that was how an angel relaxed, but perhaps a watcher had developed some human habits. The truth, of course, was that she was exhausted too. As she watched the angel sip his tea and stare at the fire, she began to doze.

The next thing she knew, it was dawn, and she was sprawled out on the couch, covered in her comforter and drooling on her pillow. Within seconds, Azza stood before her. "Ready to practice weaving, little spider?"

Bryony shot up like she was late for a job. "Why did you let me fall asleep?"

"You wanted to rest."

"I wanted *you* to rest."

Azza just smiled. He handed her a cup of coffee and a fresh croissant he had almost certainly baked during the night. She took a tentative bite and then devoured it when she discovered it was the most delicious pastry she'd ever tasted. She washed it down with the coffee, which was made exactly to her liking. "Is there anything you can't do?"

He cocked his head. "Impersonation apparently. Now come. Let's play a duet."

Chapter Twenty-Two

"It's a simple arpeggio, darling. Don't let it intimidate you." Azazel sat beside Bryony on the piano bench in her parlor. "You play the left hand, and I'll play the right." He demonstrated her part.

Her playing was slow and stilted, not at all like her father's. She should never have quit learning the instrument. All this time, she'd had a piano sitting quietly in her parlor, and she couldn't even bring herself to practice her scales. *Pretend you have an egg under your hand and you don't want to break it*, her father had told her once. She arched her hand appropriately and noticed an immediate improvement.

"Excellent." Azza's voice snapped her back to the present. "Now steady your rhythm, even if you have to slow it down. Remember this is meant to be a duet. We must anticipate each other." He began to pick out the melody in time with her playing. It was a beautiful song, one she hadn't heard before, but it immediately became familiar to her. It felt so good to hear the piano again. It had been too long since her home was filled with music. And it took an angel to do it.

An angel. Bryony struggled to reconcile herself with the fact that she was sitting beside one now, playing an instrument with him, hitting the wrong notes with him, starting over and over again with him. If she could have seen her own future all those years ago . . .

Suddenly, she burst out laughing.

Azza stopped playing and stared down at her. "What's funny now?"

"Nothing," she gasped. She wished she could have curbed her outburst, but it was impossible. The stress must have finally gotten to her. This was how she was going to save Michael? *This*? "It's just . . . I'd never have guessed I would one day be taking piano lessons . . . from an angel!" She doubled over. "It's so absurd! My life doesn't even make sense anymore." Azza's expression was impossible to read, and she recalled that he was precisely this opaque when angry. She was suddenly horrified that she'd offended him. "I'm sorry, I'm sorry." She clutched at her stomach and swallowed her laughter. "I think I'm just tired."

She wasn't sure what she expected, rage or quiet derision. He responded with neither. Instead, he reached for the keys and began picking out "Chopsticks" until she burst out laughing again. "Never apologize for laughing at the absurd," he said, "little orb-weaver."

She rocked back and tried to catch her breath. "Oh my god, I love you so much." As soon as she said it, she realized her mistake. She clapped her hands over her mouth, but it was far too late. Azazel had frozen in place, his hands poised over the keys, his lips pursed, his eyes down. Bryony quickly clarified. "I mean . . . I didn't mean it like that."

"I know how you meant it," he murmured.

What had she done? Her poor, foggy head was spinning. She'd been on edge all day, so worried she would say the wrong thing, do the wrong thing, and her worry kept tripping her up. The more anxious she became, the less able she was to self-censor, and she knew she'd made a mistake this time. She'd treated an angel as though he were just an ordinary person. She'd gotten comfortable and laughed at him, and then she'd been so relieved when he wasn't offended that she immediately ensured his offense. Azza was a monster. One did not cling to a monster as though it were a teddy bear. One did not speak to an angel as though it were one's childhood imaginary friend.

Azza tilted his head back and stared at the ceiling. Bryony watched his throat move as he swallowed. "Now," he said. "We'll do it now."

"What?"

"Now is the time. Right now." He rose from the bench without even looking at her. "Close your eyes for me, and try to remember that elusive song."

Oh! He wanted to possess her. She wasn't sure she should allow it while he was angry.

"Play," he commanded, and Bryony found it impossible to resist. She played the left-hand part and tried to focus. But Azazel's icy fingers closed over her right shoulder, and she shuddered. "Remember," he murmured. "It's a duet." He pushed into her shoulder and down through her arm, and she suddenly understood exactly what he wanted to do. She was meant to play a duet with him, but they would both be using her body to do it.

She felt the tingle and cold in her arm. She felt the weight of his chest as he leaned into her back. When the weight was gone, there was fire at her breast. She played, and it scared her. *It's only Azza,* she thought. *This is what he feels like—familiar.* She knew him. She ate with him and slept comfortably while he stood by. She laughed with him like they had a real friendship. She let him take her because she trusted him to let her go. *That's it!* she thought as he moved her right hand gently over the keys. *I trust you. That's why we're doing this now, isn't it? Because I said I loved you, and you knew it meant I would trust you this time.*

Yes, darling. His voice rang clear in her head. She didn't fight it or push it out. When the angel took her left hand along with her right, she played the piece like a concert pianist. She played the piece like her father.

The piano echoed through her empty home, sending tendrils of music to every corner. Bryony could hardly believe how well she played—how well he played. It wasn't entirely clear which of them was making the music. It was coordination. It was something that could only be done by two. It was . . . *A dance,* she thought. *We're dancing right now.*

Exactly. Now you're onto it.

Bryony felt proud, and she wondered how she'd gotten to this point in her life—the point where she was proud to be successfully possessed. Had she lost her mind? Clearly, she had.

When she felt the voice of the angel say, *Now that we know we can build the net, shall we work on creating the lure?* she didn't even wonder what he meant. She knew. She hesitated. He opened her mouth . . . And the sound that escaped her throat was unlike any sound she'd ever made in her life. It was her voice but his song, and it was in beautiful, perfect pitch. How? This wasn't her. Though she'd found a way to accept the idea of sharing her body, she hadn't yet reconciled herself to the idea of sharing her identity. Something deep inside her rebelled, and there came the sound of shattering ice behind her.

This time, Bryony didn't turn to see him. She could hear parts of him spinning across the hardwood floor. She let her forehead fall onto the piano keys with an ugly dissonance she was sure he would have admonished had he been at all able to speak.

It took him several minutes to rebuild his body. Bryony didn't straighten up, even when she heard footsteps and the creak of the piano bench as he sat down beside her with his back to the keys. "The thing is," she began, her forehead still cooling on the keys of the piano. "I can't sing. I really can't. I've never heard a sound like that come out of my mouth. It was . . ."

"Unsettling." He finished for her when she couldn't come up with the right word. She noticed his voice was fainter than usual. He touched just the tips of his fingers to the back of her hand. It was an odd gesture, but Bryony appreciated it nonetheless. For someone who'd been bound in darkness for millennia, his courtesy was remarkable. "Everyone has a weakness," he said. "If you felt true fondness for my presence and were still compelled to reject it, I believe we can assume we've found yours."

She lifted her head and rubbed at the impression the piano keys had left behind. "Do we have to sing?"

"I'm afraid so. This isn't just any fire ant we're summoning. This is the queen. The lure must be flawless." He pushed his hand through his hair in a nervous gesture she hadn't yet seen from him. When it was mussed and he didn't smooth it, Bryony grew concerned. If she'd learned anything about Azza in the short time she'd known him, it was that his aesthetic perfection would never be compromised under normal circumstances.

"How long can you keep this up?" she asked.

His smile was so obviously forced, she could barely stand to look at it. "As long as I need to, darling."

Azazel tried to sing through Bryony five more times that morning. Each time, as soon as her tongue moved under his power, she rejected him. She tried all the mental tricks she could think of. She focused on the way she felt when he made her laugh. She thought of him fondly. She pitied him. She admired him. Nothing worked. And each time he was expelled from her body, it took him a little longer to pull his own back together. After lunch, he became more frustrated. He tried every room in the house, thinking perhaps there was one in which she was most comfortable. He even tried possessing her in the bathroom, assuming she might be one of those people who was only comfortable singing in the shower. She wasn't.

By nightfall, it took him more than an hour to rebuild his body. She waited for him by the fire and wrung her hands until he came staggering into the living room. His eyes were dull, and his hair had gone from bright turquoise to a shade like yellowing paper. He was no longer his brilliant, energetic self. And worst of all, his makeup was smudged.

"One more time," he wheezed.

"Not tonight." Bryony tried to sound firm, but she was fairly certain it came out wrong.

"We don't have time to waste." He was leaning on a doorframe, and she got the distinct impression that if he tried to stand on his own, he would collapse.

"Giving you time to recover is not the same as wasting it."

Azza slouched. "We have one more day. Ash is disturbingly prompt. He won't be late."

"Then we'll just have to figure out another way to save Michael and your granddaughter."

The angel drew in a deep breath and struggled to stand under his own power. Somehow, he managed to cross the room, take Bryony by the hand, and pull her to her feet. His skin was ice cold. He looked even worse close up. He was almost transparent, like tinted, smoky glass.

Bryony stood her ground. "You can't even hold your body together anymore. Look at you. You look terrible."

"That's harsh, darling." He wavered on the spot and had to steady himself by putting his hands on her shoulders. "I won't die, you know. I'll simply lose the ability to manifest a body. It takes energy, and I haven't an endless supply. I'll be all right."

She narrowed her eyes at him and considered it. "Promise me it's painless for you."

He tried to laugh and squeezed her shoulders. "Sweet little god, why on earth should that matter?"

"Because it does," she said impatiently.

He bowed his head. "It's never mattered, Bryony."

The angel's use of her given name jarred her in a way she hadn't expected. It wasn't right. It wasn't him. Why was he acting like this? "I refuse to try again until you've recovered," she insisted. He wavered, and she gripped his wrists to keep him locked onto her shoulders.

"Don't be stubborn," he said.

"Tell me it doesn't hurt you."

"I can't." His voice was almost inaudible now.

"Then we aren't doing this until you're strong again."

He knit his brow and struggled to hold his eyes open. "But why?"

"Because you don't deserve to suffer like this, you ass!" Ah, there was her temper at last. She'd been bound to lose it with the angel eventually. She was only surprised it had taken her this long. She tamped it down and tried to reason with him. "Stop being a martyr and think about it. It won't work if you're weak. I won't be able to concentrate if I know

I'm hurting you. So what do you need to recuperate? Let's work on that for a while. No good will come of bleeding you dry."

The tips of Azza's fingers dug hard into Bryony's shoulders, and he stared down at her with that empty look that meant he was too overwhelmed to express himself properly. He stood stock-still for a moment and said nothing. Then, as though someone flipped a switch somewhere, the lifeless automaton he seemed to have become sprang into motion. He straightened up and cleared his throat. "If you'll excuse me," he said, and he walked out the front door, leaving her stunned in his wake.

She followed him. He wasn't going to just walk away now, was he? Only he had access to the demon who'd stolen Michael. Between Loki and Ashmedai, Bryony was beginning to fear she might never see her fiancé again. But the watcher Azazel had given her hope, and she wasn't willing to let go of it yet.

"Wait!" she called after him.

Several yards from her veranda, he stopped and waited for her to catch up. Then he turned to her and stumbled. She grabbed his elbows to steady him. The moonlight magnified the ethereal quality of his skin. He was wrong all over, barely holding together, an antique candy bowl. He clung to her elbows and muttered, "You shouldn't have said that."

So she had offended him after all. Well, it was only a matter of time. "I'm sorry. Ignore me. Sometimes I get frustrated and blurt out whatever's in my head. Please, don't walk away just because I was short with you."

The angel began to sink to his knees, and Bryony couldn't fully support the weight of him. He slid down in slow motion, legs bent, hands still clinging to her arms. At first, she thought his strength had finally given out, and maybe it had in a way. Because she began to feel a faint, familiar warmth, a pleasant dizziness, as though she'd just had the perfect amount of wine before a meal. And the meal was coming. *Worship.*

She slapped him before he could bow down. It wasn't a powerful slap, but it was enough to jolt the angel out of autopilot. "Don't do that," she said. She added, "Please," when she realized she was being short with him again. "I don't need it right now. I can wait a little longer." She helped him to his feet and admitted, "I'm still trying to wean off."

He staggered beside her as she walked him back to the veranda. He sat on the steps where her father used to smoke his pipe and watch the sunset. There was something surreal about seeing an angel in her father's place, but she dismissed the feeling and sat down beside him. He lay back and let one arm fall over his eyes.

She propped her elbows on her knees and stared at the ground. "Please, don't take it the wrong way, Azza. I just don't want to be a god anymore, so I'm trying to wean myself off. Michael did warn me it was an impulse for angels—"

Azazel interrupted with a groan. "It's not that, darling."

Bryony expected him to elaborate, but he fell into a long silence and she didn't want to push him. Worship was such an intimate thing. The rejection of it must feel similar to romantic rejection. She was certain it stung a bit anyway, but the thought of changing their new friendship to a hierarchical one made her cringe. Why would he want something like that? "I don't understand," she murmured.

"No, you don't." It was his only response before he fell silent for another long while.

Eventually and without warning, the angel found his tongue again. "My punishment was tailor made for me. I was bound *as* stone, you see. I became this jagged, lifeless nothing. I knew no color, no light, no beauty. But do you know what was even worse? The ugliness I heard. The ugliness was crystal clear." He choked on his memory and took a moment to recover. "I could hear everything around me—the anger, the blame, the innocent animals sacrificed in my name. I was the scapegoat for all mankind. All the evil in the world was laid at my door. It was my fault men were violent, my fault women could seduce the watchers. How they hated me—humans and angels alike. All I heard for thousands of years was their rage and the endless screaming of terrified goats."

He barely shifted, but Bryony saw the hand he'd draped across his eyes tighten into a fist. "In all those years, in all that ugliness, never once did my god look upon me and say, *Azazel . . . Azazel, you don't deserve to suffer like this.*" His last words came out as a convulsive sob.

The sound of a monster crying like a child was almost more than Bryony could bear. Finally, she understood what she'd done to upset him. She hadn't offended him. No, she'd shown mercy to a creature who'd never known a moment of it in his entire existence. Just a few words, a little courtesy, and he was finished. Loki was right. She'd conquered the infamous watcher Azazel, and she hadn't even meant to.

Chapter Twenty-Three

Bryony allowed the angel to weep a while longer. Even when his body went still and silent, she let him be, knowing he'd only lost the concentration he needed to express what he was feeling. The night was crisp and the sky clear. She was content to sit and watch the stars, but after twenty minutes or so, she began to feel a chill. Ultimately, she gave in to her desire for warmth.

"Azza," she said to the supine figure beside her. "I'd like to go inside. Will you be okay out here?"

The angel didn't answer. He still lay in the same position with one forearm resting across his eyes, his legs bent at the steps as though he were about to sit up.

"Azza?" She reached out and touched him. He was ice cold, but that didn't worry her. He'd been ice cold before, especially when he was practicing possession. No, what disturbed her more than anything else was the fact that he wasn't even breathing anymore. He'd gone completely dormant in his own body.

She tried to shake him. "Azza!" His body was so heavy she couldn't budge it. She employed her full weight to no avail. Had she been thinking straight, she might have noticed her own racing heart and told herself to calm down. She might have reminded herself that the body on her porch was a mere manifestation of the creature Azazel. Even his ice-and-fire form was just a more accurate representation and not the essence of who he was. But she wasn't thinking straight. There was only one voice dominating her thoughts, and that voice was screaming, *I've killed him!*

He looked like a corpse. He looked empty. She climbed on top of him, straddled his waist, and shoved at his shoulders. His arm didn't even drop from his forehead. "Please!" she begged. "Please, don't be dead. Please, don't be dead." What if he'd been wrong that he couldn't exhaust himself to death? What if he didn't know how things worked after so many years bound as stone? Maybe the rules had changed.

Bryony barely remembered the diagrams of CPR she'd seen aboard *Dragonfly*. Would it even work on an angel? She had no idea, but she had nothing to lose. She laid one hand over the other and interlaced her fingers at the center of his chest. She was doing it wrong, she knew, but if he was already dead, how could she possibly harm him more? She pressed down and counted, *One, Two, Three, Four, Five*. Did he need air? She tried to pry open his mouth with her fingers, but it wouldn't budge. He was like a sculpture, a perfect glass statue laid out on her veranda.

It was useless. How could she pump his heart if his skin wouldn't give? How could she breathe for him if his mouth wouldn't open? She bent over him and let her forehead drop to his chest. "What should I do? You never told me what to do. Please . . ."

Before she understood what was happening, the sculpture's arms were locked around her, and a voice, so quiet it might have been a summer breeze, whispered, "Now, now. I already told you. I won't die this way." The sculpture tugged her to his chest, and she let out a cry of relief.

"Damn it!" she shouted into his unyielding jacket. "Don't do that to me ever again."

"I couldn't help it, darling. I was simply overcome." Little by little, his skin began to soften. It didn't feel human at all, but it didn't feel as much like glass either. It was more like hard, treated leather. "Had I known it would upset you so much, I would have removed this body from your view."

Bryony went from wanting to cry to wanting to scream at him, and back to wanting to cry again. She was vacillating between compulsions so quickly she had no time to act on either one. Azazel pushed himself to a sitting position, which shifted Bryony to his lap. He didn't let go of her. He held her tighter. She might have blushed and pushed away had he been remotely human. But the way he looked now, it felt about as intimate as sitting in the lap of one of the old, stone angels around her family's gravesite. She shook the uncanny feeling and embraced him back.

"I'm sorry," he said, and she felt his breath in her hair. Thank god he was breathing again. "You were right. I should not have pushed myself so far. I thought I would be stronger. Perhaps the years of solitude have weakened me."

Finally, he admitted it. Now she was beginning to see the pride in him, which was so well hidden by his charm it was almost unnoticeable. She was used to Loki's far more conspicuous hubris. "Tell me what you need to recover," she said.

"Only time, darling. It would speed things along if I didn't have to manifest a body, but you didn't want to be alone."

She pulled back and wrinkled her nose at him. "Are you serious? You've been holding on all this time so I wouldn't feel alone? Azza, for crying out loud! I knew someone was here before I ever saw you. All the windows and fires . . . And was that you who read my letters?"

He shook his head. "That sounds more like something Ash would do, to be honest. He's far better at preparation than I am."

"Well, tell him to put them back. He left a mess in my attic." She glared at the angel, but it was meant for the demon king, and Azza seemed to understand. The energy he expended just to smile was obvious. "Now, go de-manifest or do whatever you need to get well. Just promise to haunt my house a bit so I know I'm not alone."

"I promise, little orb-weaver." And suddenly, he was gone.

Bryony knelt alone on her front porch. For the briefest moment, she regretted asking him to disappear. But a gentle breeze pushed the hair from her face, and she was sure she could smell an excellent vintage in the air. Red, obviously. Most certainly French. *Azazel.*

During the night, Bryony woke to find a warm fire blazing in her hearth. "Thank you, Azza," she said. He was still present, and he was letting her know. Bryony pulled her comforter up under her chin and wondered how anyone could hate such a creature. Then she reminded herself that she'd been one of those people. Although she hadn't singled out Azazel, she hadn't needed to. All angels were monsters. Every last one of them. But they weren't, were they? Like people, there were some who were kind, some who were misunderstood, some who'd been abused and were just trying to heal.

She spent much of the following day talking to her empty home. She kept the windows open and practiced her half of the duet. Every once in a while, she would get an indication there was someone listening. Once, she heard a thump in her attic, and when she investigated, she found all her letters put back in their right envelopes and returned to their chest. Kindness. She thought of Michael, of how it was something he might have done and how he was not with her now. He was somewhere with the demon king, and Bryony had no way of knowing if Ashmedai was as kind as Azza or as monstrous as the archangels who'd punished him.

She sat on the floor in her attic and let herself feel what she'd been bottling up all along. She buried her face in her hands and cried. "I miss him, Azza. I miss him so much, and I'm scared I'll never see him again."

A wind blew through the attic, the lid of the chest slammed closed, and Bryony could have sworn she heard a breathy voice say, "Don't fret, little god. I have an idea."

She opened her eyes to an unearthly mist forming before her. It grew thick as morning fog as she watched. Then it was smoky glass in the shape of a man, an ice sculpture with fire at its breast, and the watcher Azazel sat before her, cross-legged and grinning. She leapt up and threw her arms around his neck.

He hugged her like an old friend. "Poor, sweet child. I couldn't stand to watch you cry." He'd altered his appearance. His hair was silver, his copper-toned skin had an almost metallic sheen to it, and the new design around his eyes consisted of sharp lines in gold and red with a light dusting of orange and pink. His lips were painted gold. God but he was beautiful. He would be any photographer's dream come true, but just now, he was hers.

"You changed," she said.

"I didn't want you to get bored."

She rubbed the tears from her eyes. "I'm pretty sure that would be impossible with you."

"Well." He stood and offered his hand. She took it gratefully, and he helped her to her feet. His skin was human again, warm and alive. He'd recovered, and she couldn't completely hide her relief. "Shall we share a cup of tea?" he said. "I have so much to tell you."

Chapter Twenty-Four

"Tell me, my disloyal subject, what would you give to see your woman tonight?" The demon king crouched until his face hovered at the same level as Michael's. He was excited for some absurd reason. Likely, he was looking forward to psychologically torturing his captive, whom he'd already complained was becoming unbearably dull.

Michael leaned back and casually fidgeted with his chain. "It won't work this time. I'll know it's just you in disguise."

Ash let out a cry of mock outrage. "Already so pessimistic! I've done my job far too well. You were supposed to fight it, keep hope alive and all that." He stood and stretched his taloned feet. "Well, you'll be glad to know I don't intend to show you a fake this time. Although it was fun while it lasted, don't you agree?" He laughed. "No, I'll be taking you all the way to her house. Yours truly and your rapacious woman will be in the same place at the same time. So I'll ask you again—what would you give?"

"Don't lie to me." Michael couldn't keep hope from creeping into his voice.

"Pinkie swear." Ash extended his pinkie. When Michael refused to take it, Ash gave up and frowned. "Fine. First you need a meal and a bath. You're going to be my bargaining chip, so I need you to smell less like you've been chained to a wall for a week. As you are, she may not even want you back."

Ashmedai took him to the underground river and gave him a large meal while they waited for Michael's clothes to dry. Michael had long since given up on the idea of privacy. The cave was a locker room, but he was the only one who ever changed in it. The demon king could manifest a body in whatever form he wanted, and that form, when human, always seemed to include a suit. It reminded Michael of the first time he'd seen Loki shift from one shape to another, and how the Jötunn either couldn't shift himself into clothes or didn't want to.

"What makes you different from a shapeshifter anyway?" Michael asked. "Since I'm bound to be like you one day."

"Bless your heart." Ash chuckled. "You'll never be like me. I'm the one and only. But it's a valid question. This body is a manifestation of how I looked while I was alive." He glared at his own feet. "For the most part. My flesh isn't real, and it takes quite a toll to keep it together. I spent thousands of years perfecting it, and it still won't last as long as I'd like. A shapeshifter, on the other hand, has its own substance and can . . . well, change the shape of it, obviously. Shapeshifters never need to create a body whole cloth."

Michael's eyes drifted to the demon king's feet. They seemed to be a great source of disappointment for him.

"You're staring," Ash grumbled.

Michael looked away. "Sorry."

"It's fine." Ash shrugged unconvincingly. "It's rude, but it's fine. My curious little brother, we must teach you better manners. To answer your obvious unspoken question, it's always easiest to manifest your angelic form. In your case, that will be a seraph. The next easiest form to manifest is a body like the one you had when you were alive. It's all about familiarity, you see? You do what's easiest and dig yourself into a rut. Feet were always a challenge for me. It took less energy to manifest cherubic feet, and I got lazy. Let that be a lesson to you. Never leave the most challenging task until last." He wagged his finger like a metronome, and Michael felt like he was listening to the lecture of a particularly unpleasant schoolteacher. "Well, we all have our little quirks, don't we? I wonder what yours will be."

Michael tucked his knees to his chest.

Ash mused, "I used to wish I was a shapeshifter—how I envied them—but now I'm older and wiser, and I know better. The poor souls spend so much time in shifted forms, they tend to forget themselves. They shape their bodies to please those around them. They've got no identity of their own, you see. So be grateful for the hideous serpent in you." He cackled. "At least you know who you are."

Michael couldn't help rolling his eyes at that. The demon king wanted so badly to be cruel, but he made a terrible villain. To Michael, taking an insult or two to discover as much as he could about his own nature was a small price to pay. He realized his newfound semi-immunity to total self-loathing was due, in large part, to Bryony. She loved him as he was, and if she loved him, he couldn't possibly be as monstrous as he'd originally assumed. "Huh," he muttered. "You just need someone to love you."

Out of nowhere, the demon king punched him in the stomach. "Impudence!" Michael doubled over and tried to catch the breath driven from his lungs by the impact. "Time for a lesson." Ash stood over him and hit him hard, alternating between forehand and backhand to punctuate his tirade. "Never! Discuss! Your king's! Love life!" He spun and kicked one taloned foot into Michael's stomach. "Respect your superiors!"

Michael curled in on himself, clutching his bloodied torso, but the Aeshma Daeva wasn't finished. He made a fist, and Michael's eyes grew wide to see the sharpness of the ring he wore on his right hand. "Remember who you are," Ash said as he slammed the ring into Michael's forehead. "And remember who you aren't."

Blood cascaded down the side of Michael's face, and Ashmedai knelt to inspect his work. He took Michael by the chin and turned his face from side to side. "Good." He nodded. "Now you look suitably roughed up. That should give your woman motivation enough to see reason. Now put your pants on. We have an appointment to keep."

Michael stared up at his captor in utter disbelief. "My . . . clothes are still wet."

"Excellent." Ashmedai clapped his hands and rubbed them together. "You'll look even more pathetic." As Michael hopped on one foot in a clumsy attempt to force the other through his non-compliant pant leg, the demon king began to grow.

Michael braved an opinion. "None of this is necessary."

The demon king's voice dropped in pitch. "Oh, I think it is."

"This is Bryony you're dealing with. Even after I drew my father's sword, she defied me." Michael smiled and lost himself in the past for a moment. "She'll listen if you're reasonable, but intimidation won't convince her. I know her."

"Correction. You *knew* her. Now that Azza's gotten his hooks into her, she won't be the same."

Michael froze in the middle of buckling his belt. "You said he wouldn't seduce her."

"I said he wouldn't fuck her, and I'd still wager he hasn't. But he's definitely attempted possession by now—maybe more than once—and if you only knew how intimate possession can be . . ." The monster, now well and truly a monster, wrapped its claws around Michael's waist and lifted him like he weighed nothing at all. "If you knew, little brother, you might prefer he *had* fucked her."

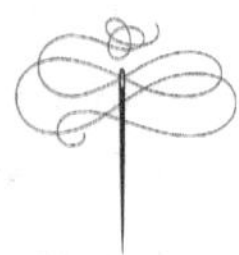

Bryony's Victorian house loomed in the night like a dark carnival attraction. How strange it was to think of such a place as home. Michael recalled how quickly he and Bryony had come to the conclusion that the place was haunted. Of course, they'd been technically right on that count.

The colossal ghost in question landed in the yard with a massive quake. Then he set Michael on the ground and began to shrink. "You claim your woman doesn't respond to intimidation," Ash said. "We'll soon see."

The back door creaked open just as the demon king took his human form and tightened his grip on the end of Michael's leash. When Bryony stepped out, Michael felt a catch in his chest. It really was her. How had he ever mistaken a cheap imitation for the love of his life?

"Michael!" She ran to him, despite the demon on the other end of his tether, and threw her arms around him. He bent over her and breathed her in.

"You're alive," she murmured. "I knew you were."

Michael clung to her and kissed the top of her head. The world was only right when she was in his arms. Lately, it had been tilting off its axis, distorting into some kind of nightmare from which he longed to wake. Had he been able to see the stars from his prison, he was certain they would have been in all the wrong places. He could no longer navigate his life without her.

A movement behind her caught his eye, and he glanced up to see a second figure emerge from the house. This must be Azazel. Michael watched the figure approach, and god help him if it wasn't the most beautiful creature he'd ever seen. The angel wore a long, elegant coat. His hair was silver and his skin glistened like copper in the moonlight. He looked like a rare jewel in the night.

Michael examined Bryony at arm's length. There wasn't a mark on her. So the angel hadn't hurt her. But had he touched her? No, of course not. Ash had been so sure. As Michael examined her, the expression on Bryony's face twisted from relief into a mask of pure fury. Her eyes narrowed at the gouges where the demon king's talons had left their mark. She blanched and then turned pink with rage. And Michael knew Ashmedai was about to get a taste of her defiance firsthand.

She flew at the demon king, claws out, screaming at the top of her lungs. "You monster! You devil! How dare you!" She swung, but Ash easily caught her by the wrist. Moments later, he had her other wrist held tightly in the same hand. He lifted her off the ground and stared at her while she kicked him. "I'll never let you forget this!" she shouted. "Never as long as I live! You're not a king—you're a bully! You pathetic *nothing*!"

Ash raised an eyebrow, and his mouth twitched into a smile. "Azza, come and do something about this yapping Chihuahua you've adopted. She's giving me a headache."

The angel—the beautiful, jewel-like figure—approached with a smooth, unhurried step. He moved like a gentle mist, which made it all the more shocking when he raised his hand and struck the demon hard. Astonished, Ashmedai dropped Bryony and cradled his face where the angel had hit him.

"Insult her again, darling," Azazel said. "I dare you." The anger in that otherwise serene face, the evident rage in that calm, musical voice was unbelievable. The reality of it erased all Michael's faith and optimism in favor of one horrific idea. The angel loved her.

Michael's world tilted back off its axis.

CHAPTER TWENTY-FIVE

B ryony pushed herself to her feet and brushed the grass off her knees. She noticed her stockings had torn and made a mental note to be angry about it later.

The demon king blinked and shook off his astonishment. "Fiery little thing, isn't she?" He clearly did not intend to acknowledge the betrayal of his partner.

"I tried to warn you," Michael said.

Bryony shot him a look she hoped would say, *Just* what *did you try to warn him about?*

Azazel finally let his hand drop. "You should not have hurt him, Ash. That was never part of our contract."

Ashmedai seemed to have been waiting for the angel to say exactly that. He smiled with a look of smug satisfaction. "Our contract is void, Azza, or didn't you realize? You changed the involved parties. Raphael was never supposed to be part of this, let alone Loki and the archangel Michael. Now you're going to sign a new contract, and I will dictate the terms."

"Why on earth would I do that?" Azazel remained cool and collected, and Bryony was grateful for it. It gave her a moment to think. She had to implement his plan carefully. She had to find the right opening and say her lines perfectly.

Ashmedai kept his focus entirely on his former partner. "You'll do it because you've attached yourself to this little minx, and you'll do what it takes to keep her good opinion. She knows about your past, doesn't she? You must have a lot to prove. Now, here are the terms of my contract. You will never help to free Raphael—*never*. That's it. That's the contract, and it's binding. Agree to it, and I'll let the whippersnapper go." He jangled the chain he had attached to Michael. "If you do not agree, I'll tear his limbs off."

The more Ashmedai spoke, the more Bryony ground her teeth. Frankly, he was an asshole, and she desperately wanted to tell him so. In the few days they'd spent together, Azazel had revealed many interesting things about the demon king, not least of which was how best to piss him off. She gave it a whirl. "You know what? You're acting exactly the way I would expect Asmodeus to act. So that's what I think I'll call you from now on, *Asmodeus*."

The demon king's gaze whipped from Azza to Bryony, and he absentmindedly tightened his grip on the chain in his hand.

"Asmodeus." She let the name linger on her tongue. "It suits you, don't you think? You're just like the stories, after all. You threaten and kill innocent men."

Deep in the demon king's throat, Bryony heard a primal growl. "There are no innocent men." And there it was—her opening. She could hardly believe it.

"Sure there are. I know lots of them."

Ashmedai showed his teeth. "Then you don't know them like you think you do. I've seen the histories of millions of men, and I have yet to see one who could be called *innocent*."

"Interesting." Bryony glanced at Azza, who nodded his approval almost imperceptibly. "Care to make a wager of it?" There was a moment when the demon king seemed to realize he'd been had. He shot daggers at Azazel, and Bryony thought perhaps the angel's plan had failed. But then Ashmedai turned back to her, and the look of defeat on his face was not one Bryony would forget any time soon. She decided to nail her victory down. "I'll wager I can show you an innocent man before the week is out. What do you say?"

"Damn you, Azza," Ashmedai hissed. Then he turned back to Bryony and drew a deep, resigned breath. "Within a week?"

"Sure." She grinned. "It'll be easy."

"And by whose standards do we measure this innocence?"

She shrugged. "By yours, of course. You're the one who can see their histories, aren't you?"

The demon king laughed so hard he almost dropped the end of Michael's chain. "You're going to bet me you can find an innocent man, as calculated and judged by me, and you think you have a chance to win this?"

"I think I have more than a chance."

"Saints preserve us!" Ashmedai wheezed. "Little brother, you didn't tell me your woman had a nest of ferrets where her brain should be. For a second there, I actually thought she'd make this challenging." He straightened up and wiped a tear from his eye. Azazel made a fist, but did not strike this time. The game had begun in earnest. "Fine, I accept your wager." Ashmedai offered his hand but snatched it back before Bryony could shake it. "First, my stipulations."

She sighed and turned up her palms. "I'm waiting."

"One. I'll not be dragged around the world to look at every random man you can get your hands on. You may show me one per day, so you should be careful about your selections."

Bryony nodded.

"Two. They must be mature, human men. No nephilim—your Michael doesn't count—no women, and no children. No one under twenty-five years."

Again, Bryony nodded.

"And three. I keep your fiancé until our wager is complete."

Bryony frowned. "Then I have some stipulations of my own. You won't leave one more mark on his body. You won't hurt him again while he's in your custody. In fact, you'll treat him well, tend to his wounds, and make him comfortable. Swear it."

The eagerness in Ashmedai's expression was almost more than Bryony could bear. He really couldn't resist a wager, could he? He was practically frothing at the mouth in his excitement for this. Who would have guessed the king of all demons had a gambling addiction? "Excellent," Ashmedai said. "Now the stakes. If I win, Azazel signs my contract, no questions asked." He grinned. "And I get to keep my little brother permanently."

Bryony started. She hadn't expected Michael to be at stake. "What do you want him for?"

"For research, of course." There was no hint of jest in the demon king's answer. "Samael's son? And I do believe the only one to have inherited his curse. He's too fascinating."

Curse? But Bryony was far more livid than curious. "Absolutely not! I'm not bargaining with—"

"We accept your terms," Azza said as he laid a steadying hand on Bryony's shoulder. "And if she wins, you'll surrender your hostage to us completely unharmed, and you'll get out of our way while we attempt to conjure the archangel Michael."

"It's a bet." Ashmedai held out his hand, and Bryony hesitated to take it. This was all moving far too quickly.

"Go on, darling," Azza said, and he was so sure, so confident that she took the demon king's hand and shook on it.

The wicked laugh that echoed in Ashmedai's demonic throat as he grew and grew sent chills down Bryony's spine. The timbre of his voice morphed into something unrecognizable as he became a beast made of other beasts. He looked so monstrous that Bryony backed into Azza's chest despite herself. And then the devil was gone, and he'd taken Michael with him.

Before she could protest, Azza bent his head and murmured into her ear. "Remember, little orb-weaver, we're only buying time. Your performance was perfect."

She felt sick. "But what if we can't summon the archangel in a week? What if we fail?"

"Listen." Azazel turned her to face him, and in the moonlight, he looked exactly the way people had believed angels looked before the massacre. The spell was broken when he tapped her on the nose once for every word that followed. "I will not fail."

"I don't know, I don't know." She was shaking all over, certain she'd made a mistake, certain this would all backfire. "What if I never learn the lure? What if I can't sing, even with your help? What then? He's terrifying, Azza. He's huge! And he isn't even bothered by the death sword. I can't fight him."

"And you won't have to." Azazel laughed. "Darling, I think perhaps there's something about our situation you don't quite understand."

She was convinced nothing could soothe her now, but she gave in and asked, "What?"

The angel drew one finger up her throat and tilted her chin back until she was looking directly into his amber eyes. "I am far, far bigger than he is."

Bryony was only a little surprised when Ashmedai, sovereign of all demons, appeared in her backyard at high noon the next day and rubbed his hands together like a cartoon villain. Azza had warned her the demon king was prompt, but she hadn't expected to be able to set her clock by him.

"Come, Samael's soon-to-be daughter," he said. "Show me your first innocent man."

"He's in town," Bryony said. She had extremely mixed feelings about the epithet the demon king used. On the one hand, it meant Ash—as Azazel called him—considered Bryony to be Michael's future wife, which would only be the case if he thought Michael had a future to begin with. On the other hand, she could think of nothing more disconcerting than the idea that she might one day be related to the Angel of Death.

"Care to fly?" Ashmedai grinned.

"No, thank you. I'd rather walk."

They walked down the lane into town, Bryony and the demon king. She thought they must have looked quite the pair, him in an expensive suit and her in a black taffeta gown. But only one pair of feet crunched on the gravel. "Why don't you just walk like a normal person?" she asked, feeling brave now that a real plan was underway.

He didn't answer.

"Don't want to scuff your shoes?" She couldn't quite keep the note of derision out of her voice. "Didn't you just manifest those into existence? Couldn't you just poof the scuffs away?"

He rolled his eyes. "You know nothing of manifestation. It's not the fairy magic you seem to think it is. It takes artistry, energy, and a great deal of effort."

"Does it?" Bryony smiled to herself. It turned out Ashmedai was easier to bait than she'd assumed. She decided to test him. "But it should be easy for you, shouldn't it? Aren't you supposed to be some kind of genius?"

"Flattery." He shot her a severe look. "I suppose Azza's been giving you tips on how to deal with me. Don't listen to him. He doesn't know what he's talking about."

She sighed. Maybe this plan wasn't going to work after all. The demon king was no fool. He was infuriating—that's what he was. "Fine. Why don't *you* tell me how to deal with you then, since I'm going to have to for the next week at least? I'm honest-to-god stumped. You don't even manifest consistently. One minute you're a monster with too many teeth and the next you're a gentleman in a suit. It's frankly weird as hell."

The demon king chuckled. "Keep amusing me, Ms. Moss, and we'll get along just fine."

He seemed to be in good spirits. Perhaps it was the thrill of the wager, or perhaps it was the pleasantness of the lane. Bryony couldn't have said, but she wasn't going to waste a moment of it. "I'll try not to bore you if you promise not to hurt the men I show you, even if they aren't innocent."

"That would be ungentlemanly of me, now wouldn't it? It's bad enough I'm about to shatter your expectations and grind your hope into dust. Why would you think I'd go around killing your friends on top of it all? You did say I was some kind of gentleman, too many teeth notwithstanding. Or was that just the suit?"

So flattery did work in a roundabout way. She just had to be less intentional about it. His good mood seemed to be holding anyway. So she asked, "Is Michael okay?"

"I've deposited him in a comfortable location and dressed his wounds, if that's what you're asking."

"No, I mean . . ." She dug her fingernails into her hands. "Is he . . . okay?"

Ash groaned. "Now you've just asked the same question again. You know you did that, right? You didn't even bother to reword it."

At this rate, she was going to wind up deliberately scuffing his precious shoes before the day was out. "You know what? None of this is easy for me. I'd hoped you could at least appreciate that, having lived so long and seen so much. I'm terrified and trying to hide it the best I can. I'm just putting one foot in front of the other"—she glanced down at her worn ankle boots—"literally. I'm one step away from collapsing into a sobbing, useless mess. So if you could just take the insults down a notch or two, I'd really appreciate it."

The words had all come tumbling out faster than she could rein them in. She was frustrated, and now she was more frightened than ever because the demon king was glaring down at her. Then his mouth twitched, and he burst out laughing. "My god, I haven't been this entertained in years. You really can't stop yourself, can you? Do go on, please. I promise not to punish you."

Bryony blushed. He was laughing at her, and why shouldn't he? The demon king had nothing to fear from her. To him, she was an insect or a Chihuahua, apparently—something with ferrets for brains anyway. She hung her head and marched on in silence.

Then Ash surprised her again by answering her question even after she'd disrespected him. "Physically, my little brother is well, aside from a few scrapes. Mentally, though, he's suffering. As you know, he's not entirely human, so he's not having an entirely human reaction to this situation. His fear of being separated from you is not insignificant."

Bryony muttered, "That's an understatement."

"So you're already familiar with his phobia." He stared straight ahead as he spoke. "His fear of uncoupling is as natural to him as a mortal's fear of death. He panics at the mere idea of it, and he knows you're currently cohabiting with a watcher—that is, an angel who has a thing for seducing women." He made a disgusted face.

Bryony couldn't help herself. "Azza's not like that."

"Oh, I assure you, he is. He has a particular reputation in fact, so keep on your guard. If he tries to get too close . . ." He shrugged.

Bryony rolled her eyes as they arrived at Ryuhei's bookshop. Then it occurred to her. "I know what you're doing."

Ash gave the shop a long look before turning back to Bryony. "And what is that?"

She planted her hands on her hips. "You want me to lose faith in Azza. You know that if I lose faith in him, I'll be more likely to reject possession. But the thing is, I can't lose what I never had to begin with. Azza and I have a mutual interest, that's all. I want Michael back, and he wants the healing sword. He may well betray me when this is all over, but I can be reasonably certain he won't beforehand because it wouldn't be in his best interest. I imagine he feels similarly about me."

The corners of Ash's bowed lips turned down even further. He opened his mouth to say something and then snapped it shut again.

Bryony was glad to have finally gained some kind of upper hand with him, even if it was just that she'd managed to baffle him more than he baffled her. He groaned. "You're entirely too cynical for your age, Ms. Moss. Believe me, Azazel does not feel similarly about you, but I suppose you have no reason to take my word for it."

She did take his word for it, though, and something in her rebelled against the idea that, between herself and an angel, the angel was the faithful innocent and she the wary pragmatist.

Ashmedai led the way into the bookshop. He'd already taken the spectacles from his pocket and was positioning them on his nose when Bryony introduced him to Ryuhei. "This is my friend"—she racked her brain trying to think of a surname to give him and finally just gave up—"Ash. I'm just introducing him around town. Ash, this is Mr. Miyamoto."

"Please, call me Ryuhei." The bookshop owner shook the demon king's hand, oblivious to the scrutiny he was under.

As they left the shop, Ash replaced his spectacles with a smug look that let Bryony know she'd lost this round. Azza had warned her to expect the loss. No one could meet Ashmedai's standards for innocence, he'd said. Bryony had to remind herself that they didn't need to win the bet to win the struggle. It just had to look like winning was their ultimate goal. "So why isn't he an innocent man?" she asked.

Ash winked. "He kicked a puppy when he was eight." It was an obvious joke, but Bryony didn't laugh. Ashmedai laughed on her behalf and patted her on the shoulder. "A man's sins are his own business," he said. "I don't divulge." And then he was gone.

Chapter Twenty-Six

Four more days Bryony failed to give her voice to Azazel, and four more men failed to meet Ashmedai's standards for innocence. Hope receded a little more each day, and Bryony was slowly crushed under the weight of her own despair. Nothing was better because she'd gotten involved. Nothing. If she just disappeared, Ashmedai would have no reason to hold Michael hostage and Loki would let go of the sword he kept for Bryony's sake.

It was evening, and she sat on her couch before a lively fire, reading a book to clear her head. Azazel slumped in the adjacent armchair, exhausted. They'd already tried to sing ten times that day. Ten was where Bryony drew the line. Any more than that and she knew Azza would begin to lose his color.

The angel was less than pleased. "We only have three days left," he said. "How are you still resisting me? We started off so strong."

Bryony laid her book open in her lap. "I'm doing my best."

"I know you are, darling." He sighed and slouched even further. "But there's something in you that can't let go, some instinct. You gave me everything else so easily. Why not your voice? No conjuration is possible without it. Not even a lesser angel would come to a circle without a song."

Her jaw was sore from clenching. Her muscles ached from tensing each time she rejected the angel. She was almost as exhausted as he was, and they hadn't made any headway. It was terrible to see him defeated. Despair was her job. He was supposed to be the optimist. But if he'd taken her role, she supposed she'd have to take his. "If we can't conjure the archangel, we'll just have to win the bet."

Azza didn't budge from his slouch. "Impossible."

"It can't be. There must be one innocent man somewhere in the world. If I knew what standard Ashmedai was judging them by, maybe I could think of someone."

Azza shook his head. "He measures their trust, though he'll never tell you so. No mortal lives more than twenty years and comes out unscathed. Life abuses you, and eventually, you begin to doubt each other. It's a different threshold for everyone, of course, but no one reaches adulthood with their ability to trust untarnished."

The air in the room was chilly from all the open doors and windows. Bryony tried not to let it show. "I thought he was measuring sins."

"Sins can be forgiven, made right, and forgotten. They're volatile that way. But once trust is lost, it's almost impossible to get back. Ash despises men for what they've done to him and to the women he cared about. He doesn't want to believe in good men in much the same way you didn't want to believe in good angels. He's bitterly angry, I'm afraid. That's why he measures innocence the way he does. In his reality, innocent men aren't allowed to exist because, if they do, his entire world will be turned on its head." The angel leaned in and propped his chin on his knuckles. "That's part of what I find so miraculous about you, darling. Your world was turned on its head the day you met me. You adapted beautifully. You changed tack the instant you realized you were mistaken. Most people fight that, but you didn't. You just accepted your new reality and moved forward."

It was perhaps the strangest compliment she'd ever received and, at the same time, the most touching. She wanted to thank him but found she'd lost her tongue, so she stared back down at her book instead.

Azza didn't seem bothered by her silence. "What are you reading?"

"Nothing." She chewed her lip. "Just some old poetry. This one's called 'Annabel Lee.' I memorized it for a recital when I was thirteen. I wanted to see whether I still knew it."

Exhausted though he was, Azazel moved far too quickly. Before she realized he'd even gotten up, he snatched the book from Bryony's lap and returned to his place by the fire. "That sounds like a delightful game," he said. "Let's play. You recite, and I'll test you. Ready?"

She was not ready, nor was she convinced this was at all a good idea. There were stanzas in "Annabel Lee" she did not think an angel would appreciate hearing. "I'm not sure about this."

"Nonsense. I adore poetry, especially recitations. Go on. Let's hear that elusive voice of yours."

She was cornered. Of course she could refuse, but he looked so unabashedly eager. His exhaustion had all but left him. He looked down at the page, and Bryony was certain he would read the poem regardless, so she began to recite. Then she came to the offending stanzas.

"But we loved with a love that was more than love—
I and my Annabel Lee—
With a love that the winged seraphs of Heaven
Coveted her and me."

She paused and glanced up. Azazel did not react, so she went on.

"And this was the reason that, long ago,
In this kingdom by the sea,
A wind blew out of a cloud by night
Chilling my Annabel Lee;
So that her high born kinsmen came
And bore her away from me
To shut her up in a sepulchre
In this kingdom by the sea."

This time, she stopped for good and felt the heat of shame creep into her cheeks. She glanced up and found Azza staring at her, waiting. He gestured for her to go on, but she couldn't. So he began to read the poem aloud.

> *"The angels, not half so happy in Heaven*
> *Went envying her and me . . ."*

It was so ridiculously on the nose that Bryony let him finish the entire stanza without uttering a word of it. *A watcher,* she chided herself. *You're sharing this poem with a watcher, an angel who actually did take a human wife because he was dissatisfied with his own world.*

"Come now." Azza interrupted her cringe-inducing thoughts. "So one poet got a few things right. Don't let it stop you. Your recitation is so much better than mine." That was an outright and shameless lie. Azazel was an angel, and his voice reflected the fact. Bryony could not begin to match it. If angels were anglerfish, their voices were the luminous bulbs they dangled to lure unwitting victims into their jaws.

Despite Bryony's hesitancy, Azza would not be deterred. He continued, and she reluctantly joined in when he came to the lines,

> *"And neither the angels in Heaven above*
> *Nor the demons down under the sea*
> *Can ever dissever my soul from the soul*
> *Of the beautiful Annabel Lee:—"*

Azza stood and approached Bryony with the book in one hand. Ashmedai's warning about his reputation echoed through her mind as the angel positioned one knee on either side of her lap and dipped his head until his mouth was inches from hers. She shrank back.

"Try to trust me," he said. "Rediscover your innocence. Take a long draft of nostalgia. Tell yourself I'm only fantasy, a dream you once had—safe, harmless, secret. Close your eyes and recite, but try to remember that old song as you do. Let it echo in the back of your mind." He held the book over her shoulder as he whispered, "Draw me closer, one word at a time."

She gulped. He was about to attempt possession for the eleventh time that day. She'd argued fiercely against it, but she knew better than to stop him. She was the rhythm and he was the rhyme. She was the lyrics and he was the song. *My god, this could work. This time, it could really work.* She'd be a fool to waste this chance. He must have been thinking the same thing. She kept her eyes closed. She knew he would change into his angelic form—that ever melting and freezing creature with fire at its breast—and she didn't want to see it. Nothing could distract her from her recitation. She was in class, and she was being tested. She could not fail.

> *"For the moon never beams without bringing me dreams*
> *Of the beautiful Annabel Lee:—"*

They spoke in unison, and she could feel his breath on her lips. It smelled of nothing and felt like winter.

> *"And the stars never rise but I see the bright eyes*
> *Of the beautiful Annabel Lee;"*

The touch of a snowflake on her tongue, the sensation of ice melting in her throat, settling deep in her stomach. And a fire at her breast.

> *"And so, all the night-tide, I lie down by the side*
> *Of my darling, my darling, my life and my bride*
> *In her sepulchre there by the sea—*
> *In her tomb by the side of the sea."*

She sang, and it was beautiful. The poem itself had become the song. She'd never heard such music before. It was as though Poe had composed "Annabel Lee" especially for this melody. She clung to the poem and the familiarity of it, how well it lent itself to the song her own voice sang. She clung to nostalgia, to daydreams and fantasy. Azazel was part of her now. Safe, harmless, secret.

At the conclusion of the song, Azza cried out in Bryony's voice, "Yes, darling, we did it! Hold on to me now. Hold on a little longer. I want to try something." He took her upstairs and sat her down at the vanity. He smiled with her mouth into the mirror and began to run a comb through her hair. Her fingers wove complex braids as though she'd been doing it her entire life. It was so natural, so easy. She didn't even have to try.

Bryony did not reject Azazel that night. She clung to him throughout the evening. They drank tea in the same body. They read more poetry. At last, they sat down together, and the angel stood without her. It felt like releasing a long-held breath. Azza immediately turned to Bryony, took her into his arms, and lifted her feet off the floor. "I knew you could do it, little orb-weaver. I knew you could." He set her down and kissed her forehead like it was the most normal thing in the world—even though he was a monster who'd just taken control of her body for hours.

She shuddered, shook the unwelcome thoughts from her head, and wrapped her arms around the angel's neck. An ally was an ally, but it was about time she admitted that she kind of liked him too.

CHAPTER TWENTY-SEVEN

Bryony didn't hesitate when Azazel asked her which angel she wanted to try conjuring first. He sat across her dining table, sipped his tea, and began to explain why they should probably avoid summoning an archangel for their first attempt. She cut in before he could finish. "Daniel!" He was the only other angel she'd seen who wasn't swallowing people alive. Sure, he'd been locking lips with the Black Armada's commodore at the time, and that had certainly disturbed Bryony to some degree. But now she felt quite differently about it.

Azza looked confused. "But Daniel's a watcher, darling. He was bound when I was."

A watcher? That explained a lot about him. She'd come to think of watchers the way she'd come to think of nephilim—as anti-angels. "He's not bound. I've seen him." She was actually excited to meet the cherub again. This time, she would face him and stand tall and not run away.

"Are you certain it was Daniel you saw?"

Bryony nodded. "At least Michael seemed sure when he told me who it was. The angel was a cherub—I remember that—and his light was very bronze."

Azza's eyes welled a bit as Bryony described the cherub she'd seen on *Dragonfly* that dark night. He muttered, "Dani," and bit back a grin. He was still staring into his tea, smiling to himself when Bryony tapped his hand to bring him back. He glanced up. "Are you sure you want to summon Daniel, little orb-weaver? He may prove a challenge. As far as I know, he hasn't spoken a word since he broke his oath to sire a child. He refused to defend himself when judgment finally came for the watchers. He didn't want to choose between lying and betraying our chief captain, so he vowed silence until silence became part of his nature. What I mean to say is, that cherub is beyond obstinate. For years, he refused to answer to the name the humans gave him. There's no guarantee he'll do so now."

Bryony just blinked at him. "I'm sorry, did you say humans named him?"

"And me. Did you think we came with these names? In our world, sound is for worship, not communication. Only our god had a spoken name, and that name was a secret revealed to very few. Even our species were named by men."

"So your species . . . What was it again?"

"Ishim, darling. Ish."

"You mean humans decided to call your kind *ishim*?"

"Yes."

"And your name wasn't Azazel before you came to our world?" He shook his head. She could hardly believe it. "Did you have anything like a name in your world?"

"I did. I still do."

"What is it?"

He hummed in thought. "Do you really want to know?"

"I really do."

"Then hold still." Azza brought his chair close and set her teacup aside. Then he leaned in and positioned one hand on either side of her face. "This will feel like a kiss, but don't fret. It's just an introduction."

For a moment, Bryony had the urge to push him away, but she was certain doing so would be intolerably rude. After all, this was just a cultural difference, wasn't it? How offensive would it be to refuse to learn a person's name? Very, she decided. While she was busy overanalyzing her situation, Azza barely touched his lips to hers and let out a long, cold breath. That was all it took.

She knew him. His true name was the memory of a feeling.

Long ago, Bryony had stood on a hillside at dawn and stared out at a frozen landscape. There were drifts of snow, and delicate icicles hung from the twigs and branches of dormant trees. Sunlight refracted through tiny ice crystals that were suspended in the air like dust. When she squinted, she saw little rainbows everywhere. A reflection of beauty. A dance of light. She'd wanted to stare at that spectacle forever.

When Azza pulled away at last, Bryony had to steady herself on the table. "That's . . ." She grappled with what to say. "That's such a beautiful name."

"Thank you." His smile was full of unmistakable pride. "If you like, one day, I'll show you the name I've given you." Bryony gaped at him. But of course he'd named her. Humans had named the otherworldly creatures that crashed into their reality. Humans had called them *angels*. Why would angels not name humans in turn? Azza chuckled at her astonishment. "Shall we summon Daniel while you remember my name? It might help to encourage trust."

"I won't forget your name," she said, and she meant it. It was like one of those names she wanted to repeat again and again just to hear the music of it. Now she knew how inadequate the word *Azazel* truly was.

He smiled and held both her hands in his. "Stay close, little orb-weaver." She looked away and breathed through the fear as he transformed into a glacial creature. She recalled his name as he melted under her skin and raced through her veins. She recalled dancing with him, playing a duet with him, singing "Annabel Lee." She gave him her body, her hands, and her voice. She gave him her autonomy—lent it, really—because she knew he wouldn't keep it. He'd never take more than he needed. He'd never ask for more than she was willing to give.

With him, building the salt circle was second nature. The words they wrote into it were like old friends. The song they sang was a familiar anthem, and the language they spoke sounded like home. When the web and lure were complete, Bryony spoke the summons in English. "I command you, Daniel, appear in my circle in fair and comely form without noise or deformity. Come now, angel—visibly, peacefully, affably—without delay. Speak to me in a clear and perfect voice."

In the dim light of her oven lamp, Bryony began to make out the shape of her prey. It filled the space. It was animal, and it was human. It had row upon row of long, sharp teeth. Its wings curled against the ceiling of her kitchen, and she had to shield her eyes from its brilliant, bronze light.

"Appear as a man within the boundaries I have drawn," she clarified. "Come now, Daniel. Speak to me. I command you." Her tongue knew the right words to say—even though she didn't—but Daniel struggled to disobey. His form shifted. His faces shrank. His claws clenched in the air. He was indeed obstinate. Then Bryony remembered something Azza had told her about the angel she was attempting to summon, and she sent a thought to her possessor. *Don't command him to speak. Respect his vow.*

She felt Azazel's smile, warm and proud. In her voice, he said, "Keep your silence, Daniel, but appear before me now."

A shape materialized within the circle, and Bryony recognized him as the same man she'd seen kissing the commodore on the quarterdeck. He manifested a physically impressive body with a broad chest, sandy hair, and sharp features. One pair of batlike wings clung to his body like a garment, crossing at his waist and curling around to his back. The other pair stretched to the ceiling and repeatedly drew her attention by scraping the plaster.

Azazel leapt into the circle, threw Bryony's arms around Daniel's neck, and kissed both the angel's cheeks with her mouth. "Dani!" he cried. "How I missed you!"

Bryony did her best to hide her horror as the massive cherub squinted down at her. *It's not me!* she wanted to shout at him. She wouldn't dare be so familiar with a stranger, let alone an angelic one. And after a botched conjuration too. She was just beginning to think she couldn't possibly be more mortified when Azza handed her body back to her. He left her hanging from the neck of a creature who was at least twice her size, even in his significantly reduced shape. She immediately let go, dropped to her feet, and failed to look nonchalant.

Azza quickly retrieved a notepad and pen and handed it to Daniel. The cherub wrote and showed the message to Bryony while he glowered at Azazel. The message read simply, *What the fuck?*

Azza laughed. "I'll brew some tea. Sit, Dani. Make yourself comfortable. We have so much to discuss."

Daniel did not sit, and Bryony mouthed an apology to him. His expression softened, and he wrote, *Fear not. I know his ways.* Then he added, *The circle*, and nodded down at the web she'd built.

"Oh!" she exclaimed. "You can't cross it. How do I fix that?"

Break it.

"Right."

She dragged a foot through the salt circle just as Azza was saying, "Now don't be angry, Dani. We needed to practice, and my little orb-weaver chose to summon you first. It's an honor really. You should be quite pleased."

Bryony cringed and tried to explain herself. "I'd seen you before on *Dragonfly*, so I knew you were one of the good angels."

Daniel cocked his head. Then his face lit up with recognition, and he wrote, *Bryony the traitor?* He stepped from the circle as Bryony's hand flew to her forehead.

"Yes, I know, I know," she said quickly. "And I'm so sorry about that. I didn't mean to hurt anyone . . . Well, except the godhunter, but you saw how that turned out for me."

The cherub winked down at her, and Bryony got her first inkling that the beast had a sense of humor. Perhaps she wasn't about to be flattened into her own kitchen floor, after all.

Daniel pulled a chair out for himself and shrank down enough to fit comfortably into it. He eased his wings around the chairback and let them droop as he sat. He seemed strangely attached to his wings. Bryony wondered why for a moment before the cherub showed her his notepad again. *How is Michael?*

Was there any good way to answer that? "The demon king has taken him and refuses to give him back."

Daniel scowled and wrote, *Ashmedai can be an asshole.*

"Yes." Bryony nodded vigorously. She was beginning to see why Raeni liked this cherub. "I agree."

Azazel set three cups of tea with saucers and sugar cubes onto the table. "Scoot." He shifted Bryony's chair closer to Daniel to make room for himself. Now she was wedged between a titan and a chimera, both of whom were capable of swallowing her whole. She hoped she wasn't letting her discomfort show. Still they had to know she was terrified. Azazel confirmed it by whispering, "I added some liquid courage to yours, darling. I hope you don't mind."

Whisky, thank god. Azza was a true friend, angel or no. She sipped at her tea gratefully while he explained everything to the cherub. He finished on a somber note. "I'd be a fool not to admit I had a hand in the binding of Raphael, but you know why I did it, Dani. Now I just want to make it right."

Daniel arched an eyebrow at his fellow watcher. *Despicable,* he wrote. *But impressive.*

"I couldn't have done it without Ash, you must know. But now Loki has demanded the archangel's release, and our host here has convinced me to acquiesce."

At the name *Loki*, Daniel rose from his chair. Bryony recoiled from the barely suppressed rage in his expression. He scribbled in his notebook. *Don't let me see that monster's face!*

Azza's mouth dropped open. "Goodness! Such passion."

Bryony felt the need to defend the cherub, whose anger, she thought, was more than justified. "Loki took Daniel's shape and made out with his girlfriend." Then she considered what she was saying. "Kind of like what you did to me."

For the briefest moment, Azza's expression darkened. He looked so troubled she almost regretted pointing out his transgression. What he'd done, he'd done to save his granddaughter's life, and Bryony had already forgiven him for it. She wanted to reassure him, but he quickly found his smile again and began eagerly questioning the cherub. "A girlfriend? Dani, this is so exciting. Tell me everything. Who is she? How did you meet her? What's she like?"

Bryony wished she could shrink down in her chair and disappear. Daniel glared at her like she'd just spoiled Santa for a room full of children. He wrote, *Not your business, Azza.*

"I suppose it's not." Azazel sighed. "So much for small talk then."

The large cherub sat back down and massaged his brow. Bryony got the impression he tolerated no nonsense, which was definitely something he had in common with Raeni. No wonder they got along so well. The kiss she'd accidentally witnessed flashed through her mind, and she blushed at the memory. It was so tender, so sweet, so private. Daniel was right. It wasn't anyone's business but his own. She gulped and missed Michael so much she nearly cried.

Azza shook off his disappointment and got to the point. "Well, Ash won't allow us to unbind Raphael, and now the precocious petal is keeping a hostage. Don't be hard on him," he added when Daniel scowled again. "He has a few good reasons to hate the archangel. Until recently, I felt the same. The trouble is, as I'm sure you know, our friends in the heavens have intentionally crippled scientific advancement. Mortals need the Angel of Healing now more than ever." The corners of his mouth turned down. "In particular, my own descendant."

Before he'd quite finished his explanation, Daniel wrote a message and flashed it at him. *And her.* The cherub pointed to Bryony.

"Well, yes, obviously."

Daniel narrowed his eyes and added, *I smell reverence.*

Azza looked taken aback. "It's not what you think it is, Dani."

Daniel stabbed at his notepad with the pen, emphasizing what he'd just written. Then he scribbled again. His handwriting was so hurried that Bryony struggled to read it at first. *You've found a new god. Does she know it?*

"Yes," Azza muttered. "And I've been duly chastised."

Now Daniel wrote to Bryony. *Good. He'll try worship again. Don't allow it.*

"Please, Dani. You say that like I'm some kind of monster." Azza forced a smile.

You are. Daniel underlined for emphasis.

Azazel said nothing in response. The history between the watchers was ancient. Bryony knew she couldn't begin to understand it, but she also knew she would never forget the artificial smile her friend wore now. It was so many things at once—fear, anger, pain. It was everything but happiness.

Finally, Daniel withdrew his notepad, and Azazel dropped his smile.

"This is ridiculous." Bryony stood and collected the empty teacups. "Azza's done nothing he should be ashamed of. He stumbled once and stopped the second I asked him to. He hasn't stumbled again. Anyway, none of this matters when it comes to getting medicine back, and that's all I care about right now. So it was lovely to see you again, Daniel, but Azza and I have a lot more work to do if we're going to conjure an archangel in two days. Please, say hello to Raeni for me."

She meant to hurry Daniel out the door, but the cherub stayed anchored to his chair and glowered at Azazel who laughed nervously and said, "We don't have a choice, darling."

Which archangel? Though Daniel had taken the time to write the question, if Bryony were to judge based on the horrified expression he wore, he already knew the answer.

Azza looked sheepish. "It has to be Michael, Dani. We need to raise Rahab."

That only doubled Daniel's alarm. *Raphael is in the deep?*

"I'm afraid so."

Jesus fucking Christ, Azza!

"I don't bind by halves." Azazel shrugged.

Daniel massaged his brow again. He looked like he was dealing with a petulant child who'd taken a prank too far. Then he began to write and tore one page after another from the notebook, laying them out on the table for both Bryony and Azza to see. It was a plan and a bold one. Daniel advised Bryony to bring all her allies to the summoning, including Loki. He made a disgusted face when he mentioned the shapeshifter, but he was determined. If the archangel Michael fought the circle, she would need every power she knew to help contain him. And they had to contain him if they wanted to survive the summoning.

Last and most shockingly, Daniel insisted the conjuration be performed aboard *Dragonfly*. The armada was close. Raeni had turned them north—against the prevailing winds—in pursuit of the healing sword, and the sea would weaken the archangel, though not by much.

Bryony could barely contain her influx of conflicting emotions. She was afraid to see the crew again after what she'd done to them, but she was eager, too. She wanted to beg forgiveness of Dara and Chuy. Especially Chuy. She hadn't seen him since she was exposed as a fraud. She'd give anything for the chance to apologize to him, but she also knew the danger a conjuration like this would put him in—him and everyone else. If it all went wrong, the archangel Michael could swallow every ship in the armada without a second thought.

Then again, if she knew the crew of the Black Armada at all, there wasn't a chance in hell they would turn this opportunity down.

CHAPTER TWENTY-EIGHT

*T*he *demon king is cheap,* was all Michael could think as he sat in one of two queen-sized beds and flipped through a woefully insufficient number of television channels. He hadn't had the opportunity to see much television in his life. These days, the technology belonged primarily to wealthier types and was certainly not to be found anywhere in the Black Armada. But now he had nothing else to do, and his dissatisfaction with the luxury mounted.

He still wore the chain leash, which he thought unnecessary considering he and Ash were now in agreement. The demon king was as short on trust as he was on cash, apparently. But Michael's wounds had been dressed, and he'd been made relatively comfortable. The room was clean enough with a faded, beige carpet and floral comforters. Though the shower was much too small, he was grateful for hot water. And though the view was little more than the brick wall of the building next door, the natural light felt like a treat. Even so, a supposed king booking a room as plain as this one seemed outlandish.

Michael's one small pleasure was an amusing little reality show he'd discovered in which brides-to-be selected wedding gowns with their closest family and frequently wept for joy when they found one they liked. The stakes were so small he could actually relax while he watched it. He could lose himself in thought and come back to it without having to figure out what he'd missed. And some of the gowns were quite attractive.

Halfway through an episode, Ash burst into the room and slammed the door. "Your woman is detrimentally headstrong," he grumbled. Then he glanced at the television, frowned, and unplugged it. "No pornography."

Michael sputtered some time before he managed to respond. "Porn . . . Excuse me?"

"Wedding gowns, for crying out loud. Do you even know what you are?"

"Yes." Michael glared at him. "I'm an amateur tailor, not a hormonal teenager."

Ash rolled his eyes. "You make clothes for women?"

"Not yet, but I thought I might. I have to make a living somehow. I do have a life outside this hotel room."

"Not for much longer." Ashmedai sat at the foot of his bed and kicked off his shoes. His talons unfolded and stretched out in a way that was simultaneously grotesque and satisfying. "Your woman and my former employer have been playing us this entire time. It's obvious they never had any intention to honor the bet. I expected to be dragged halfway around the world looking at monks and gurus and wise old priests. She's just shown me her penultimate man in this wager, and do you know who he was? Can you guess?"

Michael groaned and leaned back against the headboard. He wished he'd been allowed to see the end of the episode at least. Which gown would the bride-to-be choose? The A-line or the mermaid? He was partial to the sheer overlay himself, but he didn't hold out much hope for it.

Ash waited a moment for Michael to guess, and then gave up when it was apparent the conversation was not going to go the way he wanted. "A plumber. She chose some random plumber in her home town. She isn't even trying."

Michael muttered, "She should have chosen a carpenter."

"What?" the demon king snapped.

"It's a joke. Never mind."

Ashmedai narrowed his eyes in an obvious effort to suss out the punchline. Then he snorted and stifled a laugh. "Not funny. Listen, you impertinent fool. Your woman has been seduced by an angel—a watcher, no less. Where is your outrage? Where is your righteous fury?"

Michael dropped his head into his hands and groaned. He was tired of explaining himself. "I just find it hard to believe she's really been seduced. Azazel doesn't know her." It was a mantra Michael had repeated to himself over the last week, and by now he almost believed it. "She's not an open book."

"Oh, she's open to him." Ash half smiled, half grimaced. "Wide open. By now he knows her inside and out, literally. They've already summoned an angel together." He stood, pulled some torn notebook pages from his pocket, and waved them around. "One who works for the Black Armada, apparently. They didn't even bother to burn the evidence—just threw it out like I wouldn't come looking for it."

"Daniel." Michael bit his lips.

Ash thrust the pages under his nose. "This means your woman has been successfully possessed. They're ready to summon the archangel. She's going to break our agreement. She has no scruples whatsoever. Well, I know what they're planning now. It won't take much to stop them."

"Correct," Michael said for perhaps the hundredth time. "All you have to do is tell her the truth. She won't summon the archangel once she knows what he did."

"Not if your life is on the line, she won't." Ash pounded a fist into his palm. Then he paused and knit his brow. "But why on earth is the conjuration your focus, little brother? I just told you that your woman has been successfully possessed, and you react as though it's nothing. Where's that mad jealousy you should have inherited from your father?"

"I had a mother too. Maybe I inherited some traits from her." Little did Ashmedai know this was Michael's most fervent wish. "Or maybe I'm my own person and not just a composite of my parents."

"Fascinating." The demon king stopped pacing and squinted down at Michael. "You understand an *angel* has been *inside* your woman."

Michael felt an old heat rise up in him, but he quickly tamped it down. "I trust her." He said it as much to convince himself as he did to convince Ashmedai.

"Her?" Ash hammered one finger on top of Michael's skull. "It's *him* you have to worry about. He's the epitome of over-indulgent beauty, and I don't mean just his appearance. His personality is pure seduction, a veritable symphony of glamour and charm. He's impossible to ignore or resist."

"Really?" Relief welled in Michael's chest, and he tipped his head back to breathe more deeply. "Thank god. You actually had me worried for a moment."

Ashmedai's eye twitched. "Have you gone mad already? Has worship finally liquified your pathetic, love-addled brain?"

"No, I just know her. To be honest, if Azazel is at all the way you describe him, I'd say you are far closer to her type than he is."

The demon king stood aghast. "Unbelievable. You're no nephil, and you're no son of Samael—that's for damn sure. I must have made a mistake when I identified you."

Michael shook his head and grinned. He'd done it. He'd actually faced his own jealousy and wrestled it back down. He'd snuffed out the ghost of his father. It had taken real work, real sweat and effort to overcome his instincts, but he'd done it. With her help. He was lucky, so lucky to have fallen in love with Bryony Moss. "It wasn't me you mistook." He closed his eyes and thanked the stars for bringing him such good fortune. "It was her."

"You've been practicing *what?*" Loki's face turned bright red as he slammed his palms against the table and half stood in the booth at Martha's Café. Meeting at Martha's had been Bryony's idea. She'd assumed a familiar, public location would keep the shapeshifter from making a scene. She'd been wrong.

She cleared her throat and repeated herself. "Possession."

"Oh, I heard you. I just don't believe it." The Jötunn's icy-blue eyes flicked from Bryony to Azza and back again. "Have you both lost your minds?"

Azza sat calmly munching on biscotti and sipping Martha's best espresso, which Bryony had insisted he try. He set his demitasse down and smiled. "It's the only way to unbind Raphael, darling. You did want me to unbind Raphael, yes? I require a mortal-born body to do so."

"So use someone else," Loki snarled.

"Not possible, I'm afraid. My partner must be willing, and not even my granddaughter would agree to summon the archangel Michael. Not to mention the fact that Ashmedai is keeping a hostage and has given us a deadline. Although our little god has brilliantly extended that deadline, I still won't be able to possess another partner in so little time."

"Ashmedai's hostage can go to hell." Loki waved a dismissive hand as he sat back down, and Bryony shot daggers at him.

Azza sipped his espresso. "And so he will if he's killed, in a manner of speaking. Then you can explain to the Angel of Death why you sent his son to hell prematurely."

"It'll be for the demon king to explain why he killed him," Loki countered.

"Oh, I doubt Samael will see much difference between you. He's never been a reasonable sort. On the other hand, you can join us and aid in a rescue you yourself demanded. Our goal is to keep the archangel

Michael contained within the circle until we secure a contract with him. If the circle is broken, we'll need you to keep the ship afloat while I fight to contain him again."

"Fight?" Loki snorted. "You're not going to fight. You're just going to stand there and dazzle your opponent with perfect eyeliner."

Azza seemed to have expected the attitude. His smile was serene and settled. "Care to go again, darling? I'm up for a rematch if you are."

"Absolutely not!" Loki folded his arms and leaned back. "You have an unfair advantage in that I actually care about the future of this café and its owner. You're a mindless tornado is what you are."

Bryony took the opportunity to ask him outright. "So will you do it? Will you protect *Dragonfly*? You owe the armada that much at least."

Loki scoffed. "Of course I'll do it, Bryony, but not because I owe the armada a damn thing. I owe you and only you. If you want to let this"—he made a disgusted face—"creature take control of your body, that's your business. Just know I don't approve."

Azza stared into his demitasse. "If you truly care about the little god's safety, you'll want her possessed during this conjuration. I can move her to safety more quickly from within. If the archangel Michael feels he's been threatened, he's likely to lash out, and when he does—"

Loki cut in. "When he does, I'll bury him."

The look on the watcher's face was a cocktail of incredulity and fondness. He seemed to be growing oddly attached to the Jötunn despite everything. "You do understand the danger inherent in our endeavor, don't you? This isn't a lesser angel we're summoning. This is the general."

Loki waved away his concerns. "Angelic hierarchies mean nothing to the Jötnar. Your general doesn't scare me."

To Bryony, the false confidence in Loki's boast was obvious, but it didn't seem as obvious to Azza, who furrowed his brow in concern. "He should scare you. Just promise not to take him on alone."

"I'll wait for your signal, oh valiant one."

"Or Daniel's," Azza added.

At the name *Daniel,* Loki tried to stand, bumped his thighs on the table, and sat back down again. "I'm out."

"Because of Daniel?" Azza blinked in astonishment. "You're not afraid of the archangel Michael, but you'll pull out over a watcher?"

"I told you your hierarchies mean nothing to me. Your personal vendettas, on the other hand . . ."

"Daniel is the one who asked that you be there," Bryony assured him.

Loki grumbled, "Of course he did. Revenge is a dish best served on one's own turf."

"I'll have the death sword with me," Bryony reminded him. Loki's constant waffling between astounding courage and unbelievable cowardice made him impossible to predict. "I won't let Daniel hurt you."

"That cherub's a brute," Loki said. "It won't be as easy as taming your own personal unicorn over there."

Azazel sighed, and with an air of cool detachment, he began to trace patterns onto the table. Wherever his finger touched, the lacquer melted into a groove, exposing the pennies beneath. He said, "Because they're beautiful, unicorns are often underestimated."

Loki scowled. "You'd better be able to fix that." He was acting brave, but Bryony could tell he was beginning to regret his big talk. After all, it was Loki himself who'd told Bryony not to underestimate Azazel. Now he was leaning back in the booth, ready to run if he needed to, not quite sure where the angel was taking this. He didn't have to wonder long.

Once Azza had finished etching a small, intricate circle into the café table, he reached across, seized Loki's wrist, and slammed the Jötunn's palm down directly in its center. "Stay," he commanded. And though Loki tried with all his might, he could not for the life of him tear his hand from the circle. "Everyone seems to forget that unicorns have a weapon on hand at all times." Azza tapped the center of his own forehead. "Don't assume a beautiful creature can't fight ugly."

At those words, Loki's pinned hand began to change. It bloated, and the skin sloughed off at the tips of his fingers. Decay crept up his arm.

When his bones began to show and mold grew over his fingernails, he started to scream.

"Quiet," Azza commanded in a whisper, and the Jötunn could no longer open his mouth. "I don't think it's brute strength you really have to worry about, darling. Between Daniel and I, who do you think is more dangerous now?"

Azza flicked at Loki's hand as though it were a bothersome fly. The circle, the rot, and the mold were instantly gone. Loki cradled his hand and stared at the angel in horror. "For fuck's sake!" he shouted.

"I'm on your side as long as you're on hers," Azazel concluded.

Loki gawked at him. "You could've fooled me. Was that really necessary?"

"No." The watcher grinned. "But it was amusing. You should have seen your face." He laughed his musical laugh. "Two things I'd like you to keep in mind following that little demonstration. First, Daniel will not cross me or my allies. He knows what I'm capable of. Second, *I* am afraid of the archangel Michael. You should be too. Don't do anything reckless. We'll take him on together. Three against one. With the sea and the circle both weakening him, I'd say we stand less than a twenty percent chance of subduing the leader of the angels. But it's a chance we have to take."

Chapter Twenty-Nine

Anchored in autumn, *Dragonfly* felt more like a ghost ship than a working brigantine. Its black sails were furled tight, casting a stark silhouette against the backdrop of a gray sky. The sea was a dark shadow around them with little whitecaps slapping the hull. The energy of summer and the bustle of travel were gone. The armada was holed up in the Salish Sea for the season, and the crew was far too quiet.

Bryony hugged herself against the chill and looked around warily for people she knew. Her view was soon filled by the Black Armada's commodore, who stood before her, arms crossed, all business. She wore her usual tall boots and a black peacoat. "Where's your conjuring angel?" she asked. It seemed there would be no time lost to sentimentalities.

"Resting," Bryony answered.

Raeni nodded. "As is Daniel. He's saving his strength for the archangel." It was so strange to have angels in common with the commodore. The two of them lived in a different world now that Daniel and Azza were part of it. None of the other crew could begin to understand. "And where is our erstwhile navigator?"

Bryony cocked her head. Did Raeni really not know? "He's . . . been taken. By the demon king? He's being held hostage. That's why we have to do this in secret."

A look of worry crossed the commodore's face. Then she turned her eyes to heaven and shook a fist at the sky. "Daniel! Tell me *everything*, you dolt!" She cleared her throat and calmed herself as Andrew approached.

"The cabin is ready, Commodore," he said. He didn't even look at Bryony, and she flashed back to holding a gun to his chest and threatening to shoot him with it. She supposed she deserved one cold shoulder—at least Loki was getting the other one. Though Andrew refused to acknowledge the trickster, their juxtaposition made their similarities undeniable. Loki was a little rosier in the cheeks, a touch narrower at the shoulders, and perhaps an inch or two taller, but they could have easily been mistaken for brothers. Bryony wondered whether the shapeshifter's human body was inspired by the man she once thought of as a California Viking, but she would have to ask later.

The commodore scowled at the sky again and muttered, "I wasn't informed we were working against a demon. Ah, well." She turned her attention back to Bryony. "You know how big this could be for us, don't you?"

Bryony nodded.

"You know we're all putting our lives on the line for this? All of us."

Again, Bryony nodded, a little ashamed of how much she asked of them.

Raeni gripped her shoulder and squeezed. "Then know this. Everything you did to us, every lie you told, and every ill intention you had—succeed at this, and you'll have made it up tenfold." The commodore shook her head, and the briefest flicker of affection crossed her face. "I can't believe you survived. You and that fool Michael who wears his heart on his sleeve. So . . . Raphael it is."

The commodore stepped back and addressed her entire crew. "We're playing with the big boys today, children, and we've the rare opportunity to win a powerful game piece! Remember why you're doing this! We will not back down! This is war! Say your goodbyes while you can!" She was magnificent, as usual, and Bryony noted her machete was still at her hip, tucked under her coat like a secret between them. Raeni glanced down at Bryony with a twinkle in her eye. "That goes for you too, medic." And she nodded to something over Bryony's shoulder.

When Bryony turned around, she found *Papillon*'s tattooed captain standing behind her. He instantly grabbed her and held her in his long arms. Chuy. He'd been the first to smile at her, the first to trust her, and now he was the first to openly welcome her back. Too many thoughts competed for her voice at once, and she was left speechless.

"Chuy insisted on being aboard when you arrived," Raeni said.

"You're alive." Chuy squeezed her tight. "They told me you weren't. But when they said Michael went after you, I knew he'd find a way to save you. I knew it."

As a half angel, Michael had very few friends among the crew of the Black Armada. Many who gave everything to fight the angels did so because the angels had taken every other reason they had to live. Bryony understood the feeling. The first time she'd learned what Michael was, she'd wanted to run from him, but she hadn't. Chuy hadn't, Dara hadn't, and Raeni hadn't. Bryony was proud to be among people who could rip their hatred out at the roots when it became the right thing to do. It was something she'd not thought herself capable of, but Michael had changed her.

Michael had changed everything.

Chuy finally let her go and grinned down at her. "Well, as long as luck's on our side, we'd better tackle the scary jobs."

"Yes." It was all Bryony could do to keep from crying. "We'd better."

"Absolutely," Raeni broke in. "The captain's quarters are ready when you are. According to Daniel, you'll need privacy for the possession. I can't tell you how displeased I am that he's so familiar with the practice. He'll be explaining some things to me when this is said and done—I can promise you that. See you on the other side, medic." And she marched off to supervise her crew.

With enormous reluctance, Bryony squeezed Chuy's hand in a quick goodbye. "We'll get through this," she said to him.

Chuy grinned at her. "I know."

Before she lost her composure completely, Bryony headed toward that ornate door she'd first opened the day she met Michael. The captain's quarters were unchanged. It touched her to see that her own little bunk was just as she'd left it, as was Michael's considerably larger one. There they'd shared their first kiss. And there, on the floor, was where they'd sat while Bryony tested all Michael's needles to prove he was not the godhunter. She could almost feel his oversized hand closing around hers, the impression of his sailmaker's palm against her bare skin. She swallowed a sob and gritted her teeth. There was no time to cry.

At the center of the chart table was a glass mixing bowl filled almost entirely with what appeared to be salt. A stock pot half full of water sat beside it. It was a strange setup, but Bryony didn't have much time to examine it before a figure began to materialize before her. It was fuzzy around the edges, like a mist coming together in the shape of a man. And then it was Azazel, and Bryony was no longer alone.

The angel had changed his colors again. Now his hair was a deep garnet at the roots that faded to tangerine. Around his amber eyes, he wore a red and charcoal pattern that made her think of waning embers. His coat was a shadowy color, embroidered with gold and green thread. He looked like a forest fire in the distance, something beautiful and terrifying all at once. He took her breath away. It was probably a good thing Michael couldn't see him now.

Azza smiled and spread his arms in a quiet flourish. "Shall we begin?"

"What's all this for?" Bryony nodded down at the chart table.

"For the net, of course. As we're on a moving vessel, it'll be wise to make our salt into a paste." He pressed a finger to his lips and frowned. "You're right-handed, aren't you?"

"Yes, but . . . why?" A sudden edge of nausea crept up on Bryony. Yesterday, this had been a challenge she thought she could meet. But now, the idea that she would soon come face to face with a real archangel overwhelmed her. She groaned. "Oh god, this is really happening."

"Come now. You'll be fine. I swear I won't let anything happen to you." Azza pulled her into his arms and pressed her cheek to his chest. "This is the easy part," he whispered. His hand trailed down her left arm until it came to rest just above her wrist. "Forgive me, darling." And he cut into her skin with an invisible blade.

The sting came first, and then her wrist began to burn. The angel gripped her left arm and pulled her toward the table. She stumbled as he plunged her hand into the stockpot and held it there. "What the hell!" She glared up at him.

"To lure an archangel, one must make a sacrifice. They crave after sacrifice." He chuckled darkly. "The beasts."

Bryony looked into the stockpot and saw her own blood swirling with the water. "You could have warned me," she grumbled.

"Should I have? I'm sorry for that. I thought the pain would be easier if you didn't anticipate it."

She chewed at her lip as her wrist throbbed. The wound wasn't too big, maybe an inch at most, and it wasn't deep either. But all around it a raised pattern began to bloom. It looked like a lace teardrop. It stretched halfway up her forearm and dipped just below her wrist. The pattern was intricate, and it shimmered green and orange like oxidized copper where the light touched it.

She caught her breath as the truth dawned on her. "Did you cut me with your sword?"

He leaned down until his mouth was at her ear. "Can you ever forgive me, little god?"

She should have been angry, furious even, but she wasn't. Bryony would have given an entire limb to bring medicine back, and Azza was risking so much to help her. She didn't think he really had to. He'd bested Loki, and he could have bested Bryony, too, the instant she'd fallen asleep that first night. No, he wasn't doing this for himself. She recalled the cracks in the watcher's voice the night he finally broke down in front of her, the way he couldn't even hold his body together. How much had he suffered all those years in the dark, all because he'd changed his mind about humanity? And now he was doing it again. Azazel—a lesser angel, a defeated watcher—was willing to fight the archangel Michael alongside a powerless god and an outcast Jötunn, all for the love of the mortal world.

Azza pulled her hand from the water and pressed a piece of clean gauze to her wound. He held her wrist tight where he'd cut her and wrapped a bandage around it. Her new tattoo peeked out from beneath the gauze. She was suddenly excited to show it to Chuy, who she was certain would appreciate it even more than she did.

"How long will it last?" she asked, tracing the edges of the pattern.

"It will last as long as you love it, darling. It wants to be beautiful to your eyes."

"What does it mean?"

He touched a hand to her cheek. "It means you're under my protection. You met my weapon and walked away with your life. It means I love you."

The confession left her stunned. She stared in disbelief as Azza began to slowly pour the water into the mixing bowl and stir her blood into the salt like he was only making marzipan. There was an almost mechanical emptiness about the way he worked. Either he'd done this before, or he was overwhelmed again and could not express feeling. She guessed it was a little of both. In reality, neither of them knew what would become of them if they caught the archangel Michael in their net. Bryony could be swallowed whole. Azza could be bound in darkness for another millennium. They risked everything, and neither one of them had really spoken of it.

"I love you too," she said at last. Azazel stopped stirring and glanced up. "I mean it seriously this time. Loki would say I've gotten too attached. He says I always show my hand, but I don't care. For whatever it's worth, you're under my protection too. If Raphael binds you again, I'll spend the rest of my life fighting to free you." She tried to smile as he dropped the spoon into the bowl and stopped breathing completely. "I can't mark you or anything—"

"You already have." His voice was low and earnest. "Can't you see it?"

Bryony shook her head, and Azazel began to melt. The solid colors left his body, dissolving away like Bryony's blood in the pot of water. What was left was the man-shaped iceberg with fire at its breast and clinging snow at its hands and feet. "Will you allow me to show you through worship?" he asked.

Bryony took a step back, but Azza reassured her. "It will strengthen us both. I'll not be driven to madness if that's your concern. My heart was won many thousands of years ago, and she'll have it for a thousand more. But I've been godless for so long."

The creature he'd become sank to its knees, and this time, Bryony did not try to stop it. Instead, she focused on the memory of his name—his real name—the sun reflected on a snowy hillside, the crisp air of winter, little rainbows everywhere. "Azza," she whispered.

The watcher touched his forehead to the floor and sent waves of perfect bliss to his god. His voice was a whisper of steam, the ghost of water devoured by fire. His words were simple. "I hunger." And Bryony knew exactly what he meant. She was hungry too. She had no idea how hungry she'd been until the angel began to feed her.

Instinctively, she reached down and laid a hand on the back of the creature's head as though blessing it. Her fingers dipped below the surface of half melted ice. It felt like a river in the first days of spring—alive at last, but shockingly cold despite the warmth of the sun.

Azazel sighed at her touch. "My god was cruel," he said. "My god was unyielding and pitiless." He hesitated, and just for a moment, Bryony felt ice form at the tips of her fingers and then melt again. "I hunger for mercy, for kindness. I always have. Forgive me. Forgive me for being soft and weak, for leaving my daughters to darkness. Forgive my pride, my carelessness, my frivolity. Show mercy . . ." His inhuman voice caught, and Bryony understood that he wasn't really with her anymore. He'd gone back in time, back before his binding. This was his original supplication. "Please, don't take the light from my eyes, God.

Don't take the color from my palette. I won't fall again. I swear it. I'll never stumble again."

Bryony knelt down with him and laid her hands over what would have been his shoulder blades if he were human. "That's enough, Azza. Come back to me now."

Color crawled into his skin, and soon he was human again, wearing his forest-fire ensemble. He did not lift his head. "Will you say it?"

She knew what he wanted to hear, but she'd never been that kind of god. She provided a service, and however people wanted to live the rest of their lives was entirely up to them. It was neither her place to condemn nor forgive as far as she was concerned. But then she thought of how long the angel must have waited to hear those words from his god, how he must have longed for them while he was alone in darkness, bound as stone. She recalled how it felt to be tied to the mast of *Dragonfly* after the crew had discovered her deception, how badly she had craved understanding, forgiveness. How much greater would Azazel's craving be?

"I forgive you," she said, but she couldn't help amending it. "But fall as often as you like, Azza, especially if you're falling in love. Fall over and over again, and don't be afraid to stumble. I'll be here to catch you."

The figure under her arms shuddered and stilled. He lifted his head, and his brightly colored hair fell away from his face. Each time she saw him up close, she had to remind herself that he could only make himself this beautiful because he knew how human eyes would see him. Ash had suggested that the watcher Azazel was an insatiable creature, that he was seductive by design. He certainly could have been if that was his desire. Instead, he'd made himself into a work of art. He was the sort of beauty she might have found in the halls of a museum, hanging on the walls or sculpted into clay.

Now he looked new again, bright and stunning. He rose, stretched, and bounced on the balls of his feet like an athlete preparing for a race. His cheeks were flushed and his eyes radiant. "I feel so refreshed!" he cried. "Don't you? I feel like I can do anything." He took her by both hands, grinning like they'd already won. "*We* can do anything. Let's net ourselves an archangel, shall we?"

Chapter Thirty

Though Michael had long grown used to the angelic manifestation of cherubim, Ashmedai wasn't so much a cherub as he was a beast who looked uncannily like a cherub. He had only three faces and one set of wings, which left him almost lopsided in appearance. He lacked the cohesion of the cherubim. He was the kind of creature a child might have glued together out of bits of other creatures. Still he was formidable, and he was currently carrying Michael at an altitude that would mean certain death if he lost his grip.

Michael didn't dare move a muscle or say a word. He barely dared to breathe until he was finally tipped onto his feet aboard *Dragonfly*. Every face on deck turned to see him. He'd lived with the crew for years, and now they stared aghast, too silent, too terrified to say a word to him. The commodore's hand was on the hilt of her machete, but she didn't draw it. Michael bowed his head. There was something shameful about being presented to his former crewmates at the wrong end of a chain leash.

"I am the Aeshma Daeva, king of demons, lord of the ancient nephilim." Ash's booming voice faded as he spoke, and Michael knew without looking that he was taking his far more palatable human form. "Keep to yourselves, and you will keep your lives. This doesn't concern any of you. I have business with the angel."

Raeni squared her shoulders and lifted her chin. "I'm captain of this ship. You're on my turf now, demon, and Daniel will not see you."

"Daniel?" Ash wrinkled his hawkish nose. "It's the watcher Azazel I've come for. He's about to renege on a wager, and I don't intend to allow it."

The commodore narrowed her eyes. "Care to explain what any of this has to do with my navigator?"

My navigator. Michael could have wept at the words. Had he reason to hope Raeni still considered him part of her crew? Ash quickly shot Michael's optimism to hell. "This is my bargaining chip." He tugged at the chain for emphasis. "He's *my* subject. I'm simply utilizing what's mine, as is my right."

Raeni spat and drew her machete. Ash should not have pissed her off. Perhaps Michael should have warned the demon king about her temper while they were still back at the hotel—or not. He'd never been prouder to be part of the Black Armada. His commodore was furious on his behalf. "You don't rule him yet, demon. While he's flesh and blood, he works for me."

Ash just laughed. "Well, that is a conundrum, I admit. But it's easily solved. I could simply relieve him of his flesh and blood." Several crewmembers drew their weapons. Raeni stopped them with a gesture.

Only Dara dared to speak. "This is why you should have let me keep my gun, Commodore."

"Don't be a fool," Raeni responded without tearing her eyes from the demon king. "A gun would only insult him."

"Who says that's not my aim?"

Michael had to smile despite himself. The crew was ready to defend him. He'd never seen the like, not for his sake—never for his sake. And was that Rose brandishing a cast iron pan? Every last one of them was ready, restless and eager to fight, but Raeni wouldn't allow it. She seemed to be stalling, intentionally holding the demon king's attention.

Unfortunately for them, Ash came to the same conclusion. "This is misdirection," he growled. "Where is he?" Those sharp, hooded eyes darted around *Dragonfly*, first to the quarter deck and then to the forecastle deck, where he found what he was looking for. Movement. A dark, solitary figure crouched down, working at something. Whatever the task, it was so important the figure didn't even look up to see what the ruckus was about. With a shudder, Michael realized it was Bryony, drawing her conjuring circle. Ash started for the forecastle, but the crew got in his way.

Raeni struck first. Her machete met the demon's body with all the effectiveness of a butter knife. Impossible. Michael knew the sharpness of that blade. The demon king more than doubled in size, throwing Andrew off his back before Andrew could bury a hammer in his head. Rose struck fearlessly with her cast iron, though Ash had taken his demonic form again and was impossible to topple. Dylan charged in, but Michael shouted to him. "Don't! He'll kill you! Let the women take him! He can't fight against them!"

Dylan looked confused, but Andrew and Chuy backed away quickly. Andrew shouted to Dara and slid his weapon across the deck to her. She took his hammer in one hand and held a long blade in the other. As soon as Ash tossed Raeni aside, Dara took her place. Michael had never actually seen *Dragonfly*'s strongest deckhand fight, but he'd heard tales. She could not be stopped. Not only was she powerful, but she was fast. Ash could not keep up with her. She was a cat underfoot, weaving around his legs, cutting and digging Andrew's hammer into the creature's thighs. None of her hits made a dent in him, but Michael knew that wasn't the goal.

They were all fighting to give Bryony time.

To the demon king, the women of *Dragonfly* were little more than insects, but he couldn't manage them all at once. They were a swarm, though Michael knew it was only the demon's habitual nature that saved them. Ash could never harm a woman. Maybe the habit had been deliberate in the beginning, but now it was compulsory.

In his struggle with the crew, the demon king had dropped Michael's chain leash, and the port stairway to the forecastle deck was clear.

Michael eyed it and tensed. If he was quick enough, he could run for it before anyone noticed him. He could reach Bryony and tell her the truth about what the archangel had done. She would never go through with the conjuration once she knew. There wasn't a doubt in Michael's mind about that.

Just as he readied himself for the sprint, he felt a subtle tug on the other end of his chain. He turned back to see Loki grinning like a madman behind him. "Hello, snake."

"What are you doing?" Michael snapped. "This isn't the time. Someone has to help Bryony."

"I am." Loki laughed and drew Michael closer, hand over hand, a vicious glint in his eyes. "You *were* the demon's bargaining chip. Now you belong to me."

Michael grabbed his own chain and tugged back. "She's trying to conjure the archangel Michael. Someone has to stop her."

Now Loki was mere inches away, and he grew to match Michael in height. "Are you telling me you've sided with your captor?"

"Yes! And so should you if you care about her at all."

Loki laughed again, and his eyes lit up. "I can't tell you how happy that makes me, snake. Thank you, truly, for giving me this opportunity." Suddenly, his large hand was at Michael's throat shoving him backward across the deck. The Jötunn pinned his victim to the mainmast and wrapped the leash around both the mast and Michael. At the final turn, he opened Michael's mouth and slipped the chain between his teeth. It all happened so quickly Michael couldn't begin to fight back. "It's poetic justice, don't you think?" Loki's voice was low and angry. "Remember when she was here, tied to this mast, alone and afraid? And it was all your fault, godhunter."

Michael wanted to argue, but his tongue was pinned. All he could do was stare up at Bryony, who now stood at the forecastle rail and surveyed the mayhem. The wind whipped around her, pulling strands of hair from her hair tie and sending her skirt into a frenzied dance around her legs. In one hand, propped up like a walking staff, she held a scythe.

Michael recognized his father's weapon at once, though he'd never seen it in another human's hands. What a shape it had taken! It was intimidating. She truly looked like a god upon her cloud, gazing down at her disappointing creation, judging all of them.

"Stop!" she ordered. Her voice was two in one—a woman and an echo of steam. She was possessed. Dear god, she was *possessed*. Michael struggled until the chain began to cut his mouth. Though Ash had told him she'd already been possessed, he could not have predicted the way it would feel to see it for himself. This was Bryony, but it wasn't. She'd been stolen and something foreign left in her place.

Ashmedai was the only one to address her. "We had a bargain!" he roared. "And now you dishonor our agreement! You're a liar and a cheat!"

Bryony laughed. "But you already knew that about me, Ash darling. Remember? What else did you expect?" It wasn't her. It didn't even talk like her.

Ash gripped the rail halfway up the starboard stairway, and Michael could actually hear the wood crack. "You told me you had changed."

"And why did you believe that?" Bryony said. "Why wouldn't I have lied about that too?"

"Azza!" Ash screamed up at the shape of Bryony, thankfully completely unconvinced this attitude was coming from her. "Get out of her, you traitor, you Judas!" The demon king was shaking with rage, but he did not dare approach the death sword, not when it was being wielded by an angel. How did Azazel manage to hold that weapon anyway? As far as Michael knew, for an angel to even touch it took tremendous strength. The ability to function so close to death must have been something Bryony brought to the table. The demon king should not have underestimated her. "I want to speak to the woman," he demanded. "Give her back her tongue, or I'll torment your descendant every day until she regrets her own survival."

In one subtle shift, Bryony's whole demeanor changed. Her voice was entirely her own when she said, "What do you want to say to me?"

The demon king visibly relaxed. "Tell me it matters to you—your word. Tell me it means *something*." He shrank as he spoke, taking on his familiar, human form. "We had a bargain. It had nothing to do with him, or them, or anyone else. It was between you and I." Then he said the words Michael was certain would find the chink in Bryony's armor. "I believed in you."

Bryony leaned into the rail and furrowed her brow. Michael could hardly believe it. The demon king had actually gotten to her. She was ashamed. "Preparations don't nullify our agreement on their own," she said at last. "I haven't conjured anything yet."

"Good!" Ash spread his arms wide in a gesture that somehow meant both surrender and victory. "I'm ready to see your last innocent man."

Darling. Azza's voice broke into Bryony's thoughts. *Darling, what are you doing?*

Keeping my word, Bryony responded to the spirit possessing her. *And winning this wager. Hold on, Azza. We haven't lost yet.*

Convincing Azazel was one thing, but Bryony was hard-pressed to convince herself. This was a long shot. It was a bet against the odds. But if she was ever going to put all her chips on one man . . . "Chuy!"

The captain of *Papillon* stood back with the other men. He put a hand to his chest and mouthed, *Me?* Bryony nodded. Chuy raised his eyebrows and shook his head. He couldn't have known precisely what this was about, but he certainly had an inkling. He was frightened, and he was right to be. Everything now hinged on the demon king's judgement, and Chuy didn't likely believe in his own innocence. But what he didn't know was the standard by which his innocence would be measured. Bryony, on the other hand, did. "Trust me, Chuy," she said to her slender, tattoo-covered friend. "Just trust me, please."

She gestured for him to approach, and he did. As he climbed the stairs to meet the Aeshma Daeva, he looked particularly small to Bryony. Her heart was flooded with doubt, but this was her last chance. This was the last chance for all of them. Chuy gulped and hesitated. His eyes turned up to the demon king. Ashmedai pulled his spectacles from his pocket and balanced them on the bridge of his nose. Then he offered his hand, and Chuy, to his credit, firmly took it.

The examination took only seconds, but to Bryony, it may as well have been hours. In her mind's eye, she saw the day she met Chuy on the beach. She saw the way he smiled at her despite Andrew's suspicion. She heard his welcoming voice, the warmth in everything about him. She saw her own betrayal of his trust and how he never doubted her. Even after she lied to him and tried to steal his pendant, even after she tricked him into breaking his sobriety, he forgave her. He never once treated her as anything other than a trusted friend.

Slowly, Ashmedai's expression began to change. His eyes widened and his mouth dropped open. He was astounded. God he was undone! Bryony could have leapt over the rail and thrown her arms around Chuy's neck. The demon king's hands trembled as he removed his spectacles and folded them again.

We won. She sent the message to Azazel before anyone outside the two of them knew. Then, to Ashmedai, she said, "Your verdict?"

The demon king whirled to face her and pointed an accusing finger. "How did you know? There's no way you could have known! You're no prophet—you've only cheated again!" He took two steps up, and Bryony backed away from him.

"How could I have cheated? I'm not the one who can see into a person's past and future. I only knew Chuy a few days. You already know more of him than I ever did."

Ashmedai's cheeks darkened as Chuy found his voice and finally questioned him. "You . . . saw my future?"

The demon king let his hand fall to his side. His anger seemed to melt at the sound of Chuy's voice. And now it was Bryony's turn to be astounded because there was no mistaking the look on the Aeshma Daeva's face as anything other than pure tenderness. He answered Chuy without turning around. "No, Captain, not your future. *Ours.*" He balled his hands into fists and gritted his teeth at Bryony, the victor, who stared down at her vanquished opponent in utter confusion. For the first time since she'd met him—with his well-tailored suit and sophisticated demeanor—the demon king looked unsettled. He turned back to Chuy and frowned. "But how could she have known?"

"Known what?" Chuy backed away and stumbled on the stairs.

Ash caught him by the arm and then failed to let go again. He stared unblinking at the captain of *Papillon*, like he was seeing a waterfall for the first time in his life, like he was afraid if he looked away it would disappear. "You will break my heart," he muttered. Chuy caught his breath, and Ashmedai finally let go of him. When the demon king turned back to Bryony, his usually stern eyes were rimmed with tears. "You win." His voice was hoarse. "But however you managed it was underhanded, and you should be ashamed. Who helped you? Azza? Loki?"

"No one." Despite her triumph, Bryony felt like a scolded child. Once again, an authority figure accused her of cheating. This time, she really hadn't, but how could she prove it to someone who had no reason to believe her? "It's just . . . Chuy was the only one who trusted me from the beginning, so I thought maybe—"

"Maybe, indeed." Ashmedai quickly pulled himself together. He straightened his vest, which had not been crooked in the first place, and began to methodically button his jacket. "Well, I made a bargain, and I intend to keep it. Conjure your archangel, Ms. Moss. I will do nothing to stop you."

That was when Bryony finally heard Michael's muffled screams, but Azazel had already taken back her tongue.

Chapter Thirty-One

Michael wanted to believe Bryony's eyes had found him for the briefest moment, but she turned away without saying a word. He screamed louder, and Loki replaced the chain in his mouth with a muffling hand. "That's enough of that," he said. "Let her concentrate on what she needs to do."

Crew scrambled to secure the ship and lash down the boats, the oars, anything they had stored on deck. They knew something big was coming, but Michael was certain they could not fathom just how big it really was.

"Brace yourselves!" the demon king shouted over the sounds of frantic work. "When her song is done, she'll summon the archangel Michael, and the archangel himself will demonstrate to you why this was a terrible idea from the start. If he's not immediately subdued, he'll call to his aid a legion of angels the likes of which you've never seen. One thought from him, and they'll be upon you. Can you fight a legion with two watchers and a Jötunn?" He tapped his temple with his index finger. "Use your heads!" Satisfied with his lecture, Ashmedai took Chuy by the wrist and began dragging him away from the chaos. "You're coming with me."

"What?" Chuy stumbled after him. "Wait . . . Why?"

"Because!" Ash stopped abruptly and turned to face him. "You have no idea . . . You weren't supposed to exist. I can't let you die here. I already tried to view this event. All I saw was a wall of light. That's death. Do you understand? It was far more death than *he* could account for on his own." Ash made a sweeping gesture to Michael, and by the sudden, determined look on Chuy's face, he had to know it had been a mistake.

"Michael!" Chuy wrenched his arm free. "What did they do to you?"

Thank god, was all Michael could think. Thank god someone noticed him, someone other than Bryony, who appeared to be completely under the angel's control now. She'd already begun to sing in a strange, inhuman tongue. And worse, the song itself was so melodious, so beautiful he almost, almost wanted to stay chained to the mast just so he could enjoy it a little while longer.

Loki pulled the chain tighter, and Chuy turned back to Ashmedai. "Fine, demon. I'll go with you willingly if you free him first." He pointed to Michael, and Michael shook his head. He wanted to tell Chuy not to sacrifice himself, but he couldn't speak at all.

Ash raised an eyebrow. Michael had learned to read the demon king's expressions over the course of his captivity, and this particular expression definitely read along the lines of, *Who said anything about willingly?* But Ash knit his brow and changed course. "You're right," he muttered. "Of course you're right—you always are." He smiled at some memory of a future Michael could only begin to guess at. "My little brother is our last chance, isn't he?" The demon king strode over to Michael.

Loki tightened his grip and growled, "Back off, sore loser."

Ash scoffed. "Oh, you won't be tricking me out of a treasure today, old man. I've no intention to engage you in a battle of wits. This time, the stakes are too high. If my estimation is correct—and my estimation is almost always correct—the archangel Michael will not leave this enterprise in one piece. He must not be summoned. My little brother understands this." He nodded to Michael. "If you knew what was good for you, you'd step aside and allow him to wrest his woman from Azazel's influence. I've agreed not to stop the conjuration, but my brother has made no such promise."

Loki shook his head. "No can do, kid. I'm repaying a life debt to that woman up there. To her, Raphael is worth the risk, and to me, *she* is worth even more."

"Honorable and unfortunate." Ashmedai tapped a foot and pinched the bridge of his nose. "I had hoped to avoid another physical altercation, but I suppose this one's necessary."

Loki began to grow, and his eyes shimmered with a fiery, orange light. "You will lose."

"Of course I will." Ashmedai matched the Jötunn inch for inch and took his cherubic form. "But winning is not the objective."

The attack was so fast, Michael could not have said who struck first. Before he knew it, a cherub and an elemental were locked in a battle high overhead and flying further and further from *Dragonfly*, no doubt by Ash's own design. Bryony's song reached a fever pitch, and the wind itself responded to her call. Frantically, Chuy freed Michael from the mast and handed the bulk of his chain back to him. "Wish I could do more," he said.

"You can." Michael gave his friend a squeeze on the shoulder, hoping the gesture could somehow convey the weight of his gratitude. "Tell the others to get belowdecks and brace themselves. We're in for more than a squall if she succeeds."

The final notes of the lure hung in the air like mist. They were layered and harmonized, a siren song over the roar of the disquieted sea. Azazel had formed the net with Bryony's hands. The paste made of salt and blood clung to the ship's deck better than she'd expected. The circle's crisscrossing lines were composed of whole sentences in a language she couldn't begin to identify. One string of symbols spiraled inward, adorning the center like a jewel. *The name of God*, Azazel had called it. *Unspeakable and secret. Write it, and someone will come to snuff it out.* If they played their cards right, that someone would be the archangel Michael.

A haze of heat rose from the circle like a street mirage on a summer day. Bryony's skin tingled as though she had a fever, as though the brush of softest silk would sting her. And she knew it was time. She began the summons. "I command you—"

"Stop! Don't!" A deep voice tugged at her buried consciousness. She'd been in a dreamlike state in which everything she did was predetermined, every choice she made not entirely hers. Even her own voice belonged to someone else. But the instant Michael called to her, she woke. She whirled around to see him approach with chains in his hands. From within, Azza clung to her consciousness, but he could not compete with Michael—her Michael—who stood before her now and begged, "Bryony, don't do this. Please, it's not worth it."

"Why?" Her voice was all hers now.

Michael crouched beside her. "The archangel Michael isn't who we thought he was." He was terrified and trembling. "He's dangerous, far more dangerous than either one of us realized. Bryony . . ." He hesitated, and she cocked her head, waiting.

Azza took over her consciousness again, and this time, she didn't resist him. Dangerous or not, the archangel Michael was their one chance to get Raphael back, to get medicine back. And when she considered throwing away that chance, the only face she could see was that of her baby brother. "I command you—"

"It was the archangel Michael who ordered the massacre!" The man she loved let the truth slip from his lips like it was a dog he could no longer restrain. "Please, Bryony. It was the archangel Michael who sent them all to their graves—the doctors, the scientists, your family. You have to know I wouldn't lie about this. I was as ignorant as you a week ago. I named myself for him." He paused. "My god, I named myself for a monster."

Bryony dropped to her knees, stunned beyond speech. *Did you know this?* she asked the angel inhabiting her body. Azazel did not respond, but that was all the answer she needed. She immediately cast him out, and she heard him shatter behind her.

Michael knelt and wrapped his enormous arms around her. "Thank god I stopped you in time. Thank god, Bryony." He held her tighter, trembling. "I love you. I missed you so much." She nuzzled into him and closed her eyes to the rest of the world. It was so good to touch him again. She wanted to crawl into his lap and disappear in his embrace—in her dark and quiet hiding place—but she couldn't. Because there were two ways to resurrect Rahab, and Michael had only rendered one of them unthinkable.

The circle still sang. The conjuration was still active. And before anyone could stop her, she turned to it and shouted, "I command you, Samael, appear in my circle—"

"No!" Two voices screamed at once. Michael and Azazel. Two voices in perfect harmony, in total agreement that she'd just made a devastating, deadly mistake. The sun turned red, and the sky blackened with smoke. A sound like lightning striking too close deafened her. She screamed, and Michael covered her ears. Unlike lightning, this explosive sound and blinding light did not fade. It continued. It stayed. All the hairs on her arms stood on end. Every nerve in her body prickled and stung. The atmosphere thrummed with electricity and set her teeth on edge.

"Hang on!" Michael shouted over the storm. He wrapped his chain around the forecastle rail and kept hold of it with one hand while he reeled Bryony in with the other. For a split second, she remembered her first squall, the way he'd held her and reassured her that everything was going to be all right. There were no reassurances now.

A wall of water rose up before *Dragonfly*'s bow, and the brigantine tipped back and back, dragging its anchor until the deck was almost vertical. Michael and Bryony braced themselves against the rail. Chaos was all around them. The wave they rode was no natural thing. They were going to die. *Dragonfly* was going to capsize. Its masts would break, and its sails would shred. The crew would be tossed and drowned. What had she done? The conjuration wasn't working the way it was supposed to. Where was the seraph she'd summoned? Why wasn't he standing in her circle as Daniel had?

As if in answer, Azza shouted, "You must finish summoning him! You can't stop it now! Say the words!"

"I can't remember them!" she screamed back at him. Memorizing the summons had never been a concern because she'd expected to do it with Azza, not alone.

"Repeat what I say!" Azza commanded. "Appear in my circle in fair and comely form, without noise or deformity!"

Bryony did as she was told, but the wall of water continued to grow. She repeated *in fair and comely form* over and over again—hoping the angel might finally choose to comply—as the wave was filled with blinding light. The electrified sea rose high into the sky and touched the clouds, spinning like an enormous waterspout.

Azazel continued to shout over the wind. "Come now, angel—visibly, peacefully, affably—without delay! Speak to me with a clear and perfect voice!"

Bryony parroted every word he said. She emphasized *peacefully* and repeated the line, *Speak to me with a clear and perfect voice*, twice for good measure. The waterspout bowed over the ship, and Bryony heard the creaking of *Dragonfly*'s bones as it was tossed like a toy in a bathtub. Michael gripped her so hard it hurt. She could smell the fear leaking from his pores. The world was wrong and spinning out of control, but somehow, the little orb-weaver finished her summons. "Answer to your names: Blind Guardian, Venom of God, Angel of Death! Come! Appear before me now, Samael!"

The world shifted again, twisting back into something recognizable. Was *Dragonfly* actually righting itself, or was that just Bryony's desperate, wishful thinking? The waterspout broke apart, and the creature born of it rose from the sea like a dragon. Its body was a twisting pillar of menacing light. Its head was hooded like a cobra, but the face inside was like nothing earthly she'd ever seen. In contrast to the ophan and Michael—whose many eyes looked like distant, blinking suns—the Angel of Death had eyes of darkness, immense voids that yawned across the seraph's body, as black and empty as a starless universe. Twelve tongues of fire bloomed from the creature's back, and Bryony recognized them as its wings. They were so massive she couldn't see the ends of them as they unfolded and unfolded endlessly before her.

She had only a moment to glimpse the beast she'd summoned before her body reflexively dropped to the deck. Her hands spread out before her. Her fingernails dug into the teak like it was a grave she meant to rob. She gathered all her strength and turned her head to see Michael in the same position. To her horror, when she looked the other way, she saw the legendary watcher Azazel as prone and helpless as she was. They had all fallen before the Angel of Death, and no one came to their aid—no one could.

What was this? Compelled worship? But the deep, guttural moan that leached from her lungs and grew at the back of her throat was too familiar. This wasn't worship. No, this was unbearable, unspeakable grief. She tasted it on her tongue like an old family recipe—the hopelessness, the finality, the vacuum left behind when a life was snuffed out. Bryony knew this flavor well, and she used her familiarity to find her tongue again. "I command you, Samael, appear in my circle in fair and comely form without noise or deformity." Louder. "Appear in my circle in fair and comely form!" Louder. "Now, Samael! Now!"

Suddenly, the seas were quiet. There was no settling, no slowing of the wind or waves. It was as though the entire storm had existed only in her head, just the memory of a dream.

Bryony fought to lift her face from the deck and saw a pair of bare feet, without blemish or deformity, and a robe of rich and weighty silk that clung to a perfect, androgynous body. All of it looked as though it had been carved from white marble. Finally, she blinked up at what she could only describe as one of the stone angels that marked the oldest graves in her local graveyard. It had the traditional feathered wings at its shoulders and exquisite, almost feminine features. Its colorless hair fell just past its shoulders, curling at the cut ends exactly the way Michael's did. The curve of its chin was delicate and its mouth familiar and broad. The only thing that marked it as monstrous now were its eyes, which still had that blackness, that vast emptiness Bryony could hardly stand to see.

Then the marble statue spoke. "Am I not fair and comely enough for you now?"

So this was the Angel of Death. Bryony could only look at him for seconds at a time before she had to avert her eyes. Even in this contrived shape, something about him overwhelmed her. His voice, deliberately softened, sounded breathy and warm, like a singer who was trying to save it for a performance.

"Is my voice not clear and perfect?" he said. He was mocking her, and Bryony did not appreciate it.

Azza still lay prone beside her, all his colors faded away. The watcher was smoky glass, empty and hollow, completely overwhelmed by grief. He must have known it was coming—neither grief nor Samael's curse were new phenomena to him—but Azza had helped her finish her conjuration anyway. *He's not dead,* she reminded herself, though the sight of him in such poor condition troubled her. *He's just exhausted.*

Then she felt Michael take her hand, and she turned to see him, his cheek still pressed to the deck, his eyes rimmed with worry and unwelcome tears. In his gesture was the deepest of apologies. *I'm sorry about him,* he seemed to say, but Bryony didn't know why he felt the need. His father had nothing to do with him. In fact, the angel had abandoned him long ago—left him with no family and no home, left him completely alone in the world—and that made Bryony angry. She dug deep and found a lingering store of rage. She let it consume her until it eclipsed her grief long enough for her to answer the graveyard angel. "You look like an overpriced tombstone to me."

Samael's feet rocked forward as he crouched down to meet her. "Be grateful I've chosen a form familiar to you," he murmured. "I didn't have to take your comfort into consideration."

She wrapped her hand around the staff of the scythe—his weapon, she realized—and pulled it closer. "There's nothing comforting about those eyes."

"Ah." Samael stood, and Bryony was left staring at his feet again. "My disability, unfortunately, cannot be helped. You understand."

"Disability?"

"Did you not command me to answer to my names? Did you not list them aloud? Did you think you were simply reciting nonsense?"

Blind Guardian. She hadn't realized it was literal. A second rush of hopelessness overcame her, and she began to wonder whether she'd actually made the right choice. Summoning Samael had been an impulsive decision, an emotional one, and now she didn't know how to deal with the consequences. "Azza," she murmured to the angel who'd gotten her this far. "Azza, tell me what to say. I don't know what to say."

But it was Samael who responded. "He cannot help you now, I'm afraid. He looked too long and lost his voice. Trust me. The pattern repeats itself, again and again. You will just have to improvise."

Samael wasn't lying. Azza hadn't stirred since his collapse, and he hadn't given her any instructions on what to do after the summoning. Presumably, he would have been able to possess or advise her after she'd successfully conjured the archangel Michael. Now everything was in flux, and she was completely on her own.

The pattern repeats itself . . . What an odd thing for an angel to say—an unnecessary piece of information—and the way he'd said it . . . There was a weariness in his tone, almost as though he suffered as much as those who looked upon him. If he was suffering, perhaps he wanted this over as quickly as Bryony did. She decided to come to the point. "I had hoped . . ." She hesitated and took a deep, trembling breath. This was Michael's father. It was only Michael's father. "I had hoped you'd return Raphael from the deep."

There was a pause, and then the graveyard angel asked, "Why did you not summon the archangel Michael for such a task?"

Was he really trying to pass the buck? Bryony glowered at *Dragonfly's* deck, and the ship seemed to rock in response to her frustration. "The archangel Michael killed my family, as far as I'm concerned. I didn't want to see his face."

"Yet you wanted to see mine." Samael laughed—dear god, he actually laughed—and his laugh was as musical and beautiful as Azza's. "If your family is dead, why would you not assign blame to the Angel of Death?"

With every word he spoke, he became less of an existential idea and more of a sentient creature with a body, a voice, a personality. She thought about his question. "Death didn't cause their suffering. Death only ended it."

Samael's voice was at her ear again, but she did not look up to see him. "Do you hate him?" he whispered. "The archangel Michael. Do you despise the very idea of him?"

She got the distinct impression this was meant to be a secret confession, so she whispered back, "Yes."

The angel's sigh of satisfaction followed her answer. Of course, the best way to make an ally was to share his enemy. It seemed so obvious now that she thought of it. Then Samael surprised her. "Regrettable," he said, his voice high above her again. "He might have helped you. I will not."

What? A slow anger crept up Bryony's spine and settled in her chest. Whatever she'd expected of the Angel of Death, it wasn't childish defiance. "Do you have a choice?" she said bitterly. "I summoned you. I won't let you go until you agree to it."

Somewhere, in the back of her mind, she heard Ashmedai's warning—*he does not honor his contracts*—but it was too late to take her words back.

Chapter Thirty-Two

"Do you truly believe you've ensnared me in this circle?" Samael's voice softened, and the softer it became the more Bryony's skin crawled. The sky darkened again, and ash drifted down like snowflakes. "Curiosity alone convinced me to stay. Now you've proven yourself no different from any other power-hungry god." She shuddered, and once again, the graveyard angel's voice was at her ear. "That's right, you reek of worship. Tell me, if I swallowed you now, would you taste simply divine, or would I need to wash you down with seawater?" He chuckled. "A hint for the future. Salt cannot cage me. The sea will not weaken me. Rahab is my handiwork, my masterpiece. But then you already knew that, or you would not have summoned me."

Something heavy slipped past Bryony's arm, and a scattered crust of salt pelted her skin. She forced herself to look, though everything inside her fought against it. The white-hot tail of the creature had broken the circle. A furious, twelve-winged seraph towered above her, growing higher and higher. The Angel of Death was escaping, and Bryony had blown her only chance to bring medicine back to mankind.

He's impossible to control, Ashmedai had said. She'd been warned, and yet she'd tried to control him. How stupid. Control should never have been her first instinct. This wasn't who she was. What had become of the woman she used to be, the woman a trickster admired? Dominance was a fool's errand. Those who knew better relied on manipulation.

She had seconds to react, so she rolled the dice on her better impulses. She reached out a hand and clung to the end of the serpent's tail. Part of her expected her skin to freeze or burn at that touch, but she felt nothing unusual. The creature was smooth as an eel and subtly iridescent. It stopped dead at her touch. She shouted up at it. "Is this how you treat your future daughter-in-law?"

Once again, Samael became the graveyard angel. The clouds parted, and ash stopped falling from the sky. It was all just gone, as though none of it ever existed in the first place, and Bryony found herself stretched out on her stomach with one hand wrapped around the marble-colored ankle of the Angel of Death. It was almost laughable, how appropriate this moment had become. She should have predicted it years ago, inviting death the way she had, picnicking among tombstones and wearing a mourning veil.

Samael's face betrayed no anger, no amusement, nothing. But Bryony had learned something about angels from her time with Azazel, and she knew what she was seeing. The Angel of Death was too overwhelmed to express himself. "I wondered how you'd gotten hold of my weapon," he said. "Is my son here now?"

She struggled with whether to reveal Michael to his father, and then Michael took the choice from her. "I'm here," he said.

The graveyard angel folded his wings away. "Hello, son."

"Hello, father." Michael fought to push himself to his knees, though his hands remained planted on the deck. His black hair fell like a fringe across his cheek. "How . . . How did you know I had your weapon?"

Samael blinked his empty eyes. "An angel's weapon is like a beacon to him. It was part of me you stole that day. Would you pull a tooth and expect me not to notice?"

"I did expect you to notice." Michael's whole body began to tremble. "I expected some kind of acknowledgement that I existed at all. Anything." He forced his chin up, and Bryony saw the fight in his eyes. "I was only a child, for god's sake. I was just a child, and I had no one. I lived on the streets." Tears fell unheeded as Samael's son harnessed what had to be years of festering rage to ignore them. "I had to learn about myself by reading forbidden texts, by trial and error, rumor and insult. I was abducted by a demon, and all I could think was finally . . . finally, someone who can answer my questions. Do you have any idea how many nights I spent agonizing over what I must have done to offend you, wondering whether you even knew I was your son? So I took your weapon and awaited your wrath, your notice. You didn't even turn around. Why? If you knew I had it, why did you let me keep it all these years?"

The graveyard angel epitomized emptiness. "It was the least I could do for my son," he said. That was his answer? That wasn't good enough. Bryony dug her fingernails into the monster's flesh. Samael spoke again to Michael, though his attention was now aimed squarely at Bryony. "You did not want *me* for a father. You only think you did."

Michael clenched his teeth. "I didn't have a choice. It was you or no one. Tell me the truth. Did you know I'd inherited your curse?"

"Curse?"

"I've already paralyzed my own fiancée. More than once!"

Michael's terrifying father frowned down at Bryony. "So you weren't exaggerating your relationship with my son. I had hoped you were." And in a move that made Bryony's heart hammer like a woodpecker, the Angel of Death crouched down and pried her fingers from his ankle.

She begged, "Don't go yet."

"I won't," he said. "If my son wants his father in his life, he will get his father in his life, until he begs me to abandon him again. And he will beg for it. This is a lesson he intends to learn the hard way, and so I will teach him." Samael took Bryony's hand and helped her to her feet. His movements were so achingly slow that her thigh muscles began to burn, but to her surprise, the stone angel's touch was gentle. It made sense now that she thought about it. Death was often gentle too.

When she stood precariously before him, he blinked at her like he'd never been in the presence of a more baffling creature. "I wondered whether you would be able to stand after touching me. Have you covered your eyes?"

"No." She kept her answer to one word to hide the tremor in her voice.

He scratched his chin in a gesture that was so very nearly human, it sent chills up her spine. "Death is an old companion of yours, is it?"

"Yes."

"Then I will give you a piece of advice, from one haunted creature to another." He stepped from the circle and came far too close. "Run. Do not marry my son, and never seek me out again. If you stay, your grief will be immeasurable. He is not destined for a happy end."

God they even spoke alike. *This will end badly,* Michael had warned again and again, but he was wrong. She was sure of it. They were both wrong. She gripped Samael's hand more firmly and began to shake it. "My name is Bryony Moss. You might want to know it because I'm not going anywhere."

Was that a smile on the Angel of Death's face? It was microscopic as smiles went, but Bryony was sure she'd seen it. "So be it, Ms. Moss. It is your funeral, as they say. Now I'll give my son a word of fatherly advice, since he craves it so, and if he's wise, he will not ask me for more." He let go of Bryony's hand and turned to Michael. "Son, I was not aware you had inherited my curse. No other child of mine has, and I assumed you were the same. I cannot help you overcome it. I suggest you use it to your advantage instead, but beware. The poison is cumulative. Your betrothed appears to have developed a mild tolerance. Do not be fooled into thinking she's immune. Should you anticipate resonance, block her eyes from the light."

Bryony cleared her throat, and Samael turned back to her, questioning. "Encouragement," she whispered.

"Pardon me?" He narrowed his eyes.

"You should give him a word of encouragement in addition to advice. That's what good fathers do."

He scowled down at her. "Why have you assumed I intend to be a *good* father?"

"Because you owe him that at least." She would not back down, and Samael heaved a great sigh in her general direction.

He began, "I heard rumors of an extraordinary godhunter who struck with surgical precision. He could kill a god without touching its congregation. I knew it had to be you, and I was proud you'd made such elegant use of my weapon. I wish you to keep it, for the time being, and continue your work." Michael began to protest, but Samael silenced him with a gesture. "You will continue your work. I have a target in mind, and I'll pay a bounty in the form of the archangel Raphael."

"Really?" Bryony said. She couldn't help herself. Success was so close she could almost taste it. Then she remembered Ashmedai's warning. "But you don't honor your contracts."

Samael chuckled. "Payment in advance, you shrewd thing."

Michael was already shaking his head. "I don't kill gods anymore."

"You will kill this one. He's the most dangerous god who has ever existed."

Michael didn't ask for further details, but curiosity ate away at Bryony's resolve. "Who is it?" she finally asked.

Samael did not hesitate. "The archangel Michael."

The blood drained from Michael's face when he heard his name-sake on his father's lips. He opened his mouth several times to answer but couldn't seem to get the words out.

Samael was dead serious. "The archangel has been worshiped as a god, and it has driven him mad. I can no longer get close to him. You're a godhunter. Do your job. Put the dog down."

"I'm not . . ." Michael sputtered. "I don't . . ."

But for Bryony, the answer was easy. "I'll do it."

Michael shouted, "No!"

She pretended not to hear. "If it's me, the archangel won't see it coming."

That split-second smile crossed the graveyard angel's face again. He drew close and bent to Bryony's ear. "You do hate him, don't you?" He murmured the words like a man who'd just tasted chocolate for the first time. Then he laid a heavy hand on her shoulder. "Welcome to the family, Bryony Moss." He crouched and picked up the death scythe. She'd all but forgotten it was there. In his hands, it looked right—like he'd always had it in his possession—like Bryony and Michael had only imagined themselves taking ownership. "Interesting shape," he mused. "I almost regret changing it." Then he grabbed Bryony's arm and slammed the staff into her wrist.

Immediately, the wood of the scythe gave way. She barely felt its touch before it had turned to silver and clasped itself around her wrist. It looked like an elegant shackle and fit her like a second skin. An engraved, pearlescent disk dangled from the inside of her wrist. Bryony tugged at the band, but she could not remove it. It was all she could do to suppress her own panic. "What is this?" she asked.

"Do you not like it, my daughter? It's a charm, a prayer to St. Michael. You're going to be his biggest fan when you conjure him. You're going to cower and supplicate him. Stroke his ego. Get close enough to strike."

Bryony examined the charm dangling from her wrist. There was an angel on it—or rather the representation of an angel—that looked much like the figure who stood before her now. Only this angel was in the process of killing something. The image was too familiar. Yes, she'd seen it before. *St. Michael and the Devil.* "Is this dog thing supposed to be you?"

Samael laughed. "Yes. The great dragon laid low."

She held her wrist up to her eyes and squinted at the creature under the archangel's foot. It didn't look anything like Samael. Then again, the angel in the charm probably looked nothing like the archangel Michael. "I hate it." Bryony tugged at the band. "How do I get it off?"

"You don't. It will come off when you've fulfilled your promise." Samael reached out, and Bryony let him trace the band on her wrist. "Fear not," he said. "It won't pierce you."

She scowled and pulled her hand away. "How can you know that for sure?"

"Because it is mine, and I have sheathed it for you. When you've come close to the archangel Michael, simply draw the weapon and strike."

"And how do I draw the weapon?" She turned it this way and that. There didn't seem to be any latch to trigger.

"It will read your intention and obey, but only in the presence of an archangel." He stepped back, looking proud and enthusiastic. "Now to fulfill my end of the bargain." And without pomp or circumstance, the Angel of Death became the seraph again, rose into the air, and plunged into the sea.

Michael rushed to Bryony as soon as his father was gone. His hands went to the band at her wrist, and he began frantically trying to break it. "What have you done, Bryony? You don't make a deal with my father. Don't you know that? You never, ever make a deal with him. It's the moral of a million folktales and . . . Jesus! Somebody help me take this off!"

Suddenly, *Dragonfly* listed so far to port that seawater washed onto its deck. Michael caught himself on the rail and caught Bryony in turn. She could hear people shouting below. Azza's heavy, lifeless body slid across the deck and hit the bulwarks. She called after him, but Michael wouldn't let her go. He held her tight and doubled over her. She felt his heart thunder in his chest. The sea bubbled like a witch's cauldron, and a bright light shone up from the deep. *Dragonfly* listed back to starboard, and Azazel slid to the other side. Bryony screamed after him again.

Michael clutched her tighter. "He's fine! He's fine! Worry about yourself for once!"

Sea spray showered them both, and Bryony could taste the salt of it. Part of her was terrified, but there was another part—something emanating from the band on her wrist—that knew she was in no danger. She'd been twice marked, once by Azazel and once by Samael. And while Samael's protection might only last as long as the deal she'd made with him, she was certain it superseded almost anyone else's threat. The sea could not touch her. Never mind that she would likely be swallowed by an archangel in the near future, or perhaps Samael himself would kill her if she failed to honor their agreement. For now, she was safe.

The sea rose up, stretching into a dome like an amniotic sac. Brilliant light emanated from its center. It looked like the sun itself fought to be born, and Bryony had to hide her eyes or be blinded by it. Her body reacted the same way it had before, and so did Michael's. They both fell to their knees, but clinging together, they didn't collapse completely. Bryony found strength in the knowledge that the archangel Michael would finally pay for what he'd done. She'd make sure of it. He would cease to exist just like her family. He would be wiped from reality like the stain he was.

The ship's bow dipped as it bore the weight of the monstrous seraph that landed on it. By the time *Dragonfly* righted itself, the graveyard angel stood once again on the forecastle. This time, he did not pretend the circle meant anything at all. He carried an algae-covered, canvas sack in his hand and shook the seawater from his wings like a dog. Then he strode toward Bryony and held out the sack. "Take it. I have paid the bounty."

Bryony grabbed the neck of the sack. The weight of it was significant, but it was definitely not the size or shape of any angel she'd ever seen. "What's this?" she asked. "I wanted Raphael."

"And so you have him." Samael laughed a cruel laugh Bryony could not begin to interpret. "Be gentle with the poor creature. Azazel was not kind."

"He's in the sack?"

Samael nodded. "Do tell the watcher I have always admired his work."

The sack shifted, and Bryony had to force herself to keep hold of it. Instinct wanted her to kick it away.

The Angel of Death stood stiff and formal. "Now, to my son, I say this. I am everyone's end and no one's beginning. You did not want me for a father. But I did know of your existence, and I did acknowledge you at your birth." He held out his hand, and Michael hesitated. Samael grew impatient. "Come. I will show you."

The sack Bryony held writhed as Michael reached up and took his father's hand. The graveyard angel smiled and said, "There you are. How you've grown." He crouched down, and his hand traced a path up Michael's arm to his shoulder. There was a moment in which it looked as though the Angel of Death meant to cradle his son's face, but the moment was only illusion. Instead, he braced Michael's head with both hands, leaned in as if to kiss him, and stopped just short. Bryony recognized the gesture at once. It was an introduction. Something passed between father and son when they came close enough to share breath. She could almost see it happen. It was a secret, a shared thought, a lost moment. When Samael finally released his son, the change in both of them was palpable.

The graveyard angel stood and spoke again. "That was the name I gave you upon your birth. I have shared it with you so you understand. I will never call you by your chosen name. You already have one, and it is a far better name than the one you share with the monster you once idolized." He spread his arms and stepped back, addressing Bryony and Michael at once. "You sought me out, and I have come. Now we have a relationship, my son. Now we have a contract, my daughter. We shall see if you come to regret it."

He stretched, and he burned, and he was light, and he was gone.

Chapter Thirty-Three

The canvas sack writhed as Bryony stood. She felt stronger now that the Angel of Death had gone. It was shocking how quickly she'd become accustomed to weakness. She made a silent vow that she would never allow herself to become so accustomed again. Then she opened the mouth of the sack and dropped it with a scream that nullified that vow immediately. It was no angel. It was a snake—a real, flesh-and-blood snake—that came slithering out of the sack toward her.

"He tricked me!" As the snake came closer, Bryony's spine went rigid. Michael stood. The creature coiled around her feet, wound up her legs, and encircled her waist. It was a python—it had to be. It was huge and powerful, and she wondered how on earth it had fit in the sack. How had she lifted it, come to think of it? It was as big as she was, certainly longer, and it was squeezing the breath out of her.

Bryony lifted her arms so they wouldn't be pinned to her sides. She tried to push the body of the snake down, but it wouldn't budge. Its muscles were like stone as it coiled around her chest. She was going to die. She should never have summoned Samael. She should have listened to Ashmedai. But who could have predicted that, between the demon king and the Angel of Death, one of them would actually be trustworthy?

The serpent brought its triangular head to her shoulder and rested it there. She could not breathe deeply, but she could breathe. It didn't constrict her the way she expected it to. She forced herself to calm down. Something about the way the creature clung to her spoke more of desperation than predation. Perhaps if she was calm, it would relax its grip.

Then she heard Azazel say, "That's Raphael, darling. He won't harm you." She turned to see him standing behind her, brushing dust from his perfect clothes. He was back to his brilliant, colorful self.

"Azza, get it off me!"

"I wouldn't dare touch him," Azza said. "I'm the reason he's bound in that body. Try not to panic. He's probably freezing and wants to keep warm. I made him cold-blooded, you see? I felt it was appropriate at the time." He laughed his musical laugh.

So she hadn't been cheated after all. Still Bryony was indignant. Samael might have warned her. She grumbled, "I'm not a hot water bottle." But when the snake nuzzled into her neck, she softened despite herself. "You could at least loosen your grip," she muttered to it, and the creature immediately complied.

Michael stepped in to offer his help, but the snake hissed and tightened its coils. "I don't think he likes me," Michael said.

Azza shrugged. "He wouldn't right now, petal. He's confused, and you look too much like your father."

"Honestly," Bryony groaned. The serpent's grip was loose enough that she could walk now. It was like a coiled, fleshy corset with a head and tail.

As she crossed the main deck toward the captain's quarters, she passed Loki, who sucked air through his teeth like he'd been burned. Ashmedai clenched his jaw and balled his hands into fists. And Raeni emerged from belowdecks, drawing her machete like she meant to use it. "It's okay," Bryony assured her. "This is the archangel Raphael. He's just . . . sick, I guess."

"Then take him to the ship's hospital." Raeni sheathed her weapon.

Ash rolled his eyes. "That angel was sick long before Azza and I got to him."

Again the snake hissed and tightened its grip. "Stop that," Bryony snapped at it. "I don't usually mind snakes, but I have a very reasonable fear of angels, and you aren't helping."

She carefully descended the companionway. When she reached the ship's hospital, she closed the door behind her and latched it. As soon as they were alone, the enormous serpent began to relax. She took the opportunity to unwind it from her torso and lay it on the examination table. The animal didn't resist, and Bryony finally got a close look at it. At first, it appeared to be a bluish-gray color with silver scales dotted here and there like inlaid diamonds. But as she watched it move, she saw its rainbow sheen. "You're quite a pretty thing, aren't you? I suppose you would be since Azza made you. Can you talk?"

The snake did not respond. It laid its head on its own coils and seemed to sleep, though it never did close its eyes. She stayed with the creature for the rest of the day. She didn't dare leave it alone for fear it would disappear or someone would steal or harm it. Maybe she was being overprotective, but Raphael represented so much hope to her. He was an archangel on the side of mortals, though he didn't look like an archangel now. He just looked like a scared and exhausted animal. How many years had he been sealed away in this body?

Before long, there was a knock at the door, and she rose to address it. "Who's there?"

"It's your commodore, girl. Now open the door." Bryony couldn't help but feel disappointed. She'd wanted it to be Michael, but hours had gone by and he'd not come to see her. Perhaps he didn't want to upset Raphael further. Raeni entered the room with a tray of food, which she set beside the sink before she examined the creature on the table. "I didn't know an archangel could be bound like that," she said, grimacing. "My god, medic, what have you brought into my fleet now?"

It was a rhetorical question, but Bryony thought it over anyway. "Michael once told me that to fight powerful enemies, you have to have powerful allies."

"He wasn't wrong about that." Raeni reached out to touch the snake, and then thought better of it. "But damned if you didn't take that advice a touch too far. I won't blame you for Loki or the demon. I suppose Azazel was a necessary evil. But Samael? You're going to have to answer for that one of these days. It'll be a hard lesson you'll learn. The Angel of Death is no man's ally."

Bryony stared down at the band around her wrist. "But I think he's at least not an enemy, as long as I'm wearing this."

"Yes. Michael told me about your bargain." The commodore tsked and folded her arms. "You know a deal with the devil never ends in anyone's favor but the devil's, don't you?"

"I know." No one could make Bryony question her own decisions quite the way Raeni could.

"Well, eat something then." Raeni gestured to the tray she'd left on the counter. "And get some rest tonight. You're back on the crew whether you like it or not. Because of you, I'm a man short."

"A man short?"

"Chuy. Rose will take his place as captain of *Papillon* for now, which puts you in the kitchen."

Bryony's heart began to race. "What . . . What happened to Chuy?"

"He's been taken by the demon king. Didn't you know?" Raeni looked genuinely baffled. "I assumed it was part of your wager. Ashmedai says our captain is too precious to continue in such a 'poorly regulated operation.'" Raeni spoke the last words with undisguised derision, and Bryony got the impression she'd taken Ashmedai's criticism personally.

"No, that was not part of the wager. I would never!" Chuy was gone. Bryony was suddenly both livid and relieved because at least he was alive. At least he was alive. "What is it about abducting people that appeals to that creature? Did he say where he was taking Chuy?"

"Of course not. Did you think the demon king would make anything easy for us? He intends to keep my captain for himself, and I'll be damned if I let him. *Daniel* will be damned if he lets him because I'll damn Daniel myself."

"We'll get him back," Bryony assured her. Chuy would survive this. She had to believe it. There was something about the way Ashmedai had looked at him—that tenderness. As infuriating as the demon king's abduction habit was, she was certain he would treat Chuy far better than he'd treated Michael, at the very least. "I swear I'll get him back."

"Damn right you will." Raeni marched out the door, but she poked her head back in one last time before she left. "Time to make use of those powerful allies you claim to have gained."

Another hour passed, and Bryony was only able to stomach a few bites of food. Guilt took its toll on her. She should not have played with her friend's life. She should not have trusted his fate to a demon, no matter how many ethics that demon claimed to have. What had she been thinking?

She was sitting on a stool with her face in her hands when a voice shocked her out of her brooding. "Starving yourself won't save him, you know," it said. She looked up to see the snake had gone, and in its place sat a boy of about ten or eleven. He had wide eyes and olive skin. His dark curls intruded on his face in a way that made Bryony want to push them away for him. He wore denim overalls, a thermal shirt, and a friendly smile. He looked more like a farmhand than an archangel. But he was, without a doubt, the archangel Raphael, broken free from his animal prison. This was merely the shape he'd chosen to manifest.

"You're awake." She struggled to reconcile herself with the fact that the boy, who now gripped the edge of the examination table and kicked his dangling legs, had been a giant constrictor only seconds ago. "Are you all right?"

"Not in the least," Raphael answered. "But I'll heal in time, and I'll be endlessly grateful to you. So tell me what you want in return."

"What I want?" Wasn't it obvious? "Medicine! Oh my god, and science!" She leapt to her feet in excitement. "Please, please bring them back. We need them so badly. We need vaccines and antibiotics and surgeons who aren't charlatans. We've lost so much—so much, you have no idea." She hated the thought that she was too late to save her own family, but their deaths would not be in vain if it led her to save thousands more in their names.

"Do you not have these things anymore?" Raphael cocked his head.

That was when Bryony launched into the most disordered explanation she'd ever given for anything. She was all over the map. She couldn't keep her timeline straight. She jumped from the armada to her family, to the ophan eating an entire town, and back to the armada again. She told him everything she knew about her world, and how it had been broken like a wild horse under the whip of the angels. She told him how Azazel had helped her and why. She talked so much and so long she was breathless by the time she was through.

Raphael listened carefully. His expressions matched all the rage and sorrow and horror she felt her story warranted. When she was finally finished, the archangel bowed his head and asked, "What was his name?"

"Excuse me?"

"Your brother," Raphael clarified. "What was his name?"

Bryony opened her mouth and choked on the answer. Tears stung her eyes. No one had asked her that before. No one. She'd been asked her parents' names, her congregants' names, and the names of anyone she'd ever worked with. But no one ever asked about her brother. He wasn't important. He was just a sad underscore to her sad story. "Adrian," she finally managed. "Adi for short."

Raphael waited patiently while she grabbed a paper towel to blow her nose into and somehow managed to compose herself. "I'll teach medicine to your people again," he said. "But that's something I would have done regardless, Miss . . ." He paused and waited for her to introduce herself.

"Oh, Moss, but Bryony's fine."

"Bryony." The boy grinned. "I'm sure you already know who I am, but we should introduce ourselves anyway. It's polite, yes? I'm Raphael. You can drop the *El*, if you're feeling familiar, I don't mind. I heard you refer to Azazel informally, by the way. Have you been friends long? You must be important to him, since I'm certain he hates me and would not have helped to free me otherwise. Well, I thought you might want to drop the formalities either way, as I'm about to ask you an overly personal question. Sorry, it can't be helped. I want to repay you, and it wouldn't be fair to offer something I was already planning to give. Anyway, here I am rambling when I should just come to the point. Would you like me to mend your genetic break?"

So Azza hadn't lied when he'd told her Raphael was extremely talkative. She knit her brow. "Heal my . . . genetic what?"

"Maybe *break* is not the right word." He wrinkled his nose, and the expression was unreasonably cute for an ancient creature pretending to be a child. "You'll have to forgive me for looking too close. My senses are geared that way, you understand. I hope you do. You're a small god—I noticed that straight away—but you've a genetic abnormality that predates your godhood. It was screamingly obvious when I was coiled around you. Thank you for that, by the way. I can't tell you how freezing it is at the bottom of the ocean. Anyway, I'm sure you noticed the abnormality yourself if you ever tried to conceive."

Bryony cleared her throat and began several responses to which she couldn't find the endings. "I um . . . I mean I've never . . . I'm sorry . . . Tried?"

"I don't mean to presume, of course, but should you ever wish to conceive, you'll become quickly frustrated. To be blunt, you're infertile, but I've a talent for treating tricky conditions like yours." He interlaced his fingers and cracked his knuckles inside out with a confident grin.

It slowly dawned on Bryony just what the archangel was getting at. "I see." She was determined to suppress her blush by sheer force of will. "So if I were to . . . um . . . try, what would my chances be?" God this was humiliating. Was this what it was like to see a doctor? She supposed it must be.

Raphael noticed her discomfort and pushed a hand through his hair. "Ah, perhaps I shouldn't have manifested this body. Usually, it's less intimidating for mortals to confront a child. I don't even have to say *fear not.*" He mimicked a deep, foreboding voice, and Bryony actually laughed. "But I suppose for this conversation, I should grow up." And so he did. He looked exactly how Bryony would have expected the boy he'd been to look as an adult. She still wanted to push the curls from his face. His eyes were still wide and curious, but he was taller and his cheeks a little less round. "Better?" He stood and leaned against the examination table casually. "What I mean to say is, as you are, you won't be able to conceive a child."

"Like zero? Zero percent chance?" She could not hide her excitement.

Raphael scratched his head. "Yes. Zero percent chance, but that'll hardly matter after I fix it for you."

"Don't you dare." She resisted the urge to take him by the shoulders and shake him. "Don't ever, ever fix that. Ha!" She was hopping in place. "No kidding? Zero percent chance, all this time. I can't believe it. Can you believe it?"

Raphael looked at her as though she'd just lost the plot.

"You don't understand," Bryony said. "My fiancé—you met him—is Samael's son. He doesn't want to have children. He believes it would be cruel."

"I see." Raphael wrinkled his nose again, and Bryony was reminded of the boy he'd been. "So the very tall young man I saw is your fiancé, and Samael's son to boot? I wouldn't have believed it if he wasn't the spitting image. Well, he seems to be the responsible sort. He's no fool anyway. Is this a recent engagement? Congratulations are in order either way."

"I'll say they are! I thought I was going to die a virgin." Bryony clapped a hand over her mouth. Strange how quickly the archangel put her at ease, considering what he was.

"Please," he scoffed. "Virginity is a ridiculous concept. But surely you could have used some form of birth control? It's been around since well before I was bound." He didn't seem at all troubled by the topic of conversation. She supposed his openness was just part of his nature.

"No, it hasn't been around. That's what I was trying to tell you. We haven't had medicine since the massacre. People are using spiritualism and herbs, incense, fucking candles—sorry."

Raphael shook his head. "Curse words are also a ridiculous concept. So then, there's truly nothing else you want from me?"

"Well, there is something." She chewed her lip. "If you could promise not to bind Azza again . . . or Ashmedai." That last request was a hard one to make. She wanted to punch the demon king, but she didn't think he deserved to be bound again.

"That's something I can agree to. Anything else? You rescued me from hell, Bryony. Not punishing your friends is hardly an equivalent favor."

"Ashmedai is hardly a friend." She laughed. "Actually, do you think you could find him for me? He's taken someone I care about."

"Yes, I know. One captain left with the demon king not long after you brought me here. I could hear them talking above. Good ears, you know." He tugged on an earlobe and grinned. "Oh, the things I've heard in my time on earth. I could tell you so many stories, but I won't and you're welcome for that. Unfortunately, this particular abduction sounded more like a contract to me, and I can't break a contract. Very few of us can. Your future father-in-law is quite the rare bird, you know. Don't worry now." He patted her arm when he saw her distress. "I'm certain your friend will be just fine. Ashmedai is . . . Well, I'm sure he *means* well." That wasn't quite as comforting as Raphael probably meant it to be. "Anyway, if there's nothing else you want right now, I'll just have to be in your debt. Lucky you." He pointed at her with a wink and a grin. "So you're happy as you are?"

The question was so loaded, Bryony had to stop and think about it for a moment. "Yes, I'm happy as I am. Thank you. Thank you for asking."

CHAPTER THIRTY-FOUR

Despite being essentially untouched, the captain's quarters felt like the burnt-out shell of a place that used to be home. It represented something Michael had once known, something he'd believed in but no more. Bryony had changed so much of his life that coming back now felt like an abstraction of reality. He sat on the edge of his bunk and held his head in his hands. His entire body ached from clinging to the rail while the ship was tossed by his father's carelessness.

His *father.* So many years had passed since he'd last laid eyes on Samael. Now Michael was an adult—significantly taller, stronger, and more confident—but somehow, his father made him feel like a child again, weak and powerless. And Bryony had tethered herself to the monster, though Michael couldn't understand why. In Mexico, she'd begged him not to surrender to death without a fight, and now she'd gone and done just that, in a manner of speaking. Now she belonged to the Angel of Death.

The heavy door to the captain's quarters complained loudly as it opened. Michael didn't look up to see who it was. Only one person aboard *Dragonfly* would enter without knocking. He heard her light footsteps as she crossed the cabin floor and stood before him. He opened his eyes and peered through his fingers at her black ankle boots. He didn't want to look up and see the silver band on her right wrist or the tattoo on her left, which he now understood to be the mark of Azazel. Hours ago, while Ash removed the chain from Michael's waist, Chuy had given him a detailed recap of everything leading up to the conjuration, and Michael was comfortable with exactly none of it.

Bryony stood quietly a while, possibly waiting for him to look up and acknowledge her. When he didn't, she spoke. "I'm sorry." Her voice was so hushed, he might not have heard it had he not been hyper-focused on every syllable. "Please forgive me."

Michael finally lifted his head and saw the mark of Azazel and the shackle of Samael. "That could have gone so much worse than it did," he said.

"I know."

"You could have gotten the entire armada killed."

"I know." She bowed her head in shame.

Why was he scolding her? He wasn't really angry with her for doing everything in her power to return medicine to mankind. How could he be? No, he was angry with her for a far more selfish reason. He was angry with her for making him share. She wasn't just *his* Bryony anymore, and he was struggling to come to terms with that. But it wasn't fair to blame her for his own insecurities. He tried to temper his criticism with levity. "As it stands, I'll need to get a new pair of dividers."

Bryony let out a soft laugh and glanced down at the death sword she now wore like a charm. "I wish I could give it back to you."

"I know." He buried his face in his hands again. "My father won't let you back out of this," he said as she took one of his hands and interlaced their fingers. "You have no idea what you've gotten yourself into. I know Loki is erratic and Ashmedai is reliable to a fault. And maybe you thought my father stood somewhere in between—"

"I don't."

"He's relentless, Bryony. You can't stop him. You can only hope to evade his notice for a while, and you've just put a massive target on your back. He won't let up. He'll never, ever leave you alone."

"He's not here now." A little smile flitted across her face, and Michael couldn't begin to interpret it. Was she flirting with him? This was hardly the time, but he couldn't resist her soft, mischievous mouth. He surrendered and kissed her. It felt like it had been years since he'd kissed her last. Her lips were warm and inviting, and he suddenly didn't care about anything else. She could have intentionally drilled a hundred holes in *Dragonfly's* hull, and he'd just go on kissing her as the ship went down.

She climbed into his lap, and he flashed back to the first time he'd ever kissed her, the way she tasted that night, the scent of her hair, and the pressure of her small hands on his bare skin. How she amazed him now, this woman. This woman had taken her fears—all of them—and crushed them to splinters. She loved a nephil, tamed a watcher, bargained with the demon king, and summoned the Angel of Death. "You're so brave," he murmured. His lips never left her skin as he spoke. "I've never met anyone as brave as you."

Bryony laughed nervously. "You've met Raeni, haven't you?"

Michael held her at arm's length and looked her in the eyes so she could see how much he meant it when he repeated, "I have *never* met anyone as brave as you."

She blushed and busied herself unbuttoning the shirt he'd just put on. Her fingers found the bandages Ashmedai had applied, and she glared down at them. "He'll pay for hurting you," she muttered. "I'll make him pay."

Michael chuckled. "He thought you wouldn't listen to him if my life wasn't on the line. It was all for show."

"I don't care. It was still wrong." She began covering his chest in little kisses as she pushed his shirt from his shoulders. She kissed him once for every *ever* as she said, "No one will ever, ever, ever hurt you again and get away with it."

"Funny," he said. "I feel the same about you."

He leaned back and she followed him, kissing his mouth like she'd never wanted anything more. Her skin began to feel cool against his.

Her tongue in his mouth was like ice water, and he knew she was bringing him too close to abandon. Her hands descended, leaving little trails of coolness down his chest to his stomach, down his stomach to his belt, which she deftly began to remove. "Bryony . . ." he warned, but her name died on his tongue and was replaced with a sharp intake of breath and a moan he couldn't have prevented if his life depended on it.

It was no use. He gave in, clutched at her, devoured her. It had been too long, too terrifyingly long to have gone without her touch. He'd been so afraid of losing her, so worried she would finally realize her life was better without him. His body wouldn't allow him to do anything other than exactly what she wanted. *Give her everything.* "Wait, Bryony." He forced the words out. "Please, I don't think this is a good idea right now."

She stopped and backed away with a look of mock outrage. A nagging voice in his head reminded him what a fool he was. It sounded a bit like Ash. *Life is short. Enjoy your appetites. What are you doing, you idiot? She wants you as badly as you want her.* He fell back, panting. "Sorry," he muttered. "Sorry, I'm just . . . God it's been too long. I love you."

He smiled at her pout, and she quickly kissed the dimple on the left side of his mouth. Such a small touch, such a little concession annihilated his resolve. He rose up and kissed her harder, deeper. He was too weak to stop himself. He needed to feel safe. He needed to feel wanted. He needed to feel her body—solid and real against his—and know she was no illusion. Unthinking, he pulled down the zipper at the back of her dress and tugged the sleeves past her shoulders. He kissed her collarbone and lost himself in the taste of her skin.

"I don't care anymore," he said between kisses as he helped her out of her bodice and bra. "Forget everything I ever said about rules and boundaries. I don't care."

Her breath tickled his neck as she whispered, "Yes, you do," and pushed away from him. He could have punched himself. He'd drawn the boundaries, and of course she wasn't going to cross them. It didn't matter how mutinous he was feeling right now. She wouldn't let him throw his principles away in a fit of rebellious passion. She grinned, and there was that hint of mischief in her expression again. Michael was torn between wanting to know what it was about and needing to find out how it tasted. Her lips curled up at the corners. "Of course, you might feel differently when you know."

"Know what?" He fell right into her trap, and he didn't care. *Let her have her game. Let her have anything she wants.*

"The thing is, Raphael offered to heal me."

Michael froze. "Heal you?" His heart caught in his chest. Was she hurt or sick? What had that watcher done to her? "What's wrong?"

"Well . . ." She utterly failed to fight the smile invading her face. "Apparently, I'm sterile."

"I . . ." He took a moment to process. "Wait . . . Sterile?"

"Completely barren, I'm afraid. Raphael was certain I would never be able to have a child—'zero percent chance,' he said—and he offered to fix it for me." She paused for effect, but she couldn't pause long. "I declined his offer."

Michael curled his fingers around her waist and held her steady in his lap. Part of him wondered whether he was having one of those too-good-to-be-true dreams he so often had to talk himself down from. "Don't tease, Bryony."

She laughed. "Okay, I absolutely reserve my right to tease you, but I'm not teasing you now."

"My god."

"Yes, we've established that."

His laugh was little more than a short breath. There was no way any of this was possible. The most beautiful woman in the world sat half naked in his lap and wanted him. And he could have her. He could have her. He tried to speak but found he'd lost his tongue. Never in his life had he thought he'd be allowed happiness, love, passion like this. The rest of the world was suddenly meaningless.

"Well?" She spread her arms wide, and her body looked like a gift. "What are you waiting for? Kiss me."

He did. He let go of every worry, every fear, every childhood nightmare, and he kissed her. He cast his restraint and vigilance away like jetsam, and what he found in their place could only be described as a desperate, undeniable hunger. He held one hand over the curve of her breast and felt her shiver at his touch. She drew up against him. Her dress slipped lower on her hips. Her breath came heavy and ragged, and he knew she didn't just want him anymore. She needed him. He let her have all of him, touch all of him, use him and please him and drive him mad with desire. He met her breath for breath, mirrored her kisses, mirrored the flush in her cheeks. Then he felt it—the catch and the pull—and he stopped.

She groaned. "Not this again."

"No, it's . . ." Resonance. It was only resonance. He understood what it meant now, thanks to Ashmedai. *Block her eyes from the light,* his father had said. All of it had been humiliating, but he wouldn't have given up his hard-won education for the world. Now he knew exactly what to do. He pushed Bryony off his lap and muttered, "Protection. We just need protection." He got up and started digging through his belongings, his scrap fabrics. She folded her arms across her bare chest and narrowed her eyes at him.

He found the scrap of canvas he'd been looking for. It was black and meant to patch a sail, but Michael had a different use in mind. Then he found another, white cotton this time, gentle enough for her skin. "This should do it," he said. He returned to her, and she sat still while he folded the strips together like origami. "Protection for your eyes—to block the light," he explained as he gently tied it around her head. "I'm sorry it has to be this way."

"I'm not." She laughed. "I thought you had a stash of contraband, and you'd been holding out on me all this time. I was about to ask how many times you'd done this before."

"None." He gulped. "But now that you mention it, there's something I should probably tell you." As soon as he said it, Michael knew he should have worded it differently. Bryony's smile slipped and her body stilled. She was prepared for a blow, he realized, and the poor thing was blindfolded. "No, no. It's not what you think. I just learned something about myself while I was captive, and I thought you might like to know before we went on."

He hesitated. If what Ash had told him was true, he was about to know his fiancée better than he'd ever imagined he could. She might not want that. She might like to keep her secret pleasures to herself. He cleared his throat, suddenly worried. She waited, her dress in a bundle around her hips, her torso completely bare except for the long locks of hair that had come loose from her knotted bun. "You're so beautiful right now," he said. "And I want you—so much—but I'll understand if you're uncomfortable with this."

He could almost see her rolling her eyes behind her blindfold. "For crying out loud, Michael, just tell me."

"It's about resonance," he blurted out. "It's about me . . . resonating with you. I can't control it. I can't stop it. And apparently, while it's happening, I'll feel what you feel. All the pleasure and all the pain. Everything. I just thought maybe you might . . . not want . . ." His voice petered out because she was laughing, and he wasn't sure what to make of it.

"Are you kidding?" she gasped. "The smoke? The light? That's what it means?" She slapped a hand to her knee, but the sound was muffled by her dress. "That's so incredibly sexy."

Suddenly, Michael was glad his fiancée was blindfolded. He could only imagine how he looked, open-mouthed, red-faced, utterly astounded. *Sexy?* "You're not . . . worried about your privacy?"

"Privacy?" She scoffed. "Michael, I'm naked in a blindfold. Wait." She sat back and kicked off the rest of her dress. Then she slid her underwear over her knees and threw it to the floor. "Okay, now I'm naked in a blindfold."

Michael caught his breath a moment before reality sank in. Despite his lineage, despite his inhumanness, despite all the complications that came with him, Bryony wanted a life with him. He crawled across his bunk, put one knee between her legs, and lowered her into a pile of pillows. He let his eyes follow the line of her body. He brought the tips of his fingers to her throat and let them travel down, exploring and appreciating the softness of her skin. This was real. This was happening. He would finally understand, without having to imagine it, all those secret intimacies he'd read about ever since he could pick up a book. He lay off to one side of her, afraid he might crush her if she bore the full weight of him. She turned into him and brought him closer until his body was against hers and he could feel the shape of her.

There was a tipping point, before which Michael might have easily pulled away. It was a point he knew well, as he was ever balancing the shifting weight of his resolve. He understood that if he tipped too far over the edge, the weight and momentum would carry him the rest of the way. He had always pulled back before that moment came. But now, he didn't have to. The moment came, and Michael just watched it. Like a canoe at the edge of a waterfall, it balanced, it tipped, and it rode the current down and down.

In one moment, he was kissing the woman he loved, enjoying her with careful restraint, and in the next, he was starving for her. He was tangled up in his need, unable to separate himself from desire. As far as he could tell, she was in the same predicament, and it didn't matter. It didn't matter in the least.

"Equal ground, remember?" Bryony pushed his pants over his hips in a heated attempt to remove them. He helped her and settled himself alongside her again. She teased him, touched him, and grinned at his audible reactions. He slipped his tongue into her mouth and his hand between her legs, and he listened, measuring her pleasure by the quickness of her breath and the way she moved against him. For her, he must have been easy to read. She touched him and he stiffened, his skin heated, his fever mounted. Had he been thinking straight, he might have been a little embarrassed by how obvious he was. But he wasn't thinking straight. He was matching her, breathing with her, finding a rhythm that made her gasp.

And there was the catch and the pull. The smell of incense grew thick in the air, and the light of the seraph washed out every color in the room. He closed his eyes and felt her.

He felt everything.

It was the strangest thing, being two people at once. Guesswork was out the window. It was suddenly so easy to read her. Every shiver, every swell of pleasure, every bloom of heat she shared with him. She sent him spiraling to a place where thought and analysis vanished. Through her hands, he felt his own shoulders work as he planted one forearm over her head, wrapped his fingers around her hip, and hesitated to enter her.

"Are you okay?" she whispered.

Dear god, there was no answer for that. He groaned and managed to utter, "Yes." And she held him still, tilted her hips, and caused the breach herself.

He felt it—the heat of his own flesh within her, her need to be taken, his need to be consumed. He felt all of it until he couldn't tell who was who anymore. He pushed further, felt her discomfort, and immediately withdrew.

"It's okay," she whispered.

He steadied himself. "No, I . . ." He couldn't find the words, but it didn't matter. Resonance was precision. It ended any question of pleasure or pain. He knew everything she felt, and he was determined to put that knowledge to good use. He slid one hand under her to support the small of her back and adjust her position. And this time, he entered more slowly, more gently, little by little. At the first hint of too much, he would withdraw, kissing and tasting the rest of her body—her breasts and her bones, her throat and her beautiful mouth.

It wasn't at all like the love scenes he'd read. It was a measured introduction, like sitting too long on the beach and finding the tide had gotten too close while he was thinking of other things. Bryony's experience washed over him, a little at first, and then with more depth, more fervor. Her pleasure came to him in waves, and each ebb was as delicious as every swell.

By the time he finished his introduction and began to confer with her in earnest—deep, continuous, deliberate—Michael had already lost himself to resonance. It was so easy to let go and become someone else, someone human and fragile, someone small and evanescent. Steadily, the rising tide consumed him. He arched his back, and his body rose and fell with her urging. She moaned, and he gripped the sheets beneath her. Both his bodies—the seraph and the man—coiled and tightened, more and more, until the pulse of her climax brought and matched his own. And for the first time in his life, Michael had to close his eyes to the light.

In the moments that followed, his heart slowly found its own rhythm again, and Bryony rose up to tighten her arms around him. She squeezed him once and fell back, happy and exhausted, as the light faded. He supported himself on one arm, still afraid to crush her, especially now that he could no longer feel what she felt. He was himself again, alone in his body, and there was something so tragic about it he almost wanted to cry.

"I love you," she whispered, and the words eased him back into joy. "Mi esposo."

"Oh my god." He slid off to one side. "You're amazing. You're so amazing." It was such a predictable, ordinary thing to say—not at all as suave as he would have liked to be after the first time he made love to his fiancée.

"No, *you* are." She slipped the blindfold up over her head and tapped the end of his nose with her finger. Then she stretched, catlike and satisfied, and finally pulled away. "I should probably wash up."

He let her go, though he didn't want to. This was, of course, the aftermath few of his books ever seemed to address. He sat up in the dim light and pulled his pants back on, suddenly shy for some ridiculous reason. Still he was happy. He was so absurdly happy to just sit there, listen to the water run, and know that her warm, familiar body would soon lie beside him again. His arms already ached to hold her. He never wanted to leave her. Never again.

When Bryony extinguished the lamp and crawled back into his bed, Michael lay down beside her and draped an arm across her hips. He tugged at her protectively and murmured words he hadn't thought he'd ever say aloud, let alone believe. "If this is my life now, I want it to last forever."

She grinned. "Good. That's how it should be." Then she dropped her smile and chewed her lower lip. "Does that mean you forgive me? For conjuring your father?"

Oh . . . That. He'd all but forgotten. "You don't need to apologize."

"But I want to."

"Then, yes." He spoke against the skin of her neck, his breath stirring the whisps of hair at her nape. "I forgive you for conjuring my father, you magnificent, reckless beauty. I forgive you for everything you've ever done and everything you might do in the future." He wriggled down and pressed his lips to her shoulder. The persistence of his own appetite surprised him. "You smell so good," he added offhandedly.

She laughed. "It's just my shampoo."

"I don't care," he mumbled into her skin. "I could breathe you in forever. Please let me breathe you in forever." He was doing it again, he realized—obsessing, clinging.

"Of course you can." She patted his head, and he shifted back up to his pillows. "But . . ." She hesitated, and he could almost feel her deliberation, as though he still rode the coattails of resonance. "On one condition."

"Anything." *Anything.*

Again, she hesitated, and the nervousness her playful tone hid grew more evident.

"Bryony, it's okay." In the dark, she drew little circles on the center of his chest. He caught her by the wrist and brought her knuckles to his lips. "Just ask."

"Well, he . . . he gave you a name, your father. You know so much about me, but now I feel like I don't even know your name."

"My name is Michael," he said, still kissing her knuckles. "It's the only name I've ever known. The name my father gave me is impossible to pronounce aloud, which makes it relatively useless in our world."

"But it means something, doesn't it? Can you try to translate it?"

He traced the bones on the back of her hand as he thought. "Do you remember when I repaired your mother's dress, and you took it from my hands and wept?"

She nodded into his chest.

"I didn't know how to feel," he said. "Something about opening an old wound in you hurt me, too. At the same time, you were so happy. I realized I'd somehow given you the only gift that could have made you that happy and that sad at the same time. Had I been right to give it to you? Could I ever forgive myself or do anything to top it? That conflict was . . . not insignificant." He kissed her hair, curled his fingers around the back of her head, and held her close. "That kind of gift—that is my name."

Epilogue

In near pitch darkness, Bryony lay and listened to Michael's deep, rhythmic breathing. Now that he was asleep, she knew he would be almost impossible to wake. She loved that she knew that about him. She opened a curtain and let moonlight touch the ghost of his dimple, his slightly parted lips, his long eyelashes, and his otherwise completely average face. How it came to life when he woke, though. How his smile startled her every time she saw it. She would never tire of seeing him smile. Never. He was so beautiful.

She leaned in to kiss his forehead, and he didn't even stir. Then she got up and felt her way to her old bunk. Her only practical clothes were still folded in the drawers beneath it. She pulled out a pair of sweatpants and a cardigan, and put them on before going out to get a breath of fresh air.

Sleep would evade Bryony for hours. There was no question of that. She'd intended to find her way to the cargo hold and pick out some books to read, but before she could open the main hatch, she heard a curious sound. It was a periodic shooshing from the forecastle. She made her way up the steps. There, on his hands and knees with a bucket and scrub brush, was Azazel, swabbing the deck.

"What are you doing?" she asked, though the answer was obvious.

He looked up and smiled. "Cleaning my mess. It's the least I can do for my hosts."

She felt suddenly guilty for enjoying herself so thoroughly while he worked. "Let me help at least. It's my mess too."

He handed her the soft bristle brush. Then he wrung a washcloth and began sopping up the salt he'd already loosened. "Magic circles must always be erased, you know. Especially if they're on someone else's floor." He chuckled. "It keeps the secrets of the trade."

Salt water soaked into the knees of Bryony's sweatpants, and she was glad to have chosen a more practical outfit than the one she'd been wearing before. Azza, on the other hand, wore his standard, gorgeous, embroidered clothes. He looked wrong on his hands and knees. "Why don't you let me finish this?" she said. "You should be long gone by now. Aren't you anxious to heal your granddaughter?"

"I would never leave without saying goodbye. It's unforgivably rude." He smiled up at her. "And etiquette aside, Raphael will have taken ownership of his weapon by now. His sword is no longer free to use. Luckily, before he left, the archangel promised to heal my granddaughter himself. I wouldn't dare to presume what came over him." He winked. "But I believe he's been caught in the web of some sweet, little arachnid."

The immediate loss of the healing sword was a consequence Bryony hadn't foreseen when she'd set out to free Raphael, but she was now certain Azazel had. And he'd helped her anyway. Without any guarantee his granddaughter would benefit, without any promise Raphael wouldn't bind him in darkness again, Azza had helped Bryony. She bowed her head, ashamed of her own cynicism. Ash had been right all along. The watcher wasn't helping her for their mutual best interest. He was helping her, full stop. She finished scrubbing one section of the circle and moved on to the next. "But you should be with her, shouldn't you? You should go to her."

"Alas, I cannot. At least, not right away." Azza did not look up from his task. "She'll understand. I fulfilled my promise to heal her, and now I have other obligations."

"What other obligations?" Bryony laughed, but when the angel looked up, sober as she'd ever seen him, she stopped laughing. "No. You don't mean me, do you? You can't mean me." Azazel did not wink and assure her it wasn't what she thought, and Bryony began to scrub the deck more aggressively. "I didn't ask for this."

"You didn't have to." Azza sat back on his heels, and she bowed her head again so she wouldn't see the affection in his eyes. "A good god never has to ask for devotion."

Her knuckles whitened over the scrub brush, and she was frankly shocked she wasn't sanding down the deck as hard as she scrubbed it now. "I don't want to be a god anymore."

"But you haven't a choice, darling. You are what you are, and you need what you need. Why won't you let me give you what you need?"

She threw the brush down. "Because it's wrong!"

"Not to me, it isn't." His voice was so soft, she couldn't help softening herself at the sound of it. "To me, worship is life. I'm not human, little orb-weaver. I think sometimes you forget. I need to give worship—you need to receive it. That relationship is already in place. Let's not waste it."

"I'm not hungry." She sounded like a defiant child, even to her own ears.

"Right now you aren't, but you will be and soon. I hate to tell you this, but you won't be able to wean off worship. You may as well try to wean off food. You'll starve, darling, and it's in my nature to feed a god. Why not let your Michael believe you've successfully weaned off his worship? Let him love you as a husband, and I'll take over as your congregant. It's safer for him that way—safer for you to have an immortal source of worship." He tucked one side of his tangerine hair behind an ear. "That way, when he dies and his soul is trapped between worlds, you can conjure and employ him yourself."

Bryony stared wide-eyed despite her concerted effort to restrain herself. "Why would I want to employ him?"

"Because if you don't, someone else will. He'll be called upon by those who are too cowardly to summon the Angel of Death himself. And the work will be ugly, I promise you that. Sorcerers do not summon Samael to heal or to build. Sorcerers summon him to kill and destroy. You're the only one I've ever known to conjure the Angel of Death for the purpose of healing. It must have been quite a shock to him." He chuckled to himself.

"Fine." Bryony took the bristle brush and began angrily scrubbing at the circle again. "You can . . . be my congregant." If it was for Michael, she would do it. She would do whatever it took to save him from the kind of afterlife most demons had. "But I won't lie to him."

Azazel grinned. "As you wish."

It was ridiculous, all of it. Bryony still didn't understand, and she muttered to herself as she worked. "Why anyone would choose to worship me is a mystery I'm sure I'll never solve. I don't get it. Especially now. I'm a healing god who can't even heal anymore. I'm a has-been grifter with a stupid addiction. I'm a liar—"

"Every god is a liar," Azazel broke in. "None of them can begin to offer what they claim. You do know that, don't you? What worshipers are drawn to is the power behind the curtain, not the smoke and mirrors. Whether we realize it or not, we all crave after what is truly given, be it community or ritual, inspiration or prayer, absolution or hope."

Bryony scoffed. "I don't give anybody any of those things anymore."

"No," Azazel agreed. "Your power lies elsewhere."

"Of course it does." She rolled her eyes. "Please don't tell me my superpower is love or empathy or anything useless like that."

"Useless?" Azazel stood, angry now for some reason. "*Useless?* Get up. Stand, darling, or I'll drag you to your feet myself, god or no god." Bryony stood, and Azza took her by the shoulders and stared down at her with those incomparable, amber eyes. "Listen to me now. I'm going to teach you your worth. I'm frankly disgusted you don't seem to know it." Bryony tried to avoid eye contact by staring at the sea, but Azza wasn't having it. "Look at me, please."

She did. It wasn't difficult. If a rose garden said, *Look at me*, very few would bother to resist.

"Listen," he said. "You're worshiped by a godhunter, the deadliest there's ever been. That alone should be unthinkable." She began to protest, but the angel pressed three fingers to her lips to silence her. "Don't speak. Listen. You've earned the loyalty of a Jötunn who's most famous for his disloyalty. I was astonished when I discovered it. And now, you have the devotion of a godless watcher. My own daughters . . ." Azza paused and withdrew his fingers. She could see the pain in his expression, so she did not try to interrupt again. "My daughters want nothing to do with me, and rightly so. They're monstrous creatures, proud and cruel, and it's my own fault. They're bound in the empty place, and I'm the cause of their suffering."

Bryony wanted to argue, but Azazel preempted her. "I'm the scapegoat for all mankind, but I can't take on the sins of my own daughters. I'm useless to everyone who matters to me, except you. Why? And, little orb-weaver, most shockingly, today you conjured the Angel of Death and survived."

This was ridiculous. "That doesn't mean anything."

Azza's eyes widened. "That means everything. There's a power in you, whether you believe it or not. Your Michael, Loki, Samael, and myself—we were all drawn to it."

"Please." She shook her head. "Samael only came because I summoned him."

"You cannot force Samael to do anything. Surely you know that much about him."

Bryony glared at the watcher. "No, I don't know that much about him. I know hardly anything about him in fact. All anyone ever says is, *Don't summon him. Don't talk to him. Stay away.* He's my future father-in-law, and I've already humiliated myself and unforgivably offended him because no one bothered to tell me he was actually blind." Azza snorted, and the sound was so alien coming from him, it almost threw Bryony completely off her game. "I'm not kidding!" she said. "Did you hear what I said to him about his eyes? He won't forget that any time soon."

"He's used to it, darling."

"How does that even matter? An insult is an insult. And I probably reminded him of something terrible." She bit her lip and bowed her head. "Didn't I? Who . . . Who did that to him?"

"No one did." Azza blinked down at her, clearly perplexed by her disregard for everything else he'd said. He sighed and gave up trying to steer the conversation. "Samael was . . . How do I translate this exactly?" He knit his brow, and it only made him more lovely. "An angel would say he was 'born wrong.' He has the equivalent of several physical deformities or genetic abnormalities, if you will."

Bryony recalled what Raphael had told her about herself. She had a genetic abnormality. She suddenly felt a kinship with her future father-in-law. "A genetic abnormality doesn't mean you were born wrong. Plenty of mutations are desirable." Especially the ones that made it so you could sleep with your own fiancé without triggering his compulsive fear of reproduction.

Azazel smiled. "That's a very human way of looking at it, but to angels, Samael is an abomination. His blindness, his poison, his wings—"

"What's wrong with his wings?"

"There are twelve of them," Azazel said matter-of-factly. "Seraphim have six. Can you imagine a human with eight limbs?"

"Of course I can. We have traveling shows. People pay good money to see that sort of thing."

Azza's mouth twitched, and he nodded, stifling a laugh. "Curiosity is one of the things I love most about humans, despite the tendency of some to exploit it. Most angels are not curious. They don't explore and question. They only serve or dominate. Without a hierarchy, they don't even know when to breathe. Samael exists outside the norm, which means he exists outside the hierarchy. He's the essence of change and impermanence, so to angels, Samael is hideous."

"That's absurd." Bryony pulled away from Azza, rejecting the ideas he communicated as though they were his own. "I mean, he's an angel, so I wasn't particularly happy to see him. But I'm not going to pretend he wasn't impressive and . . . well, honestly, kind of pretty for a seraph. Anyway, how are more wings a bad thing? They're *wings*. They're beautiful by default."

As she spoke, Azza brought a hand to his mouth in a vain attempt to contain his laughter. Before she was quite finished, he was doubled over. He shook his head and clutched at his stomach. "Stop," he gasped. "It's too much."

"What's so funny?" She glared at him.

He slapped her on the shoulder. "You, darling! How can you say such things to me and never once think to say them to *him*? You really are the worst flatterer I've ever known. Ah, you could have confounded him so easily. Imagine his reaction!" He cackled again.

"It's not flattery." She was not enjoying this conversation at all. "It's the truth."

Azza stopped laughing instantly. Somehow his expression went from hysterics to sobriety without a moment of transition. It was always unnerving when he did that. "Then tell him next time you meet him, and promise you'll let me watch. I've never seen him flabbergasted, and I won't miss my one and only chance."

Bryony promised nothing. "And another thing. There's nothing 'wrong' about being born blind. It happens to humans all the time. If I'd known that was why his eyes looked the way they did, I wouldn't have minded them. I just thought he'd manifested that way to intimidate me."

"No." Azza shook his head. "He's always had trouble manifesting eyes, which reminds me. Do ask to see Ash's feet next time you see him. I want your reaction to them as well—and his reaction, come to think of it."

"This is so stupid." Bryony sat as angrily as she could manage. "I don't make a point of knowing exactly how each type of angel is supposed to look, so none of you are wrong to me. You're all just angels."

"Good. Tell him."

"That's not a compliment." She knelt and went back to scrubbing. "I mean you're all terrifying as far as I'm concerned—or you were, I guess, before I got to know you personally. To me, the Angel of Death doesn't look any more monstrous than the rest of you. I doubt he even means to paralyze everyone who looks at him. He probably hates it."

"*Tell* him."

"Tell him what exactly!" she snapped.

Azazel crouched down and tilted his head until he could look beneath her curtain of hair. "The next time you see Samael, tell him you think his wings are beautiful. Start with that."

"He'll just think I'm making fun of him."

"He won't." Azza sat on his heels and took the brush from her. "He'll believe you. Trust me. Your sincerity is deafening. Even when you're lying, you're somehow sincere about it. So, little orb-weaver, tell the Venom of God you think he's beautiful. Catch him in your honeyed web. I swear to you, he won't know what to do with himself—not if it's you—because you're . . ." He knit his brow. "I can't translate this. Forgive me. I have to show you."

Before Bryony quite understood what was happening, Azza had placed a hand on either side of her head and brought his mouth to hers. He breathed ice into her, and she heard him loud and clear.

It was a feeling she knew well. One winter, when she was a child, she'd taken a shortcut through the woods on her way home and quickly lost track of her surroundings. The day was overcast and getting darker, and her little heart beat faster and faster as the realization that she was truly lost finally settled in. She feared she wouldn't find her way back before night. She wondered if she would ever see her family again—or would they find her lifeless body in the woods? But against all odds and just before nightfall, young Bryony had spotted a glowing, yellow orb through the trees. She knew it at once as the cobwebbed porchlight of home, but that night, it meant so much more. It was better than hope. She'd cried at the sight of it. She'd run to it, eager for the familiar voices of people who loved her, eager for hot chocolate and a warm hearth, and so very eager to snuggle down in her own bed and rest at last.

Azazel pulled away, and Bryony reached up to her cheeks to feel the tears the angel had somehow drawn from her eyes. What he'd communicated to her was *home*, but not just home—it was *home after it has been lost*. "What was that?" she asked, though deep down, she already knew.

"Your name." He pressed a palm to her cheek and smiled a warm, beautiful smile. "In our world, you're called after what you most resemble. You're called after the feeling you evoke. I named you for your power, little orb-weaver, and it is a million miles from useless."

Her name. But it wasn't just a name, she knew. It was a big idea, a big truth she was only beginning to understand. *Home after it has been lost* did not teach her something about herself as much as it taught her something about the creatures she feared. "Oh my god." She brought a hand to her mouth and stared up at Azazel. "You're all just lost, aren't you?"

The watcher closed his eyes and touched his forehead to hers. "Yes, yes, yes, darling. Lost and terrified. Now you understand. We need to be found, merciful god. Find us, if you can. Draw us out, and show us home."

Acknowledgements

They say writing is a solitary endeavor, but this time around, I had so much encouragement from family. I want to thank my mother, in particular, for her early support of this series; my father, who championed my childhood writing; and my sisters, who helped cement the importance of found family into my world and fiction. None of us are blood related, but we've never questioned our familial bond. I love all of you.

To the people on social media who helped me get the word out about A Tyranny of Angels: Thank you, thank you, thank you! More than once, I was brought close to tears when I learned that strangers actually cared about this passion project of mine. I can't possibly express how much your support means to me.

And to Mika: The world lost you far too soon. Learning of your death hit me harder than I ever imagined it would. I wish I could have told you how much you gave to Azazel. He is who he is because of you.

A Tyranny of Angels

Book 1: Godhunter

Book 2: Speak of the Devil

Book 3: The Evolution of Angels

https://www.isobellynn.com